First edition 2025

To my husband. I love you! Thank you for dreaming up this story with me, for honoring the parts of me that are deeply ingrained in Myla's healing journey, and for being a man who I have always felt safe with. I love dreaming and making exciting new worlds with you! The world needs more men like you, which is why I gave Myla a Bryar.

To my parents. Thank you both for always nurturing my creativity, reading my short stories, and giving me the confidence to say "I can do this."

Naomi, Alex, Chelsea, Ray, Abbey, B, and Jazzy, and Allyson: each of you played a fundamental role in the success of this book. Thank you for cheering me on, for reading the unpolished versions, and for being the best hype team a girl could ask for. I love you all.

To my beautiful friend and editor, Amber with Bibliobean Books, I did not believe in miracles until I met you. Now I do. Thank you for diving into ATBR with me. I simply could not have made it to publishing day without you. Welcome to my ribcage, I hope your nest is very comfortable.

Rae. I adore you. Thank you for casually volunteering for what was, frankly, an insane undertaking in the time frame you were given. The fun facts have been real. May your leather jerkin never be too tight for a full range of movements.

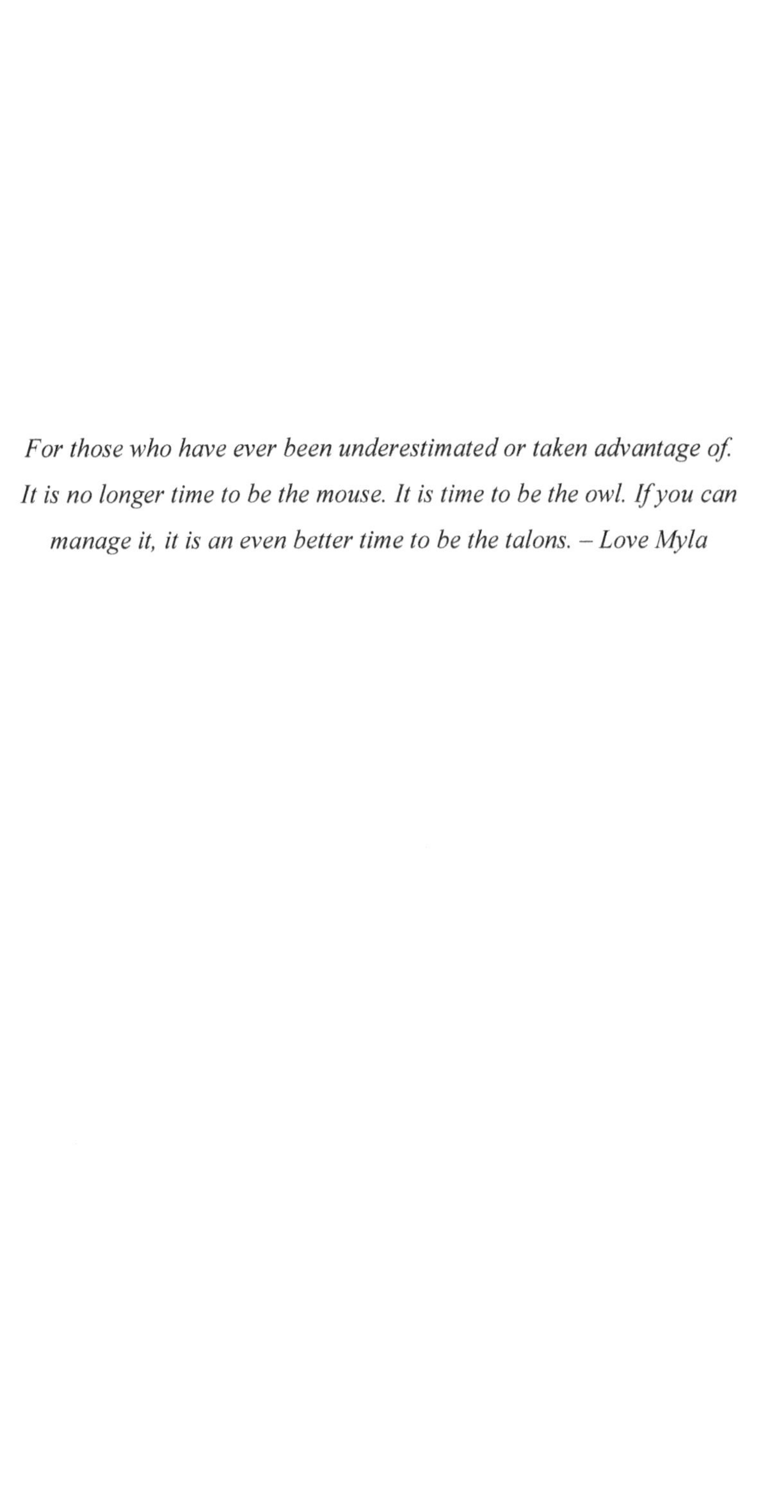

For those who have ever been underestimated or taken advantage of. It is no longer time to be the mouse. It is time to be the owl. If you can manage it, it is an even better time to be the talons. – Love Myla

Content Warnings

This story contains some content which may be triggering, traumatic, or uncomfortable to read.

Listed below are the subjects I believe may be difficult for some readers. I want my readers to always feel safe while experiencing my stories. If a specific trigger seems especially concerning to you, please reference the smaller text for context clarification. Otherwise, skip the smaller text as it may be a spoiler to the story.

Off-Screen Sexual Assault *READ ONLY IF YOU NEED CLARIFICATION— OTHERWISE SKIP TO AVOID SPOILERS
FMC experienced S/A in the past. There are no flashbacks nor is it described in detail. It is referenced and mentioned on more than one occasion.

Mentions of "R*pe" *READ ONLY IF YOU NEED CLARIFICATION— OTHERWISE SKIP TO AVOID SPOILERS
The word itself is used, and it is distressing to the FMC.

Unintentional Self-Harm *READ ONLY IF YOU NEED

CLARIFICATION— OTHERWISE SKIP TO AVOID SPOILERS
Due to supernatural influences, the FMC is subject to experiences in which she has no control over her body. These experiences lead to accidental / unintentional self-harm.

Pregnancy *READ ONLY IF YOU NEED CLARIFICATION— OTHERWISE SKIP TO AVOID SPOILERS
FMC is pregnant, and this is a pretty relevant & frequently mentioned portion of the plot.

Child in Peril (I promise, the child is okay!) *READ ONLY IF YOU NEED CLARIFICATION— OTHERWISE SKIP TO AVOID SPOILERS
FMC has a bad dream where the villain of the story forces her to self-harm in a way that also harms the child. She wakes from the dream to realize all is well and her child is okay. This specific scene begins in Chapter 14 if you would prefer to skim over it.

Woman in Peril (She is okay, too!) *READ ONLY IF YOU NEED CLARIFICATION— OTHERWISE SKIP TO AVOID SPOILERS
FMC is subject to a curse which is potentially life threatening and strips her of her autonomy. She is alright!

Mental and Emotional Abuse *READ ONLY IF YOU NEED CLARIFICATION— OTHERWISE SKIP TO AVOID SPOILERS
Topics of emotional and mental abuse are confronted. They are explicitly described as abhorrent things and in no way are they presented as forgivable or justifiable. The FMC does battle with understanding "why" at times, but these feelings are resolved.

Other potential warnings which require no explanation:

Violence, Death, and Gore

Sexual Content

Sexism

Prologue

"I have heard you called 'The Queen Who Bleeds Stars'." Something that might have been a compliment, were it not delivered by a fallen Fae God, haunts the captain's memory.

He pictures her, standing in the throne room. A Ruthless Queen. A Queen of Wrath. A Queen Who Bleeds Stars. A Queen who teeters dangerously on the edge of just *bleeding.* If he does not find answers on this mountain today, she will bleed it all—the stars, the wrath, the ruthlessness; but most importantly, her life, and her memories. It will all bleed out, right into the palms of the Blood Stealer.

It is a thick curling mist; the kind that tricks you into thinking a shallow breath is caught in your lungs. The skeletons of trees have long since been stripped of their foliage, and nothing living has been seen in two days. It is difficult to tell if the shadows in the snow are blackened cliffsides or the slumbering beasts that belong to the Blood Stealer. There is nothing to suggest to a soul that hope lies nearby; and yet, if their plan goes accordingly, hope there is.

The group of three has been swallowed in the mountain's crevice, a test of mental and physical fortitude well underway. The two heading up the rear, quivering from both cold and fear, follow their bold leader, hoping his confidence is enough to deliver them to the Seer. Though he is thigh-deep in freezing snow and the possibility of crashing beneath the surface into an unseen and deadly cavern is fair, Captain Bryar Monroe presses onward with unwavering conviction. For death is imminent, whether delivered by a nasty fall here, or because fear dissuades him and he returns to the wreckage that is home. There is no choice but to move onward and hope the Gods and Goddesses favor him. Or more so . . . favor *her.*

When at last the mouth of the cave appears, wide and gaping with sharp icicles forming teeth overhead, the weary travelers cease movement. Motivated as he is, even Bryar is taken aback by a deep, eerie chill running down his spine.

Who lurks within? Some accounts claim she is a sightless beauty, her pale irises lost in the whites of her eyes. Others tremble as they tell of her ghastly face, sunken into itself and shrouded in the blackest of matted tendrils. In any regard, all descriptions of the Seer are scarce, as those who conquer the mountain are few. As far as Bryar is concerned, *any* accounts could simply be tavern fables, and he has wasted precious time.

There is only one way to find out, he thinks to himself, ignoring the bickering of his peers behind him.

"I am not going in before you. I have more to live for," Rhyland spews, running an exhausted hand over his dark, frozen features.

"That is quite a comforting reflection of you as a friend," retorts his lifelong friend and danger-detector, Callum.

"Though I value you deeply and will miss you when you are gone, I have aspirations which I am not ready to give up on, Cal. I am not dying here today."

Callum snorts and draws a dry length of cloth from his pack which he wraps around a stick to make a torch. Brows pressed together, Bryar watches, amused, a spark of fire tingling at his palms.

"If you mean bedding that boy from the market," Callum scoffs. "I would not sacrifice your best friend for it. I do not think *that* will happen." A hot glow of fire appears from his palm and sets the torch ablaze. "In any case, do not talk about me like I am already dead— "

"Callum," Bryar interjects, holding two hands ablaze before him. "Why are you making a torch?" Bryar can answer his own question. Training for the king's guard drills it into a soldier that they cannot rely on their magic for everything; thus, they are required to do everything without magic, saving their abilities for only the direst of moments. Callum takes to the rules better than most.

Rhyland rolls his eyes, watching as the two men exude a supernatural heat, melting the snow around them. "I get it. I am the only one here without *massive* flames to throw around. Can we get a move on now?"

With a brief, nervous smile, Callum snuffs the useless torch and ignites his palms. "You might not be able to light a torch, but you can make me forget this Gods-awful experience once it is over, and I will thank you for it."

The entrance carries a freezing draft of wind, a gale that welcomes doom into the darkness, ushering them deeper. Each step inward feels like a gamble. Does the Seer truly live in this Gods-forsaken cave on the side of a thankless, frozen mountain? Or are they walking willingly into the mouth of some hungry beast? A beautiful face in his mind overpowers concern and Bryar disregards his doubts, urging Callum and Rhyland to keep close. It is a mere dozen steps later when his light extinguishes, and Callum and Rhyland find themselves standing alone.

When Bryar was a boy, he and his friends would jump off the highest cliff point along the edge of the bay, diving into the depths of the ocean. That feeling of your heart catching in your throat as you catapulted yourself into the dark oblivion of the ocean is the closest feeling he can conjure in comparison to this. One moment he is braving the unknown with his comrades, the next he is free-falling into a black state of mind, suspended in nothingness. Then, she is before him.

The Seer is neither beautiful nor is she a hideous sore upon the eyes. She is entirely faceless. Although, the form is there, the features are not. Black hair, long enough to engulf her entire being, shrouds her body, leaving only a pale orb visible, where her face should be.

"Forgive the assault on your person," her silky voice breaks the silence. "I welcome only those with dire need into my presence."

"I imagine my companions' needs to be as great as mine," Bryar answers, thinking of the questions Callum has for the Seer. Bryar attempts to collect his wits, though greatly distracted with the question of whether he is standing or floating. The sensation of not *actually* being here is overwhelming. Is this truly a physical location, or has he simply fallen through her portal?

"You forget," she whispers, sending chills past his shoulders, "I see all."

"Forgive me," Bryar responds. "I am weary, and . . . I fear, short on hope."

"Then ask your question," the Seer insists, long fingers reaching out to brush his forehead. He hesitates, wishing that for all the many miles and days spent hiking up this awful mountain, he had thought more carefully how to ask what he needs to know. Be it weariness, desperation, or something deeper within the most concealed parts of his heart, the simple question asks itself, before he has time to ponder it.

"How do I save her?"

The orb of a face grows gaunt, and the white grows whiter. The air chills, and yet Bryar is overwhelmed with the heat growing in his middle, as the pressure of the Seer's power saturates what already feels like a small space. Her voice lulls in and out of silky sweet and a deeper one, the prediction of the Gods flowing through her.

"You can not save her."

For the briefest moment, Bryar's heart slumps deeper than his shoulders do. To have braved this perilous journey, and find it is a fool's errand, feels like a sharp dagger to the stomach. But then, she speaks again.

"It is you who will be saved, washed in a purifying fire. And because of *her*, it is a great many who will be saved. After a thousand burning ravens fill the skies with their embers."

"But how? And who? And a thousand—what?"

"Bryar Monroe." She breathes his name as though it is something forbidden. "She does not need anyone's help. What she needs, she will find already within her."

Defeat hangs heavy in the air around Bryar. "So, we do nothing then?"

"You do as you have always done. Forsake not your convictions, and in the hopeless months to come, do not be divided. But most importantly, though you say you are short on it, have hope."

Bryar's journey back to his comrades is a fitful one, his consciousness plagued by the memory of his queen. The moment which set his feet upon this treacherous mountain path. Only to return to the queen and tell her she already has everything she needs inside her. It is laughable. Nevertheless, it is what he has been given, so they better damn well find an effective way to use it.

Chapter 1

"The Dowager Queen." She is announced, and it is a fucking joke if not downright insulting. Calling her a *dowager* is how they all get away with *owning* her every move, even though she is very much the ruling monarch. Willing or not. With an agitated sigh, Myla enters her conservatory, the place she has taken to holding council. The room is a dome of glass with old vines meandering upward. Lanterns hang from the ceiling at different heights, gently illuminating the room from the night sky. An abundance of lovingly grown plants, herbs, and fruit trees flourish in the large room. A thick, green and gold ornate rug cushions the stone flooring beneath their feet, a kindness in the colder months. When the conservatory is not being used for gore and warfare strategies, it is an astoundingly peaceful place. When ugly old men in ugly sagging tunics are not there, it may just be her favorite room in the entire palace.

With an air of bristled defiance, she had told her confidants that the Council Room was a dismal place, but the truth was, it simply smelled like her decapitated husband. She felt as if the room exhaled his very essence each time she stepped inside. She would be so ambushed by memories and guilt that focusing on making vital decisions for the sake of the kingdom was futile. But a strong queen would never admit her heart was sabotaging her head, so she simply said the conservatory was a more cheerful place to plot murder.

"Be seated." She issues the command with less patience than intended, her nerves simmering just beneath the surface. Across from her, the grim face of her father inspects her for weakness, no doubt adding to the tally of times she has seemed 'un-queenly' in the recent months. A sense of failing before she has even begun picks at her, and she wills the disgust on her face to retreat.

With an outward breath and a subtle grasp of the thick satin of her skirt, she checks her tone before speaking again. "What news is there from the farmlands?"

A gray and grizzly-looking man, with a scar interrupting the otherwise thick growth of beard, speaks. "Our emissary has yet to return, Your Grace. I fear we have had no word."

"Another loss," she mumbles, dragging a heavy finger across the shiny surface of the oak table beneath them. A tremor within her, like a sounding alarm, threatens to disrupt her pretense of composure as Lord Heron delivers the grievous news. It is subtle at first, a twitching in her hands followed by her fingers curling around the hilt of the dagger concealed beneath her skirts. News of the defeat, delivered by the imbecile across from her, makes her want to plant the dagger in his neck.

Myla swallows and forces her shaking hands to withstand the

overpowering urge, clamping her fingers tight around the edge of the table instead. Now is not the time for an . . . *episode.* Now is the time to ignore this almost instinctual need to relocate to the Seam, the point beyond the black mountains where the Blood Stealer amasses his army and hoards his strength.

Men have been going missing for months now, no doubt sheep added to the Blood Stealer's flock. Of all the faces gathered around the table, hers is the most concerned. An unbecoming feature on one who is supposed to have the answers. *What would Caius do?* A silly thought. If Caius were here, this would not be an issue. His death is the cause of it all. *Bastard.*

"Your Grace?" Heron probes. "Shall I send operatives to assess the situation and report back directly?" A sharp tilt of her chin is all that is need for him to leave the room to execute his plan. The rest of the council is seated, awaiting instructions. After two years of ruling in her husband's stead, Myla feels this should come easier—the questions and solutions ought to materialize within her. And yet, with her waning supply of power and energy, nothing is easy. At all times, there are eyes on her, looking to her to deliver them from the consuming chaos of the Blood Stealer. A feat she feels unprepared to do.

"Council is adjourned for today," she blurts, to the dismay of all. "I fear we shall find no solutions, and I need to have some private conversations before moving forward." All at once, her scowling council disperses, leaving only she and her father in the room.

"What are you doing?" he fumes, his gray-peppered beard failing to hide the scowl contorting his mouth.

"I am taking a break," she snaps, slamming the conservatory door behind the final councilman, closing them in for what feels like a long overdue tiff.

"Queens do not take *breaks,* Myla."

"This one does," she retorts, perching herself on the edge of the comfortable sofa. "We have lived and breathed strategy to no end for a week, Father. I will have no more of it until tomorrow."

"You will do as you are told!" he bellows, his words threatening to crack the glass overhead. Red lines his eyelids—whether anger or exhaustion, Myla does not care to know. He is always angry at her; he always has been.

The door opens to her Captain of the Guard rushing in at the commotion, hand on the hilt of his axe. Myla holds a hand up, stopping him before he enters further. "I am fine, thank you." The guard retreats, leaving them alone once more, and Myla turns her attention to her father, an iron ferocity etched into the creases of her face.

"You are the one who made me a queen, Father. If you wanted to control me, you should have thought about that before giving me the power to *ignore* you." Without giving the bewildered man a chance to respond, she waves a dismissive hand his way. "You are excused. And Father?" Her words stop him, just before he storms from the room. "Send for my friends."

With a roll of his eyes and an exaggerated huff, he leaves, no doubt begrudged at her replacing the council of the men *he* has chosen for her with her trusted friends.

As soon as the door closes behind him, Myla turns on her heel and makes for a more secluded part of the indoor garden. A small path winds to the furthest corner, heavily shrouded in overgrowth. There, Myla's altar sits. Small offerings lay at the feet of the Goddess. Today, Myla places a jar sealed with wax there and closes her eyes. She begs the Goddess to give her strength, and patience. She then moves to the sofa, where she sits, awaiting her friends' arrival.

"Myla?" The first of the group arrives not ten minutes later. The young queen watches as concern fills her friend's eyes. Elsa assesses the situation, watching as Myla sits, dignified but slight in stature, on the velvet green sofa tucked beside the window. Fatigue engulfs her like an unwelcome blanket, an appearance she struggles to hide more and more—one she has been suffocating beneath for two years.

"Well . . ." Elsa whispers, sitting in the space beside her. "The fucker has nothing better to do than taunt you from afar today, does he?" Her eyes, though sincere, spark with a rebellious resistance only Elsa can conjure. Nevertheless, her pale-blue irises are rimmed with the glisten of tears at the sight of her friend and queen, bearing it all with an unshakable indifference.

With a bolstering breath, Myla smiles and responds. "I feel his pull almost daily now," she admits, a calloused inflection almost dismissing the statement itself. "I only wish I could return the favor and taunt *him* from afar." She smiles reassuringly as the door opens and another enters, dread emanating from his entire being.

It is the captain, no doubt still enraged by her father's display, not ten minutes ago. He stays silent and stands nearby, maintaining the role of bodyguard. His is a commanding presence—locks like warm, inky waves tumble across his forehead and the immaculate dress of Captain of the Guards, always evoking respect.

"My . . . my power is trickling from my veins. I wake up and it is spent already. What I am not expending myself to protect us, he is taking. I have impulses, and fighting them daily is exhausting."

The door opens one last time, admitting Callum and Rhyland, the former taking a seat beside Elsa, discreetly grabbing her hand. It is Rhyland who speaks next, an exhausted swoop of his hand brushing a stray hair from his bronzed face. "You are carrying something much heavier than just a war, Your Grace. There must be answers and solutions that do not always involve you taking the brunt of it all."

"Tell that to the room full of council members I just dismissed." Myla laughs, pressing a palm to her forehead in exasperation.

"Allocate, that is all we are saying," Callum adds.

Elsa nods in agreement and continues to listen as the man beside her offers solutions. "I will go to Titonfall and inquire about our progress there. It is time I check in anyway, see if we are any closer to infiltrating the Seam. At the very least, we will have more information on how his strength is growing. It is better to know than to wonder."

"In the meantime," Elsa adds gently, side eyeing both men as though to rally their support, "is it time to consider letting the child come?" Myla bristles, leaping to her feet. Her friends exchange weary glances, and it is clear Elsa regrets raising the topic.

"How do you expect me to allow my child to be born into this?" Myla gestures around them, to the palace and beyond; to the hundreds of miles Caius's mere breath protected, and death doomed. "I can not protect anyone, let alone a child. I will not risk our final living Restorer to relieve my own suffering."

The captain nods in agreement, cautiously shifting from his role as her personal guard to that of an old friend, speaking finally, "while bringing forth the child may seem logical, I fear we can not overlook his, or her, lineage. As Caius's heir, this child is already in grave danger . . . should anyone find out."

Myla had discovered the pregnancy a week before Caius died. It was a week of joy and dreaming, a week where he was entirely pleased with her—she had finally done what was the duty of every queen. The days felt more effortless, a feeling which was quickly snuffed. The wreckage left behind in the wake of his murder was tumultuous, and Myla decided then, she would not allow her child to be born into uncertainty, nor would she announce the pregnancy at all.

For the last two years, she has been expelling much of her magic keeping her pregnancy dormant. A task she does not plan to reverse until she has made the realm safe, and as a result, her child safe. The sacrifices of motherhood, so one would say.

"But," Callum hesitates, "how will you have the energy to sever ties with the Blood Stealer if all your energy is going to this?" He gestures to her belly, still slender and keeping her secret well hidden. "You can not do both."

"So, it seems," Myla huffs. "I can not sever ties with him anyway. How can I allow my child to be born when I, myself, am a threat to it? At any given moment, the Blood Stealer could instruct me to annihilate my kingdom from within, and I would be but a pawn at the mercy of his whims! What would you have me do? I am at a standstill."

A chilling silence falls upon the group. The usual conclusion to a conversation they have had many times over the last two years. A sense of hopelessness once more brings noise to the quiet, induced by dead ends and unanswered questions.

"My recommendation, Your Grace," Captain Bryar speaks again, "we continue to say nothing of this. Not to a single soul." He gestures to their friends, satisfied only by their understanding nods of compliance. "Should this information fall into the wrong hands, it could mark the end of Caius's lineage. It would certainly be death for you." He looks directly at Myla, looking for confirmation that she is listening. The straightening of her shoulders and the slow breath she takes, followed by a nod, is answer enough. They will continue to keep her secrets and seek answers to questions they can not ask.

It is before dawn when Myla's eyes flutter open. Earlier than she usually rises, a warmth deep within calls her from her slumber. Something contrary to the fatigue and anxiety which usually keeps her abed past sunrise. At first, she is pleased by the unusual surge of energy, then with a groan, falls back into her pillows. A lazy hand lifts and with ease, she summons a trickle of light from her palms. *Shit.*

She presses a palm to her stomach and visualizes her magic pooling deep within her womb, creating a shield where the child will be suspended, yet again. The magic untethered overnight as it has done so many times before. In the safety and relaxation of sleep, her weary body instinctually reclaims its flow of magic, releasing the grip on her womb, and she is forced to exert that much more energy to place a hold on the growth. Today will be exhausting; she can feel it in her bones already.

Myla stands, untangling her legs from the thin material of her white nightgown, and makes her way to the balcony jutting out from her bedchamber. The palace and the town beyond are peaceful at this hour. Precious few are awake, and those who are move with purpose. No reason to dally at this hour. The palace guards patrol diligently below, several in view in the gardens alone. A few younger soldiers, it would seem, pass playful shots of magic back and forth. One guard launches a gust of air toward the other, deflected as the recipient of the assault crosses his arms, forming a translucent shield about his body. The sight is a relief; Myla knows her home is well protected, though she must speak to Bryar about the unnecessary expenditure of magic.

The moon glistens off hundreds of rooftops while torch and lantern light casts swaying shadows. White peonies are illuminated, and strands of light dance on the ripples of the water in the canals. It is beautiful. The ivy sneaking up the sides of the terracotta palace walls, hiding the wear from weather and cracks of settling, reminds Myla that this building has stood hundreds of years, and shall stand hundreds more. The palace is not simply old, it is ancient.

Which is an irony to many of the locals who live within New Falkmere. The true Ancient Palace is located in Old Falkmere where the ruins of the first palace sink slowly into the earth and foliage.

The New Falkmere palace sits perched upon a jetty of cliffside, waterfalls tumbling and etching paths in the rocks downward. If one is not looking directly at the palace in daytime, it may be easy to miss, for it is overgrown with creeping ivy, moss, and wisteria. Faded stone peeks out here and there, but the most noticeable part of the palace is the drum tower at the forefront, its crenellations—an unusual pattern against the natural backdrop of the forest—surround it. Many windows and balconies offer a view out, and when the night is black, lights spill forth, creating a magical glow.

The entrance is protected by a gatehouse, which gives way to a magnificent arched door with intricate cuttings of a raven perched on a sword adorning its rim. On either side, stretching along the wall, lining a pleasant pathway, is a row of blind arcades. The ornate decorative arches are kept clear of foliage, so the ravens' torches within them may burn free from obstruction. From the gatehouse, framed by two small watch towers, is a curved stone bridge, closing the sizable crevice of earth which separates the palace from the rest of the city. The tumultuous thundering of the falls below casts a mist, almost constantly shrouding the palace.

Her hands move to her belly, a place they are familiar with resting now. "If I have any say in the matter, this will all be yours, and you shall rule it well." With a gentle pat, Myla moves to her dressing room and dons a robe before ringing for her lady-in-waiting. The slip of a girl hurries in within minutes.

"Good morning, Fern," Myla says. "I would like my tea, please. And send for Captain Monroe."

Upon delivering the tea, and Bryar, Fern is dismissed, visibly mortified to be leaving her queen alone with a man. Myla smiles to herself, trying not to embarrass the girl further with a departing statement such as "*You know I have been alone with men before; this one is no exception.*" Myla holds her tongue instead, and offers Bryar a cup of tea.

"Your Grace," he remarks with a reserved smile once the door shuts behind Fern. "How can I be of assistance? Is something amiss?" His dark eyes are still heavy with sleep, and Myla feels a tinge of guilt for waking him on his night off. His usual post is outside her door, but twice a week, he sleeps through the night, undisturbed.

"No," Myla lies, hiding her fatigue well. "It is only a small matter." Before Bryar can reply, she continues, "I was hoping we could discuss the soldiers. I just saw a few down below in the gardens. *Playing.* With magic. That is energy we can not afford to expel so needlessly."

His broad chest rises as he inhales deeply. His jaw is set firmly. "I will address it, Your Grace." It is likely one of fifty things he might address in a day, as her captain.

Satisfied, Myla nods before speaking again. "I believe it is time we send the Raven's Veil into the Seam again, or . . . perhaps the Ashborn should be summoned."

With a less formal tone this time, Bryar is quick to answer. "Caius would never forgive me if I got you tangled up in any of that. Bringing the Raven's Veil into the situation will take our standstill and turn it into battlefields within days, Myla. I do not see how they can truly help right now." *Myla.* He knows better. "Your *Grace,*" he corrects. "As for the Ashborn, they have not been known to mingle in the matters of Falkmere for centuries."

"Caius would know that I am a lost cause already if something does not change quickly," Myla replies, trying to keep her voice steady and unconcerned, a tone which does not quite fit the words accompanying it. "And the Ashborn are going to find the matters of Falkmere on their doorstep if they do not pick a side soon."

His gaze locks with hers and she thinks he almost reaches for her hand, then hesitates. "You are not a lost cause," he replies simply. "The Ashborn may be, but you are not."

Myla smiles, hiding the doubt behind a sip of her tea. "Were Caius still here, he could have broken my Blood Bond. Without him, there is no way. We must kill the Blood Stealer or . . ." She does not finish. They both know it ends in her unwillingly betraying her family, her friends, and her kingdom. The traitorous mistress to the Blood Stealer, and mother to his wicked offspring.

"The child is Caius's," Bryar objects. "If you allowed it to be born, it would carry the gift, as every Restorer has before . . . you remember what Sir Roderick told us. The child you carry is likely immortal, if the prophesy is true."

"Yes, but to wield it, to *know* to wield it, this child would need to be much older. I do not care what Sir Roderick told us; I believe that was all just a story. Not an actual prophesy. In any case, this child's chances of surviving to young adulthood in the current political climate are slim to none. In every case *but* this one, I will choose my kingdom. I will not, however, sacrifice my child, or risk its life in hopes that it is immortal."

A silence falls between them. With Bryar unwilling to enlist the help of the Raven's Veil, and Myla unwilling to bear the child, solutions feel slim to none.

The crackle of her hearth mixed with the fading tension draws Myla back into the earlier comfort. With time, she glances back at Bryar who, for the moment, is entranced with the flames. For one who wields flames so beautifully, he never seems to lack amazement in the smallest of them. Even a bedroom hearth. Maybe he knows something about them she does not.

"Perhaps you could catch him unaware and send him to face the Gods in a fiery blaze," she speaks finally, visualizing the masterful destruction of their foe at the hands of the powerful man before her. It is a satisfying vision.

The corners of his mouth turn upward in a faint smile. "I fear the Gods would judge me, for I would thoroughly enjoy that," he answers.

"I do not believe that the Gods have never delivered vengeful justice and enjoyed it. They would understand the sentiment."

Changing the subject, Bryar shifts in his seat to face her squarely. "When this is all finished, what will you do?"

"If I live to see it, Gods willing, I think I will just be grateful to still be alive. I am not sure how to plan life after this. Once I defeat the Blood Stealer, I have an entirely different foe in my father."

"You will live to see it, and your father will learn to submit to your reign."

"Always the optimist," Myla teases. "Careful. You are reminding me of a much younger version of yourself."

"If you recall, we promised one another we would always see that version of each other." He gazes at her in a way he has not for many years. A way he has not dared to, since she was betrothed to Caius. A red-hot glow begins to emanate from his being, a response she has seen many times before. His emotions churn beneath the surface. "And," he adds, not wavering in gaze for a second, "you will live to see it, you will be happy, your child will be safe. I will not allow anything less than that."

A weight settles on Myla's belly, a feeling she has not experienced in many years, and has unsuccessfully tried to ignore with Bryar, since the day she met him. Something they are teetering dangerously close to the edge of with this early morning dalliance. Averting her gaze, she nods resolutely, her voice taking a cooler tone than before, a sign the conversation is over. "As captain of my guard, I should hope that is where your commitment lies."

A fleeting look of amusement crosses his face, and he stands to take his leave. "I shall be just outside, should you need me, Your Grace."

"Wait," Myla insists, turning to walk toward her dressing room. "Will you train with me this morning?"

His expression is blank and his eyes briefly twitch toward the door. "Sparring?" There is an instant tension in the room with the word *spar.* It used to mean many things to them, not always the act of swordplay.

"Mm-hmm," she replies modestly, assuming an air of obliviousness. "Without use of my magic, I fear I may be at a disadvantage as of late. I should stay in practice."

Sparring is innocent. Training with her Captain of the Guard is equally so.

To those who do not know their history.

"Yes, Your Grace." The captain's nod is stiff as he turns to leave. "I shall wait for you in the arena."

Before long, Myla has donned a slim-fitting pair of trousers with straps and buckles up the thigh intended to hold daggers and vials. Paired with a form-fitting leather vest over a billowing white tunic, and a tall pair of black boots, she is fit to out-maneuver the captain. Or at least try. She has not been able to out-maneuver him since they were teenagers.

Nevertheless, she arrives at the arena flanked by two perplexed guards, no doubt questioning why the queen is sparring with their captain and not one of her ladies, such as Elsa, who is Myla's usual sparring partner, but now joins only to watch.

Light barely peeks over the tallest point of the mountain which casts its shadow over New Falkmere. It is a mere golden streak of light, meandering over the darkened clouds and trailing overhead where the opaque moon still hangs in the sky, slowly fading with dawn's light. In the center of the arena, the captain already lunges at a wooden dummy, swinging a heavy broad sword over his head. He has discarded his long cloak and heavy armor and stands now in his base uniform of black trousers with a fitted, leather jerkin.

He spins in a forceful lunge, warming his muscles to the exertion and in turn, meets her gaze. For the briefest of moments, her mind plays tricks on her and his chiseled features soften. His curls fall a little looser and the stress lines on his forehead fade. The stubble on his jawline disappears and his green eyes brighten with the loss of a decade of grief. He is no longer a twenty-nine-year-old man. He is an eighteen-year-old boy, and she has just walked into the blademaster's for practice.

Her belly flutters, but she forces a stoic expression, crossing the arena with dignity and no outward signs of nostalgia.

"Places," she piques, twitching an eyebrow and pursing her lips together.

The captain does as instructed, and teeters slightly from foot to foot before finding his balance and bending slightly at the knee, ready for her attack.

Myla also finds her center of balance but wavers slightly, worried what might occur when the shock of their metals meet. She stands a breath away from him, a proximity she has intentionally avoided for a long time.

Never mind that. This is ridiculous. Myla lunges, her fore-foot burying itself in the dirt a few inches from where he stands. Dust from the sudden skirmish is disrupted and the sharp *clank* of steel on steel reverberates off the stands around them. Bryar deflects her attack, sidestepping expertly, his blade now lowered at his side. He does not advance as he used to, catching her off guard or knocking her to the ground. He waits for her attack- waits for her instruction like a proper Queen's Guard.

Oh, I am your Queen now, so you can not fight me properly? Flushed with immediate frustration, Myla glares at him. "Have you lost your love for the fight, Captain?" she growls, lunging at him again. This time with more aggression. Her fists tighten around the handle of the blade and every muscle in her arms engage, ready to lower the blade with as much force as she can muster.

He chuckles slightly, raising his blade to block her attack. The weapon jars violently in his grasp, the shock from her assault clearly far more than he anticipated. With a startled grunt, he staggers back before finding his footing. This time, he leans into her and their blades lock. Using his gauntlet as a shield between his flesh and the blade, he braces his weapon as she swings at him again with a frustrated grunt. Bryar now slides his blade in a downward thrust, breaking their lock and Myla stumbles backward.

"Do you concede the battle, Your Grace?" His tone is anything but formal. It is teasing and familiar, and sends an unwarranted smile across her face.

"Never."

The flashing of blade against blade catches the sunlight over and over again, met with grunts and shrieking metal as they push against one another. Their weapons move in unison, swinging in what becomes a familiar pattern of attack and block, time and again. It is the sort of harmonious brawl that begins to look like a dance. A dance that could only flow so effortlessly with the years of practice they once had together. On the sidelines, arms crossed, Elsa watches with a slight smile hanging from the corner of her mouth.

Myla pivots against another assault and twirls with the blade fully extended. Her blade makes contact with his and they both pause, muscles burning with exertion. Panting and pressing into the lock as hard as she can, Myla blows a wisp of hair from her face and takes note of how close their faces are. Shoulders and forearms pushed against one another; she can smell him.

The all-too-familiar scent teases her with more memories.

"Your Grace," he whispers, his voice trembling between gritted teeth. "You do not seem as out of practice as I thought you might be."

Boring a disgruntled glare into his green eyes, Myla pushes harder against his sturdy frame. "There was a time when you could not best me, if you recall."

"I recall many things," he admits, bracing against her added pressure. The blades slip slightly, sending another shriek of cold steel into the air.

"And yet here you are, barely holding me back." Myla flinches at the coyness in her own voice, but does not allow her stone expression to change at all.

"Maybe I do not want to hold you back." His resistance lessens and the release of his muscles against hers, still engaged, causes her to lunge forward, smacking flush into him. Briefly, Myla finds a firm arm around her waist. To anyone watching, it could be excused as him ensuring his Queen does not suffer a fall. But to her, the hot pressure of his fingertips in her side is unmistakable.

With a slight gasp, Myla steps back immediately, her side still warm from his touch. "That will do for today, Captain," she says. Her voice, traitorous and trembling, does not carry the severity of a queen. Instead, it is soft and pliable and startled.

Myla hands him her blade, averting her gaze from his, and turns to join Elsa. She is grateful they have stopped, for a quivering in her hands begins to takeover, and all she can think about is using her blade to actually kill Bryar. *Courtesy of the Blood Stealer,* she thinks, clamping her hands together.

Her friend's shimmering blue eyes dart between captain and queen, before she leans in and whispers, "I am not so sure that was swordplay." She links her arm with Myla's. "It looked more like foreplay."

Chapter 2

Watching men amass into carefully aligned units, forming a deep blue blanket across the courtyard, the inner bailey, the outer bailey, and beyond the drawbridge into town perimeters, is intimidating no matter how many times one sees it. Tens of thousands of troops, not an inch out of line, ready to march with a single word. Lethal dignity fills the very air Myla breathes as she watches Bryar shout commands, his soldiers respond in maneuvers they have clearly practiced countless times.

It was always Caius's custom to host a military inspection every year before the Oath Ceremony. A grand affair. Dignitaries and political figures, aspiring lords and ladies alike, all descend upon Falkmere to swear fealty to the reigning monarch, as well as to take awe in the impressive military force. Really, as Caius once put it, it is a pissing competition. No one would dare to stand against her when her army is on display like a giant heaving beast against the surface of the earth, ready to strike at her command. It sends chills through her just looking at it. *I have built and maintained this, and they still have the nerve to call me a Dowager.*

Now, Myla carries on her late husband's tradition. This is the second time she will hold her breath as Caius's subjects commit themselves through blood oaths to her. Last year, when all but two of his supporters came to uphold their oath, Myla was humbled with both gratefulness and a sense of unworthiness. This year, despite the quivering within her body, she is determined to present herself as a queen worthy of every drop of blood. Feasting, drinking, and dueling are to take place for a week. Myla wonders how she will find the energy to host into the early hours, then turn around and present various military officials with medals and favors on two or three hours of sleep.

"Your Grace." A page hands Myla the reigns to her saddled mare, a beautiful, raven-black beast who has been a faithful friend since childhood.

She will spend the next two hours riding the perimeter of her army in the company of several council members—her father included—as well as the Lord and Lady of the Riverlands, while they discuss lumber trade deals.

As the small group exits the courtyard, beginning their visual assessment of the troops, Myla is keenly aware of Bryar and twelve of his best soldiers taking up the rear once they have passed the drawbridge. How he can shift so effortlessly from the casual man she sparred with earlier, to this version, a lethal head of military with thousands of soldiers looking up to him, is beyond her.

He is clad head to toe in heavy, crucible steel armor that has seen many battles. A battle axe is strapped securely to his back. He, along with the rest of the army, wears a heavy cloak in the Queen's Blue. Caius had said it was the color of her eyes. On his breastplate is the crest of a raven perched atop a downward pointing broadsword. Myla's symbol as queen.

When her mother sat beside her father during betrothal negotiations, she spoke words Myla will never forget: "*My daughter is as cunning as a raven. She should be treated as such.*" Caius took her words to heart and distributed the symbol of the raven throughout the entirety of the kingdom. It was a romantic and fierce gesture, the motive for which is not lost on her now. *Nothing quite like showering a woman in attention to distract her from what is truly happening . . .*

Myla returns to the palace, with a few moments to spare, before feasting begins. Fern helps her right her hair and smooth the wrinkles in her bodice caused by the tight riding habit. Once alone, she reaches to the very back of her vanity drawer to retrieve a vial of opaque liquid; a tonic her brew mage concocted to help sustain her magic during longer days.

Myla decants a healthy splash into her afternoon tea and sips. Her view of the gardens below is usually uneventful, but today . . . with a giggle, she gawks wide-eyed. Her guests are enjoying themselves already. Two young ladies, foolishly assuming that the hedges shield them from voyeurs, are tangled in each other's reckless embrace. One appears to be from the western region of the realm, perhaps near Titonfall. The tattoo of a mountain range down her back, paired with the heavy boots she has discarded, are a giveaway. Myla can not make out where her partner hails from, and without inspecting an indecent amount, she is unable to, and thus she returns inside her chambers.

She must gather every drop of strength and control she can muster before she stands in a room full of hundreds of men and women. It would be a shame to slaughter them all at the whim of the Blood Stealer.

Too soon, Myla enters the throne room. Pillars fifty feet tall line the edge of the room, a dozen to her left and another dozen to her right. Each pillar is the circumference of at least three men. Caius's great-grandfather was a collector of books, so when he had this room designed, he was adamant the pillars would have ornate shelving carved into them. Now, decades later, the throne room is home to over ten thousand books.

Along the highest point of the ceiling, chandeliers mounted from the beaks of raven gargoyles illuminate the massive room. The ceiling itself was painted the Queen's Blue four years ago, yet another reminder that Caius intended Myla to rule equally alongside him, at the forefront of his peoples' minds. Or that is what he wanted it to look like.

At the furthest end of the hall sit two thrones. Both in the shape of ravens, partially outstretched wings forming the backs and armrests of the thrones. The council suggested, about six months prior, it was time to remove Caius's throne. They believed its presence somehow made her appear weak and still grieving, as though she were in denial. Myla promptly dismissed the suggestion. What she did not want to tell them was she is not ready to accept that she bears this responsibility alone.

She now sits tall on her throne, to the left of Caius's, watching guests trickle in at a steady pace. Her sharp eyes miss nothing, the disheveled couple slipping in as discreetly as they can manage, parting ways without a word. Lords and tenants alike, wearing their finest tunics, all there to swear fealty. Her father parting the crowd like he himself is king and they are an ocean of nuisances, stooping before her throne with a reverent bow.

"I am glad to see you will at least respect my rule when there are people watching, Father," she hums, not bothering to whisper for his sake. Her eyes continue to take in the room, barely glancing at the man before her. It is an intentional disregard; one she hopes will humble him. He remains knelt, unable to move without her permission. Myla's lips turn in a satisfied smile and after a minute or so, she lazily flicks her wrist, allowing him to stand.

"Tonight, of all nights, daughter, you should know I respect your rule." He seats himself at a table near her, close enough to hear any conversations she might have throughout the night.

The room fills rapidly. Sounds of conversation mixed with that of bards telling the tales of kings past and wars sooner forgotten, barely tap the fog of her mind. Another side effect, courtesy of the Blood Stealer. There was a time when Myla was not as much of an observer, but knowledge is power, she has heard repeatedly, and so she watches, despite the ever-present grip of tension her foe has on her.

Seated at a long table to her left is a gathering of lords and ladies, as well as many of Myla's Council members. Lord and Lady Valen of Titonfall raise chalices of sweet wine to one another and Lord Valen leans to whisper, making his wife emit a deep and genuine belly laugh. On the opposite side of the room, important military officials, Bryar included, sit wearing solemn faces. *Discussing assault tactics, no doubt,* Myla thinks to herself.

As she takes in the faces of those gathered this evening to swear fealty, Myla is grateful to see so many. This year alone, they attempted to storm the Seam with hopes of weakening the Blood Stealer. Their army was flattened with a devastating loss of two thousand men. Since then, Bryar's special forces, the Raven's Veil, have been in and out of the Seam countless times, collecting information and undertaking stealthy attacks on smaller targets. He has more recently forbidden any killing behind enemy lines, after men began succumbing to the Blood Stealer more frequently during skirmishes.

Despite the tumultuous happenings of the last half a year, all of last year's subjects have returned. *That is what happens when they do not know their queen is on standby until the Blood Stealer summons her*. The morbid thought sends a shiver down her spine.

When Caius sat safely on the throne, and his Restorer abilities were keeping the Blood Stealer subdued to his own territory, it was simple to keep the plague of the Blood Stealer at bay. Anyone found to be under his influence was brought directly to the King, who would cleanse the victims with Restorer's Magic. Now, without that solution, anyone found to be under the Blood Stealer's influence is executed on the spot, so as to slow his powerful growth. Myla wonders who among her trusted officials would be the first to raise a hand against her, should they discover her secret.

Across the room, the door swings open to another familiar face, though older than the last time she saw him. His chin length hair and gray stubble beard are well groomed and the decorative blade at his side still gleaming. Wearing a fine black tunic with silver details at the wrists and neck, he strides in, oozing the humble confidence she has known from him for a decade now. Myla stands, a thrill in her heart dismissing every instinct to remain the dignified queen. Descending the steps from her throne, Myla parts the crowd and stops just feet away from her old friend.

"Sir Roderick." She tempers the excitement in her voice, though the gleam in her eyes betrays her.

The older gentleman smiles back, bowing with the utmost reverence, a glimmer of pride in his eyes. "Your Grace," he replies, waiting for her motion to stand upright. "It has been many years. I heard of your . . .

status change, and thought to myself: what an honor to have taught the future queen to defend herself."

"I am so pleased to see you," Myla replies, taking Sir Roderick's hand. "I insist you sit near me. I should like to speak with you more this evening. I am afraid I have business to attend right now."

He smiles with a nod of understanding. "I see another friend." He nods toward Bryar, who watches with a visible swell of joy. "I will sit by him for the ceremony, and I shall speak to you after."

Myla returns to her throne, a loneliness sinking over her. Every single person is here on duty, something she is so grateful for. However, at each table, friends sit with friends, while she sits alone. Bryar and Sir Roderick shake hands firmly and exchange a brief hug. Old banter seems to ensue without delay, and Myla diverts her gaze, lest someone notice her jealousy, her longing to sit with them and feel as though she belongs, the way she used to.

As the sun sinks beneath the horizon, casting an eerie twilight over the grand hall of the palace, Myla stands, her movement commanding silence to fall throughout the room, her presence both regal and foreboding. It escapes not a single soul how beautiful she looks. As all eyes settle upon her, she appears tall and resilient, a young woman deserving of the attention she receives. In the flickering candlelight, her flowing brown hair is highlighted and cascades in soft waves down her back, framing her delicate, yet strong face with high cheekbones and a set jawline. She carries a stoic roughness in her eyes, put there by years of treading water. They are a deep, icy-blue. They suck you in like a whirlpool in an angry ocean of unspoken thoughts you would like to know, but never will.

Still wearing the dress she chose this morning; she is certain she made the right choice. A hunter-green gown hugs her form, an elegant and precise tease, the fabric shimmering subtly as she moves, reminiscent of the dense forests surrounding her realm. The gown's intricate embroidery features meandering vines and various creatures, a nod to the unpredictability of nature, as well as the strength of a queen who is equally at home in her court *and* the untamed wilderness, though the latter is not commonly known.

As she moves, the fabric whispers against her skin, and the modest neckline of her dress validates her seriousness. A piercing black crown, crusted in smoky quartz and obsidian, jets upward in six slender spindles, and black peonies are arranged between the points, giving her a feminine ferocity. Looking over her throne room, across the faces of those called to her attention, a look that seems to say, *"you can not hurt me, for I have died and come back again,"* whispers across her stoic features.

The air is heavy with the scent of roasted meats and spiced wine. The flickering candlelight creates shadows that dance ominously across the stone walls. Tonight is not merely a feast, but a ritual steeped in ancient tradition: the oath-swearing ceremony, where loyalty is proven with blood.

With a raised chin, Myla examines her people, the magnificent and menacing slant of her eyes taking in every detail, preparing herself for at least two hours of standing, listening to oath after oath.

Lords and ladies, clad in their finest silks and velvets, approach the dais with trepidation, their eyes flickering with a mix of reverence and awe. Each vassal bears a token of their loyalty—a jeweled bangle, a sleek chalice, or some simple, yet significant trinket. As they kneel before her, the air thickens with tension, and their voices rise in a haunting chant, pledging their fealty with a reverence that sends shivers down the spine. One by one, they prick their palms with the cold steel, allowing a single drop of blood to fall onto the altar, a crimson symbol of their commitment to the crown, and the price of loyalty in Myla's realm.

As she accepts each offering, her hand is steady on their shoulder, her gaze piercing their souls, binding them, not just by a spoken oath, but by the magic spilled from their veins onto the altar before her.

Elsa stands before her now, jaw set firmly, hand unshaken. She pierces the soft flesh of her palm, slicing through scars from many years of oaths, allowing blood to spill upon the altar. Ever a faithful friend and loyal subject, Elsa kneels at Myla's feet, expressing devotion and commitment of the sincerest kind.

Behind her stands Bryar. His increasing proximity, paired with the purpose of the evening, brings heat to her cheeks. *Nothing like a man spilling his own blood for you, after spending the last several years pretending his affections were only for the crown.*

Resisting the urge to smile as he steps forward, Myla lowers her chin in the same reverent nod she has shared with the last eighty-five people. Yet, this nod feels different. The way her stomach twists, as he flays open his own palm to bleed for her, feels different. The grimace of slight pain, matched equally with eyes that scream, *"I would not have this any other way,"* speaks in a different language to her than any of the other oaths before.

It reminds her of a night they shared many years ago, his words haunting her as he kneels before her now. *I would burn this lifetime and every other lifetime to the ground. I would watch my life caught in a fire, all for you.* When his lips part and the oath drops from his tongue like a sacred vow, only they two know, something else in her stirs.

"This Raven Throne, where loyalty binds,
I kneel here; our fates entwined.
With sacred vows, spilled blood we share,
If death is true, I pledge this prayer.
In darkest times to stand as one,

My body, your shield 'til my breath is gone.
By dagger's point lest I be disgraced,
I swear allegiance in this sacred place.
For every drop that stains the ground,
A vow unbreakable, forever bound."

With his oath is complete, he gently places a black curved dagger upon the altar, his gift to her. The hilt is exquisite, fashioned into a leaping fox. The tail is the butt of the hilt, intended to curl around the wielder's fist, and the hungry mouth of the fox being where the blade appears, sharp and menacing. *He made this . . .*

Silence claims the room, waiting for Myla to accept his oath. Eyes locked, the space between their breath is thick. Myla fears any closer and they might implode into a visceral inferno. Nonetheless, with a trembling hand, she gestures for him to stand. *It is just a kiss.* She bolsters within and leans to press her lips to his cheek. To the room of onlookers, Myla is merely accepting one more oath. Between Bryar and her, it is clear in the way the air catches at her lips and her hand instinctively brushes his as she leans closer, this is more than just a vow of fealty. It is a reminder.

When the final vow is uttered, a heavy silence envelops the hall before erupting into applause, the sound reverberating like thunder, a testament to the loyalty forged in the blood of every man and woman in the room. Blood drips from the altar now, trickling down the steps leading to her throne.

In this moment, standing at the head of the room with every single eye on her, responsibility weighs heavy.

They look to her for answers she does not have.

Feasting has commenced when Sir Roderick approaches the throne, kneeling before her, his fist wrapped around a white cloth staunching the flow of blood from his palm.

"As promised, Your Grace, here I am."

Myla laughs at the formality, something she is used to from all but her old blademaster. "Come." She gestures for him to stand at her right and observe the room with her. "What do you see?" she asks, as he takes his place.

Sir Roderick scopes the room, no doubt attempting to predict the next moves of those he studies. It is in his blood to know where people are going next. "I see potential," he says finally, eyes fixed on one table in specific, full of military officials saluting to something. "I see hope." His gaze shifts to room in general, before turning back to her. "But I also see fear . . . for you have the fate of the realm crushing you."

She shivers, eyes flickering to the space behind him, not wishing to meet the inquisitive gaze of one who knows her so well. "You see a great many things, in so little time," she responds stoically. "Did you know all those years ago, that it would be me?"

He sighs, and Myla watches his hands fold before him resolutely. "I had my suspicions after your *display* in the garden. But of course, we all knew without a doubt after your aptitude test." He passes a sorrowful gaze her way. "I must admit, as your instructor, it both broke my heart and thrilled me at once. I watched one reality crumble and another take form. I knew if anyone could do it, it would be you."

Myla scoffs, gesturing to her court. "And you still think that?"

Without hesitation, Roderick answers, "I do." After a moment of silence, he grins. "I wonder at the humor of the Gods."

"Why is that?"

"They saw fit to tangle the threads of your fate with his." He nods toward Bryar. "First in my training arena and now here." He gestures to the great throne room. "In this palace, where so much power limits even the threads of fate."

Myla's stomach twists and she has half a mind to reprimand him for speaking so freely. Instead, she leans into the familiarity which has always been the nature between them.

"You turned a blind eye to much all those years ago."

His beard twitches as his jaw clenches, a smile subdued. "I mind my own business."

"But you did not," she corrects.

"I suppose not. I did not see what everyone else saw. He was not *just* a blacksmith's son, and you were so much *more* than a nobleman's daughter. The rebel in me wanted to give you both a safe haven to *be* so much more than what others allowed." He tenses now, glancing from her to where Bryar sits, intently watching the exchange. "I can see now what a mistake that was, and I can only apologize for allowing false hope to grow where there would only be ruin and hurt."

"How are you feeling?" Elsa asks as she curls into the cushions of the green sofa. She looks like one of the delicate creatures you would expect to find in the conservatory. Perhaps a vision of the ancient fae.

"Gods, I feel like I stood for three hours while countless lords, ladies, and military officials swore their lives to my cause . . . *wait*," Myla giggles. "Yep, that is exactly how I feel." Her body aches, but a budding sense of contentment dulls the discomfort.

Elsa rolls her eyes, followed quickly with a playful smile. "Yes, but how did it *feel*?"

"Different than last year," Myla allows, a subtle nod of

acknowledgment to Elsa's underlying question. "Much different."

"That is what I thought," Elsa chirps excitedly. "You looked to be enjoying yourself this time. Last year was just . . ."

"I was scared," Myla admits. She stood up there last year with a trembling body and a soul filled with doubt. Memories from the year prior, when Caius had been slaughtered before his entire court, were all that ran through her mind as they pledged to her.

The Blood Stealer had descended on his black wraith, fueled by the magic of thirty thousand unwilling donors. Visions of the handsome, yet vicious, man known as the Blood Stealer maneuvering his razor-sharp wraith like a puppeteer across her husband's throat, will forever be etched in her memory. His inky eyes, hooded by deep-black brows and a thirst for blood, insatiable.

As Myla had reached for the hand of her dying husband, the wraith left a cut along her wrist, carrying her blood directly to the Blood Stealer. Leaving her cure lying in a pool of his own blood, dead. He took the life of such a powerful man in a fleeting moment and left Myla in a situation far worse than death: a situation which teased death but refused to deliver on the promise.

Myla is jolted back into reality, her eyes instinctively graze the scar on her wrist, the one that did not kill her but certainly took her life. *No. That was not the day that killed me. Maybe, it was just the day that marked the end of what killed me . . .*

Elsa clears her throat. "Join the living, darling. There is no point chasing the dead down rabbit holes." She is right, of course. Elsa, more than anyone, has seen the darkness a woman can lose herself in after such gore and tragedy.

"I saw it, you know."

"Saw what?" Myla asks for clarification, meeting Elsa's

crystal-clear gaze.

"I saw the look in your eyes, when Bryar swore his oath."

She takes a sip of her wine, a look of innocence fleeting across her features, as though she has not just pranced into forbidden territory.

Myla squirms beneath the scrutiny of her friend's gaze. The conversation she has expected for a while, now here, feels daunting and personal. "There is no point in discussing it, Elsa. I am the queen."

"Yes," Elsa admits. "An unmarried queen, with no lover. It is the most preposterous thing I have ever heard." The woman snorts, swallowing another heavy dose of wine. "Hell, if I was queen, husband or not, I would probably be fucking half of Falkmere and asking the king what he planned to do about it.

"Yes, and you would be headless within a fortnight."

"Not as *headless* as I would have been, if I had not fucked half of Falkmere . . ."

"Elsa," Myla gasps, ignoring the flowery innuendo and instead studying the lanterns hanging from the conservatory ceiling, then the stars beyond them. Anything to avoid the direct gaze of her friend. "There are risks to taking lovers, you know."

"Oh, you mean pregnancy?" Elsa laughs. "Darling, it is a little late to be worried about that."

"I know," Myla says firmly, "but the question of legitimacy to Caius."

"Myla… you have been pregnant for two years, and the only people who know are your immediate friends. It seems to me, that legitimacy will be questioned until the child proves, through their power, who sired them, and you know that. I do not think you are afraid of being questioned. You are afraid of repeating the same hurts. You are afraid of betraying your dead husband."

Myla stiffens. "It is not that. I know in my heart that to love is no betrayal . . . I am afraid to appear weak, or as though my priorities are not in order." Which is exactly why this conversation is futile. No amount of friendly coaxing is going to change her mind. Her situation is already precarious without adding a forbidden lover into the equation.

Elsa scoffs. "You ask any man in that hall tonight where on his priority list *fucking* falls, and it would be priority number two, right beneath loads of power." She pauses, not daring to meet Myla's gaze with her coming statement. "Are you afraid of . . . being physically hurt?"

Myla flinches, drawing her attention to the empty bottom of her wine glass. "No, why would I?"

Elsa nods with an annoyed twitch of her eyebrows, "Not ready for that topic? Noted. So, it is having a more responsible priority list than a male monarch. Let us unpack that, shall we?"

Despite Myla's instinct to argue that it is different for women in power, she merely laughs, grateful Elsa has chosen not to pry. "I think some of them have more power than they do good looks. Fucking might be priority number one." The girls' laughter fills the conservatory and lighthearted conversation cleanses the heavy space.

Chapter 3

It is an hour later when Elsa retires, giving Bryar, who stands guard outside the conservatory, a sly smile upon exiting. One he does not acknowledge, his eyes fixed dutifully ahead, hands resting, relaxed but ready, on the hilt of his axe.

The door closes behind her, a healthy divider between she and him. *I might need a new personal guard.* She thinks back to what Sir Roderick said to her. *I can only apologize for it.* Crickets chirp just outside and fireflies dance in the trees in the furthest corner of the indoor garden. *I can only apologize for it.* A trickling of the fountain accompanies the song of crickets, but otherwise, there is a deafening silence. A silence begging to be broken with whispered confessions and bated breath, an inclination so contrary to her commitment as queen. *I can only apologize for it.* Even Sir

Roderick sees the folly in their past. There can be no future.

Instead of succumbing to the temptation of the man outside, she lifts her palm before her, redirecting her energy. "This is where my focus should lie," she mutters to herself, urging her magic forth. Two years of siphoning her magic to her womb has taken its toll on what used to be a limitless supply. Though she tries, she can not manage to form even a pool of light without relinquishing the hold on her womb. Sparks, like extinguishing stars, speckle her palms, then drift slowly down her forearm until dissipating to nothingness. Another futile attempt.

Dropping her wrist limp at her side, Myla reclines back on the sofa. The sound of soldiers walking past outside the conservatory sends a disruptive *clank* into her tranquil silence, a memory is sparked.

"Well done," Sir Roderick exclaims, patting Bryar on the shoulder firmly. His kind eyes graze the distance between he and Myla, smiling at her as she leans panting, sword gripped between her sweaty fists. "You are both exceptional students." The blademaster takes the swords from each of them, returning the weapons to their places on the rack before gesturing for Myla and Bryar to sit.

Myla does as instructed, grateful to take the weight off her weary thighs, but all too aware of the proximity to Bryar this creates. He sits on the bench beside her, leaning his forearms against his knees as he hunches. She finds satisfaction in the way he swallows air as though he has been kicked in the gut. She has exerted him; he is no longer her superior with the blade. For now, they are equals. Pursing her lips to hide the smirk forming across her face, she turns her attention to Sir Roderick.

"Tomorrow we shall double the time. I believe you are both ready to wield heavier weapons for a longer duration. Our goal this next month is to extend your stamina. There is no telling how long you may find yourself

in combat, nor who you might encounter." Sir Roderick turns to his desk, leaning over a textbook. His students sit in silence, waiting for him to continue. When it becomes clear he has concluded his lesson, Bryar turns to look at Myla, his boyish face alight with curiosity.

"Tell me more about the magic of the Gods."

Myla shifts slightly, the thud of her heart gaining speed as she realizes she is leaning toward him, rather than away from him as propriety would demand. "The headmaster spoke on it in class yesterday."

"I know," Bryar says with a grin. "You told me. That is why I want to hear more. I know you did not tell me everything."

"I did not have time," she replies with a slight smile.

"So, tell me now." His eyes dart to where Sir Roderick is, clearly ignoring their interaction. "Please, I want to know."

A tinge of guilt threatens to erase the warmth collecting in her middle as she breathes the same air as he. She is privileged to learn so much more than Bryar on account of her status and finances. He is lucky to even be here, learning the art of the sword.

"Alright," she whispers. "The headmaster says common magic is not gifted on account of status, but that many nobles have only that. Whereas some commoners throughout history have been known to have ethereal magic, or magic of the Gods even. It is not a matter of social standing that determines what tier of magic one receives, but the gamble of the Gods' will."

"There is not much of the Gods' magic left, is there?" he asks, his tone a bit too loud with excitement, catching Sir Roderick's attention.

"That there is not," Roderick replies, turning to face his pupils. "Have you not learned of the tiers of magic?"

Bryar shrugs, glancing down at his boots before shaking his head. "I know of it. My father simply does not tell me as much as I want to know."

Through a few comments of this sort, Myla has come to realize Bryar's father, a well-meaning man, seems to be restricting the world of magic from his son. To what purpose, she has yet to learn.

Roderick gnaws at his lower lip, deep in thought. "I have not much time before my next lessons begin, but I shall answer your questions now, as long as you both are sworn to secrecy. If the headmaster knew I was giving out additional lessons for free, he would find a replacement for me." A severe look passes across his kind features, warranting nods of agreement from both of them. "Alright," he continues. "What do you want to know?"

Bryar briefly looks to Myla, excitement written on his face. With a nod of encouragement from her, he speaks. "I want to know why magic has anything to do with the king not marrying."

A stillness fills the room, Bryar's bold question clearly catching Roderick off guard. Myla's brows furrow, and she too, turns to the blademaster, curious about the answer to this question she herself has never considered.

Clearing his throat, Roderick nods, beginning to pace the circular stone room as though he walks on unstable ground. Perhaps with this question, he does. "His Grace is said to be a part of a much larger prophesy, spoken by the Seer on the mountain when he was born."

"What prophesy?" Myla blurts, asking what she and Bryar both clearly think.

"Well," Roderick says, kneeling before the two of them, "a prophesy to eradicate the Blood Stealer." Silence settles over the trio, the blademaster observing his students' perplexed expressions before continuing. "You see, the Blood Stealer went undetected for centuries as he built his strength off the magic of mortal men. By the time our kind realized he was here and troublesome, it was too late for any simple solutions. He had consumed the blood of far too many—"

"But where did he come from?" Bryar interrupts.

"Oh, that is simple," Myla retorts, surprised he does not know. "He is a fallen Dark Fae God."

Roderick nods in affirmation. "Precisely, Lady Alerys. And when he fell from the graces of his fellow Gods, he took to the mortal world, quietly consuming us one by one. Now, we know the only magic which has ever been known to weaken him is that of a Restorer, although we found it could not kill him entirely."

"Why?" Bryar challenges, his dark brows pushed together.

"Because it is the only equivalent magic to still be found in our realm. Magic of the Gods, channeled directly from the palms of the Gods above and down through the veins of our king. However, it does not overpower the magic of the Fae Gods. In any case," Roderick redirects the conversation back to their original topic, "His Grace is the only being left known to channel the magic of the Gods. Therefore, he is the only one capable of stunting the Blood Stealer.

"When His Grace was born, the Seer prophesied that in our lifetime, a bride with the magic of the Gods would be found for him, and together they would bring forth a child of incomparable abilities. The existence of that child would be the end of the Blood Stealer. For this very reason, the Institute of Mystic Arts exists. Why do you think the King himself attends every single aptitude test? He is waiting for the day his bride reveals herself."

Myla scowls, thinking of the poor girls walking in here with hopes for their future, not realizing they are all on display to the king, a mere fulfillment of prophesy. "You mean the day someone accepts the King's ransom and turns a poor girl in? Is that all?" Her stomach sours at the thought, aware that deep within, she is likely one of very few girls who do not see the honor in this prophesy, but the prison.

Roderick answers with a deflated sigh. "The Seer spoke of this woman's abilities and how she would not only be a potential vessel for the King's heir, but should the Blood Stealer entice her, she could secure his line of darkness instead. It is said that once this woman be revealed, she is at greater risk of calling the Blood Stealer's attention to herself, for she will decide the fate of our realm. Will we be ruled by the light magic of the Old Gods or will be we ruled by the dark magic of the fallen Fae God?"

Roderick concludes his lessons by encouraging them to understand as much of their history as possible before sending them on their way. Together, the two scale the spiral staircase leading up to the main floor of the Institute before either of them speaks.

"He says you should understand as much of our history as possible," Myla whispers to Bryar as students pass them in the halls. "He says that to you like he did not just have to give you a lesson behind the headmaster's back. It is not fair that having enough coin is what determines what parts of our history you can or can not know."

Bryar shrugs, smiling down at her. "I know more today than I did yesterday. I can not complain."

Myla's eyes lower, and she finds herself absently chewing her nails, nervous to speak should they be heard. With a discreet gesture, she encourages him a step closer before whispering, "Yes, well I can." Her blue eyes narrow, a seed planting itself in her mind. "I can meet in the afternoons, just before supper. I shall teach you everything I learn. Meet me tomorrow, and I shall bring my notes from all of my classes so far. You can keep them for a few days to catch up, we will begin meeting every day next week."

It is not a suggestion, and Bryar knows it. Myla will not take 'no' for an answer. If she is to be educated, then so is he.

Myla could lose herself in memory, an indulgence she allows more regularly than she cares to admit. For the past is where her happiness lives. Tonight is no exception. The memory threatens to lure her down the more secret paths of what her and Bryar's meetings would become.

That is, until six Council members and Myla's flushed father come pouring into the room. Their faces are a mix of ashen concern and rage.

"Forgive the late disruption," Lord Sorrin offers hoarsely, though it is clear he is not sorry at all. His voice is cold as the officers form a strategic standing circle around him. He unfurls a detailed map of the realm, the parchment crisp under the tension of the moment, and decisively points to a location fifty miles west of the palace with a pudgy finger. "Here, just before Titonfall. The Raven's Veil reports the Blood Stealer, accompanied by a small army, is advancing toward us. We have a strict timeline of forty-eight hours before they reach the palace gates."

A visceral jolt of shock courses through Myla. Thoughts of her own blood staining these floors, dripping down the Fae God's chin within the week, flash unwelcome through her mind's eye. Gathering her resolve, she steadies her voice, projecting confidence amid the turmoil. "A small army, you say. What are their estimated numbers?"

Sorrin casts a glance to his right, where Lady Jameson stands, visibly fatigued and road-weary from travel, yet composed. "My scouts estimate the hostile forces to comprise approximately two hundred combatants."

Turning to Bryar, Myla furrows her brow, urgency lacing her tone. "What is the status of our border defenses?"

"I currently have nine hundred troops deployed along the perimeter of New Falkmere," Bryar replies, his voice resolute.

"Can we allocate another five hundred?" she inquires, her mind racing through the logistics.

Bryar nods firmly. "Your Grace, we have an additional thousand available. We have been fortifying our defenses, in preparation for this very reason, over the past two years."

"Well done," she praises, careful not to make direct eye contact lest they see right through her formal tone. "Please arrange for five hundred more troops to be dispatched to the city borders and fortify the palace defenses immediately," Myla commands, her eyes narrowing with determination.

Sorrin interjects, his tone authoritative. "Your Grace, I recommend we also distribute our forces to the outlying villages, perhaps we send troops to protect the monks, should he pass through that way?"

Though, it is unlikely the monks will be disturbed, Myla nods in agreement before she glances at Bryar to confirm he understands her orders. "Execute the plan, but instruct our forces not to engage in combat unless provoked. There is no need for more unnecessary bloodshed," she commands. Bryar acknowledges with a brief bow and swiftly exits the room, instructing the guards stationed outside to remain with her in his absence, ensuring her safety as the preparations unfold.

As the evening wanes into early morning, the atmosphere within the conservatory-turned-war-room grows increasingly tense, a palpable weight settling over the assembled officers as they begin outlining defensive strategies. Myla, though outwardly composed, feels a tempest of emotions swirling within her—fear, dread, and a gnawing anxiety that the Blood Stealer might not only come for the realm, but for her specifically. *The prophesy also warns that he may want me for other purposes . . .* This is what she expects. It is a wonder he has allowed her to continue in any sense of normality after Caius died.

The looming question in the back of her head remains: why wait this long? Memories of whispered tales and fearful glances surface in her mind, reminders of the devastation that followed in the wake of Caius's murder. The Seam grew in strength and the raiding of smaller villages peaked for several months as the Blood Stealer continued his rampage. It was only after Bryar led an army to intercept him at Titonfall that the marauding slowed. Bryar had flattened much of the Blood Stealer's army with fire alone.

It is unlikely his fire will have the same effect this time, but Myla can not help but hope that between herself and the more gifted in her court, something will prove effective.

As plans are formulated for repositioning troops and reinforcing fortifications, she struggles to focus, her thoughts drifting to the implications of the upcoming conflict. The Blood Stealer has been known to dispatch his blood-thirsty wraith and claim control of hundreds of victims in mere minutes. Should he be coming to Falkmere with the intent to battle, without the Restorer's magic, they are as good as dead—or puppets. Though she hates to give the order, Myla instructs for any recently deceased citizens of New Falkmere to be burned so the Blood Stealer can not reanimate them while he is here, as he has been known to do.

The officers debate logistics and troop movements, discussing the best placement for archers and infantry, while Myla's heart races at the thought of the enemy's approach. She imagines the chaos that might ensue if the Blood Stealer breaches the palace walls, and the devastation it could bring to her people—and her. Each mention of strategy raises her pulse to a deafening pound, like battering rams on the palace gates, she fights to keep her composure, knowing her role as leader requires unwavering and selfless strength.

Caius used to tell her that Falkmere was made of two castles, the one they reigned in and the one that was the mind and body of the monarch; a fortress as impenetrable and well-guarded as the dwelling itself.

Determined to uphold this philosophy, Myla steadies her breathing, answering questions and giving instructions with a pretense of ease.

As discussions turn to the potential for a flanking maneuver and the necessity of proving a fallback position, Myla's mind races with strategies of her own—not just for the defense of the realm, but for her own child's survival. Will he sense the power of the child growing inside her? She resolves to stand her ground, to fight not only for her people but also for her child. As the shadows lengthen and the reality of impending confrontation looms ever closer, Myla is eerily aware she has been cornered into a situation which will demand that she choose: her people or her child.

The Blood Stealer, a fallen Dark Fae God, prowls through the shadows, a sinister figure and a friend to darkness. His presence is both chilling and magnetic, an eerie call to sacrifice one's blood to his cause. His skin, pale as moonlight, starkly contrasts the deep crimson of the blood staining his hands and lips, remnants of his most recent claims. Eyes like obsidian pools glint with an unsettling hunger, betraying a predatory intelligence that infiltrates the very souls of those who dare meet his gaze. He moves with a silky grace, each step calculated, as if the very ground beneath him trembles in recognition of the malevolence he embodies.

Around him, the air thickens with an aura of dread, a palpable reminder of the countless blood oaths he has consumed in his relentless pursuit of power. The Blood Stealer feeds not just on blood, but on the latent magic coursing through the veins of his victims, drawing forth their essence to amplify his dark abilities. With each drop he drains, he binds their will to his, transforming them into unwilling thralls, mere shadows of their former selves, compelled to serve his insatiable appetite for dominion until he has drained them of life and their body fails them, inevitably resulting in death. Sometimes self-inflicted.

Myla chews her thumbnail, envisioning the devastation left in the wake of the demon she knows marches toward her now. Is he coming to kill her, or claim her? As of right now, Myla is the only woman in the realm known to have the magic of the Gods on her side. If the prophecy Sir Roderick taught she and Bryar years ago is true, that means the Blood Stealer may want her for her womb. *Gods, just let him kill me,* she thinks sarcastically.

"You need to rest." Elsa appears around five in the morning, dressed for the day and bearing a cup of mulled wine. "You are no good to anyone worn, ragged, and weary." Elsa presses palms to Myla's shoulders, releasing a syrupy warmth of calm healing into her veins.

Myla smiles at her friend, accepting the drink. "Yes. You are right. I think I shall retire for a few hours. If I am needed, please come wake me. Will you send Fern in to help me undress?"

Fifteen minutes later, after a heavy dose of restorative tonic and the warmth of the mulled wine in her belly, Myla sinks into the feathered folds of her bed.

Chapter 4

As he grows closer, Myla can feel the supernatural pull, an urge pulsing through her veins to surrender her throne, surrender her palace, and run to him. A darkness lying in wait, always torturing the back of her mind, taunting her with the knowledge that he is imminent. He is coming to either kill her or claim her body. Either way, his approach means only one thing for her: this child is in great danger.

Those around her are also in great danger. Myla wakes from a fitful sleep with the urge to kill. Soldiers posted around her, the target of her violent intentions. The Blood Stealer seems to plot against her already, wanting her unprotected and easily accessible.

Soldiers line within the palace grounds and beyond into the streets of the city. Everywhere you turn, the flash of Queen's Blue is moving back and forth. It is no secret war is brewing; that has been clear for a long time.

Though it is midday now, Myla would not know. From the moment she rose, she has been in the Archives Sanctum, accompanied by the scrollwarden, searching for any clues for defeating the Blood Stealer. Though Myla conceals her secret from the scrollwarden, the elderly woman can still prove useful in pulling any texts from the shelves that contain information on their foe. Myla now flips through the texts, desperate for something to stand out as an obvious solution.

Without Caius's magic, there seems to be no way to break the blood oaths which have already been stolen. If they try to kill him without breaking the blood oaths, they will have him and his rapidly growing army to contend with, no doubt adding to it with every wounded soldier.

Myla has heard rumors the Blood Stealer has been known to engage in small skirmishes, but rather than killing his victims, he will only wound them, consume their blood, and expand his army by several dozen at a time. Soldiers have been known to change sides mid-battle, which is why Myla insists there shall be no battling if it can be helped.

I have resisted his call; perhaps we could find a way to implore his army to resist as well, she considers absently, flipping pages back and forth as though the answer will appear before her with encouragement. "I have heard of some victims in the past being able to withstand his attempts at control. How was that achieved—can we replicate it?" Myla asks, hoping to learn more of her own situation, as well as find a possible solution.

The scrollwarden, an ancient-looking woman with crow's feet at the corners of her eyes, shakes her head resolutely. "In the past he has been known to claim more powerful victims. There were those who were fortunate to have a more potent magic in their veins, who seemed to withstand him a little. The victims he recruits tend to have minor magic abilities and thus, no power capable of withstanding him at all. An intentional selection, I presume."

"So, one's ability to resist is merely a privilege of ability?"

The scrollwarden nods, a grim expression flashing across her wrinkled features. "Indeed, Your Grace. What an unjust system, is it not?"

He must be allowing me to live in some semblance of normalcy so I will thank him for his lenience when he arrives. Myla lets out an exasperated sigh, picturing the Blood Stealer attempting to win her over on account of not fully controlling her.

Well, he will not hear a 'thank you' from me.

"I need to meet with the brewmage. Perhaps he can brew something to help reinforce the weaker wielders."

"The magic you seek can not be manufactured," the scrollwarden warns. "You can not fabricate a gift from the Gods."

"Perhaps not, but none will thank me for not trying, not even the Gods," Myla responds absently while flipping through piles of records. The history is vague. Though stories of the malicious and beastly magical bloodline are sparse, those she can find prove unhelpful. Every record leading to the same dead end: one must wield Restorer's magic to unharness victims of the blood oath and defeat the stealer himself.

"Keep searching," Myla instructs with a grateful nod. "I must look elsewhere." She climbs the steep stairs leading out of the Archives Sanctum to the back of the throne room, where servants are polishing the floor and dusting bookshelves. Tall wooden ladders leaning against the pillars support people higher up, tending to the harder-to-reach books.

"Rhyland," she calls to the young man who leans against one of the pillars, flirting with a guard.

He bows briefly, then straightens as she approaches. "Your Grace." With a bashful whisper, he looks sidelong at her. "*That* did not go well. I really wish my morals did not keep me from wiping his memory."

Myla grins, shaking her head in a pretend state of judgment. "You need to stop searching for love among the guards."

Rhyland flashes her a condescending smile. "Says the woman hopelessly in love with a guard herself."

"I am not . . . in any case," she quietly replies with a smile. "I remember a time when you claimed to love him as well."

Rhyland grovels. "Remind me to wipe that memory too . . ."

"You have been saying *that* for ten years," Myla answers with a laugh. "I think you enjoy giving me your secrets." Myla looks to the cleaners overhead and with a more serious and formal tone, she addresses him. "See to it these people have harnesses. We do not need a repeat of last time."

Last year, when one young idiot was cleaning the top of the bookshelves, a flighty housekeeper did not notice as she backed into his ladder, knocking him fifty feet to the granite floor beneath. She spent the day mopping his blood and fragments of his skull up, Myla had insisted on safety harnesses being worn from then on out.

Rhyland, abashed at the oversight, bows once more and demands the workers bring themselves down at once. He then glances over his shoulder at her and whispers, "Also, who says anything about looking for love, Your Grace? Perhaps I would settle for a friend these days."

The words rest uneasy where they land with Myla. There used to be an effortless bond between herself and her friends. Now there is a barrier which seems to have pushed the wedge of duty between all of them, to an extent.

Now, more than ever, she wishes they could all find their way back to that effortless place. Problems were easier to solve back then.

Shaking off the nostalgia, Myla passes quickly through the throne room and makes her way across the palace, past the barracks, and into the

Alchemy Chamber where the brewmage leans manically over a thick, leather-bound book. His pale hair is pointing in complete disorder, and three vials are suspended in the air to his right, bobbing up and down with the motion of liquid bubbling within.

The brewmage is a young man, younger than many of the lords and ladies of the realm have dared to employ. But Myla, having questioned the loyalty of Caius's original brewmage, made it her goal to employ a trustworthy one.

It had taken many weeks of tracing lineage and reading applications before Myla had selected Alaric. Though he was young, he had graduated the Institute of Mystic Arts with brilliant scores on all fronts and came highly recommended by his tutors. Myla had met with a large string of brewmages who all seemed qualified, but Alaric was the one she connected with. He is the only one outside of her friend circle she has dared share her secret with. Mostly on account of necessity.

Myla, taking in her surroundings, is at once enveloped by the earthy aroma of herbs and the faint sweetness of blooming flowers. Sunlight filters through a large, circular window, illuminating the room with a warm glow and casting intricate shadows against stone walls, adorned with climbing ivy and hanging moss. Statues of the Gods line the walls, telling stories from eons before their existence. Brightly colored tinctures also line the walls, each labeled with handwritten notes in flowing script, detailing their uses and effects.

Around the chamber, shelves made from ancient wood are filled with glass jars of vibrant colors, each having dried herbs, roots, and flowers—chamomile, lavender, and sage among them. A large wooden table sits at the center, its surface cluttered with pestle and mortar, dried leaves, an assortment of crystals that sparkle like dew in the morning light, and a large, leather-bound grimoire. It has been left open, its pages filled with sketches of plants and notes on their magical properties, inviting Myla to explore the secrets of green witchcraft that lie within.

In one corner, a small herb garden thrives, pots overflowing with greenery and delicate blooms, leaves glistening from a recent watering. A gentle breeze wafts through an open window, carrying the scent of wildflowers from outside making the delicate wind chimes—crafted from bone and glass—tinkle softly in harmony. Across the room, a bubbling cauldron sits atop a fire pit, steam rising in wispy spirals, infused with the rich scent of simmering potions.

Everywhere she looks, the symbiosis of nature and magic is palpable, creating a serene yet vibrant atmosphere that speaks of ancient wisdom and the art of herbal alchemy. All of it is new since she banished the earlier brewmage. Alaric has brought the alchemy chamber to life.

Myla notices black runes lay scattered, divination having occurred recently.

"What do the Gods tell us?" she asks, levitating a finger above the energetic runes, not daring to touch them.

"Your Grace!" he quips, hastily bowing before handing her one of the bobbing vials. "I have replenished your tonic!" He glances to the runes, his red cheeks flushing, "And they say we are royally fucked."

Nodding to the vials, Myla rolls the one he handed her between her fingers. "I am grateful." She smiles and tucks the tonic into her bodice. "Royally fucked is no news to me. Perhaps next year they will say something different." She pauses, flipping a rune over now, hoping to erase their messages. "I am afraid I must disrupt whatever it is you work on."

"Your will is my command," Alaric replies, waiting for her to elaborate on her needs. He fidgets, eyes darting to and fro with distraction. Myla has always noticed he lacks the ability to be still, always moving, always driven with purpose and a need to accomplish every task before the day's end.

"Do you suppose there is a way to replicate or manufacture, you might say . . . the Restorer's magic?"

His shoulders sag slightly, and he reaches out to retrieve the other two vials, slow and careful in his answer. "If it were as simple as making specific kinds of magic, I believe we would have conquered this already. Sadly, the best I can do for you, Your Grace, I have already done."

"I was afraid you would say that," Myla replies. "I am on the hunt for solutions. I am afraid it will not be a matter of defeating the Blood Stealer, but of putting up a good fight," Myla admits with trepidation, the reality of the situation weighing heavy. "Could you perhaps brew something that amplifies my magic or increases its longevity more than the one you have already made me? I do not wish to die easily and be the laughter in a bard's retelling when this is all over with."

Alaric chews his lower lip, eyes darting from herbs to vials and the books on his wall. "Might I beg Your Grace to give me a few hours? I will try what you ask, but I will need time to reference several manuscripts. I am afraid the strength in the tonic I have made already was a feat. I doubt we have access to the ingredients needed to make a stronger one."

With a nod, Myla hesitates and asks a final question. "How long do you suppose it would take one to train in dark magic before being able to stand against the forces of the Blood Stealer? He has so many tied to him."

Alaric grins. "Against the rabble? You have nothing to fear." He hesitates. "But, once dark magic is introduced into your being, it is challenging to rid yourself of it. You already carry burdens you should not, Your Grace. Perhaps it is bold of me to say, but I would not muddy the pond with dark magic."

His response, while reassuring, does not settle well with Myla. The majority of the Blood Stealer's army are victims, certainly not there willingly. The concept of killing them with a flick of her wrist feels like a cheap and unnecessary death. Myla drums her fingers aimlessly on the apothecary table, taking one last glance at the runes before leaving. *Royally fucked.*

Having left the Alchemy lab with little to go off, Myla was on her way to her chambers for a brief rest when her father had intercepted her, insisting there was more she should be doing. There is always more. When he had promised her in marriage to Caius, he told her of the pleasantries and privileges she would enjoy as queen. As he belittled her today, she found herself spewing, "Where are my pleasantries and privileges if I can not simply walk to my own chamber without being berated by *you?*"

Since her mother died shortly after her marriage, the relationship between Myla and her father has grown substantially more tense. Her mother always served as a buffer between Maverick and his daughter. Now, with no buffer at all, they are like sharp daggers grinding against one another, each desperate for the deeper cut.

As a result of this bitter encounter, she has retreated to the gardens, and at last, Myla finds herself seated on a stone bench, hidden behind the ancient, draped limbs of a weeping willow at the furthest end of the garden. The grass beneath is trodden from years of visiting. Here, Myla leans back, her eyes falling closed, and the sound of a babbling brook behind her is nature's lullaby. In the distance, the sound of soldiers training, a sound that should be comforting, is merely another reminder of impending doom.

"You should not be here alone," a familiar voice chides. Myla does not open her eyes; she does not need to to know who stands before her. His presence, the sound of his voice and weight of his steps advancing is an immediate reminder of the last time they took to the willow tree as a hiding place. Myla's father had just signed a betrothal agreement with Caius. At the time, Myla was fearful and heartbroken. She knew Caius was a good and kind king but had no way of knowing how he might serve as a husband. And she knew he was not Bryar.

As the marriage outlines were drawn up, Myla had watched with glistening eyes as Bryar stood, resolute in his role as the king's guard, behind his master, unwavering. His jaw set in a firm clench, Myla believed he was balling his fists and biting down on his own tongue to refrain from objecting.

Once Myla was dismissed and Bryar could escape unnoticed, they met beneath the willow tree. It was there they had lain together for the last time, promising for both their sakes, as well as that of the kingdom, they would forsake each other forever. There would be no more secret rendezvous. They would no longer exchange warm gazes across the room. Under no circumstances would they compromise her position as queen nor his as the King's Guard.

So, he has become a phantom to her, someone she sees and pretends not to. Now here he is again, where she has hidden so many times in the last five years, wondering if he ever did the same. Daydreaming of their concluding moments here.

"How did you find me?"

"You are predictable, and consistent, fortunately for me. What kind of Queen's Guard lets his queen wander unattended." The latter is spoken as a sort of chastisement disguised as concern. He hates when she wanders off without him or at least *someone.* Myla opens her eyes to see him turn dutifully, back to her, watching the grounds before them. The branches of the weeping willow skew her view of him slightly, but she can make out the way his shoulders heave in a worn-out sigh and his hands rest heavily on the axe at his side. She laughs slightly, and he turns to look at her between the branches, eyebrows raising in question.

"What is so funny?"

"You. Carrying that axe."

"Why is that?" he asks.

"Because we all know it is purely decorative. You do not need it."

"No," Bryar agrees. "Unless I get fatigued in battle and can not channel magic."

Myla purses her lips, picturing the one and only time that has ever happened to him. Caius's death weighs heavily on all, but Bryar holds the grief of the soldiers who died trying to save their king. The battle which ensued once the palace had been breached was a devastating one, and Bryar fought honorably. Myla will never forget him walking into the throne room where she sat sobbing over Caius's body. He was covered in blood from head to toe. A long slash to his ribs and the remnants of human tissue on his axe were proof enough of the way he fought to save his king and soldiers.

"I visited the brewmage," Myla says to shift the topic. "His runes say we are royally fucked."

Bryar smirks and cautiously steps within the enclosure of the tree. "It is nothing you can not handle, Your Grace." He stares at the ground between them, an invisible barrier keeping that distance greater than either of them would like. "What if I asked you to go to your family's estate and wait somewhere less obvious until we have more answers. Until we have a better plan?"

Myla shakes her head, standing as if she has been stuck with something sharp. "You want me to run away? You, who is the least cowardly person I know, is asking me to be a coward?"

Bryar shakes his head in fierce contradiction. "No, Myla. I am asking you to stay out of harm's way, until we know how you can best protect yourself, and the child."

Myla shakes her head. "I will not leave. I swore to protect this kingdom, and that is what I plan to do, even if it kills me."

An irritated growl escapes Bryar, and he reaches out to grab her arms, his brows furrowed and concern drawing a sharp line in his jaw. His touch, though an angry one, is electric, and Myla feels a surge of passion rush through her being. He has not laid a hand on her in years.

"*If* Myla?"

Myla. Not 'Your Grace.' Myla.

"You say *if* like we have some plan just seconds away from falling into place. You say *if* like your death is not a real possibility!"

Attempting unsuccessfully to jerk free of his grasp, Myla glowers at the man before her. "*You* say *if* as though I have not been living this very real possibility for two fucking years! I am exhausted, and I want it over with, *Captain Monroe.* Whatever *that* looks like, I can not continue like this. Let it kill me; see how much I care."

He releases her, running his hands across his face in exasperation. "You might not care, but . . . there are those who do, and will not hear you talking like this. I hear you." His voice is softer now, though still edged with desperate reasoning. "Consider, you carry the heir. The last being to possess Restorer's blood. If you die, it dies and hope for a life without the Blood Stealer dies as well. And while it may seem selfish to bring personal feelings into the equation, I do not want to watch you die unnecessarily." The final plea is spoken cautiously, his hands gripping the hilt of his axe as though he needs something, anything to occupy them, lest he should burn the garden down, in rage and fear.

Myla takes slow, deep breaths, trying to untangle fear from reason to make sense of what should be done. Being pigeonholed into a corner with very few solutions, none of which are good, does not give a queen the appearance of control. Which of course, stands to reason, for she has none at this moment. "Captain, I do not believe I am seen as a queen to be feared. I am followed and respected because I was Caius's wife. These people do not fear me."

"I do not see that as a bad thing."

"It is not," Myla agrees. "Until I run off into hiding and am a coward on top of it. How will they follow me then?"

Bryar shakes his head fervently. "Being seen as a coward and actually being one are vastly different things. Do you care how they see you more than you care to survive?"

"A queen must care how she is perceived."

"So, we tell them you are seeking answers from the Gods, and you will return shortly. Assign a regent in your stead. And then we take you somewhere no one will look for you, and I will go to the Seer and get answers for you."

Myla gasps, resisting the urge to reach out and take his hand. "You can not. I could not allow you to make that journey on my behalf. Many have not returned; I could not bear that." Regret fills her middle the moment her final statement is made. In an effort to rectify the sentiment, she speaks again. "I see enough men die on account of my rule. I will not see any of those deaths be for hopes or whims."

"We do not have a choice," Bryar huffs. "Without some clarity from the Gods, I am afraid of the mess we might make here, following our own judgment."

Myla knows he is right. Without answers, they are left to gamble and hope they make the right choice. The Gods know already how—or even if—she will defeat the Blood Stealer. "I shall go with you, then. I shall seek these answers for myself. That is not your responsibility."

He takes a deep breath and nods. It is clear he is relieved, having been successful in his purpose. "Go ready your things, Your Grace. Pack light, and we will leave in an hour."

Together, they appear from the cover of the willow tree and navigate the garden hedge maze back to the palace where life is more abuzz than when Myla left it an hour ago.

A figure draped in a heavy cloak runs toward Myla, throwing back the hood. Callum is revealed, breathless and flushed with exertion. "Where the hell have you been?" He looks from Bryar to Myla, then rolls his eyes in agitation. "You have maybe fifteen minutes before the Blood Stealer arrives. I nearly killed my horse trying to get here before he did."

Myla freezes, dread rushing through her. Could this be it? Could this be the moment her fate is decided? "How large is his army? Was the earlier report, correct? I thought he was not set to arrive until tomorrow?"

Callum shakes his head. "Less than two hundred. I do not think he has come to fight. It looks like a peaceful envoy. But he travels much faster than he did according to yesterday's reports, so *make haste.*"

Myla glances at Bryar, her furrowed brow asking the silent question: Could that be? Of course it could be. The answer is simple—he has not come to kill her; his intentions are far less merciful.

"What makes you say it appears to be peaceful?" Bryar clarifies.

It is at this moment Lord Sorrin and Lord Heron join them, both fully armored and clearly ready to stop the threat.

"Because," Callum answers, side eyeing the new arrivals, "he is leaving much of his army outside the city limits. He did not even progress half of them through our barricade. They are simply . . . making camp. Last I saw, he was approaching with only eight guards."

"Royally fucked," Myla growls, turning away to make for her chamber. "Send for Fern and tell her to make haste. We have no time to spare. When the Blood Stealer requests an audience," Myla turns to face Bryar, her expression stone and unreadable, "you are to let him in."

Chapter 5

Pounding at the door, much like inside her chest, causes a trembling in Myla's core. Her limbs feel feeble against the stress of anticipation. Timidly, Fern opens the door to the face of Maverick. The tall and fearsome man pushes past her young lady-in-waiting and stops nearly toe to toe with Myla.

"You have let the dark one *himself* through our defenses and into our home?" he bellows, gripping her wrist as though she is an insolent child. "Have you learned *nothing* about the duties of a wise queen? Have you listened to anything I have tried to teach you in the last six years?"

Myla's nostrils flare in rage and her body tingles with a need to eviscerate her father on the spot. "How *dare* you barge in here, trample over my maid, and speak to me in this manner?" She turns her back, facing her mirror as though he is invisible, adjusting her appearance one last time.

"I have no choice but to chase you all over this palace, cleaning up your messes!"

"What messes, Father? Name one thing I am at true fault for beyond not kowtowing to your minuscule fixations?" Myla's voice is raised now, sounding the alarm to the captain posted at her door.

Red faced and enraged, Maverick's hand raises, ready to strike his daughter for her insolence. Bryar steps through the door in time to halt his swing, his hand clamping tight around the angry man's wrist. Eyes boring into the blacks of her father's, Myla brushes past him, certain to force him out of *her* way with a sharp nudge of the shoulder before eyeing her captain. "Have him removed," she hisses, and without further instruction, Bryar drags Maverick away from Myla.

Concern on his face, Bryar looks over his shoulder to where she stands, seeking permission to speak.

"What is it?" she asks.

"Your presence is requested in the throne room, Your Grace," he says, his head bowed. Eight more guards now stand behind him, ready to escort her right into the mouth of the enemy.

Caius had custom armor made for Myla as a wedding gift. She had never needed use of it, so it sat on display in their private armory. Today, she dons it, along with her crown, sharp and spindling points reaching several inches above her head. A chill cascades down her body. The bodice of the war-plate is cold, virgin metal with no battle experience to warm it. Delicate etchings of wild things—such as foxes and ermine—and foliage twist across the breasts and belly of the armor. A feminine touch.

As she walks, surrounded by her guards, her height is no longer a matter of how tall she naturally stands, but the way she carries herself, a towering symbol of infallible strength equally matched by feminine demure. Ornate black shoulder guards resembling crouching ravens cover her shoulders, transitioning smoothly into bracers and a chainmail top. With each step, the rustle of her chainmail skirt, shrouded in a deep green satin, announces to all that their queen passes.

Fearful eyes line the halls, looking to her for solutions. Prayers muttered as she passes, prickle her ears to listen. Whispers of "May the Gods be with you, Your Grace" are echoed over and over. Servants and children alike watch with horrified faces as she passes. A comforting nod from her evokes sad smiles.

They think you are going to die today; what a lovely bode of support.

Everything moves in slow motion and a million thoughts pass through her mind the closer to the throne room she gets. Tension hangs in the air unlike anything she has felt since Caius was killed. Whereas his assassination was a blow to all, leaving a reverberation of shock looming over the kingdom for weeks, the very breath she and her court breathe now stings with the promise of deadly poison. A sentiment promised in the way her body trembles uncontrollably. *He is here, and he wants me to feel him.*

"Her Majesty, Queen Myla Alerys of Falkmere, the Dowager Queen!" She is announced with a confident shout as the giant, iron doors of the throne room swing open, making way for her and the guards beside her.

Knelt in suspicious reverence before her throne, back to it and face turned downward in her direction, is a shockingly handsome man, who Myla swears is dripping black venom from his pores. Flanking either side of him are two massive wolves. Their coarse fur is as black as ink, and they stand partially crouched. The scruff of fur behind their sharp shoulder blades stands on end and they watch her approach with vigilance. They seem to communicate with their master, snarling in response as he orders them to lie down with a simple wave of his hand. Though she can not see it, she *feels* it. She can feel his pull deep within her. Negotiations have already begun.

Hair darker than ink is pulled back into a twist at the nape of his neck, a few stray locks falling around his forehead. Black stud earrings pierce his pointed ears, a dead giveaway to his Fae background. A long scar travels from the upper left of his brow down to his chin. His dark eyebrows are furrowed as he looks directly through her into her soul, searching for secrets perhaps. Or is he sniffing out fear to feed upon, like the wolves which stand guard beside him?

Whatever it is, Myla refuses to satisfy the hunger. Her face is unreadable as she walks directly past him without so much as a glance and twists fluidly to sit on her throne, the green of her cloak, a stark contrast against the black of her armor, ruffles like a train at her ankles.

"Blood Stealer." She hisses his name making it clear she has little taste for it on her tongue. "To what do I owe this *intrusion*?"

With the effortless unfurling of a snake, he stands, his hands raised slightly in protest at his side and his massive black cloak shrouding the majority of his being. "Come now, darling, surely you have heard it is not nice to call names."

A charming and charismatic smile steals across his face. To many, it might appear dashing, alluring even. To Myla, it is unnerving. There is a loss of vitality forming within her, a sickening feeling of inhibitions lulling and impulses spiraling out of control. A need to fall into his arms takes over as she grows lightheaded, struggling to stay composed.

"Allow me to introduce myself formally," he continues, taking account of the dozens of guards flanking her left and her right, one of them being Bryar, hand on hilt. "Lord Vesperian Shayd, at your service, Your Grace." The words *at your service* are hummed like an ancient vow, one Myla has unwillingly partaken in.

The only sound behind her is an unwelcome snicker from Elsa and an almost inaudible whisper of, "I would like him to be at my service." *Gods, I really need to talk to her about her inappropriate timing.* Myla ignores the lewd joke, speaking clearly.

"And what are you doing here, Lord Vesperian?" She steadies her voice and lackadaisically relaxes her fingers across the hilt of the fox dagger which she has sheathed at her waist. "For your coming unannounced is a gross lack of decorum."

The Blood Stealer smiles, flashing a row of straight, white teeth behind deep-red lips. "I should imagine you have been expecting me for some time now. Have you not felt the call?" Myla bristles, and the entirety of the room falls silent with questions and confusion. He continues, throwing Myla's stomach into a lurch. "Your blood tasted delicious." He does not get one step closer before Bryar and twenty other guards have drawn their weapons. Myla holds up a hand, commanding a pause as the Blood Stealer ceases his advance.

Unconcerned, Vesperian glances slowly from the soldiers back to Myla. "It made me wonder...how the rest of you tastes." A devilish grin creeps across his face and does not waver, even when Lord Maverick barks protest to the gross address of his daughter.

"Mind your tongue! You speak to your queen!"

"Mind my tongue? Yes, I intend to," he agrees with a suggestive smile. "My queen. One whom I have allowed to live here in peace, undisturbed. Surely, my darling, it has not gone unnoticed, how I have not forced you to do anything?" A wolf beside him flexes, rolling its huge head back to nuzzle his master. Vesperian runs a palm fondly over the large head which reaches past his hips.

Myla stays silent, eyes studying the commanding figure, which is so different in appearance than he was the night he killed Caius. He takes a different form in battle, it would appear.

No one dares speak. No one moves. The energy in the room is balanced on the trembling shoulders of Myla who struggles to master the urge to run. Finally, she works up the courage to respond.

"Again, Lord Vesperian, I ask: why are you here?"

Lord Vesperian straightens even taller than before. His eyes wavering to none, fixed solely upon her. He speaks to her as though he is not in a room full of fifty men and women. "When you have lain in bed at night these past two years and felt me calling to you, tell me, did you touch yourself? For it was I who gave you that urge."

An intense heat to her right threatens to boil the throne room in a river of molten lava, and in her peripheral, Bryar seems to be emanating his rage in waves of heat and smoke, the spectacle catching the attention of her court.

"Did you even know that was me calling you? I have wished not to dominate you but to plant in you a seed of longing. Together, I believe we can bring unity to the realm . . . and the tension between us."

At this, Myla scoffs, standing with a fury that threatens to level the room. For the first time in years, her fingertips spontaneously tingle and a ringing in the back of her head signals the slow leak of magic trickling forth. "You speak to me like your whore?" she demands, taking a threatening step toward him, her eyes burning with rage.

Lord Vesperian lowers his head in what could be mistaken as a respectful bow but is nothing short of mockery. "The opposite, Your Grace. I *wish* to speak to you as a wife and my co-ruler of this realm." Wicked intentions reflect within his eyes, his message clear: marry me and we shall be allies. Deny me my wish, and I will flatten you. He has come to claim her and fulfill his prophecy.

Dread washes over Myla in an instant, and the space in her chest where her heart should beat feels still. Any semblance of composure hangs on by a thread, and the shift of the room is born of both discomfort and betrayal. The truth has been revealed, Myla watches the faces of her subjects and her council members contort with anger and distrust.

Yes, witness my shame. Here it is, the scandal I have hid so well for so long. Your Queen has betrayed you. Embarrassed and angry in one, Myla diverts her attention from the looks of horror, to the evil incarnate before her. *Their feelings will have to wait.*

"You propose marriage? To what end?" The very impression of entertaining his proposal sends a handful of lords and ladies, Maverick especially, into a fit of protesting, a lunging mass of anger moving a few steps forward with alarm, stopped only by the drawn weapons of her guards. A few, Bryar included, summon balls of magic which levitate in their palms, ready to stop those who may feel justified in crossing her.

"You are a powerful woman," Vesperian attempts a compliment, which is sorely lacking in authenticity. "I am a powerful man, yet I have chosen not to use the full extent of that power on you. Surely that allows me *some* sense of decorum which you suggest is grossly lacking. Should we marry and rule here together, I offer you more power than you could possibly imagine building on your own. I offer you protection."

The Blood Stealer consumes her body with his eyes, a slow glance first up and then back down, pausing at the space between her legs as though she is a meal offered up before him. "I offer you the gift of your own free will. Marry me, and I will release you from our sacred blood tie."

The tension which previously threatened to unravel the dignity of her court snaps with his declaration. An unmanageable crowd of both angry and concerned courtiers scream profanity, pleas, and threats her way, ceasing only when she raises a hand to demand silence. Her fingers themselves feel heavy above her head and the blood behind her eyes threatens to drain, potentially leaving her an exhausted weight of flesh on the ground. The rustle of a gown to her left brings comfort and strength, a reminder that despite the teeming crowd before her, Elsa stands nearby. Myla can feel a vibration growing between them, Elsa's gift of healing giving her a wave of strength.

"Your proposal is most unexpected," Myla corrects her voice, softening and drawing from an untapped reserve of sensuality. She allows her eyelashes to droop ever so slightly over her eyes, their deep blues devouring the Blood Stealer with deception. One slow step at a time, she descends the perch where her throne sits, inching closer to the devil of a man before her. "I will admit," she whispers as she stands close by, his ear a mere inch from her lips. "I am intrigued."

She lures him in with a syrupy-sweet guile, her fingers brushing lightly across her collarbone and a smile threatens to wipe the smug look from his face, born from a sense of accomplishment. *What a fucking fool.*

"And which part intrigues you most?" he asks. "The promise to bring you power and freedom or . . . the promise to taste you."

Ignoring the filthy advance, Myla offers her hand, which he accepts, pressing his lips intimately against it.

"A queen is wise to weigh . . . all the benefits. I must beg of you a day."

"A day?" he nearly growls, pacified only when she presses a finger to his lips in silence, slowly tracing downward toward his broad chest.

"Surely, you see how I must explain this to my subjects," she gestures with her eyes toward the seething courtiers behind them. "I never told them what . . . was between us." She straightens the collar of his black leather vest, matching his familiarity.

The phrasing of her last statement seems to satiate him, suggesting she is a willing participant and not a victim, twists something in his dark mind.

"A day then," he agrees loudly, looking past her shoulder to where the ground at Bryar's feet smolders, a black smoke coiling around him. "Perhaps you should do something about your overzealous guard; he seems to be ruining the finish on your flooring."

Myla conjures a modest giggle, not daring to look back lest her countenance waver. Vesperian leans in, pressing a familiar kiss to her cheek, his hand lingering on the small of her back long enough that Myla fears he may be able to feel the tremble beneath it. Then at last, he turns back, flanked by dazed guards. Their faces are all confusion, looks of being somewhere with no recollection of how.

"Should I detect anything amiss when I return," he says with a swift twist back to face her. "I shall use you to annihilate your entire kingdom." The threat is spoken with a fond smile, sickeningly sweet in spite of the message therein, and it is in this moment, Myla visualizes what it might be like to call upon the Gods and reduce her court to a pulp. The intrusion is not an imagination of her own making, but Vesperian's warning. He will use her to kill them all; the message is quite clear.

When the doors close behind him, Elsa rushes to Myla's side, offering a hand.

"Your Grace?" Lord Sorrin spews, clearly speaking for the rest of the courtiers. "What is the meaning of this!"

"Surely you do not mean to align yourself with that vile monster!" Lord Heron bellows.

Lady Reacher scoffs, the next to speak out. "The laws are clear!

Anyone found to be under the Blood Stealer's influence is to be put to death." Her declaration is met with far too many shouts of agreement and nodding heads.

Myla snaps around, facing the woman head-on and taking note of the room full of men ready to oppose her. "It would be *most* unwise to threaten me while speaking of laws, as threatening your queen is *also* punishable by death."

She turns to sit and something on the back of her neck prickles, a sense of disgust. She sees their faces both grim and confident in defiance with eyes like heartless beasts, shredding her for sport. There is nothing that suggests these men have ever respected her nor submitted to her rule. In spite of the years she has given to their wellbeing, ensuring fair and just treatment of all, and nurturing the financial health of New Falkmere, they are, all of them, vultures. Likely awaiting this moment for years.

"We do not question a queen; we question a widow—a *dowager!*" Lord Heron speaks again, his hand reaching for his blade with alarming confidence.

"Surely," she hisses, turning to face the room squarely, "you do not mean to unsheathe that weapon in my presence, Lord Heron." It is no question; it is a command which he hesitantly abides. To draw a weapon in the presence of their queen is a death sentence of itself. It seems none in the room are law-abiding citizens this day.

Lord Sorrin, however, is not so easily intimidated. He takes a bold step forward, turning to address his fellow lords and ladies. "I fear we *must* draw blades!" he encourages the crowd. "It seems our leader, one whom we swore fealty to not two days ago, has deceived us!" Ringing in her ears, screams of magic, those in the room seconds away from summoning theirs. "Will we stand by and allow this woman to lay claim to a throne, once so revered and held sacred by King Caius, when she herself has disrespected it and *lied* to us!" he shouts, raising his arm high, rallying the mob forming for him.

Bryar pushes past her, leading the Queen's Guard to form a barrier between her and the angry body of courtiers before her. "I command you in the name of the queen: stand down!" His axe is held ready to swing and flames form at his fingertips, slowly engulfing the hilt. A wall of impenetrable magic forms, a harmonious continuation of each guard's magic and a barrier between herself and those rioting on the other side.

"We will not stand down when this so-called queen has sat on that throne for the past two years, a mistress to the Blood Stealer!" Sorrin spews.

Horror washes over Myla, followed quickly with boiling and insatiable rage. A burden she has carried in solitude for years is now twisted as the grossest of betrayals, and it is serving as an excuse for these men, who have always been uncertain of her, to speak of her as though she is not there. To speak of her as though she is a choice and an easy problem to eliminate.

Slowly glancing from Elsa at her left to Bryar on her right, hoping and grateful to see loyalty in their eyes, she swallows hard and presses a finger to her temple. *They doubt you. They doubt your convictions. They doubt you will enforce your reign. They doubt that you are loyal to them and this throne.*

They would not dare contest a man.

A palpable tremor ripples through the air, an unsettling wave that sends shivers down the spines of all who see it. The source is Myla, a force of magic long dormant, now stirring with a dreadful fury, fueled by the anger of injustice. All fatigue and weakness melts away at the mercy of her righteous anger, and her magic flows unbridled.

The heat radiating from Bryar is a seething cauldron, his own magic bubbling violently beneath the surface, ready to erupt while Elsa stands close, her hands radiating a glow of energy meant for Myla. Both Callum and Rhyland have moved to her side as well, Callum's palms raised in flame and Rhyland rolling his shoulders, ready to swing his blade. Here they all are, shoulder to shoulder, as they so often used to be. Only now, it is their lives at risk, not simple propriety.

"You dare to plot against me?" Myla hisses, her voice a chilling blend of calm and menacing as she draws from the courage of her friends alongside her. "In my own throne room, as I stand here before you?"

It begins slowly at first. The way the light in the room seems to separate into individual grains, traveling in currents to where she stands, replaced by an unnatural darkness. Her web of veins adjoins in a hypnotic spark of starlight traveling across the skin of her arm until a searing light pools at her fingertips, pulsating with a malevolent energy seeming to warp the very air around her. As her tension and power swell, the light blinds and illuminates her form, like a dark goddess of wrath.

The years of watching them whisper behind her back, while applauding her directly, pulls a vile hatred from the depths of her heart. To have leaned so heavily on people who swore to protect her, to follow her, only to watch their backs turn the second she is forced to prove herself to them, is nothing short of an insult. Directly before her, the very image of anger and disappointment, is her father, his own fist closed around a blade.

It is in this moment, Myla realizes she is not only fighting a battle against the Blood Stealer, but a larger one right here between herself and her father.

If they want it, any of them, they will have to take it.

"Stand down now and leave with your lives," Myla commands, taking a threatening step in her father's direction, though her eyes pass over the faces of her council as well. The message is clear: they have crossed a line, and there is no forgiveness for that.

"Stand down and leave Falkmere in the hands of a traitor?" Maverick laughs, clearly not concerned by the brewing of his daughter's magic.

"Tell me," Myla retorts, "when have I ever betrayed Falkmere? Am I not here? Have I not listened to your guidance and made good decisions for our kingdom?"

Sorrin yells, clearly trying to start a riot, "You let the Blood Stealer walk right in—"

"And I will stop him! The question is, will you help me?"

"Not like this," Maverick says, his hand now flying to the hilt of his blade.

The palace walls tremble, vibrating with the power building in her voice, a sound that twists and contorts, becoming shrill and deafening.

The Voice of The Gods, a force which Myla has repressed for years, now claws at her lungs, begging for reprieve. The muscles in her neck tighten around the urge to release the deadly scream. Myla's body tenses with the need to temper the violence brewing inside her, already evoking a response of terror from her court. "Stand down now, lest you face the consequences of defiance," she commands, watching as her words only fan the flames of treachery. "Have I been so complacent as to make my own Council believe they can defy me?" The quaking of her lungs deepens now and her voice contorts to something that is not her own, but the Old Gods' above. The pillars quake, books falling from their high shelves, tumbling to the ground, a few knocking the people below them senseless.

Lords and ladies alike collapse to their knees, shrieking in agony as terror stretches across their faces. Some cover their ears, desperate to block out the cacophony of her fury, while others shield their eyes from the blinding light radiating from her body. Lord Sorrin, trembling and fallen, tries to meet her gaze but recoils in horror, shaking his head fiercely. A trickle of blood travels from his ear to his jawline, blending in with his dark beard.

"No—no, I—" He raises his hand in what appears to be a remorseful surrender, but a glint of malice flickers in his eyes. In a heartbeat, his outstretched palm seeks to command the very weapon at Myla's waist. Myla has only ever seen him use his ability to seize anything with the flick of a wrist in relaxed settings such as a dining flute, or a quill in the council room. The fox dagger trembles loose from its sheath, but it is futile.

In an instant, the scorching, blinding light at Myla's fingertips is drawn back into her being, radiating from every pore like a million living stars. Her eyes, once a comforting blue, morph into a blinding white, more searing than the sun itself. With a swift, deliberate motion, she raises her hand, and that light snakes like a noose around Lord Sorrin's throat, snapping his neck with a sickening crack.

A scream erupts from the crowd, a raw, primal sound that echoes off the palace walls. As weapons are rapidly sheathed, the sight of their usually quiet and gentle leader now transformed into a figure of dread leaves her subjects trembling in fear. Many retreat toward the door, their courage evaporating, while a few, consumed by a twisted loyalty, prepare to follow Sorrin into death.

Myla conjures another wave of energy, the air thick with tension. A guttural battle cry pierces the atmosphere, accompanied by a heat that slithers around her like a snake. From behind, she feels the shocking sensation of an inferno unleashed and a fiery blast igniting the back of the throne room. Myla turns just in time to see a charred figure, arm raised with a sword overhead, consumed in a small hell by Bryar's hand. The flames lick hungrily at the air, still engulfing the burnt body. A threat bellows from his lungs, his palms still molten red and ready to send more to face the justice of the Gods in the afterlife.

"Those in the great hereafter will not suffer the company of men who died as cowards!" he bellows, commanding men and women alike to stand down. The room stills, and fear is as potent as the smell of charred flesh.

Myla stands now not just as the Falkmere queen, but as the embodiment of a gravely underestimated woman, her magic a reminder of the dark tempest living within her, ready to rain destruction upon those foolish enough to oppose her wrath; something her council seems to have forgotten.

"I *am* your queen and I was chosen to be so for a reason. But I command no one to serve me," Myla speaks once more, her voice returning to normal. Those who are still in the throne room quiver on their knees, few daring to look upon her. "Any who do not wish to honor their oaths further will be allowed to take their soldiers and leave. You will be met with no harm. But you are grossly mistaken if you believe that my quiet these two years past are an indicator of complacency. Leave with your honor but do not stay and believe I will abide any treason beneath my rule."

A unanimous tilt of heads as men and women alike, surrendering to her rule passes over the room. Callum approaches Maverick, ripping the blade from his hands and Rhyland shoves the begrudged man to his knees in forced submission. Bryar whispers behind her to a few of his men to have the bodies removed and returned to their families, while Elsa, following Rhyland's lead, passes through the crowd, pushing stragglers to their knees and forcing a few heads lower before she herself also lowers into a kneel. *Unnecessary, Elsa. But I like the gesture.*

Myla takes a trembling breath and speaks once more, a final statement. "I see your fear. Know that I have felt it too, for a long time. Know that I have remained true to my commitments and true to *you,* in spite of this affliction. Should I be unable to resist the Blood Stealer, I will willingly relinquish my claim to this throne. I have no intention of unifying myself with that man. Bear in mind, will you, though I do not wield Restorer magic, I am his equal in potency. I shall not succumb to him easily."

Her words are strong and unwavering as she addresses her subjects, ignoring the near-visible rage which ripples around the stiff frame of her father. "Let this here," she gestures to the devastation surrounding them, "serve as a reminder of what I can and will do, should any dare to threaten me." At this, she does make eye contact with the man, not breaking it until he lowers his, in submission. "I am still the queen you swore oaths to, and I will answer to *dowager* no longer. Make your decision."

With nothing left to say, Myla descends the steps of the throne room, the crowd parting for her as she passes through, no longer seen as a shadow quivering in the background in the wake of her husband's death, but a queen to fear, in her own right.

Once again, evening wanes and Myla finds herself standing in the conservatory, surrounded by the rest of her council along with Bryar, Elsa, Callum, and Rhyland who, when he is not flirting with every man and woman who crosses his path or running the household, is the map maker of Falkmere but specifically, the Raven's Veil. His talent in penmanship, illustrations, and having an eye for the memory of landscapes, has served many missions well in the past years.

He holds in his hands an unfurled map, "The Raven's Veil is amassed here." He jabs a gloved finger toward a plot on the map. "If necessary, Callum could have them here in two days."

"Two days is not fast enough," Lord Heron interjects. "The Blood Stealer is expected tomorrow afternoon."

"If I may," Elsa speaks up, "is there any sense in fooling the Blood Stealer?"

"How so?" Myla asks, curiosity piqued.

"When he returns tomorrow, Your Grace will agree to the marriage." Her proposition is met with tension, as well as a slight increase in temperature as Bryar's disapproval mounts. Maverick moves to speak but Elsa rolls her eyes at him before continuing. "Once he is appeased, he swore to release you from your oath. Perhaps, once he is well enough convinced you are comfortable in your alliance, you can cut his throat while he sleeps or slip poison into his glass." The final statement has a coy edge to it; Elsa has always been one to play dirty if that is what it took. In most cases, Myla has admired that. In this case, it makes her uneasy.

"You suggest I climb into bed with the Blood Stealer and poison him," Myla objects, absently chewing her nails as the stress amounts. "Poison will not kill him."

Elsa shrugs, a smile twitching at her lips despite the glowering of everyone else in the room and the scoffed protests of the council. "We all have our crosses to bear, Your Grace. At least yours always seems to come with outrageously handsome men. Poison might not but a slit throat will."

Bryar clears his throat. "Permission to speak, Your Grace?" Myla finds him interjecting at this exact moment jolting. She already knows that he will contest anything that requires her sharing another man's bed. *This is a fucking cross to bear.*

"Granted," Myla remarks, matching the formal tone.

"The Monk's monastery is half a day's ride from here. It would be a good place to take refuge. The Blood Stealer can not marry you if you are not here when he returns."

"And when he does arrive to find me gone," Myla argues, "imagine what he will do to those who remain." All, including Bryar, nod in agreement, though the latter seems more invested than a Captain of the Guard ought to be. Fortunately, Myla is the only one paying him attention, so the sentiment goes unnoticed.

"We have enough forces," Maverick interjects, ignoring the glare Myla passes his way. Though he stood down, it is not lost on her that her father was ready to kill her. "I believe it is time to face this beast and bring an end to him once and for all." His words are calm and calculated.

With piercing eyes, Myla stares fiery holes into his forehead. "Without Restorer's magic? Careful, Father, if I did not know any better, I would think you wanted him to kill me. That would be a large steppingstone for you." She turns away to face Elsa. "I do not like your idea, Elsa." Myla speaks with a firm conviction which does not in any way accurately reflect how she feels inwardly. Her hands tremble as she laces her fingers together resolutely. "But I fear there may be logic to it." She dares not meet Bryar's gaze as she speaks, lest her resolve should falter.

"Excellent," Lord Heron adds sarcastically. "But what of the army he will no doubt bring with him? Are we expected to welcome them into our halls?" He turns to Bryar, whose chin is upturned stoically, and his expression is unreadable. "What say you?"

Long trained in the art of watching Myla walk into bedrooms with other men, Bryar seems to have found his composure, or perhaps his ability to disassociate is shining through. Regardless, with all eyes on him, none are the wiser to the deeper emotional objection he currently experiences.

"His troops are no better than the undead. They are a nuisance, but in their dazed state, no logic accompanies their motives. The kitchen maid could kill them with a fork. I will move my small, local force of the Raven's

Veil into the palace with the assignment of discreetly picking off his soldiers when possible."

Myla cringes disconcertingly, troubled to think of innocent people being killed. Regardless, it seems this will all end in tremendous bloodshed. "Please, make those preparations at once," she instructs, knowing it is best that the following conversation happens without his presence.

With a bow, he is gone, and a silence fills the room, all in attendance waiting for her to speak again. For a moment, Myla loses herself in the atmosphere. Her eyes flitting from plant to plant, light particles reflecting off stone, the way the lanterns bring out the greens and reds in the room, a red she fears will resemble her flayed body, should this plan go amiss. "For this ruse to be convincing, I must become unrecognizable to you," she says, low at first, then gaining confidence. "I wish for my actions to be so convincing that you are all alarmed. I need to know that no matter how questionable my devotion to him becomes, I have you all at my back."

Solemn nods bob across each head in the room, an understanding of what must be done, bringing forth a deep sense of grief and sacrifice. Even on the face of Maverick, Myla finds a grim solemnness. She continues, not wishing the moment to last any longer than necessary. "Lord Elias." Myla looks to a younger gentleman. "I task you with hiring gravediggers to acquire a dozen or so fresh corpses."

Elsa gasps. "Myla—I . . . Your Grace. Why?"

"I can not imagine that if I were to seriously look at my courtiers, and tell them I was happily aligning myself with the Blood Stealer, that there would be no bloodshed. It must appear as though there was a quarrel over the matter, and my court is in submission after I demonstrated what would happen to any more who defied me. The throne room is already a mess. We shall hang the corpses from the pillars of the throne room, and when he returns, he will ask about it."

Myla's stomach violently churns, a tug within her, a reminder from the Blood Stealer no doubt, a twinge that says "*I am thinking of you. Are you thinking of me?*" Angrily, she grips the sides of the long couch to her right, waiting for the wave to pass, before speaking again. "See to it, Lord Elias," she commands gently, watching as the man reluctantly removes himself.

"Elsa, find Fern and Alaric. Meet me in my chambers in half an hour." She turns to her father with a dismissive wave of her hand. "You, leave."

With the last of her companions out of the room, unable to object nor be privy to her instructions, and Maverick none the wiser to something he would no doubt take advantage of, Myla takes a final deep breath and looks to the rest of her council. "Should my plan fail, and you sense the Blood Stealer is truly controlling me, I know I can count on the remainder of you to stop me." Her words thicken the air of the room. Lady Rivenna, Lord Elias's wife, speaks to clarify, though the suggestion is lost on none of them.

"Stop you . . . Your Grace?"

"Kill me," Myla speaks clearly with a confident tilt of her jaw, so there is no confusion. "I will not be his puppet; my powers being used against my own people. Should he claim my impulses completely and you find I am a threat, kill me."

Fern and Elsa are given strict instructions on remaining unreadable, should they find themselves in the presence of the Blood Stealer while tending Myla's needs. With a convincing environment being of the essence, Myla is certain her fickle courtiers would perform fine. It is those closest to her she is afraid might give away their ploy. With Alaric currently brewing her an extra supply of energy revitalizing tonic, there is one person left to speak with, and Myla fears this will be the hardest conversation.

A knock sounds at her door. With Fern and Elsa intentionally dismissed, Myla answers the door herself. Bryar stands, hands relaxed on the hilt of the axe at his side. "You sent for me, Your Grace?"

Breaking her rule of no-contact, she takes his hand and ushers him in, closing the door firmly behind them. "Take off your armor and sit," she instructs. "You are off duty tonight."

"Of all nights, Your Grace," he answers, "I can not rest this one."

"Please, Captain," she begs, the furrow in her brow softening. "I do not wish to face this when there lives a rift between you and I." Hesitantly, and aware she is crossing many of the boundaries put in place for herself, Myla reaches to unclasp his cloak. Bryar stiffens at her proximity, his eyes looking resolutely past her, his breath catching. Careful not to touch him directly, she frees the cloak and sets in on the chaise before her hearth. "We must speak. Please sit with me a while."

Bryar accepts a glass of mulled wine and sits, his face unreadable but the energy buzzing around him alive with turmoil. "I have done as you ask. Assassins will be at their posts throughout the palace within the hour."

Myla smiles gratefully and sits next to him, aware the space between them is but a few inches, closer than she has allowed in years. "What I will ask of you is too much. I have not been blind to your lo—your loyalty, these past years, and I am no fool to think they have been easy on you," she speaks gently, careful to keep her hands occupied in her lap to avoid unnecessary contact that she is certain would break her resolve. Deep green eyes like the forest at midday, gaze back at her, unreadable. "I must convince him that I am truly amenable to his alliance. There must be no question of it. If he doubts for a second, we will all fail, and I believe the consequences will be devastating."

"And what of leaving, *Myla*?" he snaps, his anger finally boiling over. Her name on his lips is electrifying, sending a shock through them both, yet he does not recoil from his argument. "We had a plan."

"Yes," Myla pleads, not at all surprised by the bitterness vibrating from his being. "Surely, you see I can not leave now."

"I see leaving might be conflicting, but I thought it would be an easy choice when faced with the alternative. It was one thing to know you were taking Caius's bed. You had no choice in the matter, but this?" He points to her bed a mere ten feet away. "You will be welcoming your husband's murderer into your bed to touch *your* body?"

Myla swallows hard as tears blind her. "Captain Monroe, my body has not been my own for a long time. First, it was Caius's, and then there was a child within me—one I *do* want to protect still! And then . . . then the Blood Stealer laid claim to it through that *fucking* blood oath." Her words spill out in an emotional unburdening, anger and grief alike married together. "Whether he has my body in my bed, or has my body through my uncontrolled actions, he *has had* my body for two years, and I want him to have it no more. If I must share his bed to convince him of my loyalty, so that I may kill him while he sleeps, so be it!"

Bryar stands and pushes his palms into his temple, eyes closed and what appears to be an internal battle taking place. "And if he does not keep his word? If you have tried all this, and he still does not release you from your oath?"

"Then, I will try to kill him in spite of it and hope I am strong enough to resist any urges *not* to kill him."

Bryar clenches his jaw as he moves to leave the room, before he turns on his heel to return, standing directly before her. His hands closing around her face, earnestly drawing her attention to something deep within him. He speaks with fervor, leaving no question of how he feels unanswered. "I hate this, Myla. Believe me when I say, I know none of this has anything to do with me, and that *constantly* seems to be a consequence of station. I am tired of being forced to sit back and watch the woman I have faithfully *loved* for ten years be passed off as another man's pawn. I would have defied your father and taken you from court five years ago, had that been a possibility, but I want to be with someone who is not already married to duty with no regard for herself!" He releases her, heaving an inward breath before grabbing his cloak to leave. "I respect you and have always admired your commitment to your people. But that commitment must end when it compromises your wellbeing and your sense of self."

His voice lowers and he speaks with confidence, his eyes fixed on hers. "When you married the king, I swore to protect, my heart broke, but I knew we both acted from a place of duty and loyalty. And when your husband, my king, died, I grieved with and for you—for the uncertainty you felt. And as you suffer now, I suffer with you, for my heart has always been *your* heart.

"As my queen, you can command me to leave now, to go wage your wars and kill who you wish, even to watch you throw yourself away for the sake of this kingdom. I will faithfully ensure that you live to see the other side of this. Not, because I am sworn to the crown, but because I *still* love you. But I will not stand in this room any longer and accept the insult of your soft words as you try to pass them off as *compassion*."

A wave of both hurt and anger wash over Myla as she watches him head for the door. Angrily, she throws her wine glass to the floor, disregarding the shattering glass and the spray of red in every direction, an ironic visual representation of their imploding relationship. "Are you so damn arrogant to assume this is easy for me? You are acting like a victim right now, while I am trying to right wrongs!"

"I am no victim, *Your Grace*. I stand here willingly. But you are about to make yourself one, and I will be left having to clean up the mess."

"Well, if you are so sick of protecting me, of cleaning up after me, then go protect someone else," Myla hisses, taking several steps toward him, uncharacteristically angry. Bryar faces her squarely, his jaw set, fumes of smoke beginning to permeate the room, as his own anger amounts and heat boils in his fists.

"You say that as if I did not just swear a fucking oath to you two nights ago, Myla! I am the idiot who just . . . follows you around, hoping that one day you will see *me* again!"

"I do see you!" Myla nearly screams, planting her hands in his chest, pushing him further from her. He stumbles backwards knocking her washbasin off its pedestal. Painted glass shatters, adding to the carnage on the floor.

"Then say my name," he challenges. "Stop calling me *Captain,* like it somehow erases our history."

Myla freezes, sucking her bottom lip inward and digging her teeth into it. His name, something she tries to keep out of her mouth, out of her head, and most importantly, out of her heart.

"*Say it.*"

"I can not."

"What are you so afraid of?" he asks, his head shaking as though he is looking down on a child who has once again disappointed him. "Are you afraid you will remember what we used to be?"

Her voice trembles as she speaks. "I am not afraid of remembering—I did not forget. I have *never* forgotten that before him . . . there was you." Her voice breaks, though anger still presides over the room, in spite of her words. "And for a while, the grief and guilt of his death held me back from you. Then, when that was gone, it was only fear. Fear of adding this to the long list of things I already can not control." She hisses the last word, taking several steps backwards, moving away from him. A futile attempt, as he only follows her, closing the small space between them. "This is something we have never been able to control, something that we barely harnessed when I was married to Caius, and beyond. But now . . . now I am afraid. Afraid of how sad I have become, afraid that if I spend whatever days of my life I have left fighting against something that has always been such a source of joy and safety, that I will have nothing to smile upon while I lie on my death bed." Myla presses a hand to his chest, another barrier between them, a silent warning, as if to say: *stay back if you do not want to be hurt again.* "It is for those reasons, and so many more . . . *Bryar* . . . that I have to protect us and—"

Bryar stops her mid-sentence with a firm kiss, his tongue slipping through her parted lips to press against hers as they share the same air. The passion dissipates their anger. His touch, foreign yet still familiar, is a gentle reminder of the safety she once held so dear. All thoughts of arguing are snuffed and replaced with a need to prove something to one another. To prove they do not still care and yet, in the same breath, they do. To prove that everything will be alright, though it feels as if it will not. The way their bodies move against each other, reminiscent of a battle, each hungry with desire and unwilling to surrender their stance on the matter.

Myla shudders, releasing a gasp of realization, she is unraveling her carefully woven defenses. She parts their lips to look up into his eyes, fear strikes deep inside in her soul when she sees the depths of his desire inside, she sees it painted across his face, sees it embedded deep within his being. She reaches out to touch his broad chest, longing to fall into him, to find that safe space they spent so many years hidden in. The barrier of armor between their skin is suddenly torturous, as the years of carefully constructed restraints crumble with the slightest breath of permission. The flickering candlelight casts a warm glow over his chiseled features, highlighting the anticipation of something so long awaited in his gaze.

These once-familiar expressions, gentle touches, and private rendezvous were something they never felt the need to resist—the natural innocence of adolescence never caused them to question it. Bryar had touched and lain with Myla, the nobleman's rebellious daughter. But Myla the *queen,* of an entire realm, is a new territory to explore. Their connection burns hot, a forbidden ember that has been left smoldering to die for years, waiting for the day she would give it oxygen, give it the slightest permission to spark.

As their eyes lock in a silent exchange of longing, Bryar's hands slide down Myla's sides. The brush of his fingertips, nearly mistaken as accidental, the whisper of a touch sending shivers down her spine. She leans in closer, her lips dangerously close to brushing against his once more in a tantalizingly slow dance of desire. He need only bridge the gap, then that passion which she imagines frequently, that passion which she has replayed in her head many times from years ago, is sure to be uncaged.

"We should not be doing this," Bryar whispers, voice thick with both yearning and apprehension. He presses his brow to hers, his breath heavy with the disappointment that can only come from self-denial. "If you knew how I have missed you," he continues, his strong fingers tangling deep into her hair, gently pulling her closer. "I do not want to do this if it is something you will regret and I will loath later."

But Myla only responds with a soft, breathless moan, her fingers tangling in his hair, all of her self-imposed rules and emotional barriers crumple to her feet. "I have many regrets in my life, but I never have and never could regret *you.*"

That is all the encouragement he needs. Those mere inches no longer exist. All of the years of yearning for one another and missing one another begin to unravel the second his mouth finds hers. A shudder of respite and pent-up longing is released between them. The taste of him is intoxicating, a heady blend of longing and passion with a touch of kerosene that ignites the fire deep within her. A longing that has lain dormant and undisturbed, cracks wide open, and Myla is reminded how exceedingly small she feels in his embrace. Overcome by a sense of urgency, and an ache growing between her thighs, Myla presses her hips to his, irritated by the thick belt and chainmail padding the sensitive space between them.

As their lips meet in a desperate kiss, the captain's hands move over her body with a reverence born only from years of unrequited worship. "You are the queen," he breathes against her skin. His lips find a soft spot on her neck as his words plead for reason amid their heated tryst. But she only responds with a soft moan, her hands fumbling with the fastenings of his uniform as they both give in to the undeniable pull between them.

"I was a girl to you well before I was a queen. Do not forget who it was that made me a woman." As the layers of clothing begin to fall away, revealing his muscular chest as well as new scars, Myla's breath catches in her throat. A mangled twist of skin slashes across his right side, the tense ripples of his abdomen causing it to rise and fall, silvery in the firelight.

Every inch of him is a masterpiece, a testament to his strength and his long-suffering dedication to the crown. Her crown. She leans down to press lingering kisses along his jawline, trailing a path of heat and desire down his neck and across his collarbone. Bryar's hands roam over her body, his touch igniting a symphony of sensations that reverberate through her very core. It is as though he is swearing an entirely different sort of oath to her now.

The room is filled with the sound of their ragged breaths and the soft rustle of fabric as they surrender to one other. Amid the vulnerability is a palpable understanding that they are crossing a line which can not be uncrossed. A space they have both safeguarded and resisted reopening is now cracking wide open into something sure to be catastrophic. It is a moment of pure, unadulterated desire, a fleeting escape from the constraints of duty and honor that always rip them in separate directions.

Bryar's hand begins to trail up the space between her rib cage, fingers grazing the curve beneath her breast. A trained finger slides between the material of her neckline. Confident in his advances, his nimble fingers inch closer to the fastenings at the nape of her neck, ready to disrobe her entirely—and the dress falls to the floor, leaving only her dressing gown and corset. The act sends an unexpected cold sweat through her body as a memory—like a nightmare—invades her mind, causing her to flinch.

Bryar steps back, alarmed. "Are you alright?" He searches her for any sign of pain but finds it only in her eyes. "Should I go?"

Myla takes a deep breath, gazing at the man before her. The *safe* man. The man who has never hurt her, the man she has longed for for years. *He* is not the cause of her nightmares. Shaking her head, she pulls him close once more. "Please, do not leave me."

With little time to think, Myla finds herself splayed across her bed with Bryar caressing her arms above her head, his mouth attentively pressing kisses to the space where her neck and shoulders meet. All thoughts of their argument slip away as the warmth of his body, hard against hers, brings a sense of weighted comfort in the midst of conflict.

"Bryar, stop," she breathes with absolutely no conviction.

He loosens his grip on her wrists and lifts his face to hers. "Do you want me to stop?"

He would stop, if she asked, and that knowledge alone prompts an enthusiastic, "Absolutely not." Myla shakes her head and revokes her statement, lifting her lips to meet his, her breath hitching as his free hand travels down her abdomen and past to where he can firmly grasp a handful of her gown, drawing it slowly upwards. Bare fingers against the inside of her thigh send shivers through her as he draws slow, seductive designs against her sensitive skin, inching closer and closer to that space between her legs. A blaze heats his fingertips, fueled by his innermost desires running away with him. The sensation both scorches and chills, igniting a desperate craving for relief.

His touch, at last, is euphoric, dismissing every one of her fears and concerns with the intentional brush of his fingers. Immense pleasure building within causes her to attempt an escape from his grasp, but he holds firm, his eyes searching hers as she surrenders to his all-consuming touch. Myla arches her back, pressing as close to him as she can manage, her mouth fixed upon his in a kiss she wishes could last forever.

With shaking thighs and a need to feel more, she arches her body closer to his. “Let me touch you,” she whispers, gasping as his expert fingers vanquish her over and over again.

“No,” he growls a response into her ear. “You may be in charge outside of this room, but here, tonight . . . I am.” The words are thrilling and the need to be at his mercy is overwhelming. Myla resists his restraint no more, fully allowing herself to be submerged in him. When at last his efforts elicit a loud gasp from Myla, her body tensing beneath the throbbing pleasure between her legs, his fingers uncurl from around her wrists and his lips linger on hers for a second longer.

When she regains her breath, still intoxicated by his touch, she nips at his lip and moves to straddle him. “Your turn,” she whispers against his mouth. He shakes his head slowly, moaning beneath the pressure of her teeth.

“Not tonight,” he says, smoothing stray hairs away from her face. “This was for you, not me.” For several minutes Myla lies, steadying her breath, while Bryar is sprawled next to her, his hand holding tightly to hers, both of them afraid to let go.

In spite of the relief brought on in the last ten minutes, Myla can not shake the feeling of doom hanging over her like a storm cloud ready to drown her. No amount of bliss locked away in this room can spare them from the grief that always seems to await them outside.

Reluctant to move away from him, but aware of the rapidly passing time, she stands and begins picking up shards of splintered glass from the floor. Bryar joins her and together they consolidate the sharp pieces into a tightly woven basket, normally intended for laundry. Myla will have Fern dispose of it later. Guilt pulses through her.

"We have never behaved in such a manner," she says finally, addressing the disaster around them. "I hate this."

"We have never tried enduring such an impasse," Bryar responds coolly, fixing the tousled bedding and putting his shirt on. As they pass the next few moments in silence, both knowing their little tryst has solved nothing, Myla turns away from Bryar, trying desperately to hide the shake of her shoulders as she silently sobs into her hand, an overwhelming wave of fear for the following day washing over her. Or perhaps it is fear for the reality of losing him right when she feels he is returning to her.

"Bryar . . . you should not spend any longer holding your breath for me. I do not believe I will be here much longer."

"It is not too late," Bryar pleads, standing close behind her now, a firm hand sliding around her middle, pulling her into a hug from behind. Myla allows her head to fall back against his chest. "We can leave now and come up with a plan that does not include giving yourself to that animal."

She turns to face him, a gentle hand smoothing against the stubble of his cheek. "I can not. I must do something to fix this mess before it consumes Falkmere. I understand this may very well be the final straw for us." Her voice cracks, and a sob brings pause to her words. Taking a slow and steadying breath, Myla continues. "Please, stay with me tonight. If it is the last time you look on me kindly, I would like to make the most of that time before you loathe me."

Bryar pulls her into his arms, holding her tightly. His body trembles, and she wonders if it is for anger or grief. Perhaps both. Firelight glints off the tapestries hanging from her walls, and candles dance in the corners. On any other evening, her chamber would feel warm and welcoming. This evening, to Myla, it feels like the prison of a young woman failing at being a queen.

Elsa is sent for, her face unreadable as her eyes bounce back and forth between he and Myla. "How can I be of assistance?" she asks coyly, taking note of the basket of shattered glass. Her eyebrows arc slightly before picking the basket up. "Do I even want to know?"

Myla sighs running a palm across her forehead. "Please help me out of my shift and into a bath, Elsa."

Elsa smirks. "I will fetch a basin and return shortly to help you." In another ten minutes, Elsa returns, followed by a few servants bearing heavy buckets of water and another two dragging in a large bathing tub. Elsa dismisses the servants and begins pouring the water in the tub, which is placed before the hearth.

"If you will excuse yourself," Elsa says gently, still eyeing Bryar who now stands peering out the window. "I will help Her Grace bathe now." Elsa expects Bryar to remove himself and is surprised when he turns back, stepping close to Myla, and taking the final bucket from Elsa. "I will handle the rest. Goodnight, Elsa."

A bit of red flushes Elsa's cheeks, and she looks to Myla for guidance.

"It is ok, Elsa. Please be discreet about this."

Elsa nods assuredly, placing a quick kiss on her friend's cheek. "Always, darling. I will come in Fern's place in the morning." And then she is gone, sure to close the door firmly behind her.

Rough fingers move her hair over her shoulder, finding the laces at the back of her corset. Bryar fumbles with the ties, clearly not well-versed in undressing a woman.

"Bryar," Myla whispers, letting a brief sigh of relief escape her lips as the corset loosens, allowing a full breath. "How long has it been since you undressed a woman?" There is a hint of laughter in her voice.

He chuckles slightly before tossing the corset to the floor beside them. "I suppose it would be the last time I undressed you by that tree."

Stunned, Myla turns to face him, clutching her thin shift to her chest. "You have not—"

"No," he interrupts, placing a hand in her bath to test the temperature. Waves of heat radiate from his hands until steam rises from the water. "I had no desire to."

"You mean . . . not at all in the last five years?"

Bryar gazes unabashedly at her, seeming to take no note of her thin shift, only her. "Myla, I never have and never will crave another. It will always *only* be you. Now, take your clothes off."

Myla shrugs the shift off and it slips to the floor, leaving her naked before him. Accepting his hand, she steps into the hot bath and sinks her aching body thankfully into its warmth. Bryar pulls up a stool and sits behind her, moving her long hair over the rim so he can brush it. One slow stroke after another, he works through the tangles and curls until the brush passes through it without resistance. At which point, he nudges her to sit upright. Tenderly, he dips a cloth into the soapy water and proceeds to sponge the suds across her back and shoulders.

Myla closes her eyes and leans into his touch, letting a small sigh slip when he presses a line of warm kisses across her shoulder and up her neck until he finds her jawline. She turns to him with a smile, their lips finding each other again.

Though she can sense his yearning, no number of gentle touches or kisses can persuade Bryar to do anything more than sleep. After an hour of lying side by side, talking and lazily kissing one another, Myla drifts into a peaceful sleep, Bryar's arm draped heavily over her.

Chapter 6

The sun has barely risen when Elsa returns, and Bryar is already gone. Myla sits on the edge of her bed, her knees pulled to her chest, eyelids hot with tears.

"I did not expect to find you crying this morning," Elsa gasps, sitting beside her friend. "Whatever is the matter? Was he not as good as you remember?"

Myla laughs unbecomingly, swiping tears from her cheeks with the backs of her hands. "Though, it may be rather unbelievable to hear, *that* did not happen last night."

Elsa nods, a look of understanding passing across her delicate features. "Oh, I would be crying too, in that case."

"Oh, Elsa." Myla finds herself lost between laughter and tears.

"No. I am unraveling. Can you not see? I should not be feeling everything so deeply. I should be up, dressed already, and finding the strength to fool the Blood Stealer. Instead, I am crying in bed because I can not see Bryar standing with me through this. What kind of queen faces the potential annihilation of her kingdom with tears for a man?"

"Queen or not, you are still a woman. A woman who has endured unkindness at the hands of a man."

Myla flinches a knowing look passing between them, before she averts her gaze from that of her friend.

"If I were sitting in your position right now, I would cry for the loss of the safest man I have ever known, and it would not make me less of a queen. Nor does it you. Might I also add, you have spent five years *not* crying when the rest of us would have. You are overdue, my dear." Elsa pulls her to her feet and together they move to her dressing room. "Any man able to stand by and watch his woman be married to another who misuses her day in and day out for three years can handle a couple days of this," she says finally, confidence in her voice.

"How can you be so sure?" Myla asks, bracing herself as Elsa cinches her corset.

"I just am," she replies. "I love you, and so I must tell you, these next days will be hard, and if you want them to work, you can not be distracted by Bryar's feelings. He will be hurt, but he can handle it." She hesitates, pressing a calming hand to Myla's back. The energy seeping from her palm into the queen's body is a healing balm, soothing Myla's nerves.

Wishing to move on from the conversation, Myla selects a fierce black dress and allows Elsa to help her into it. The collar is chin high, an intricate lace design which jets in a sharp point to her naval, exposing the shadow of her breasts. Black silk sleeves clasp at her wrists and the skirt cascades over her hips, gathering at her feet like a black pool, the sleek material exposing her curves. Black embroidery across the dress depicts flying ravens. Sharp black boots give her height, and Elsa finishes the look with dark eyeliner and red lipstick, a 'look that could kill,' or so she describes it.

"Now, your crown." The black points embedded with obsidian, smoky quartz, and peonies catch the light, demanding attention.

Myla and Elsa stand together, gazing at her reflection, neither one quite ready to depart the safety of her room. "I have to ask," Elsa says, her voice barely above a murmur. "What *is* your plan?" She swallows hard and moves Myla to face her. "The Blood Stealer seems the kind of man who will have no respect for rules."

"I know that," Myla answers. "I am prepared for the most awful of things, Elsa. I do not really care what happens to me, so long as this all ends with the Blood Stealer dead."

"Yes, but . . . should I find him in here, what do you want me to do?"

Myla swallows hard and looks down to the clasps at her wrists. "Exactly what you did last night when you found Bryar in here. Act like it is nothing. And leave."

Elsa's blue eyes shimmer with tears but are chased away by a stoic nod. "I am behind you."

Myla enters the throne room, her eyes casting briefly across Caius's throne. She gestures for a few soldiers to join her beside it. "Store this in the treasury and have the older one brought in." Their faces are written with shock, no doubt in disbelief she is having the throne removed after so long, but still, they are quick to heed her instruction.

The palace is buzzing with gasps and murmurs of disapproval when Lord Heron enters the throne room, a servant dragging a cart of bodies behind him. Lord Sorrin's mangled and ashen corpse lies contorted on top; hollow eyes rolled to the back of his head. Myla feels a lump form in her throat. Of course, having a Council member hanging behind her throne will sell her story better. Nonetheless, it feels callous.

"Your Grace." Lord Heron bows. It is not lost on her how his demeanor seems more submissive this morning. In fact, the eyes of her courtiers more swiftly fall to the floor in reverence than they ever have in the past two years. "Perhaps I can persuade you to remove yourself while I oversee this unpleasant task?"

Myla clasps her hands before her and shakes her head resolutely. "No," she answers, ignoring Bryar's entrance as he delivers swift instruction to his men. Rows of soldiers pass through the room, a few falling into formation behind her throne, others relocating to various places in the palace. "I have delivered this dreadful sentence; I shall suffer to see it enforced."

So, she does, watching with solemn anticipation as pale-faced servants hoist the bodies, hanging three behind her throne and five on each side of the room approaching it. Somewhere within, the last pieces of her girlish innocence seem to wither and die with this dreadful act. She begins to wonder if there will come a time when she will regret the choices she makes now. She reminds herself that they are made in the name of survival. But at what point is surviving no longer worth it?

The completed task is a bleak sight, even the strongest of stomachs would lurch to see it. Accompanied by the foul stench of death and the rubble from yesterday's fight, Myla stands at the head of the room. She looks to be the queen of death itself; it delivers a frightful sense of darkening. On an average day, the sound of bards and the scent of warm wine would fill this space. Her courtiers would converse at ease. Now faces, heavy with the fear that they may be the next bodies to adorn the walls, dip in and out of the shadows. Of course, this is the desired effect. For her plan to work, Myla needs her subjects to be afraid. It must appear as though she has lain ruin to her own household in the face of defiance and changed its course to align with the Blood Stealer.

It is midday when the thundering of hooves can be heard from beyond the palace gates. Myla steadies her pulse with an extra draught, swallowing it quickly until the warmth of the alcohol seeps into her bloodstream. Her head feels lighter and the dancing lights of the black candles begin to blur together. Dulling her senses ever so slightly feels like the best way to betray herself without resistance. Not that Vesperian would restrain from doing that himself anyway. *Asshole.*

Mere moments pass before the Blood Stealer enters the throne room. His powers demand more of her than yesterday, for the pull in her chest nearly convinces her she is not pretending, this ruse now feels real. *Look at him, so handsome. So . . . alluring. The swing in his step makes it look like he is dancing across the floor, coming to sweep me up and carry me away. Snap out of it. Do not be an idiot. He killed my husband. He is killing me. He would want to kill my child if he knew about it. I do not want him. He* wants *me to want him.* Myla allows a stream of defensive affirmations to flood her mind, centering her train of thought against the attack that is his poisonous aphrodisiac.

A hush claims the court as he walks with slow determination toward her, flanked once more by his wolves and an entourage of dazed guards. Those who watch from their huddled corners exchange fearful glances with one another as they make themselves small. It is as though they avoid being seen to avoid being *used.* He does not bow. Instead, his eyes devour her from afar, not ceasing in their consumption the closer he gets. He seems to not even notice the bodies and ruin around him, a sight he must be well accustomed to.

"Your Grace," he says at last, stopping only when he stands

directly before her, looking down at where she sits. She has leaned intentionally into her throne, relaxed by all appearances, watching him from beneath her thick lashes. "You look ravishing."

She allows an easy smile to tease the corners of her lips before standing. Reaching out, she pushes him to his knees, forcing him to look up with a finger tipping his chin. "Lord Shayd, I see you left your manners outside." Her voice is coy and flirtatious, a sentiment which sparks delight in his darkening eyes.

"Vesperian to you, Your Grace," he replies, dark eyes casting downward in reverence.

"Then I must ask you to call me Myla," she answers, urging him to his feet by the collar of his jacket, certain to pull him a step closer so they share the same breath. "I have considered your proposal."

Vesperian stands tall, his hands resting casually on the hilt of the blade at his hip. "And what have you to say in response?" Only now do his eyes wander to the bodies hanging behind her. A glint of pleasure passes across his face, and Myla hopes that means he is taking the message in the manner it is intended.

Oozing confidence and a faint breath of sensuality, Myla answers, her voice low so only he can hear. "You asked me a question yesterday . . . of the most intimate nature. Do you recall?"

His eyes dart to the space between her legs and with a lick of his lips, he nods. "How could I forget. The question plagues me nightly."

At this response, Myla feels herself wavering, tortured by what she must say next. *This would be a great time to feel your dark pull, Vesperian. You really need to work on your timing and not make me do all the heavy lifting.* The pull on her remains silent, as if he were giving her a choice. One of many lies to come from him.

She musters every ounce of courage inside and steps closer to him, tracing a gloved finger gently along his jawline until it finds his lips. Her finger grazes across them, separating them to gain access inside, she brushes the tip of his tongue, making certain her eyes flicker there in mock intrigue. In her peripheral, a tense Bryar stands, staring straight ahead, appearing as an unfazed and dutiful soldier to the crown.

"Two years ago, you rescued me from a most dull arrangement. In the many nights following, I have felt your pull." She lowers her eyes and speaks the unspeakable. "Thoughts of your power have plagued me nightly. Thought of our power . . . *together.* So yes, I did touch myself as I thought of you. A man with such *gifts,* claiming what he wants, myself included; how could I not want what we might create together, what we might *own* together. A union to be *feared* after too many years of being underestimated." Myla removes the finger and releases her grip on his chin before she takes one step back, her perfume wafting and the sway of her body carrying his attention. "Do you see how they look at me? They do not see a queen. They see a widow. My father." She nods to where Maverick stands, his stern expression the very picture of disapproval. "You see, he created a life for me which I did not like at all. I should like to return the favor." Myla cringes inwardly as the latter is whispered, exposing more truth than she intended. Another impulse, courtesy of the Blood Stealer before her.

Vesperian, handsome as he may be, reeks of lust and power. His words are repulsive, but promising to her cause. "Am I to assume this is you accepting my proposal?" he nearly growls, primal like a starved beast, stepping forward as though to claim her right here for all to see. Everything about him is refined, from his well-manicured hair and nails, to the precise lines of stubble along his cheeks and jaw. His eyebrows are set in a relaxed line across his brow while the eyes beneath them tell ancient stories. At a glance, he could seem cocky and boyish, but up close and intimate as he is now, she can see it. This man is centuries old, and carries knowledge and guile that she could never hope to hold for herself. He is power. He is an apex predator, ready to strike should his attempts to claim her falter.

Louder now so all may hear, she speaks. "It would be an honor to align myself with you and bring unity to our people and territories. I accept your proposal, Lord Vesperian." Those in the crowd who are not privy to her plan seem to quiver in the wake of her acceptance. Eyes dart back and forth, searching for others who seem equally stunned. The courtiers need not look far before finding their bewilderment reflected in the eyes of their peers. The gore hanging behind her throne seems to be the only repellent which staunches any potential resistance. Gasps of shock and fear fall into something even more terrifying: silence.

When Caius had proposed to her publicly, all a ceremonial nicety as the official proposal was nothing more than him shaking hands with her father, and she had accepted, he had kissed her hand and thanked her for the consideration. Myla is not sure what she had expected, but as Vesperian steps closer, his hand snaking down the small of her back, she is momentarily stunned. Unwilling to waver now, she checks herself, pressing close to him, unresisting when he meets his lips with hers, his tongue delving inside her mouth. She matches his advancement, her fingers wrapping around his collar to hold him close, and in turn, kissing him back. It feels like the deepest of betrayals, knowing the man her heart beats for is mere steps away. Myla reminds herself that not only is this just the beginning of her sacrifices, but these sacrifices are for her people, and Bryar is one of those whom she hopes to save by suffering this.

Vesperian marks his territory before all. The gesture can not be mistaken as anything less than claiming her for all to see. Myla allows it, mindful to seem open to the encounter. When he pulls away, his face brimming with lust, Myla is grateful to not taste the bourbon and blood on him any longer.

"My Lady," he speaks, tipping her chin upward with a threatening finger. "I am besotted." He casts a glance over the room, taking note of the eyes sinking into him and then to the bodies overhead. "It seems I missed a show."

Myla laughs lightly before slumping into her throne. "Your proposal was not welcomed by all." A young page offers her and Lord Vesperian a glass of wine each, which they both accept; Myla takes a long sip before speaking again. "I squashed any sign of resistance and made sure the survivors were well aware of what might happen should they defy me." The words are lackluster and seem to care little of the souls belonging to the corpses. "Do you think I got the message across?" The question is quipped like a small joke between the two of them and followed up by an insensitive giggle. Myla is repulsed with herself.

Lord Vesperian grins, his flash of white making it hard to believe he is a consumer of innocent blood. One could mistake his gaze as riveting, intoxicating even. Perhaps that is his strategy. "Consider me impressed, dear. I felt there may be a ruthless queen beneath the quivering widow, and I am deeply pleased to have been right."

"You, of all people, should understand biding one's time." Myla answers, a dual meaning, for she reminds herself this is a temporary arrangement. Her eyes travel slowly to the bit of chest exposed beneath his black tunic. The place she plans to embed a knife. There is a twisting black tattoo—his wraith, she believes. From what she can see of the marking, the wraith is tattooed in a way that gives the impression of impaling Vesperian's heart. A grim piece of artwork to put on one's body, even for a fallen Fae God.

"It seems you are my match in that area," he remarks, sitting in the throne which was brought in earlier. It is magnificent, with etchings of thorns and skulls seeming to tumble from the base. It was Caius's father's throne before. Myla would rather Vesperian sit in her father-in-law's throne than that of her late husband, who died at his hands. She swallows hard, grateful to have removed Caius's. There is a rush of whispers and murmuring building throughout the room, courtiers in disbelief that Myla should allow this man to sit upon the throne. In any other circumstance, should a betrothed display such disrespect, she would have them removed. Today, she must allow it. More than allow it though, she must punish her courtiers for questioning it. *If it is a ruthless queen he wants . . .*

Myla stands swiftly, demanding the silence and attention of all in the room. "I see it in your eyes," she hisses, her fingers pulsating in and out of a clenched fist, magic convulsing in small orbs between them. They respond to her fear now. "You question me. You question him. But you shall not!" She takes a few swift steps forward, her advancement clearly frightening those closest to her. So many familiar faces, who have often looked upon her as a trusted queen, now tremble before her. She has had tea with these people, she has walked the palace gardens with them. Now, she threatens and terrifies them. *Better this than death or enslavement.*

"Have you seen my new decor?" She waves a dismissive hand toward the dead. "I believe there is room for more, and the bodies of those who defy me would be the most breathtaking additions."

Lord Vesperian bellows a deep laugh before standing beside her. "No, my love, look upon the sheep. See how they tremble. They will not bleat . . . lest I *eat them.*" He licks his lips, a thirst visibly forming and that awful black mist of his wraith seeping from his veins.

Chills prick every inch of her body. Of course, he would threaten to rob them of their free will. That is his most potent weapon of choice. Rather than succumb to the vile twisting in her belly, Myla joins him in sadistic laughter, carelessly turning on her heel and returning to her throne, lowering herself weakly into it, his proximity already draining.

By nightfall, the Blood Stealer's men have descended. At Myla's command, arrangements for them have been made in the barracks with her soldiers. Myla trusts that Bryar has briefed his men well and none will truly sleep without a peer on watch. The Blood Stealer has been taken to Caius's old chambers. She could avoid Vesperian sitting on her dead husband's throne. There is no logical reason she would deny his sleeping in the King's chamber were she truly aligned with him and planning to make him her king.

Thus, she stands in the heart of a room she has avoided for years, watching the dark man before her direct servants to place his trunks beside the bed. *The bed.* A fragrance fills her senses, or the memory of a fragrance. Oakmoss. That is what Caius used to smell like. On that particular night, he reeked of it. In his drunken state, his words landed with a harsher sting than usual. *Stop it.* She diverts her gaze from the bed, ignoring the memory of fingers around her throat, holding her in place. *"Just give me an heir, Myla. That is all I ask of you."* With a shudder, Myla turns around entirely, facing away.

"I have ordered a feast in your honor," she says, smiling sweetly at Vesperian, who tests the mantle with the swipe of his finger, pleased to find no dust. "I must go ready myself, but I look forward to seeing you there."

"A feast? You indulge me," he hums threateningly, watching with thirst as she leaves the room.

Walking down her own halls has never felt so threatening. Unfamiliar soldiers patrol, dressed in the crimson red of Vesperian's house; some alert, others appearing dazed. His banners have already been strung up on the walls alongside hers; a single drop of red, presumably blood, is framed by ornate black detail. Myla interprets them as the curling of his black wraith around the blood of a victim.

There are no safe nooks to carry on a private conversation now. Myla can not even fathom how she might feel safe sleeping tonight, even with Bryar standing post.

Her steps hasten with the rate of her heart, as she hurries down the corridor to her chamber. Shaky hands throw the door open, and she quickly slams it shut behind her, pressing her back to it and taking several, steadying breaths. Elsa already waits within, and at the sound of the doors she appears from the dressing room, her face pale and concerned.

"Oh, thank the Gods you are here," she says with a relieved sigh. "You were marvelous. Startling, *terrifying*, and marvelous." These words are spoken more confidently as she grasps Myla's hands within her own, holding her friend close. Myla smiles at Elsa despite the turmoil within. Nothing about this feels marvelous.

"I only hope it proves worth it," she replies, working at unfastening the buttons of her gloves and removing them from her balmy hands to dip her fingers in the warm washbasin. Once finished, she sits before her vanity, allowing Elsa

to fix her hair. Elsa hesitates, her fingers nimbly tucking Myla's dark hair into an elegant side twist, scooping the curls from the front of her face and leaving the majority of it swirling down her back. "I overheard the Council discussing something. Bryar and I both heard it . . ."

Myla jerks her head swiftly to face Elsa. "What was it?"

"It was of your instructions . . . you told them to kill you, should they doubt you are yourself." Elsa's voice inflects with betrayal, though her actions stay on task. Turning Myla's head foreword, she ties a headdress of raven feathers over the crown of her head, secured by a black ribbon at the nape of her neck. Obsidian and smoky quartz spears, like the ones of her crown, are fixed in the center of the headdress, as well as a few more black peonies for fullness, creating a dark and celestial look. "I want you to know," Elsa continues firmly, "there is not a fucking chance *either* of us are going to let that happen, and that is a deal he and I made together so you best believe it. I can not believe you trust a single soul in that room not to take advantage of your *request.*"

Myla bites her lower lip to keep the tears at bay. "Elsa, you have to see the logic in it."

"Your logic is rapidly running out of space for the heart, Myla." Elsa snaps, her voice an octave higher and her face hard. "You know I support you; this was my idea to begin with, and it is brilliant, but if you believe for a second, we are going to let you disguise suicide as martyrdom, you are a damn fool. Bryar is angry at you."

"He will have to live with his anger a bit longer and—Elsa! Suicide? Suicide would have been confronting him when he first walked in here yesterday. I am trying to make sure we *all* survive this!" Her hands fall instinctually to her belly, and Myla takes a steadying breath.

Elsa nods slowly and helps her unclasp the lace collar of the dress she wears, exposing the skin from her chin to her lower ribs. "For self-control." Elsa slides an onyx gemstone ring in the shape of a moon onto Myla's forefinger and then a matching necklace around her throat. The perfecting touch, a statement piece, is tied around her waist: a full skirt to layer over the form-fitting one creates depth to her silhouette. The skirt is made entirely of the sleekest black raven feathers, allowing a mesmerizing swish with every step. Myla parts the slit of her first layer and straps the fox dagger to a garter at her thigh.

"There." Elsa stands back and admires her handiwork. "What did that monster call you? Ruthless?" She smiles, nodding in approval. "A Ruthless Raven Queen. Get revenge for Caius, okay? Get revenge for yourself. But know we will not allow this to end in your death." Elsa places her hands on either side of Myla's head, and with the gentlest vibration of her magic, healing energy slips peacefully into her being with the delicate touch that can come only from a healer. Sometimes, Myla doubts if Elsa should be a lady-in-waiting when her true talents lie in the gift of healing and revitalization.

"Thank you," Myla says, holding her friend's hand to her cheek. "I do love you so. Please be safe tonight." Myla stands, taking one last look in the mirror at her violently dark reflection, seeing there, someone who could and would kill anyone for those she loved.

"Elsa?"

"Yes?" Elsa asks, watching Myla attentively.

"What if I am not doing any of this for Caius?"

"Then, I would tell you to get twice the revenge for yourself."

Myla takes a deep breath in and checks her posture in the mirror, something the blademaster once told her echoing in her mind, a reminder to stand tall.

"This is how you should stand. Sword or no sword in your hand, stand tall, Lady Myla. You have no reason to walk through this world cowering."

Chapter 7

Black candles are lit at uneven heights overhead, some hanging from the ceiling, others from sconces on the wall. The lighting is darker than Myla would prefer for a celebration, but considering the nature of the party, she supposes it is fitting. Long tables have been brought in and line both sides of the long throne room. Courtiers and visiting lords and ladies sit, mingling uneasily. An air of pretense fills the room as her subjects seem to act on cue, unsure of their moves but knowing they must comply. Black furs have been thrown across both thrones as padding and warmth, for the evening has grown cold.

"Her Majesty, The Dowager Queen!"

Someone forgot to tell the master of ceremonies that I am not going by that anymore . . . Myla is announced but a scoff quickly follows, and she can see, already reclined in his throne, is Vesperian. He is dressed in black leather. His forearms exposed where his tunic is rolled, revealing crimson red tattoos in the shapes of bodies, covering the majority of his arms.

"I think dowager is a title we should retire. Do you not agree, my Queen?"

I suppose Vesperian will do it.

Myla tips her chin upward, walking slowly toward him, certain the look on his face is one of sinful lust at her soft, exposed skin, which no doubt glints in the candlelight.

But it is not his gaze that thrills her.

Bryar's is the look she must pretend once more not to see. How beautifully he wears his jealousy *and* admiration.

"What should I be called then?" Myla asks coyly as she ascends the steps to her throne, allowing one last flicker of a glance in Bryar's direction before settling on Vesperian's lap.

"Something that includes Shayd, do you not agree?" he replies, a large hand squeezing the thickest part of her thigh in greeting.

Myla pauses, running familiar hands through his hair. "For that to hold any weight, I would have to be your wife first."

The thin line of a smile passes over his face, and he hands her his glass of wine to share. "Three days should be enough time to plan a wedding, do you not agree?" He leans forward, offering her a chalice and urging her to drink. Reluctantly, she does. "And until then, perhaps we can sample what is to come." He presses cold fingers to her collarbone, allowing them to explore the dips and curves of her body, pacing the ridges of her breasts before resting on her belly where the fabric unites. His eyes turn upward to meet hers. "There is one issue though." His voice is louder now and Myla tenses, already unnerved by his touch.

An overwhelming intoxication suddenly fills her senses. Moments before, he was disgusting to her. Now, as she studies his features, she is drawn to the depth of his eyes, the ridge of his upper lip and the way the light across his scars is both ferocious and attractive. His breath is spiced, and the cologne he wears must be an aphrodisiac. She catches her breath and against her will finds herself pressing against him with enthusiasm, eager to please.

"Whatever is the matter?" she asks, her impulses not to be denied as her hands caress his chest in spite of her brain begging her not to. She presses soft lips to his ear. "Tell me, my lord, what issue do you speak of."

He grins. "I like how you respond to me." Then he stands, pushing her from his lap, and gestures to a young woman sitting at one of the tables. Myla recognizes her as the teenage daughter of one of her Council members. "The issue is that traitorous bitch."

Myla flinches at the language, as do many around her. "Whatever has she done?" she asks, feeling a reaction within her, not his magic, but hers. Anger simmering beneath the surface and threatening to bite like the snapping jaws of wolves.

"She was speaking to a friend before the celebration began, speaking on her *concerns* regarding my presence." His words are calculated as his hands raise at his side, a blackness forming in the skin of his palms. "Come, child. Step forward."

Myla's throat swells and turns dry as cotton, watching as the girl stands. She seems small and far too young to be here in the first place. "Vesperian," she coos, placing a hand on the rigid shoulder in front of her. "The words of a mere girl are no threat to us. Send her away for the night and let us be done with the nuisance."

The Blood Stealer turns to her, the irises of his eyes framed with crimson now and the small wraith forming between his hands growing violent and wriggling in his control. "I do not suffer insubordinates to go unpunished beneath my rule."

Myla forces a relaxed smile, allowing the light at her own palms to form. "Neither do I. I must be the one to punish her." Eyes full of terror, the girl before her trembles, her fingers laced together in a fervent plea. "Please, Your Grace . . . I—I was merely frightened. Surely you see we all are."

Lord Reacher, her father, and the Treasurer on Myla's Council has rushed to her side, his body partially shielding the girl's. "Do not harm her, I beg of you. She meant no disrespect."

Although her heart begs her to show mercy, Myla retires the thought, aware of how Vesperian watches her with anticipation. This is a test. The dead bodies on the wall were not enough. He has to see her in action. With a breath of a prayer, begging the Spirit Mother to give her precision, Myla allows her magic to trickle, first to her palms, then her fingertips, and finally, through her pores, until all the light in the throne room has been summoned to her body alone. Flecks of golden light seeping and collecting like a tether in her hands, blinding all around her. The use of magic costs her dearly already, and Myla can feel the magic relinquishing its hold on her womb, a problem she will have to rectify later in the evening.

For now, she calls upon the Gods to bring their trembling wrath upon her court.

Better their wrath than Vesperian's.

"I was clear," Myla speaks, her voice a booming echo of what it usually is, no longer sweet and assertive but distorted and angry, the light within her coiling and ready to snap. She has used her power to kill before but never has she tested its precision. She does not wish to kill the girl, only scare her, and make a spectacle of the situation. "You may accept my word as law, or you will die. I implore each of you to consider the very real consequences of defying me!" Myla hopes they interpret the duality of her message. If anyone strays, it will not be her who kills them; it will be the Fae God beside her.

Her guests grasp their ears, some seeming to try and tear them from their heads, the rasp of her voice stabbing deep into their brains and evoking screams of agony. Others abandon all care for their hearing, covering their eyes from the angry light. With a flick of her wrist, her light furls around the ankles of the girl, suspending her upside down in the air. A chilling scream pours from the girl's lips as she catapults fifty feet upwards, and pleas for mercy mixed with apologies are frantically sobbed.

Everything inside Myla wants to turn her magic on the Blood Stealer, but this is a game of waiting and biding her time. In order to defeat him, she must catch him completely unaware. Instead, she channels her energy into controlling the thread of burning light so as to not knock the girl senseless on the stone pillars. "Should anyone find it necessary to speak against me again, know that death will be the consequence, *not* humiliation." Myla lowers her to a few feet above the ground before releasing her. She falls into a defeated slump, her parents rushing to help her up. As Myla's light fades, it is replaced by a sinister darkness growing larger between Vesperian's hands.

"Myla, my Ruthless Queen," he says with a laugh. "That was spectacular. I have heard you called The Queen Who Bleeds Stars . . . but to *see* it, that is something else." He toys with the wraith between his hands as though it is a pet needing attention. "I can see your goodness will be difficult to supplant."

There is no time to think or even intercept. It is faster than a blink or a sharp breath, shooting across the room like an arrow. The black wraith cuts through the girl's cheek, met with a river of red leaking from her face. Vesperian is consumed inside the darkness of the wraith, one moment standing beside Myla and the next, reappearing alongside the shrieking girl. Her father lets out a cry, a protest, begging for his daughter's life. Vesperian, void of feeling, seizes her by the throat, his hand sliding against the blood already spilling down the neckline of her dress.

"Why would I kill her," he asks, "when controlling her is far more entertaining?" He leans in, his tongue gliding across her cheek, lapping drops of blood from her face. The blackness around him grows, coiling and pulsating as the girl's minor magic feeds his main source. A look of disassociation washes over her, an absence of thought or feeling replacing what was moments ago, a young woman full of life and fight and opinions.

She is a shell.

She is *his* shell.

And she never saw it coming.

Horror devours the crowd, silence claiming all but her parents, who weep. Lord Reacher lets out a beastly scream, raising a hand above his head ready to attack. It is a futile effort. The conjured wraith pivots from the Blood Stealer's being and lops his head off with one lethal slice.

Myla flinches and her chest constricts, everything inside her screaming at what a mistake she has made. Not one night into her plan, and he is already claiming lives and wills.

"Margot, Matteo." The dark Fae God gestures to his wolves. "Eat." To Myla's horror, the command is obeyed, and the large wolves descend on the fresh kill. The sound of ripping flesh and famished wolves is sickening. The urge to scream is snuffed when he turns around, searching for her approval. Something inside her suddenly worships him, a congenial expression forms, and she finds herself leaning against him, wiping traces of blood from his chin. "Your power is *exhilarating*," she says breathlessly, hoping to pass off her distress as being awestruck. "Let the servants clean this mess, I am famished."

Signs of conflict and casualty are erased by servants who clearly wish they were elsewhere. The remainder of the guests fill their plates, not because they appear hungry or happy to, but for fear of finding themselves on Myla's wall. Myla reclines in her throne, a laissez-faire cover for the waning of her energy. The proximity to Vesperian is draining her in spite of the tonic poured in her wine and a few subtle recharges with Elsa. Nothing could prepare Myla for the way she now feels sitting next to him. Both fatigued and helpless, yet happy to be so. She finds herself doing and saying things that feel a betrayal to herself, to Elsa, to her entire court, and especially to Bryar.

Between feasting and drinking and exchanging scandalous promises with Vesperian, the night drifts on in a drunken haze. When Myla comes to, in a moment of sanity, she finds herself draped across Vesperian's lap, his lips to her throat and his hands exploring up her legs all while her guests and subjects sit watching. Attempted conversation and music from the bards seem dulled beneath the heavy blanket of intoxication poisoning the room at Vesperian's hands.

Myla wants to stand, to remove his hands, to walk out. Her body is frozen in place and a strange longing inside her defies her logic. At their feet, between Margot and Matteo, like a cowering dog waiting for orders from her new master, is Lord and Lady Reacher's daughter. Her eyes seem empty as glass, nothing laying beyond them but a possessed soul in a helpless trance.

Those also under the Blood Stealer's control seem to be responding to the drunken and lustful energy. Myla realizes his control is not always a conscious instruction. Anyone tied to him by blood oath is like the root systems to a tree, connected to all the others, communicating, and responding as one. If he feels drunk, so do they, and if he feels rage, they also feel rage. And as Myla is rapidly discovering, his arousal seems to be theirs as well. Men and women both under his control make indecent advances on those around them, matching his pace and even his gestures until the room spins out of control in a landscape of scandal and nakedness.

Myla inclines her head, hoping to see a friendly face, yet the blur around her grows until Vesperian is the only person she can see. The sensation strikes fear to her core, fear she might respond the wrong way and be another victim to his wrath, but also fear for responding the way he wants and being his victim in an entirely different way. His voice is the only voice she can hear, though she swears her friends try and speak to her. She can not hear them, only him. She feels isolated from those she trusts now, and no matter where she turns, all she can see, feel, and hear, is him.

How can something so enticing feel so terrible once inside it?

Get it together. Myla wills herself to stay focused on the risks and rewards of this endeavor. With trembling hands, she cups his chin, pulling him in for a warm kiss, the alcohol on his tongue potent. He is drunk. This is her opportunity to excuse herself without raising suspicion. "I fear I do not know up from down," she giggles, letting her fingertips gently explore his handsome features. "You must excuse me; I need sleep if I am to properly entertain you tomorrow."

He growls protests into her neck, hungry fingers digging into her hips, but his words are slurred and as he slumps further into the throne, she considers herself excused.

Myla stands, wobbling beneath the effort. Voices and music alike swirl around her resembling a tempest, threatening to throw her off course. The stairs seem a daunting task, let alone the walk to her chamber, so she is grateful when Elsa finds her side, a firm hand bracing beneath her elbow and guiding her through the haze of movement. Vaguely, Myla is aware of Bryar taking up his position behind her, following protectively.

Proximity to him is unusually warm. He ripples with rage.

Within minutes, as they slowly put distance between, she and the Blood Stealer, Elsa's magic seeps into her veins, and Myla feels a lurch in her stomach. The letdown of his control is not unlike recovering from too much drink. Upon entering her chamber, Myla trips over her own skirts and falls to the ground, vomiting onto the ornate tiles.

Elsa gasps and Fern rushes over, wiping the corner of Myla's mouth with her apron. "My Lady," she coos sympathetically. "Let us get you out of this dress."

"Wait—" Myla holds up a hand to stay her ladies and presses shaking hands to her belly. The first attempt to redirect her magic comes to a disappointing, sputtering halt, as does the second. A third and final attempt is warm and calming as that sacred space halts its weaving of life. Breathlessly, Myla peers up from where she crouches and manages a weak smile. Though only Elsa understands what has occurred.

The two ladies help her into a thin shift. Fern stands before her door, though it is barred, and Elsa instructs her to intercept anyone trying to enter.

Elsa sits behind her in the large bed, running a comb through her dark hair and whispering comforting remarks. "You are performing beautifully," she begins. "The doubt and fear you see around you . . . it is temporary. You have to keep focused on the end goal."

Myla nods slowly, nothing in control beyond her breathing. Her thoughts come in waves of confusion with nothing clear enough to form a cohesive stream of consciousness. "Elsa, I did not realize it was going to feel like this."

"You could not have known."

"No, but . . . I think Bryar knew."

"He has an irritating way of always being right—do not tell him I said so," Elsa interjects. "It does not mean you were wrong. You can both be right in this case."

Fern peeks around the corner. "Speaking of Captain Monroe," she says sheepishly. "He is talking outside the door, asking for me to let him in." She looks at Myla, concerned by the ashen queen before her. "Do I . . . uh . . . let him in?"

Elsa stands, moving past Fern. "I will handle it."

"I can not let you in right now; she needs space."

Myla can not hear his words, but his tone is distressed. She wants nothing more than to let him in, to feel safe beside him, but with the Blood Stealer down the hall, it is too risky.

"I will give it to her." After the door closes and latches, Elsa reappears around the corner. She runs an exhausted hand over her face before speaking. "He says he is by the door tonight, and I am to give this to you." She slips a piece of paper into Myla's hand, which she carefully unfolds.

"You have survived worse. You will survive this, and we will too." —B

A hint of comfort glows and Myla folds the parchment and slips it inside the shaft of her pillow. "I guess he loves me still," she says with a slight smile.

A look of confusion washes over Fern's face, and her mouse-like nose scrunches in question. "The captain? Love? Still—*what?"*

Myla and Elsa share a brief laugh before Elsa speaks up. "You are in it now, kid. If the secret gets out, we will know it is you."

Fern grins slightly. "Oh, I knew he came in here from time to time. I just thought it was . . . at Your Grace's discretion, you know? I did not realize it was love."

Elsa bellows, clasping her hands in a gleeful clap. "Fern, what do you know of such things?"

Fern simply sighs and sits down on the chest at the foot of Myla's bed. "Firsthand? Nothing . . . and I should like to keep it that way, given how miserable it seems to make a person." She grumbles the last sentence before continuing, "Can I do anything more for you, Your Grace?"

"No, thank you Fern," Myla responds with the sincerest smile she can muster.

"I will retire then, Your Grace."

Myla shakes her head, reaching for Fern's hand. "It is not safe. You will stay here with Elsa and me. If I could bring every lady in the palace into my room to protect her, I would. Keeping you and Elsa safe will have to do." With her free hand, she grasps Elsa's and looks between the two. "Thank you both for your help. I could not manage without you."

As Myla falls asleep, she reflects on Bryar's message. How can he love her after watching her mold like putty at the whim of the Blood Stealer? A warmth fills her middle, stirring like a summoning. Though Myla wants to believe it is brought on by thoughts of Bryar and their earlier encounter, she is afraid it is the call of the Blood Stealer. As of right now, she can not be sure of the authenticity of any feelings.

And that is the most terrifying realization she could possibly come to.

The three girls drift to sleep on the comfortable plumes of Myla's bed. Despite the uncertainty hanging thick in the air, Myla finds peace in sleep. So, when she is awoken to a knock on the door and Elsa shaking her awake, nothing short of disoriented can describe her being, as Vesperian's voice coos from the other side of her door.

"She is my fiancé; I will see her."

Myla's skin prickles and she flies out of bed, sending a prayer to the Gods that Bryar watches his tongue.

"She is asleep." Bryar's retort is barely audible, though the defiant inflection is unmistakable.

"Shit," Myla hisses, allowing Fern to pull a dressing gown over her for modesty before she flings the door open, attempting to erase all signs of annoyance from her face.

"Lord Sha— Vesperian . . ." She greets him with a slight smile, ignoring the reddening of Bryar's axe as his hand sears the metal.

"You have a most dedicated bodyguard," he hums, his piercing eyes dissecting Bryar with suspicion. "You might consider giving him different instructions when it comes to me."

Myla tenses as her words say the exact opposite of what she feels and wants. "It is alright, Captain Monroe, allow Lord Vesperian to pass."

Bryar steps aside dutifully, though the glower he burns into Vesperian's back as he passes is murderous, sending a brief thrill through Myla. Vesperian is about to close the door when he sees Elsa and Fern in company. He smirks, gesturing to the door. "You are both dismissed. I should like a private moment with my fiancé." Myla glances briefly at the watchful wolves trailing behind Vesperian. They are unnerving and she wishes she could think of a reason for them to not be allowed in her chambers.

Both girls exchange anxious glances, briefly looking to Myla for final instructions. With a nod of encouragement, sure to keep a pleasant smile on her face, she glances at Elsa.

"Return in ten minutes. I would like to dress for the day."

The latch falls in place with a loud *clink* as the door shuts behind her ladies, and Myla feels more vulnerable than ever. Vesperian stands with his back to her, watching the flames in her hearth lap at one another. He is already dressed and his hair combed neatly, though the stubble along his jawline shows this morning. He wears a loose black tunic tucked into form-fitting trousers. The sleeves are rolled, exposing tattooed, sculpted forearms.

"I trust you slept well?" he asks, turning now to face her with a sinister look etched in his dark features. Dangerously handsome or not, standing alone with him is a terrifying and unwelcome way to wake up, and truly highlights the 'dangerous' element in the equation. Questions and concerns in equal proportion pulse through Myla's mind while the unexpected proximity to him is an assault on her already tapering energy source. The wave of overwhelming senses is an immediate onslaught, forcing her to sit. She is careful to do so slowly so as not to reveal her fatigue.

"It is an unexpected pleasure," she says methodically, ensuring that every syllable can be mistaken as an invitation. It is vital he sees her as unfazed. Her fear is his feast, so she will starve him. "What, or whom, do I have to thank for your presence so early?"

Vesperian sits on the chaise beside her, a hand toying with the material draped over her knees. "I believe negotiations and a marriage contract must be drawn up today. I wanted to pay you the respect of discussing it all privately before we sit before both Councils."

His statement is threatening. Discussing things privately removes the logic and input of her Council members. Not that she needs it for this scheme, but in any regular situation, this interaction would be unheard of. One more show of defiance in the Blood Stealer's score book. "What a splendid idea," she responds, taking his hand in her own. "I am eager to plan our reign together."

His smile is fleeting and lacks genuine depth. This is where his agenda comes into play. This is where her ruse succeeds or fails. Sweat forms behind her knees, and she must consciously choose to keep her legs still beneath the mounting nerves.

His next words are alarming. "I believe it is essential to our cause that in addition to a wedding ceremony, there must also be a coronation for myself."

Myla shivers and the pulse in her neck rises as he watches her response intently. "I was thinking the same thing," she agrees beautifully, caressing his fingers between hers in a manner that could be mistaken as loving. "If our people are to unite, so must we. If our people are to respect us both, we must be seen as the rightful monarchs, together. Most importantly, we must bring the rule of this realm beneath one banner."

His expression screams lust for power, the tilt of his chin, the way his dark hair falls into his eyes as he smolders, pleased at his success. Everything about him, from the scars to the fragrance, the silk of his voice, even the very air tremors around him, it is all masterful deceit. A more trusting woman might be fooled by his refined looks and even tone. "Dominion of the entire realm, I approve . . . half of your Council will move to my palace, while a half of mine will relocate here. A king regent will be established on my behalf there as well, so my agendas may be enforced while I live here with you."

If Myla accepts all of his conditions without proposing any of her own, it will raise suspicion, so she interjects, "I believe a queen regent must also be established within your palace. I must be seen to have power and representation in the Seam as well."

Myla envisions the Seam. She has never been, but the illustrations in her textbooks were enough to send chills through her. A barren wasteland engulfed in a choking haze and guarded by unnaturally large wolves. Much like the ones he now commands here.

Vesperian nods. "I acquiesce . . . though, there is the matter of your large army, as well as *whose* banners we will unite under. There must be but one royal seal and one *army,* lest our unity be questioned."

"These are all cosmetic changes you propose," Myla answers sweetly. "I can not say I care one way or the other. What of my army, though?"

His eyes fixate on hers and darkness manifests physically, exuding from his very pores until the room feels like an abyss closing in on Myla. His power manipulates her energy, suddenly draining any will to resist or argue further propositions, she feels inclined to agree to whatever he may suggest.

"It is customary for my soldiers to swear blood oaths to me," he says in a hypnotic voice. Myla knows very well what he proposes. The blood oaths her subjects swear to her are quite different from his. She does not consume their blood, feed off their power, or control their actions and impulses.

Which is precisely what he wishes to do to her army of thousands upon thousands of troops.

"The day after our wedding, I will begin accepting blood oaths. Your army is substantial, and I believe it will take many weeks to carry out. It is exhausting business. Those who have yet to give their blood oaths will be detained until it is their turn so we have no deserters."

Accepting blood oaths. He means stealing them. Myla stands slowly, moving toward a decanter of wine and pouring it with a trembling hand which she prays he does not see. She offers him a glass and swallows hers swiftly before responding. "Of course. That is most logical. I should expect the same gesture from your soldiers, however. They will kneel before me and swear fealty."

Vesperian nods, his eyes lowering to her exposed collarbone. "Anything for you, my Queen."

Myla suspects negotiations have ended when his hand brushes a trace of wine from her bottom lip with his thumb, which he proceeds to lick reverently. His gaze does not waver from hers. Instead, in spite of the silence, his unwillingness to avert his eyes feels like noise, sirens screaming in her head to move. Her legs twitch in an effort to walk away but the motion does not follow. At an almost inhuman rate, he stands, jerking her close to him, the hand not currently grasping a wineglass slips slowly down her back until it slides dangerously low, groping her from behind.

"My Lord." Myla forces a giggle though a rage building in her lungs begs to scream profanities at him. "It is important I maintain my virtue until we are wed."

He slowly digs his fingers into her flesh, silencing her protest with a kiss which nearly draws blood between his teeth. His breath is hot as he speaks in slow demands. "My Ruthless Queen has virtue?" His hand trails from her back to her front, teasing the ribbon at her neckline which holds the slip in place. "You told me yourself; you have thought of me in your bed. There is no place for thinking now, let us *do.*"

Vesperian drops the wineglass, and it shatters before the hearth. Myla feels the spray of wine on her feet and legs but has no time to assess the damage to her slip. Both of his hands now firmly grope her, pulling her against him. His teeth dig into her neck gently, nipping as though to coax her and his lips travel in icy kisses up her neck.

The very place Bryar kissed her two nights ago.

Sucking in a breath, Myla places both hands on his chest, urging herself to be steady. "I have imagined what we could be countless times." Her response is breathless and she ignores the tingling sensation crawling up her thighs entirely against her will.

Another game the demon before her plays.

"But there is a tension here," she whispers, allowing her lips to brush against his, hoping to tease him enough with words to satiate his desires. "I should like to let it grow so I may enjoy you to the fullest . . . as my husband." The words taste rotten in her mouth, a betrayal to her very core, yet ones that seem effective as his hand retreats slightly, allowing her dress to remain in place.

"Darling." His voice is like the edge of a sword, sharp and threatening, but there is a hint of coy appreciation there. "I have never purchased a horse without riding it first. A wife seems to be no different, by my calculations."

Shock ripples through her body, threatening to spill out her fingertips, inciting a battle she is not ready for. Of all the times she has been treated as a man's pawn for profit, Myla has never been compared in value to a horse.

Trial run or not, he needs me alive.

She calls his bluff. With a slow, calming breath, Myla presses her lips in slow kisses along his jaw. Finally meeting at his mouth in a tense battle, their lips move against each other's. In a calculated risk, knowing he is a lover of danger and conflict, Myla grasps at his throat while the other clutches his shoulder. She presses her body flush against his while her lips murmur against his ear. "I am no horse, my lord," she answers. His response is exhilarating. He tenses and his throat bobs—*is that fear?* She continues, urging every fiber of her to prove convincing. "I will have you know, I ride, Vesperian. I am not *ridden.* You shall wait to have me, and when you have me, you shall forget every other woman you have ever held. Do you understand me?"

His large hand, cold as iron closes around the wrist grappling at his throat and jerking himself free. A flash of anger is replaced with curiosity and eagerness. He licks his lips and takes a step back, smiling as though he has just won a battle, and she is his vanquished trophy.

"I understand you perfectly. Do not be fooled though, my Ruthless Queen. Two nights from now, I will not be the only one forgetting all others."

Seconds later, before Myla can respond to his promise—or a threat, as it feels—Elsa returns. She brings Fern with her, carrying a steaming basin of water for a bath. Myla looks once more at Vesperian, allowing her eyes to travel up and down his body before she extends a hand for him to kiss.

"I look forward to your demonstration of many things," she says, watching with implied pleasure as he kisses her hand not once, but twice. "Including the power of forgetting."

The door closes behind him and his wolves, taking with them the air of confusion, a sensation of wanting and not wanting all at once. Myla ignores the prying eyes of her ladies, not wishing to expose a single detail should sharing her encounter cause her resolve to waver. That is a response she simply does not have time for. Feeling will have to wait until she has managed to somehow overthrow the monster himself.

Kill the devil. Care later.

Chapter 8

Myla exits her room an hour later, bathed, dressed, and drunk. Elsa supplied another decanter full of a well-aged wine and together, the three girls drowned their worries in the red of their glasses.

Now, she appears, ready to navigate the day and all its complexities.

Bryar still stands at her door and everything inside her wishes to turn and speak with him, but fear for his life stops her. Their only interaction is the slight brush of fingertips as she passes through her door before moving ahead of him to fall in stride with Elsa.

"I need you to deliver a message to Alaric for me." Myla slips her friend a small scroll, which is quickly concealed in her bodice. She then turns to Fern. "My green chemise, the one I wore on my wedding night with Caius. Have it washed and pressed and lay it out for me tonight."

"Your Grace?" Fern asks, astonished, her expression mirrored on Elsa's face and Myla can all but feel the jealousy boiling off Bryar. She stops in her tracks, turning so all three of her companions can see the severity of her features. There is no room for mistakes, now more than ever.

"I must have your trust in this," she demands, briefly aware of dazed crimson soldiers approaching from the other side of the corridor. "Tonight, I will have Vesperian in my chamber—I will be safe," she interjects before Bryar can protest. "And you," Myla looks at him with a determination that could silence most any objection, "you will be by my door, ready to enter it should I cry out; do you understand me?"

His nostrils flare and a glint of something born of anger and pain settles into the souls of his eyes. "Yes, Your Grace."

The bitterness in his response goes unnoticed by none.

There is no misinterpreting the chill forming between Myla and Bryar, causing Elsa to turn, facing away. Fern follows suit and Myla lowers her voice, allowing the Blood Stealer's men to pass before speaking.

"Bryar," she whispers, her hand brushing against his briefly. "Do not burn your life down for me. Not tonight."

A slight smile tugs at the corner of his mouth, followed by an exasperated sigh. "Perhaps tomorrow?"

"Yes." She nods. "Perhaps tomorrow."

Myla's aunt had been married to a cruel man. As a young girl living in her parents' countryside estate, years before coming to court, she watched how her aunt would cower when her uncle entered the room. Myla's mother had seen it too and offered her a position in their home, with a convincing excuse to give her husband which might compel him to allow her to leave. By all accounts, it should have been simple, or so it was in the eyes of a young girl. Myla always wondered why her aunt did not accept help or seek out situations that would make her life easier.

Now, Myla finds it impossible to hold a private council meeting. With Vesperian fixated on her every move, it occurs to her that complacency is not always chosen. Just as her situation in the last two years was mistaken for weakness, as the day progresses with her unable to speak to her trusted advisors, she assumes they wonder at her actions now. *Complacent queen,* they must be thinking. No. Not complacent, simply stalked. Watched, like the prey she is.

Vesperian paces through the throne room, giving instructions to all who pass on wedding happenings, as well as drawing up contract revisions. Myla stands, peering out the window overlooking the courtyard. Soldiers below converse, and messengers pass correspondence back and forth.

Nothing seems out of place, *if* she ignores the beast at her back. He currently leans against a pillar, flipping through one of her books with his panting wolves at his feet. It is unnerving.

Luncheon has been served, most of which went untouched by Myla. Servants have removed the bodies from the throne room and a coat of wax polish is applied to the tile flooring. Every ray of light reflects on the floor and dust particles are meticulously removed. As it happens, the wedding celebration for the marriage of a widowed queen and a blood consuming demon is no small affair. The guest list is shocking.

Myla is nearly stunned as she watches furniture hauled in and out, moved, rearranged, or disposed of entirely. A sculpture to honor their marriage is already commissioned, the artist paid well to have it delivered the morning of the wedding. Every time Myla attempts to remove herself, Vesperian finds a reason for her to stay, from tasting cakes to coordinating wedding attire; he has accounted for every second of her day. If Myla is to succeed in her plan, it will be entirely because Alaric receives her message and takes action himself.

Myla is presented with a missive as the sun is setting and candles begin to flicker through the palace, glinting off the dark gothic mirrors intended to give the illusion of secret nooks, something Caius's father had installed when he was a boy.

Thirty-seven pages of their marriage contract, written out by one of Vesperian's glossy-eyed secretaries. Myla is relieved as Vesperian sets it in her hand, an idea mounting. "I will meet you for supper. I must look this over and get my council's signatures."

With a passable reason to leave his side, Vesperian seems unfazed, allowing her to slip away while he continues to sort out with his own personal captain how best to 'accept' blood oaths from Myla's soldiers in the most expedited manner.

Yes, Vesperian. Shall you chain them all by the neck and hold them in place while you sink your teeth into them? Or perhaps have the smithy design the realm's longest blade and slice a hundred hands at a time, collect their blood into one bowl, and drink of them that way? Myla mocks as she walks away, ignoring the surge of desire in her which longs to stay beside him and feel his breath running up her thighs.

Calm yourself, you traitorous whore. She almost laughs to herself, turning out of the room with a sigh of relief.

The hall leading to the conservatory is dark, the stewards having yet to light this corridor. "Someone is slacking," she mutters, wondering what is taking him so long to keep up with duties. Her question does not go unanswered long for a muffled squeal ahead catches her attention, pricking her ears to listen closer.

Apprehensive at first, she steps around the corner to see Callum giving orders to have a body quickly disposed of. A man wearing the armor of the Raven's Veil discreetly flings the limp body over his shoulder and makes off with surprising stealth. "Thank you, Callum." She amends her earlier statement. He must have instructed this corridor be unlit to serve as a trap.

As Callum nods in answer before taking his leave, Myla finds herself grateful for a moment to lean against the wall, undetected, and orient herself. Bryar stands several paces behind her, not moving, nor speaking. He has assumed his duty of just her bodyguard beautifully, and she finds it both irritating and admirable. Reaching into a pocket concealed in the voluptuous folds of her gown, she runs her hand over a selenite bundle, allowing the herbs and stones to gently pass under her fingertips. The protective and calming qualities, immediately impactful. After a moment of breath-work, visualizing her blood coursing evenly through her veins and her body still with decisiveness, she turns to the captain, motioning quietly for him to approach.

"Under no circumstances do our soldiers remove their armor. If one must bathe or change, others will watch his back. I believe Vesperian will go to nefarious lengths to *steal* as many souls as he can. He tells me he plans to do it ceremoniously after our wedding, but I do not believe him."

Bryar nods, understanding his command. "It will be done."

"Good," Myla replies. "What of the assassins? How many have they claimed?"

"Twenty-two dead, Your Grace. My men move undetected so far."

She feels relieved. At least something is going according to plan. "You amaze me," she says thankfully, grasping his hand briefly before moving the conversation along to more important matters. "Alaric is drugging his army. He has spent all day concocting a serum which will stunt any magical abilities. He believes it is not powerful enough to subdue

Vesperian, but I think it may dull his abilities. I need you to get a dose from Alaric and give it to Fern and tell her to pour it into the cup on the *left* in my chambers."

"Drugging him?" Bryar whispers, his tone inflating with concern. "This is your plan. To *drug him?*"

"Yes . . . and no," Myla confesses. "I will drug him, making sure he is in a relaxed state through whatever means necessary. Then I will strike when he is confident I am on his side. Whatever the outcome of tonight, I refuse to make it to that black wedding of his."

Bryar's eyebrows perk slightly, and Myla almost detects a smile. "Well, at least we agree where that is concerned."

Myla returns the smile, a tinge of pain behind it. "You shall come to no harm on my account. It is an order."

"Myla," he says confidently. "Take away my personal feelings. I am sworn to come to harm for you if that is where my oath takes me. I can not do what you ask; it goes against my oath to you. It goes against my oath to Caius."

Myla shudders, wishing her words could sway him, but in cases such as these, he has never been the swaying type. She shall have to settle for something else. "Then . . . promise me you will not die angry at me. If it all comes to that, you and I failing. I can not meet my end without your love."

His cheeks dimple with a sincere smile, a beacon of hope in her dark day. "As long as I do not meet my end without yours," he replies softly. He raises a gloved hand now, pressing the back of his fingers to her cheek where he caresses her.

"Never," she breathes, leaning into the touch.

As much as Myla wishes their few moments of peace in the dark corridor could continue, footsteps approach, no doubt her council. Her next words are fervent and rushed.

"Whatever you hear inside my room tonight, it is not what you think. I heard when you said you are tired of me choosing duty over you, and I will not betray us tonight."

She hears his breath hitch, but his only response is a stoic nod and three powerful words: "I trust you."

With the doors of the conservatory locked and Bryar standing guard outside, Myla and her council are able to speak freely, though voices stay hushed as the eerie feeling of being listened to lingers. The papers of the marriage contract lay untouched at the center of the table, Myla is open about the fact she has no intention of this situation outlasting a wedding between herself and Vesperian.

"Your Grace," Lady Rivenna speaks. "You intend on confronting him yourself this evening? Do you believe that to be wise?" Her words are not spoken as a challenge; true fear seems to drive the question to the forefront of the conversation. There is no longer the air of defiance she felt from her council a few days prior. They may not like her these last few days, but their respect for her grows.

"I believe it is when he will least expect it," Myla reasons. "But, no, I can not say with all certainty that it feels wise at all. Is any of this wise?" she responds, carefully rolling a quill between her fingers, knowing Vesperian will expect signatures to the contract when she returns to him this evening.

"I can not say your behavior at all, seems wise." Maverick speaks, the only voice of contempt toward his daughter to be found in the room. "I imagine the late King, your husband, would be appalled."

Eyes drift anxiously from him to Myla, no doubt waiting for her wrath to succeed the previous comment. Myla runs her tongue over her teeth, silencing the words which beg to be hurled her father's way. Instead, she looks to the other faces in the room. "Would anyone like to offer helpful advice or should we waste our precious time listening to my father's useless insults?"

Myla presses the quill into Maverick's hand. "Insults do not kill father. If they did, you would have killed me long ago. Do you know what *does* kill? The Fae God who expects every signature to be on this contract. Including yours. He *definitely* kills." Myla raises her eyebrows, watching as Maverick reluctantly leans over the contract, adding his signature to the list.

Lord Heron exchanges uneasy glances with his fellow members before speaking, seemingly on behalf of them all. "We have a plan, Your Grace. If you will hear us out?"

Chapter 9

Myla wears a simple green dress, nothing astonishing to draw attention. The neckline scoops just above her collarbone and modest sleeves button at her wrists. The skirt is full, concealing any shape she may have, and her hair is pulled into a sleek bun at the nape of her neck. More than anything, Myla wants to get through her night of charades without having to fend off advances from Vesperian. Taking an innovative approach, per her council's advice, Myla imagines their message is on its way this very moment, hopefully carried by a swift raven. Lady Reacher now stands before her in the throne room, eyes swollen from hot tears and her body slight with disparity.

"Please, Your Grace. Tell me what has happened to Ariel."

There is no straightforward answer. To show sympathy and admit that Ariel is being held in a discreet room, drugged into silence by Alaric until the Blood Stealer's demise, would expose her plan. The more people knowing of her true stance, the higher the risk of an unplanned exposure. Myla can not be sure Lady Reacher's late husband exposed their plan to his wife, and therefore, a callous response is the only safe one.

"Your daughter is being punished for her insubordination." The words taste like rusting metal on her tongue. Never once in her five years as queen has Myla treated her subjects like pests to be dismissed. She comforts herself by focusing on the task at hand. In a matter of twelve or so hours, this should all be over. *Hopefully, I am still here to see that*, Myla thinks morbidly.

"She is . . . she is a good girl, Your Grace." Tears swell down the sunken cheeks of the new widow, piercing the dagger of memories into Myla's heart. The hopelessness, the directionless wandering. The first days of widowhood are bleak.

"Lady Reacher," Myla seethes, certain the darkness forming in her eyes, despite the desire to comfort, does not fail her. "Unless you wish to leave your daughter an orphan, I suggest you silence yourself." It is not an empty threat whatsoever. Desperate people do desperate things which usually lead to unbearable consequences. *Says the Queen of Desperate . . . something, I am wise to remember.*

A harrowing cry slips from the poor woman as she turns away, making her way out of Myla's presence, leaving guilt and an urgency to right things in her wake. The silence does not last long, however, for the vigilant fiancé, Vesperian Shayd enters, his hands hidden behind his back in a cunningly mysterious way.

Afternoon light glints off the dark streaks of hair brushing against his forehead and lines of scars travel across his arms and neck. In the daylight he is the epitome of a handsome, misunderstood villain. Only, he is not misunderstood, merely unstoppable. He is handsome, dangerously so, making him lethal for an entirely different reason than one might expect of the Blood Stealer.

Elsa's poorly timed joke rings in her ears. *You can be at my service any day.* He is a deadly sort of alluring. The kind that lures you in, convincing you that it is your idea, then completely ruins you, right after he has devoured your values, leaving you hollow and helpless. If he were to have been a woman, one might refer to him as a siren. Unfortunately for him, his voice does not captivate her.

"You hide something from me," she says, tilting her chin toward his concealed arms, unease stirring in her middle.

"Show me, or I will be forced to make you."

A dangerous smile melts the frost of his icy features. "That sounds rather tempting, darling. Unfortunately for me, there are no cuffs on my bedposts—the late king seems a dull fellow. In any case, making me do anything might prove hard for you."

Her middle constricts with the lurch of her breath. His effect, not her own. She reminds herself the insatiable attraction is fabricated, a temptation of his own design. "Making *you* do what I want though," he whispers, moving closer and closer with an inhuman precision, appearing to glide. "I could make you fall to your knees now and beg me to take you to bed. I could make you cut your own throat with the dagger I know is hidden beneath your skirts." His hand trails down her waist, knotting a handful of silk between his fists. Myla swallows, her lips parting as she licks her dry lips, anxious for something to moisten them. *Stop it.* Even his threat of a gruesome murder feels exhilarating. Arousing, even.

"Shall I lift up your skirt and see what else you hide from me?"

Gathering her wits, painfully aware of the uneasily shifting guards in the room, Myla forces a demure smile and presses a hand to his chest.

"Only if you show me what you hide behind your back. Is it for me?"

He lets out a slow, playful sigh before revealing a blue vial the size of his little finger. It is corked and sealed with black wax making it look like something she and her mother would make with the druids. "On the topic of controlling you," he continues, "do you know what I hold here?"

Myla shakes her head. The contents of the vial are a deep velvet crimson. There is a pulsing glow within it, clearly not a naturally occurring element. "What is it?" Myla asks, having an uncontrollable need to reach out and seize the vial.

Vesperian retreats, shoving the vial into his pocket before linking his fingers with hers, holding her closer than proper. Not that anything proper has occurred inside these palace walls in a week. Her mind escapes to thoughts of Bryar's fingers, then back to the present. Her body is unwittingly responding to Vesperian's pull, allowing him to own her, should he wish to. *Fingers are fingers.* The thought is jolting, and Myla attempts to reason with herself. *He wants to own you, you fucking moron. Stop being weak.*

Vesperian's words are enough to bring her back to reality. "It is an oath reversal which my healer concocted at my request."

Myla stiffens, feeling delirious at the prospect that her cure is mere inches away. This thing which has plagued her existence for the last twenty-four months could be cured today, if only she can get her hands on that vial.

"Careful," Vesperian whispers, his lips flicking her ear. "You are going to hurt my feelings if you look like you want that any more than you already do. More than you want *me.*"

Myla checks her breathing before placing a tender hand on his cheek. "You can not blame me for wanting to know my feelings for you are my own."

He grins, a finger teasing her jawline until it presses firm into her lips. "Tell me more. About those feelings."

Gods. Myla knows she must convince him. That vial, acquiring it at all costs, must come before her pride. She grips the collar of his leather vest and turns him around, pushing him backwards until he sits stunned in her throne. A dark gleam circles his pupils as though his very life source is being fueled. Of course, it is. Lust, longing, and praise are his favorite meals. *I will be his fucking main course if I need to.*

Myla moves nimbly until she straddles him where he sits, his chin level with her breasts and his breathing suddenly shifting dangerously close to anticipation. "I can not sleep," she whispers, holding his head still by a handful of thick hair, her other hand tracing promises into his throat before slowly moving lower toward his belt. "I wake up wondering where you are, willing you to appear next to me. The seconds you are away from me, I feel like I can not breathe, like I never drew a full breath until you arrived here." She pauses, allowing the words to fill every crevice where his ego is starving, lapping up her attention like a pathetic dog. Seeing him here, so helpless beneath her grip makes Myla wonder what exactly she has been so afraid of.

"So, I feel everything. I feel the places you are, and I feel the places you are not. I feel the places I wish you were. And I can only wonder if those are feelings you gave me. I long to feel them and know they are mine." Her lips meet his, teeth grazing his plump bottom lip and allowing his tongue to explore her mouth, slowly and lazily. His lips move from hers to her chin and downward to her collarbone where he pelts warm, venomous kisses. A thrill surges through her body, an alarming sensation which she knows is her nervous system coordinated with his. Myla tries desperately to separate her mental response from the physical, allowing him to be convince. If she can not own her body, she will try to own her mind.

This endeavor grows increasingly challenging as his hands trail down her, finding a hold on the back of her thighs and moving her body against the hardening in his pants. Myla lets out a subtle moan, one that is not lost on the devil beneath her.

"Good, my Ruthless Queen," he coos in her ear, praising her response, words which exhilarate and evoke a satisfied melt from her. "I wonder what you would say if I took you to bed now." He moves a hand to her exposed thigh, inching upwards, closer and closer to that sacred space which feels hungry for his touch.

"Vesperian," she moans into his neck, angry at herself for feeling so wildly out of control and so deeply intoxicated by the monster who murdered her husband. Yet, the euphoric sensations pulsating through her body begs her not to stop his conquest. His fingers nearly graze their target, prompting a desperate gasp when the door of the throne room slams shut.

Myla flinches, something jolting her from the spell, and she stands, blue eyes swelling with regret when they fall upon the furious gaze of Bryar.

Foolish. She chides herself. A queen's guard is rarely far away; of course he was going to find her. Myla feels a shiver of guilt wash over her.

"Bryar—"

"Bryar?" The Blood Stealer stands, his eyes narrowing in on the space between the captain and his queen. Myla fears the raw energy flowing there may be detectable by Vesperian, and she quickly corrects her tone.

"Captain Monroe, you approach me unannounced?"

Bryar's jaw grinds as though he is chewing his words before spitting them out. "Is that not my job, Your Grace? To protect you?"

Vesperian laughs, a threatening hand landing on Myla's shoulder. "*Ah*, the overzealous guard who would not let me in your room."

Myla attempts to match his casual demeanor, laughing mockingly with him. "It is. Troublesome, really. He has nightmares, I hear, from when you killed that idiot I called a husband." Shame infiltrates her very essence, and averting her gaze, she silently asks Bryar's forgiveness. If only he already knew what was concealed in Vesperian's pocket.

Judging by the shadowed look on his face, Bryar is teetering on the edge of questioning the ruse himself. Is that not what she wanted? For everyone to believe she had surrendered to the power of Vesperian? If he is convinced, should not the Blood Stealer himself be?

But he is not.

Suspicion breeds rapidly as the Blood Stealer takes stock of it all; the way the tiles crack beneath Bryar's heating feet and the inferno boiling at his fingertips, which cause the handle of his axe to grow red-hot. The weapon wilts like a flower before Bryar even seems to notice the way his rage builds upon itself, bringing destruction of everything, including her plan.

Vesperian's angry, snake like eyes dart to her. Sweet features washed away in a rush of pale, and the darkness she had exuded replaced with what truly lies beneath: fear.

So, he feasts.

"Tell me, Myla . . . my *stupid* queen. Did you intend on marrying me and then letting *that* vermin between your legs behind my back?"

Myla trembles and attempts a recovery. "Stop with your nonsense, Vesperian. Your jealousy is ruining my mood." If he was not already angry, her tone may have been convincing, but a black wraith begins to form at his hands, giving Myla the sick feeling she has just failed. He allows the otherworldly creature to slither around his hand and wrist like a pet snake, and something about his being shifts from devilishly handsome to absolutely terrifying.

Here is the creature who slaughtered Caius.

His eyes burn a deep crimson, a blood thirst amassing deep within as he anticipates his next kill.

"If my suspicion is nonsense as you say," he goads, "then prove it, and I will give you this." He pulls the vial from his pocket, its brilliant blue catching in the daylight through the tall arched windows in a vast contrast to the black swirling at its base. It shines like a beacon calling to her. "The captain's life for your cure." Vesperian presents his ultimatum like a prize, his ivory teeth flashing a smile coated in mockery. The wraith grows larger, a swirling demon summoned by the Blood Stealer to cut Bryar's throat, just as it cut Caius's. Pressure constricts Myla's throat as if an invisible being grapples at her, silencing any protests.

Realization washes over Bryar, and he wears an odd look. Defeat? No. Resolve. Flames engulf his fists as he stands partially crouched, ready to meet the Gods in a shower of black and flames.

He will sacrifice himself for my cure . . .

"Killing you myself would be too quick," Vesperian hums as he seats himself in Myla's throne instead of his own. Margot and Matteo sit on either side of him, panting hungrily. No doubt anticipating their next meals. "I am in the mood for a show." He pats his lap, summoning Myla to sit. A test. "Come, my Ruthless Queen. We shall watch my loyal men battle yours. An experiment. Who is stronger?" It is not an experiment. It is a threat.

Myla does as he instructs, the pounding in her chest dulling every other sense and she watches as six of Vesperian's soldiers lull from the shadows.

He can kill them easily . . . if he wants to, she comforts herself, watching Bryar straighten and rolls his shoulders, ready to slaughter. He holds a borrowed sword now, taken from one of his men, his axe lays distorted on the ground next to him.

He does not look her way, though her eyes are fixed only on him, and Vesperian's on her.

The six Seam warriors close around Bryar slowly at first. Slow enough that with every step, their calf-length chainmail sounds like gentle chimes in the wind. The crimson of their tunics stands out against Bryar's pure black ensemble, but his is the only coherent expression. His green eyes dart from one foe to the next, assessing which to lunge at first.

He makes his choice and the battle ensues. It is mayhem. The way lifeless soldiers lunge and are met with a deafening ring of metal. Bryar's arms heave overhead and with an angry snarl, he lowers his blade into the undefended back of an opponent. There is a crack, followed by a short, agonizing scream as the soldier is flayed open from behind.

Myla winces as bone shatters and blood gushes in rivers from the body, creating a slippery surface beneath Bryar's boots. He dislodges the blade from the man's spine in time to parry an attack from another soldier. It is a flash of steel and blood.

To Vesperian, it becomes obvious rather quickly that his men are no match for her lethally-trained captain.

So, he pushes Myla off his lap and stands, urging another rush of soldiers to join the fight. Myla watches, wanting nothing more than to see him summon his flames and melt their foes. But she knows he will do no such thing.

Though he puts up a fight for the sake of convincing Vesperian, he plans to die for her. Myla knows what he looks like when he is slowly conceding a battle. Their years of training together amounted to a time when she could not best him. But from time to time, he would let her win. Just as he begins to allow them to win.

One soldier, whose face she can not see behind his black helmet, swings a heavy broad sword just slowly enough that Bryar should catch it.

In every other circumstance, he would.

This time, he does not. It slices into his shoulder. And as a second flash of blades threaten to fall on him, he responds too slowly.

He wants her to remain silent, to let him fall on the sword for her, and to claim her cure. That is his goal.

Perhaps a stronger queen would allow it. The solution to her problem could cost only one life.

But to her, it is a life too dear.

Myla feels a shriek explode from her lungs, and as quickly as it began, her plot to defeat the Blood Stealer ends, replaced with a desperate need to stop the fall of the blade, even if her ruse is revealed.

The moment seems to pass in miserable slow motion. Though it is early in the day, night descends upon the throne room. The power of the Blood Stealer summoning darkness itself, black particles falling from the night sky to shroud them in an inky fog. The darkness sucked from every shadow within the palace walls, collecting there in the throne room. Guards spill into the throne room, wearing panicked and helpless expressions and shouts from somewhere beyond sound an alarm, all within the palace instantly alerted to the impending disaster. The Blood Stealer's wolves leap at an unsuspecting guard and sink their beastly teeth into his throat, silencing a gargled cry. They proceed to feast on the warm flesh of the guard.

"The Queen and the Blood Stealer will battle." "Send help." "Run." Words bleed together. Courtiers with minor magic seem to flee while those with major magic rush in, all halting behind Bryar, a standstill before them pausing any advancements.

Myla begs her magic forth, and yet something, like a cork blocking her supply, stops its rise. Her veins feel flaccid, and her screams are empty, no rage magic following. It feels as though now, when she needs them most, the Gods abandon her.

A ringing douses out all other sounds save that of Vesperian's laughs. Ringing and a demon's laugh is all she hears. This is the same way she responded when he came to kill her husband, panic dousing the fire of her magic. Somewhere between the tears and the wraith's swirling vortex, she sees the faces of her court, of Elsa, and of Bryar, now with a pile of corpses at his feet. Blood spills from his arm and he watches her with pleading eyes, though he knows his plan has also failed.

Her father pushes between them, eyes wide with something that should be fear but is not. *He wants me to die, so he can have my throne.*

Callum, Elsa, and Rhyland now group together, each holding a weapon to stave off attacks as they come. They are screaming something, those words falling on deaf ears. She can not even hear the way her soldiers now clash against the Blood Stealer and blood flows through her throne room like an undammed river. Sprays of it pelt the walls and the books and even herself. *Wake up.* She urges herself, clenching her eyes shut and visualizing the birth of her magic. But something else penetrates her mind's eye. An orb in the womb of the earth. Small and flickering. Something holds it in place, veins of magic like the roots of a tree. "It is time to wake up," she whispers, her eyes opening to see confusion written on the face of the Blood Stealer. His brow furrows and then arches in an annoyed roll of his eyes.

"So, it is to be the captain and the queen. Lovers dying pitiful deaths today." His words are hissed, a contortion of his regular voice, and Myla wonders who speaks now, he or the wraith. Maverick's eyes widen as he glances from Myla to Bryar, a sense of realization washing his features, changing quickly from shock to rage. Perhaps he is thinking back to the evening his daughter confessed she was no longer a virgin, complicating her betrothal to the king. Myla feels a tinge of deep-seated betrayal and anger growing into something nastier. *In this moment, of everything that could bring anger upon him, that is what does it.*

Echoes of her friend's words pierce the veil which seems to deafen her, and she barely makes out Elsa's words: "Use *all* of your magic."

And just like that, the magic roots suspending that orb in her womb retreat, dissipating into her veins, her entire body flashing, like a volt of energy has flared from within. The sensation is sickening as the child in her womb quickens, no longer hanging in a time continuum, waiting to be. Myla once more reaches within her depths, calling upon light, and righteous rage.

The Blood Stealer repositions at this, his gnarled hands lunge backward, about to lose the wraith on her, when her voice cracks, a booming, thunderous command. A primal scream boiling within her throat and flooding beyond into something terrible. Rubble from the ceiling shakes loose, cracking down upon them, and her body is engulfed in a blinding flash of light which launches in sharp fragments toward Vesperian.

In a trained, fluid motion, he disintegrates into a million black wisps, joining with the wraith in a whirlpool of abysmal shadow and chaos, reappearing behind her. Something hard slams into her back, knocking the wind out of her and catapulting her body several feet away. The cold tile smacks into her cheek and somewhere beneath the screams and shouts, Myla hears gasps as well, followed at once by the shuddering of summoned magic in mass amounts. The atmosphere begins to crumble beneath the pressure of the conjuring.

Assertive, Bryar bellows orders to his knights and somewhere in her periphery, she watches as rows of blue surround her at his command. "*Protect the queen!*" A futile effort, she is certain.

Myla pushes herself to her feet, turning in time to see her council and various courtiers forming a wall with their bodies, hands extended as flashes of magic overpower the senses. Bricks are compelled to wiggle loose from the walls as one wielder's mind causes a chaotic flurry of heavy and sharp objects to hurdle in the Blood Stealer's direction. Another conjures clairvoyant magic to anticipate Vesperian's next moves, intercepting a teleportation in Myla's direction.

It is a violent and catastrophic cacophony, disorder laying waste to the usually regal throne room. Books of all size and variant colors tumble from different heights, streaking the black veil with vibrancy as they are used as weapons, thrown to and fro at their targets. Myla is overwhelmed with urgency to be in all places at once. Before her, Bryar is in a half-kneeling position. His cloak is singed and in tatters and a soot collects on his already black armor as fire magic rages from his being in the direction of two dozen of Vesperian's dazed soldiers. Their bodies sear like cold meat to a hot iron. The screams are sickening, even more so than the stench.

Elsa crouches over the convulsing body of a courtier, a young man with fair hair. His identity is not easily detectable as a gaping wound has split his face in half. Elsa's skin is tinted a healer's lavender. In spite of the chaos around her, she stays calm, trying to heal the man seizing upon her lap, no doubt begging for his life. Myla cringes, knowing it is futile. Soldiers cloaked in the Queen's Blue spill in from every direction, blades, and magic flashing furiously.

The greatest need lies at the feet of the Blood Stealer. Carnage piled beneath and behind him as he moves with a swiftness unmatched by any. Blood sprays from the helpless bodies of his victims, caught off guard as they slash at the air before him where he stood, only to be assaulted by him from behind. His methods are the strategy of a coward, though in efficiency, she can not argue he has the upper hand.

Vesperian faces away from her, caught in the crossfire of Lord

Heron and one of Bryar's assassins' magic. It is ripples of blue, interrupted by a violent fire which blasts a small crater into the tile flooring. Myla catches her breath, thinking for a moment he may be subdued as she loses sight of him in the mayhem.

The black of he and his wraith appear to constrict inward until there is nothing left, and all at once, the black is ejected. Sharp spears of inky mist pivot in every direction, lodging themselves in a dozen victims before dissolving and recovering mere inches before Myla in the shape of a man once more.

Trembling with a violent flush of power, Myla's magic seethes to the surface, deadly rays ready to be loosed, when Vesperian reaches out with a gloved hand, as cold as frost, and seizes her throat. His eyes flash a look of finality. His free hand lifts to eye level now and the wraith condenses into a single swirling orb, threatening to reach out and impale her.

"You could have had it all, my Ruthless Raven Queen." His words are a mere echo of a human, carrying more of his demon's voice as he delivers her final rites, accompanied by the mournful and threatening howls of Margot and Matteo. "I shall henceforth consider this the greatest tragedy; to see a masterpiece such as yourself lose herself and sacrifice her greatness, for the likes of her captain."

His hand tightens and a fog threatens to claim her mind. There is movement, flashes of light, billowing smoke, and the heat of flames. The ground trembles and her logical brain tells her that her court and Council wage valiantly behind her, though fear within whispers. *It is the demons below. They are waiting to welcome you into their belly.* Somewhere, Myla senses sound—shouting, but nothing audible reaches her ears, which seem to be weighted in a dark magic, urging her to surrender. A foul force binds her arms to her side, unable to conjure her magic and with her throat constricted, she can not call upon the voice of the Gods to channel through her.

"Be sure to tell that joke of a husband hello when you see him," Vesperian whispers, toying with the shape of the wraith between his fingers. "It would be wise to leave out the part where you are fucking the guard who let him die."

Fury builds, a will to defy all, to defy the vile creature before her, to defy her acceptance of death, and to defy the dark Gods themselves.

Most importantly, to defy that she has anything to apologize to *any* man for.

Searing heat gathers at her throat where the Gods' voices batter and, in spite of the tension between Vesperian's fist and her neck, Myla's mouth falls open. A crack of thunder, an ominous cry of a thousand angry voices demand her release.

From the core of her lungs, the Gods command fear and submission of every living thing across Myrnith. Even the Blood Stealer himself is flung backward briefly, the wraith retreating within him. A horrified look is quickly replaced by shock and something sadistic: thrill.

Vesperian moves to stand, but in ancient tongue, a young female from within the tangled chaos of the crowd compels the black chandelier overhead to snap loose of the chains suspending it. The Blood Stealer lurches backward, barely missing the sharp spikes of iron, which instead shriek violently on the tile. It is enough of a distraction for Myla to feel herself yanked into the dark corridor behind the thrones.

"Run!" Bryar demands, his hand tight on her arm. Myla glances backward to see an entirely different beast of fury forming around Vesperian. The wraith contorts, angry to be defied. Within the swirling of the blackness, visions wash in and out, opaque against the dark magic. Sight of destruction and death, the screams of his victims replaying, fuel for the monster as it grows larger and larger, intending to consume every being in its wake.

"Bryar, no!" Myla pleads, trying to jerk her arm free of his iron grasp. "Look!"

Blue chunks of ceiling fall, crushing and crippling those beneath it. A row of Council members stand shoulder to shoulder, their arms extended creating a wall of energy, flame, and any other power they can call upon to hold off Vesperian. She knows every name, every face. She can see them clearly and hear their voices as they swear oaths to her. Oaths to honor, to serve, to protect. Myla realizes they are merely stalling him for her escape. Anyone in that throne room is surely damned, any remaining are there of their own free will, a sacrifice for her life.

At the furthest end of the throne room, Callum, Rhyland, and Elsa stand together still. Elsa's eyes meet hers and she mouths one word: "Go."

Tears swell in her eyes as Bryar, visibly distraught, drags her by the waist toward the dungeons.

"Stop fighting me," Bryar growls angrily, yanking her into an embrasure alcove. "I swear to the Gods, I will knock you senseless and carry you out of here myself if I have to, Myla!"

"They are dying!" she sobs, trying to turn back. Frantically and out of breath, she pleads and shrieks. "Elsa is in there, Bryar! Elsa and Rhyland and Callum—" Panic threatens to claim her being as visions of her friends sliced in half tease her imagination.

"Fuck, Myla! Do not let them die in vain then!" It is not a request. As the sound of mayhem and murder pierce the air, accompanied by the shaking of the ground beneath them, Myla is thrown over Bryar's shoulder and carried out of the palace.

Chapter 10

Myla's mother used to tell her heartbreak was the worst emotion a human body could endure, that it left its mark in deeper ways than scars ever could. Having felt heartbreak on multiple counts, Myla disagrees now. She now knows, guilt is a far worse feeling. Guilt, and heartbreak paired, however, is a bitter coupling.

A sob catches in her throat. They have been traveling for an hour, the rocky terrain and towering mass of trees engulfing them into the nothingness of the land. Every bit of her wants to turn back and meet the morning, dead alongside her people, her best friends, and even her father.

Unfortunately, Bryar is well-versed in the stupidity that propels grieving people, and he trudges behind her, watchful of her every move. Turning back is impossible with him as her escort. In any other situation, being his prisoner would seem exhilarating. Tonight, it feels like a betrayal.

Myla thinks back to a few hours ago. *Imagine, you thought you could win this.* Visions of her father, being so fucking useless, plague her. Though, he is most likely dead now, the terrifying realization that she does not care weighs heavily. His face when he heard Vesperian refer to Bryar as her lover. It was not the topic a father watching his daughter face her death should have focused on. *I have always been his steppingstone. Of course, my death would not affect him. I already cleared his path into the throne room. I made him a queen's father.*

"We need to stop and find shelter soon." Bryar breaks the silence and her dark train of thought, increasing his stride to move alongside her. His hand finds hers, helping Myla up a steep incline. "Let us make for the cliffside."

Myla follows in silence, ignoring the ache in her feet as well as the cramping in her stomach. "You mean Druid's Cave." A place all-too familiar. She shivers, sidestepping a fallen tree blanketed in richly colored moss.

The sun has hidden its face behind the mountains, and fireflies have set the forest aglow. It is peaceful, considering the circumstances for their journey, but not even the magic of the forest can move Myla's mind from the cold that must be settling over her palace as she moves further away. Her throne room, where subjects pledged fealty to her a week ago, now their crypt. Bitter tears sting her red eyelids as visions of Elsa lying dead on the cold tile sabotage her mind. She remains trapped in this tortured thought until Bryar stops her.

They stand, partially shrouded in a thick mist at the base of the mountains, an ancient location the druids visit for their Wheel of the Year sabbats. Myla used to visit here with her mother often, before her father was made a member of the Council. Witchcraft was not frowned upon, but a king's Council member certainly could not have a wife and daughter who were known to mingle with the old pagans. Their visits to Druid's Cave became less frequent, and always under the cover of darkness, after his promotion to society.

Standing here now, the earth feels solid and familiar. Sacred ground for sacred purposes, and she, an unworthy visitor.

"The cave you brought me to." Bryar points ahead at the gaping mouth of the pitch-black cave. "It seemed more welcoming the last time we were here."

Myla brushes past him, briefly taking note of the tatters his cloak is in before trudging past. "I suppose that is what hiding like cowards does. The last time we were here was for a celebration, not because we abandoned our friends and family to death."

Bryar seizes her hand, stopping her with a small lurch. "You are not a coward." His eyes catch in the moonlight, reflecting earnestly. "You are brave. He would have killed you if you had stayed."

Myla faces him squarely, her chin tilted in defiance. "Tell me, Bryar. What good is a queen who will not die alongside her people? What good are my people's oaths to die for me, if I will not die for *them*?"

Bryar frowns and releases her hand, clearly angered. "What good is a dead queen? What good is a dead queen to the child inside her womb who is our only hope of truly cleansing the realm of the Blood Stealer?" It is his turn to walk now, leaving her behind in the darkness of the old trees. "Your people died with honor. Do not rob them of that honor by loathing your survival."

They enter the cave, and Bryar kneels to coax a flame into the circle of stones, which has warmed many travelers and worshipers before. At first, the spitting of embers fizzling at his palms does not strike Myla as odd. Within seconds, however, his hand glows like an iron from a smithy's furnace and the blaze erupting is massive, causing Myla to step out of the cave entirely.

"What the hell—" she coughs, choking on the smoke wafting out of the cave.

Bryar exits, shaking his palm and cringing, the heat clearly more than he is used to. "I did not mean to do that."

"I can see that!" Myla exclaims, reaching to examine his hand. "Are you okay?" Her eyes travel to the wound in his arm, tied with a strip torn from his cloak.

"Yes," he mutters, walking back into the cave. "Wait there. I will get the fire started and bring you back in when it is ready."

Soon enough, Bryar has it warm and illuminated inside the cave. The lick of the fire heats Myla's face and causes her shadow to dance on the smooth rock alcove behind her. Across the fire and lying on his side facing away from her is Bryar. He is silent and unmoving, though the grip on his sword tells Myla he is still awake. She has never felt anger toward a person she loves the way she does now.

Myla replays over in her head how he pulled her from the palace, listening to her shriek objections and beg him to put her down. Her pleading fell on deaf ears, as he took her further and further away from the very place she was most needed. Even now, she looks on him and feels the deep cut of betrayal, knowing any attempts to return would be intercepted. Her loyalty is to her people and his is to her.

They are silent, Bryar pretending to sleep, and Myla sitting, leaning against the wall of the cave, her mind drifting in and out of anger and memories.

Like the day she was taken to the Institute of Mystic Arts by her father. Or the evaluation of her natural abilities, which propelled her right into the arms of Caius. Her parents beamed with pride as the Grand Mage had told them a Conveyer of the Voice of the Gods had not been documented in a century. Her gift was a sacred honor; it was the kind that changed her course entirely. Before that day, she was not the kind of match the king was looking for. A king with ethereal magic needed a queen of equal power. And suddenly, there she was.

"Bryar," Myla whispers, watching as he slowly rolls to face her. "I wish I had listened to you and never gone to the Grand Mage."

A slight smile threatens to erase the glum look on his face. "I had more exciting plans for you that day." They both smile, and Bryar sits up, jabbing the toe of his boot against a displaced log, probing it back into the fire. "This was the right path for you," he says. "You were meant for this. The Gods will not fail you."

"I am not afraid of them failing me, Bryar."

"Then what?" he asks.

"I am afraid of me failing them." She places a hand on her belly. "I am afraid of failing her."

His brow furrows. "Her? How do you know?"

Myla smiles, offers a slight shrug, and responds, "It is just a hunch. And I do not want to fail her, like I failed Elsa today. And every other person I left behind." Myla's voice cracks, a fresh wave of sobs slipping through her stoic cracks. Bryar moves to sit next to her, his strong arms pulling her into him.

"Myla, failing is allowing yourself to become small and breakable. Failing would be to stop trying. Elsa would never want you to give up. So, honor her by getting up in the morning and doing whatever you have to do to see the sun set again and again and again until Vesperian lies dead at your feet."

A gentle hand strokes the crown of her head, brushing dark wisps of stray hair out of her face. No response is necessary. He is right, though his truth is a painful one. Persevering is painful, and this night, Myla wonders how she will wake and walk further from her people.

"Did you see how my father looked today?" Myla asks, allowing her head to slump against Bryar's shoulder. "I have questioned his loyalty for a long time now, but watching him in the throne room today has shed new light upon it."

"He certainly was not trying to help you," Bryar answers, taking a deep breath of frustration. "I have questioned his motives for a long time."

"A long time?" Myla probes.

"Since he stepped into the privy Council."

There it is. The truth, stripped to its bare form, a naked beast Myla has averted her gaze from for many years. "My mother passing so soon after I married Caius was crippling, you know. I recall feeling as though for all of my tears, my father did not weep enough."

She feels Bryar nod. "Well, Maverick has proven many times, his only care in life is to die with a title."

"One would think 'husband,' 'father,' or even 'lord' would be enough," Myla scoffs, "but it seems he needs more, even if it costs him both his wife and his daughter."

They awaken to the sound of chirping birds outside the cave. The sun beginning to illuminate the silhouettes of the forest, its golden breath whispering just barely inside their hideout. "We will arrive at the monastery before midday," Bryar says as they appear. "If they survived, Callum and Rhyland will know where to meet us."

Myla cuts him off, surprised. "How would they know that?"

"When the Council told me of their idea to send word to the Ashborn for help, I thought we might need a backup plan." He glances sidelong at her, something dangerously close to annoyance written on his face. "They have not been known to help humans since the fall of Old Falkmere. I did not expect them to help this time. So I told them, if anything went amiss, where I would take you."

Rage simmers in the depths of her belly, but Myla takes a deep breath, steadying her voice before speaking. "You made an escape plan because you did not think mine would work?"

Bryar walks on, his shoulders square but his head shaking dismissively. "Be angry, Myla. But do not forget I have spent the last five years learning when to act as your friend and when to act as your guard. As your friend, I wanted to believe that plan would work. As a guard who swore your safety to your husband, I had to have an alternative plan."

"Friend," Myla scoffs beneath her breath, trudging reluctantly behind him. "Your fingers really spelled *friend* the other night."

He turns sharply on his heel, his change in trajectory catching her off guard, his eyes blazing.

"Stop."

One word, a command which leaves no room for bickering and a word which in any other case would see a guard hanged for insubordination. He has no need to elaborate; his tone and face says it all, and Myla instantly feels like a child.

"Start walking, Myla. The monastery is the last place anyone will look for a pagan queen."

"I am sorry . . ." she says, shamefully following his path once more.

"Yeah, me too," Bryar answers stoically. "You are not the only one here who has lost people, Myla. I just had to pick between saving my queen and saving two hundred young men I have been training from pages and squires for the last ten years."

His words are like spears of ice to her gut. *Of course.* It had not occurred to her that the men who made up the mass body of guards to her, were names to him. She has had enough trouble distinguishing the hundreds of courtiers who want intimate friendships with her to have sorted out who was who in the barracks. To Bryar, men like family died next to and for him yesterday.

"You know," Myla says, wiping a fresh onslaught of tears with the back of her hand. "Elsa had this reoccurring dream that she was naked in the mountains being—and I quote her words, not mine— 'ravished by an army of Valkyries and a dozen of the old Gods'."

An unexpected laugh slips from Bryar, and he glances briefly over his shoulder to flash a weak smile. Myla rolls her eyes, trying to muster a smile in return. "I hope it was not a dream, but a prophesy of her afterlife." Together, they both laugh. An attempt to summit the feeling of loss and grief that has chased them into the morning light, and will no doubt continue to be their shadow for a long time to come.

The monastery is tucked in the base of the mountains. It is hidden from the world by a tangle of trees and overgrowth, accessible only by a narrow and tumultuous path along the base of the mountain. Myla can only assume he knows of this secluded hideaway through his guild of assassins. From above, during their descent, she watched as humbly clad men moved back and forth. Some herding goats and chickens, while others harvest from a small garden. Many seemed to sit and deliberate in prayer. Now, as they approach and the finer details come into view, the aura of the monastery exudes peace. Etchings of their god are carved into the stone above the arch entry way, mesmerizing chants heard from within.

What catches Myla most off guard is the friendly and familiar greetings Bryar receives from every other monk they pass before entering.

"You are well known here," she remarks, taking stock of the dark interior of what appears to be their place of worship.

"It is a safe place to stop between the palace and the Riverlands. Callum's uncle is the Abbot here and was able to assure our safety and asylum."

An old and wrinkled man with kind, gray eyes approaches, leaning heavily on a worn cane. "Captain," his voice quivers with age. "I am always pleased to see you. Who is your companion?" He nods toward Myla, who looks nothing like a queen now, disheveled as she is.

"This is Mistress Myla Alerys." He introduces her as a noblewoman and not the queen, a calculated decision should they want to sleep here tonight.

"Welcome," the man smiles. He does not bow, does not refer to her as any more than an average woman. It is refreshing. "I am Martin, the Abbot of this humble monastery. I hope you will be comfortable here."

"A pleasure," Myla curtsies and follows as Bryar leads her to a bench before an altar, where statues and offerings lay. It is a strange arrangement, however, from what she is used to seeing. There is a bowl of bread bits, a string of brown beads, their sacred book of scripture she recognizes, but the grotesque depiction of a sacrificed god seems vulgar, even compared to her Gods' love of war and bloodshed. It strikes something solemn in her. A faith where gods die for their people, rather than the people for their gods, is a curious notion. Her faith honors death in battle. Bryar takes note of her observation and smiles.

"Their god came to wash the filth of man from this earth and replace it with a little holiness in us all." He gestures with a tip of his chin back toward the sacrificed man. "Fascinating, is it not?"

Myla nods and sits down, her attention drawn back toward Martin, who offers them a tumbler of wine.

"Mistress Myla," he addresses her. "I am not sure if the captain has informed you, but the use of magic is prohibited here. We ask that you do not violate our space with the energy. We, each of us, have the same gifts you find anywhere else in Myrnith, but we believe in managing our day-to-day tasks simply."

Again, Myla nods, finding she is weary and willing to agree to about anything that promises a quiet room and a bed to fall into.

As though seeing into her thoughts, Martin smiles softly and extends a hand. "You look exhausted, my dear girl. Allow me to have a room made up for you. I am afraid you will find them simple. But they are clean and private."

An hour later, Myla lies in a steaming bath she drew for herself. There is one small window overlooking the climbing mountain, a view she gazes upon wearily through half-opened eyes. Her bath water is tinted with blood and dirt; a warrior's bath, as she once heard Callum describe it. The crimson swirls with the ripples of water against her hands, gently coaxing the current back and forth. Mindless and weightless, she exists, knowing there is more to come, but unbothered by it just yet.

Cocooned here in an oasis, unfamiliar but somehow comforting, Myla imagines this is how the child within her has felt these past two years. For the first time since unharnessing the child, giving it leave to grow, Myla looks down at her exposed belly, examining it for change. There is none to be found, no proof the baby is even still there. But the waves of energy within are palatable. It is a feeling she has not yet felt, something that would have felt gradual and unnoticeable had this taken a natural course.

To think, this child might have been walking and talking at this point. Myla shudders and lifts herself into a sitting position, correcting her thought process. *She would likely be dead.* Vesperian would not have allowed Caius's Restorer's bloodline to carry on. Even now, Myla fears that may very well be the child's fate.

No. Her fingers press into her belly, hoping the child can sense her. "I would not let that happen to you."

Myla exits the bath, feeling drowsy from the heat, and after drying and donning a simple shift provided by the monks while her garments are washed, she stretches herself across the bed. It is not yet supper time, but Myla does not care. Promises of food or drink could not lure her from the sanctuary of a deep, peaceful sleep. One which she falls into, welcomed by visions of her mother playing on the floor of her palace chambers with a small child: her child. From behind, all she sees is a small bobbing head of brown curls; a piece of her already manifesting itself in the child.

The monastery is quiet as nightfall descends. Most have retired, and those that remain are sequestered in quiet groups for prayer. Bryar sits by the hearth reading a letter when Myla joins him, drawing his attention away from whatever message he holds. He glances briefly at her cotton shift cinched at the waist with a length of leather and then smiles at her. "You look rested. I checked on you earlier, but you were as good as dead."

Myla sits on a stool next to him, teetering slightly on the uneven legs before finding her balance. "I do not even recall falling asleep."

Bryar nods toward the parchment in his hands. She notes now that it is a map. "We need to go to the Seer, Myla."

While the treacherous journey to where the Seer has lived for an unnatural length of time sounds unpleasant, Myla knows he is right. They need answers, and she will have them. "Let us go in two days, then. You will be no good up there with a fresh wound."

Bryar simply nods in agreement, his eyes drifting to the crackling fire before them. Absently, he chews his lower lip, mind busy with thoughts. "Have you noticed my abilities seem a bit . . . out of control lately?"

Myla furrows her brow, leaning closer in, her elbows on her knees. "I think it is always been more potent than the average fire wielder." Images of his axe wilting in his hand, or the explosive flames the night before, calls into question her answer, but she does not amend her statement lest he should worry.

He shakes his head, glancing sidelong at her. "Yes, but lately it feels like it is constantly simmering beneath the surface, ready to implode at the slightest disturbance."

"And it has not always felt like that?" A stupid question really. Myla has seen him angry a handful of times through their childhood and never once did his anger start a fire at his feet.

"No."

Myla briefly places a hand over his, careful to not shock the monks with their indecency. "There is no shortage of stress right now. I am sure that is all it is."

He nods, seeming to accept the explanation. They both know it is bullshit.

As the candles burn low, monks trickle out of the main hall until only a handful remain, silence mostly filling the empty air. Myla and Bryar's low whispers are all that disturbs the quiet. Though they both know there is no point in planning any retaliation against the Blood Stealer, Bryar humors Myla as she aimlessly mulls over one potential solution followed by another. Knowing she is tucked safely away in this monastery while that dark scourge stains the ground of her kingdom is sickening. Those who did survive are no doubt his playthings. Myla can only imagine he spent the day claiming oath after oath, cutting a devastating line of victims through the town and beyond.

"What of this antidote he speaks of?" Myla states after some hopeless silence. "Surely, his is not the only healer who could craft it."

"No," Bryar agrees, "but obtaining his blood is likely the challenge."

"Perhaps we could send some of the Raven's Veil to the Seam to search for more?"

Bryar watches the flames diligently, as though taking his eye off them might cause them to explode and flatten the entire monastery. After some thought, he responds.

"Once we return from the Seer, I will figure out how to get word to a few of our best, and they will go in search of an antidote. I doubt he only had one made."

Myla lets out a small sigh. "There," she whispers, looking down at her stomach. "Some hope at last."

Bryar smiles slightly and reaches past the space between them to take her hand. "You will solve nothing with worrying," he says, his face heavy with exhaustion. "We have our next steps laid out. Let us follow those, and leave the rest up to the Gods. They will not forsake us."

After another hour of deliberating and considering other courses of action, Myla retires to her room.

Chapter 11

At first, Myla thinks it might be the monks praying outside her door when the sound of a boot scuff brings her head from the flat pillow. At the turning of the handle, she sits upright, drawing the heavy linens over her chest. Quietly, the door creaks open, and Myla is grateful for the fox dagger on the bedside table; otherwise, it may be difficult to abide by the monk's request of no magic within the monastery walls. Alas, with a breath, she relaxes at the sight of Bryar entering, bearing a humble teacup on a chipped saucer.

"It seems all of their cups are chipped," he whispers with a tired smile, handing her a steaming cup of chamomile. Myla gratefully accepts.

"You have brought me my evening tea," she acknowledges warmly.

"Well, without Fern. . . someone has to see to it you get a good night's rest."

Bryar leans against her hearth momentarily before taking note of the dying flames, which he resuscitates with a few logs and some patient stoking. "No magic, they said," he mutters. "So, we do it the normal way."

"You know, most people have to start fires and tend them the normal way," she teases, savoring a long sip of her warm tea. "We do not all have the gift of fire and constant warmth."

Bryar smiles briefly at her before checking that the shutters of her window are secure. "This should keep your room warm most of the night. The shutters are locked, and I will stand guard by your door tonight." Myla nearly sighs in exasperation at this man's level of commitment.

"You will do no such thing," Myla argues, standing to place her half-empty cup on the mantle. "You said it yourself: a monastery is the last place anyone will look for pagans like us. You have had a long day, and we make for the Seer in two days. Rest." Myla pats the bed. "Sit with me for a while, at least."

Bryar takes a deep breath and absently grinds his jaw, weighing the risks of abandoning his post before looking back at her. "Only for a bit," he responds, sitting with a sigh.

Hesitantly at first, she moves alongside him and begins working at the fastenings of his armor, helping him shed layer after layer of weight. Exhausted to the core, he sits, allowing her to help. When at last his armor, tunic, and boots are discarded, she moves to the cut on his arm, unwrapping it. In silence, she tends the wound, washing it with clean water from her basin and rewrapping it.

When she finishes and stands back to examine her handiwork, his eyes, rimmed with tears, knock the wind from her. After stripping the hard, cold warrior down to his barest self, nothing remains but a grieving man.

A lump catches in Myla's throat and she presses a palm gently to his rough cheek, wiping a tear with her thumb. "Bryar," she whispers, "tell me what you need."

He says nothing. Instead, she is stunned by the raw vulnerability as his arms wrap around her waist and his head presses against her chest. Though he makes no sound, his shoulders shake with sobs. Myla wraps her arms around his head, holding him close, hoping if she hugs him tight enough, she will hold his broken pieces in place.

"I am so sorry," she whispers into his hair after a while. "I wish I could take your hurt."

He pulls back now, looking up at her. "Hurting is what makes us human, Myla. I do not want it taken away; I just do not want the guilt."

The same guilt she felt earlier. "You have nothing to feel guilty for."

"Our best friends are likely dead," he heaves, "and so many men I trained from boys were slaughtered. If I had not walked in . . . I have everything to feel guilty for."

A stinging sensation forms, and Myla blinks quickly, ridding her eyes of the tears. "I am so sorry." She chokes on the words, and it is Bryar who now wipes the tears from her cheeks.

"It is not your fault," he insists adamantly. "We were all just doing our jobs, you included."

"Doing your job is not supposed to hurt this much," she answers, cupping his hand against her face and leaning into his touch. "I am so tired of hurting all the time. For once, I want to feel something other than pain."

His hand lingers, held in place by hers, and the sorrow on his face is replaced by a deeply starved look. Her skin pebbles with exhilaration as his countenance shifts. She is all at once aware of the thinness of her nightgown and the way little is hidden with the glare of the fireplace passing through the thin material. Bryar swallows hard, looking up at her as they are still fixed in what was only moments ago, a comforting hug, but now feels different.

"Take my pain tonight," she whispers, pressing her forehead against his, "and I shall take yours."

"Myla." His brow furrows and she can feel a tremble pass through him as he battles temptation. The following is nearly laughed, "We are in a monastery right now. I bet a year's wages it is a sin to these people for us to even be alone right now. Not to mention . . ." He clears his throat. "You are nearly naked here in my arms already."

Unabashed, Myla leans to press parted lips to his neck and whispers, "Then I guess it is a good thing I pay your wages, we do not worship their god, and you have seen me naked before." Slow and calculated, Myla pushes him flat against the bed and moves on top of him, her thighs pressing on either side of his firm abdomen.

Bryar's body quivers with desire as her soft lips leave a trail of fire along his neck, and one delicate kiss against his mouth, causing his breath to hitch. His hands, filled with longing, grip her hips, drawing her body flush against his, and the taste of her lingers on his lips as he breathes her name.

"*Myla.*"

His hand is firm and possessive on back of her neck, drawing her into a slow, attentive kiss which melts her body against his like warm honey. From the nape of her neck, Bryar's hand slowly travels down the contour of her back, barely grazing her with the tips of his fingers as he chases the tension of her muscles away.

Her hips sway intentionally now, rolling forwards and back against him until he hardens beneath her. His response is exhilarating and quickens her breath in slight, raspy gasps. What was slow, soft and hesitant turns to fire, sparks kindling into a lapping blaze.

Between breathless kisses and roaming hands exploring the dips and curves of his sculpted body, Myla finds the self-control to pull away from him, her eyes fixated on the green of his. He studies her back, looking deeper than a gaze should allow.

"I have spent five years catching glimpses of you, waiting for a brief smile and thriving off it alone until the next smile or the next word—and they were never enough to heal me," she whispers, hoping the dead do not hear.

"Heal you?" he asks, tucking a loose curl behind her ear.

"To heal the shattered mess that was made of me when my father told me it could not be you." Myla leaves no time for a response, silencing whatever he is about to say with a kiss, her tongue moving with his. His body radiates heat, not the natural kind, but the kind that awakens through magic when his body does.

Bryar wraps strong arms around her and in a fluid motion, he sits upright, linking his arms beneath her so he can stand. Stunned, Myla grips his sides with her legs, holding on tightly as he pushes her against the wall with an unintentional *thud,* then lowers her to her feet.

His mouth finds her neck, then her shoulders where the shift still covers her. He kisses her gently there, then with a nimble flick of his fingers, he nudges the material off, watching, satisfied, as it slips to the floor at her feet.

For a moment he stands back, examining her, his hunter's eyes expertly taking stock of the ways her body has changed and matured. A hand traces the rise of her collarbone, drifting lower and lower until he cups her breasts, massaging them reverently, causing warmth to pool between her thighs. Myla licks her lips hungrily. Her gaze travels from his chiseled midsection to the taut bulge of his trousers and hunger turns to insatiable starvation.

Sensing her need, his hands stroke lightly up and down her sides, teasing her senses. His magic, simmering now, steams from his body, coating hers in a hot mist, leaving her skin slick and glistening in the firelight.

At last, Bryar's fingertips find a hold on her hips as he drops to his knees before her. The fluid motion sends flutters of anticipation through her stomach, and she lets her head fall back against the wall, waiting for his kiss there.

His attentions begin against her belly, slow kisses awakening her. Each shift of his hands, holding her in place, stokes a fierce heat in their wake. An intoxicating kind that makes his touches more electrifying, nearly burning her but not quite. Myla tangles slender fingers through his thick mess of curls, urging him lower.

He growls a laugh, looking up at her. "You are not in charge here," he reminds her, pressing his thumbs to the inside of her thighs, nudging her open. "But I have been a patient man, and I do not want to wait any longer. So, I will oblige."

It is a gentle kiss at first, slow and tender followed by an expert flick of his tongue against her core, already honeyed with warm arousal. Myla's head falls back against the wall, her lips parted as he coaxes breathless, desperate moans from her. The stubble on his cheeks grazes the sensitive skin inside her thighs as he drowns in her pleasure.

Myla is on the brink of combusting already when his hand moves upward, his fingers adding to the aching until there is a shock wave of throbbing tight around them. She gasps, one hand bracing her body against the hearth to her left and another knotted in his hair, supporting her trembling thighs.

Bryar leaves her with no time to recover before he stands, a strong arm sliding around her waist and guiding her to the bed. Careful not to create too much noise and alert the pious men just outside the room, they lower themselves into the comfort of the bed. Bryar's hands waste no time in pulling her close, her red-hot skin coated with sweat from his heat, and that of pure ecstasy.

A soft moan escapes her as she sucks in a needy breath, but he silences her with a firm kiss, his teeth gently bearing into her bottom lip.

Eagerly, she drags her nails down his chest and fumbles with the laces of his trousers, frantic for their union. Myla pushes him to his back, and he concedes control, peering up at her.

"Do you hurt still?" she whispers, taking him in her hand and stroking upwards, and down again until he throbs in her hand, evoking a deep moan from him.

His head falls back, and he nods. "Terribly."

With a touch as soft as velvet, she repeats the motion, satisfied as he grows even harder. Leaning to press her lips to his, she whispers, "And now?"

"Unbearably," he growls, nipping at her lips.

Trembling with anticipation, Myla moves forward, aligning her hips with his before slowly lowering herself onto him. The first thrust is deep, and coaxes a unanimous gasp from them both.

"How about now?" she asks finally, an ecstatic smile stretching across her face as he simply responds with another passionate thrust. "Good," she replies, digging fingers into his chiseled abdomen. "But just to be safe," her hips roll forward in unison with his in a slow tease, her thighs flexing as she moves up and down around him.

His entire body tenses as he pushes himself into a sitting motion, drawing her against him so his mouth can find hers, then flipping her onto her back so he once again commands the pace and rhythm. There is a harmony their bodies create, moving together in a tangle of touches and kisses, thrusts, and moans. Bryar masterfully evokes gasps and whimpers from her. Myla reaches above, grasping the solid headboard to brace against the force of his body worshiping hers, pushing deeper and deeper inside her with each forward motion, until it is difficult to tell where she ends and he begins.

Sunken gloriously in the pillows and linens of the mattress, Myla digs her teeth into her lip to remain silent. Despite her best efforts to refrain from crying out, begging him to move with her deeper and faster. The throbbing between her legs is euphoric and demands she moan his name. Passion and pleasure lay claim to the bed, like a battlefield where their magic unfurls from their bodies, mingling unbridled. Myla's light illuminates them and Bryar's proves the bedding superfluous.

When at last, like a thunderous roll, pleasure at her core spills, and the earth itself ceases to spin on its axis, Bryar is forced to press a hand gently over her mouth, hushing her. An endeavor that proves futile as he reaches his own release and his body shudders while her name falls from his lips reverently.

Myla doubts they will have a place to sleep tomorrow night if they were half as loud as she suspects.

He does not remove himself at once, instead, panting and both coated with sweat from the warmth of his magic, slow kisses stoke the flame.

"Do you think they will forgive us if we repent in the morning?" Bryar asks once their breathing has steadied. His question is met with small giggles.

Elsewhere in the monastery, a humble row of monks is knelt heads bowed, praying with sanctimonious dedication, none the wiser to the religious experience taking place in the room above their heads.

Myla teeters on the edge of sleep, resisting the call only to bathe in the feeling of Bryar's hands absently gliding up and down the side of her naked body.

Silently, Bryar draws designs across her skin the way he used to when they were younger. Myla presses a light finger against his temple. "Will you tell me what you are thinking?"

He rolls to face her head-on, the glint of the fire creating sharp lines across his disciplined body. "You said you broke when your father said it could not be me. Do you mean you asked him?"

She nods slowly, lowering her head into the crook of his neck. "Yes, I did."

"You asked your father if you could forgo a marriage to the king for . . . someone untitled?" There is a glint of humor in his voice.

"When he told me I was to marry Caius, I cried. You know I do not do that much, so father was suspicious. I am afraid he dragged the truth from me. I never told him it was *you,* but he knew there was someone."

Bryar stiffens. "How much of the truth did you tell him?"

Myla tilts her head upward to land a quick kiss before answering. "I left the more delicate details to my mother, who had to ensure negotiations did not include checking my virginal state. I cried myself sick for two weeks. And when the wedding day arrived, I cried once more, then never again."

His arms tighten in a comforting embrace. "I could not tell by looking at you. You were very . . . stoic from the wedding on."

Silence follows as Myla considers admitting stoicism had nothing to do with it; it was a matter of survival. "Caius knew about it all, you know."

"About me?"

"Not you specifically. I did not want to risk him reassigning you, or worse. But there were times we would drink too much and tell each other things we never would when we were sober. I learned those were the times it was safe to tell him that my heart missed another. He did not seem to mind."

Perhaps because she was merely a means to an end for him. Her heart did not matter at all.

Bryar strokes strands of her hair down her back, watching her lips move as she speaks. It is clear he tries to work that out in his own mind, wrestling with something deeper. "What an odd arrangement you had with him," he says finally. "I never would have guessed he was the kind of man you could admit that to."

"It was not love, that was for sure," she answers, barely loud enough for him to hear, afraid the Gods might strike her dead for her ungratefulness. "Friendship maybe, honesty, yes. But I never loved him." Myla rationalizes all of the things she wishes she could say, but is too scared to admit, hoping if she gives them an explanation, they will not hurt so badly.

Bryar is silent before speaking again, his words calculated and carefully chosen. "I was supposed to stand guard beside your chamber the night of the wedding, during the consummation viewing."

Myla gasps, sitting upright. "You were not!"

"I *did not*," he clarifies. "I was drunk in the cellars and ended up being on squire training for a month as punishment." His eyes travel past her collarbone to her exposed breasts and, before speaking again, he reaches out to draw her closer. "Never mind any of that. I am in pain again and need my cure."

Chapter 12

"In a *monastery?*" Myla jolts from sleep at the sound of the door closing, Bryar discreetly exiting and leaving her tucked away. A rush of gratitude washes over her at the familiar voice of Callum just outside her door, muffled now. Bryar says something inaudible, but she can hear Elsa's name followed by a sob. Myla sits upright, a sickening anticipation settling over her. *Who else is with him?*

She dresses swiftly, pulls her hair in a loose knot at her neck, and exits the room, stepping out in time to see Bryar gripping his friend's shoulder supportively. For being such a big man, Callum seems so small beneath the quaking of his shoulders. His face twists as grief devours him whole and he falls against his comrades. Together, Bryar and Rhyland comfort their friend as he admits the agonizing reality. Rusty hair brushes his forehead, and he shakes his head in disbelief, eyes gleaming.

"The ceiling came down," Rhyland says quietly, as Bryar looks to him with questions.

Shaking with a rush of denial, Myla approaches slowly. Rhyland glances at her, his head dropping in a bow. Bryar stops him, whispering something; no doubt telling him of her concealed identity.

"She is not with you?" Myla asks, grasping at Callum's sleeve. "Elsa is not with you . . . what of my father?"

Grief crumples the man before her like a flimsy piece of paper, and he simply shakes his head. "I tried," he chokes before turning and leaving the building.

Rhyland is about to follow when Bryar grabs his arm. "Let him go, he needs to be alone." There is a knowing in the way he says *needs*. Like he has felt that need before.

The room seems to spin with the shocking finality of what Myla knew in her heart, but had hoped was wrong. The miracle of the men standing before her should be a relief, and it is, but it is outweighed by the crippling thought: *how could they leave without her?*

As though reading her mind, Rhyland speaks. "I barely got Callum out of there. It was hell unleashed. I have never seen such bloodshed and wreckage in one place. But all he could do was scream her name. He ran right toward the Blood Stealer and almost got his head cut off before I could get ahold of him and drag him away." He stumbles over his words. "I am so sorry I could not do more. For Elsa or your father. I lost sight of him when the ceiling came down as well. I do not believe anyone could have survived that."

Myla nods, her vision blurred with unshed tears which she wipes away before they can free fall. She struggles to find words, so she says nothing. The fact is, there is nothing to say, and all in company know it.

Wearing weariness and grief, Rhyland lowers his eyes and draws his long dark hair to a twist at the back of his head, revealing a layer of closely shaven hair beneath, then moves toward a table spread with food and drink.

It is Bryar who finally propels the conversation. "We will visit the Seer." His words are hushed to avoid prying ears. "I believe she can bring clarity and direction to our path."

Rhyland groans and glances between she and Bryar, finding seriousness on both their faces. Letting out a sigh and pressing his dusty palms exhaustively into his brow, smudging layers of dust over his brown skin, he concedes, "Let me sleep first?"

Myla smiles weakly and nods. "We leave tomorrow morning. Rest today."

Rhyland retires to Bryar's room to sleep, not wanting to inconvenience the monks by making up another room. With Bryar's assurance that he will not need it, Rhyland collapses in an exhausted heap, sure to sleep the day away.

The hours pass and Callum is nowhere to be found. Bryar seems convinced he is well, but most likely taking the space to grieve after their journey. Their convalescence seems to be wasting time, and Myla wants nothing more than to pack up and make for the Seer at once.

Instead, she finds herself kneeling in the garden, helping a quiet monk remove weeds. He is sworn to silence—or so Martin tells her—so she, too, partakes in the wordless task, finding comfort in the cathartic act of wrenching overgrowth out by the roots.

With each violent rip upward, she envisions one of Vesperian's limbs separating from his body. Dirt dislodged and flung in various directions replaces the vision of his spraying blood, her imagination sufficiently quenching her need to brutalize the demon, or her father, though she chides herself for resenting the dead.

Let the Gods do their work, her mother would tell her. The Gods can not bring Elsa back, and for that, she curses them.

In the back of her mind, tucked a little deeper than her hatred, are memories of last night. Scenes that replay in her mind without her permission, and she feels shame for allowing herself to be distracted by something she should not be at such a time. If Elsa were here, she would say sex is the cure for all. Elsa had been a woman who celebrated with it, a woman who experienced both defeat and anger with it. If anything, Elsa would have been pleased to know her demise resulted in Myla finally acting.

She smiles at the thought and leans back, settling in the dirt, her face turned upward toward the sky. Her dark lashes falling shut over her blue eyes, and she wills the energy of her friend to join her. *I wish you were here. I wish I could tell you everything. I wish you could tell* me *what you are thinking. I wish I could tell you I am sorry.*

Myla opens her eyes to find the monk looking kindly on her, a small smile curving his thin lips. He says nothing but nods slowly and points to the sky. Myla looks upward to see a raven passing overhead. Whatever that means, in his faith, she has no clue. But Myla chooses to interpret it as a message from Elsa. *Carry on.*

Myla glances back at the monk and nods toward the raven as it soars out of sight.

"Do they mean something to you?"

He tips his chin in an affirmative response then returns to his work. Myla finds his silence fascinating, and somewhat appealing, having the choice to simply not speak, even when spoken to.

"Will your vow of silence last a long time?" Again, he nods, so Myla continues. "My best friend died two days ago, and it is my fault."

His eyes grow sad, and dirt covered hands reach out to grasp hers. His head shakes 'no' this time.

Myla smiles weakly and eyes him sidelong. "No . . . it *is.* And my father. He died, and I am not sad for that."

The monk glances over his shoulder to where Bryar sits, pouring over a map, occasionally staring at the mountains. He tips his chin in question.

"Yes," Myla answers. "My friend died helping him save me." The monk's hands tighten around hers, and he gives her a melancholy smile, followed by a final pat before he returns to his work.

"You seem like the sort of person who would have helpful things to say," Myla says. "It is rather inconvenient you had to take a vow of silence during my visit."

At this, the monk laughs, giving her a brief nod of agreement before pointing back toward Bryar, suggesting she talk to him.

Her cheeks flush, and she shakes her head. "Since you are sworn to silence, I will confess: talking to him right now does not seem to lead to *talking*."

The monk's eyes narrow but his face does not hold judgment. He wags his finger but continues to smile at her.

"Yes," Myla agrees. "He *is* good to talk to though."

The old monk cuts her off, wagging his finger again, and Myla realizes she does not understand what he is suggesting. Her brow furrows as she studies his face. Once more the monk points to Bryar, encouraging her to *see.* So, Myla observes. His eyes bounce across the map, moving back and forth searching. Then he looks up, studies the terrain before dropping the map to the ground, a hand pressing wearily into his brow. He looks worn thin and distressed.

Myla glances back at the monk, who she finds is studying her. "He is struggling too. You think I should talk to him?"

Pleased, the monk smiles and then promptly returns to his work, pointing to his own ears.

"I should listen."

He nods yes, and then gathers a basket of weeds, taking them to discard on the forest floor, leaving Myla sitting in the dirt alone. Given the sadness of this morning, Myla has not had a moment to speak with Bryar. Last night cured nothing. Of course, they both knew it would not. But looking at him now, she sees how truly defeated he appears. Against the backdrop of the ancient and massive mountain he intends on climbing, even he appears small.

Myla stands and brushes the dirt from her linen dress. "It is just a mountain," she says, teasing. "I do not think glaring at it will make it smaller."

Startled, he quickly turns to her, flashing a half smile before retrieving the map from the ground. "Damn, I will need to come up with a better plan, then."

Myla sits beside him, absently smoothing the wrinkles across her legs. "Something troubles you."

He holds up the map, pointing to a location. "This is us." She nods and follows as his finger moves to the tip of the mountain on the map. "This is the Seer."

"Yes?" Myla acknowledges, confused where the problem lies. "I do not understand."

"It is a long journey, Myla. In your condition—"

"Stop," Myla whispers. "It is out of the question."

"We need to be realistic," he retorts, looking at her head-on. "Myla, you are with child. An important child, I might add."

"Are they not all important?" Myla challenges him with a faint smile followed by a sigh, hoping he will not press the matter.

"You know what I mean. This child may be our only chance at putting an end to the Blood Stealer," he insists. His boyish eyes, soft and safe as ever, bore into her and beg her to concede the battle. "It is too great a risk."

Myla shakes her head fiercely and takes his hand, urging him to see how very determined she is. "I am coming, Bryar. I need to speak to the Seer."

With a grimace of disapproval, Bryar averts his gaze, clearly not pleased with her. "You are stubborn," he whispers after a moment with gentle eyes resting on her belly. "You must be careful. That child has the magic to free you, and I want nothing more than to see you free."

"*She*," Myla corrects with certainty, ignoring the exhilaration she feels at his concern. "She has the power to save us all. I know. I would not do anything to hurt her."

"Are you afraid?" Bryar asks cautiously. "To raise her alone, that is?"

Myla's eyes fall to the ground. Does she dare to admit it? Looking at him, his handsome and harsh features, and the way he looks to *see* and *understand*, not to simply look, persuades her to full transparency. "I am not afraid. I know I have everything she needs. I am hoping if we make it out of this, I will not *have* to do it alone." She does not dare look at him. After last night, Myla feels it is important to raise the topic.

Silence follows and he scuffs the dirt beneath his boots, deep in thought. Finally, Bryar clears his throat and the furrow in his brow sends a fleeting tinge of dread through her, quickly erased when he finally assembles his thoughts into a cohesive response. "I never knew my mother. My father did not talk about her. But when I was four, he started accepting invitations to the seamstress's for supper. I thought he was just taking me somewhere for a decent meal, but after a while I noticed he smiled a lot around her."

A fondness passes over his face as he tells the tale. "He married her when I was five. I was pleased; it meant I never went more than a day with a tear in my clothes, and my belly was always full of a dinner father did not burn." Together they laugh, and then Bryar concludes his response. "She was my mother, and I loved her until the sickness ate her alive and made her body sink in on itself." Myla recalls this, watching him as a teenager grieving the death of Alice the seamstress, consumed by an illness where her bones were too heavy for her lungs.

Bryar stands and dusts the back of his pants before turning to face her, his expression earnest. "You do not have to make a child to raise it. You just have to love it . . . and *her* mother is easy to love, which means she will be too."

Bryar simply smiles at her, before walking back inside the monastery, her deeply hidden fear dissolving. Caius's death brought many uncertainties and sadnesses, including the idea that she would have no one to celebrate her child's moments with.

In an instant, Myla stands, chasing Bryar inside, stopping him as he turns down a stone hall toward his room.

"You can not just say that to me and walk away," she says, not giving him a chance to respond before she falls into his arms, holding onto him as though her life depends upon it. Wordlessly, his arms cradle her there, both ignoring the glances of the monks who pass mumbling their prayers and chants. A warm hand gently caresses the small of her back, holding her close in return. His embrace is sturdy, unwavering, and she finds herself comforted in his refuge.

Callum returns before the sun sets. His jaw, stone solid in the form of a grimace, and eyes rimmed red. But his voice is level and composed when he speaks, addressing them upon his entry. “When do we leave in the morning? I have questions for this seer.”

“At dawn,” Bryar answers, watching his friend move past, sitting alone at the end of the table. His deep olive skin is ashen; he appears sick with heartbreak.

Rhyland, not long awake, lets slip an exaggerated groan, peering depressively at an empty mug which holds wine. “I am to set out on a treacherous journey in the morning, and I do not even get a decent glass of ale beforehand. Just this—” he tips the mug, watching a few drops spill onto his palm “—weak brew . . .” He takes another glance around the room with a grim expression. “Not to mention every man here is celibate. No ale and no bedmate before I quite possibly *die.* This is the grimmest crock of shit never to be sung in a bard’s tale.”

Myla rolls her eyes, content with the herbal tea before her. She is, however, less than impressed with the mutton on her plate. Something about it smells rancid. Nobody else seems bothered though, so she takes small nibbles to not offend their hosts.

The men carry on conversations, slightly drowned out beneath the monastic humming, providing ‘contemplative entertainment’ to the monks. While the men disregard the songs for their conversations, Myla is entranced. This monk is younger than the rest. He is likely younger than she, and a dull ache in his eyes suggests he is here because there is nothing left for him out there. His song is in a language she does not understand, but gauging the yearning on the faces of the others who do listen, she can only imagine he sings of peace and hope. Something she feels rather short on.

A glance at her companions, and she can see it written on all their faces. Peace and hope are nowhere to be found. Callum is leaned over his plate, nudging the food in various directions, never once taking a bite. Rhyland looks as though he is about to fall asleep where he sits, and Bryar stares into the flames, lost in thought. Sadness is palpable, driving a cold dagger of grief into the fresh, Elsa-shaped wound in her heart.

Not wishing to call attention to her tears, Myla steps outside to get some fresh air, her stomach deeply unsettled. The door has almost swung shut when light pools out behind her. Callum follows close behind and wordlessly, he pulls her into a trembling hug.

They stand together, more family than friends, and they cry. The lighthearted boy she grew up with, would never have stood here crying. But that boy had never experienced heartbreak, whereas the man here now is crippled by it.

"I will not insult you by asking how you are," she whispers after a moment.

Callum loosens his hold on her and steps back. "Nor I, you." His eyes travel upwards, taking stock of the sky above. Anything to avoid Myla's piercing gaze. "The last of her I saw, she was helping people. She was always helping people. Helping people brought her joy. It was her life. And it was her death." He smiles down at his travel-worn boots and shoves scarred hands into his pockets. The hands of an expensive, trained killer attached to the body of such a loving human. "I can not decide if I am angrier at Rhyland for taking me from her . . . or at myself for not being by her side when it happened."

Myla shakes her head as tears choke her. "Callum—"

"Myla. You are the only person who loves her as much as I did.

You can not tell me you do not feel the *exact* same way."

Myla cups a hand to her mouth, unprepared to face the rush of agony. Traveling and strategizing and sex is an amazing distraction from a broken heart, but it is no balm for confronting it. "I think I will never forgive myself," she whispers, pressing her hand to her thundering chest in an effort to still the phantoms which seem to stampede inside, aching to be released. "There was too much magic . . . the institute spoke of too much energy in one place." Myla recalls the lessons she sat in, urging a wielder to be mindful not to saturate the atmosphere. "There were over a hundred souls in the throne room, and every single one was wielding. I should never have allowed it."

Callum's eyes fall shut, and with a solemn shake of his head, he speaks. "Exactly how do you think you could have stopped that? Every single person there knew what they were doing and they all—Elsa included—would cave the room in again if it meant you escaped."

Myla nods, sucking in a breath in an effort not to lose herself completely. "Callum, I am so sorry. I never wanted to be the one people would die for."

His light eyes, illuminated by a thick row of tears, meet hers, and he speaks in all confidence. "Well, you are. Do not cheapen their sacrifices by loathing the life the Gods have given you." Callum sighs, touching her shoulder, as if to share whatever fortitude he has to spare, then adds in a most hopeless tone, "I am sorry we lost her. And I am sorry you lost your father."

Callum returns inside, leaving Myla to collect herself beneath the healing light of the moon. Her mother used to take her 'moon bathing' as a child, and even into womanhood, and every month when she bled, her mother would take her to bathe naked and wash in water charged beneath the moon. It was to fill herself with the unfailing wholeness of nature as her body shed what it no longer needed. Her mother told her it was to remind her body that she is never empty.

Caius caught Myla in the gardens once, bathing naked beside the willow tree. She thought he would be alarmed by her practices, her body's curved edges glistening in the candlelight. Instead, he was curious, asking questions and showing his support. That is how she later told him she was pregnant. *There will be no moon bathing for me this month, or for many more it would seem.* He was elated and she was relieved he no longer had a reason to summon her to his chambers.

Her mother also taught Myla how the Gods have written every single individual in the stars. She would say that those placements mold them as humans. "Ground yourself," she used to say. "You can not be manipulated if you are in tune with yourself and the Spirit Mother."

Before the encroachment of the Blood Stealer, Myla had never found failing in this. Even now, *with* the tug-of-war Vesperian plays with her, standing here barefoot against the raw pulsing of the earth is healing. It tightens the knots she has always tied with the Gods and the Spirit Mother. Tonight, it makes her feel as though she can reach past the veil, into the spirit realm to touch Elsa, knowing her dear friend can finally smile on the faces of the Goddesses who have guided them since girlhood.

Myla kneels down, lifting her skirts so her knees press into the moist soil of the earth. She lays her palms flat and closes her eyes, visualizing the white light within her nuzzling into the ground, planting her roots and growing from there, tangling with those of the natural world. The internal and external aches buzz with warmth before fading away, leaving behind a calm certainty: what is meant for her, will be hers.

Chapter 13

Myla lays awake, watching a moth flutter against the ceiling, lulled by the breath of the man sleeping beside her. Once more, with Bryar to blame this time, her clothes lay in a pile on the floor, recklessly discarded beside his.

Something her father said shortly after Caius's death keeps her awake. "*You must remarry, Myla. Soon. Falkmere needs a king.*" He had presented her with a written list of eligible nobility to which she had responded, *"If I marry again, Father, it will be for love."*

The frustrated man had slammed his list fiercely on the council table before her and announced she was at liberty to do so, but it would not be as queen. If it were just a matter of Myla and her personal wishes, abdicating the throne would be of little consequence to her. She never wanted it to begin with. Carrying the king's heir now, she realizes her position is far less negotiable.

Myla shifts, turning to face Bryar. By daylight, there is something fierce about him. To a stranger, his sharp edges, broad shoulders, and menacing stare might come across as frightening. Here, washed softly by fading firelight without the pretense of a soldier, he appears vulnerable. The thought that falling asleep beside him may be a fleeting reality turns her veins icy, visions of her stoic loneliness flash through her mind. These visions haunt her as she drifts off to sleep and beyond, her dreams taunted with memories of days turning into years where his touch grows foreign.

And when she awakens, Bryar is gone.

"Surely you saw *something,*" Myla demands, looking at the dismayed collection of monks who exchange glances and confused shakes of their heads. "So, three loud, clanking soldiers just slipped out here during breakfast and no one noticed?" Myla feels a compilation of fear and rage build in her chest, further statements from Martin, unhelpful.

"Mistress," he continues carefully, "I would venture to remind you they are assassins, not clanking soldiers. I prayed with the sunrise and saw no one leave. I fear they left well before daylight."

"One of them *is not* an assassin and has the stealth of a damn cow!" Myla declares exasperated and aware that assassin or no, Bryar has gone to the Seer without her.

"Fucks me, and then leaves while I sleep. Despicable." Wide eyes in a sea of brown habits fix upon her, Martin's expression especially horrified. "I apologize," Myla adds swiftly, but she is not in the least bit sorry. The crowd of scandalized monks begins to disperse until only a few remain. One of which is her silent friend, whose eyes twinkle in amusement.

Myla looks to Martin. "What is his name?"

"Ethstan," Martin begrudgingly answers before also removing

himself. No doubt to pray for her.

"Ethstan," she whispers, leaning toward the grinning monk. "I do not think you belong here," she sighs before accepting a plate of flat-cakes from him. "I told you, talking to him is not ending in *just* talking—before you point to your ears, Ethstan. I *did* try listening."

He grins in a dopey sort of way, making his already large ears protrude further and his thin lips stretch, exposing mostly bare gums. Waiting until the last of his companions has left the main hall, he reaches into the drooping sleeve of his habit and reveals a letter, handing it to her.

"From Bryar?"

He nods and shuffles away, leaving her to rip it open alone.

Do not be angry with me. Everything I ever do is to protect you. I had a bad feeling about you coming with us, and I could not ignore it. I promise to return in a week. Stay with the monks. You are safe there.

-B

Myla grinds her teeth together, a mixture of anger and disappointment brewing. She wanted to ask the Seer so many questions, not just about defeating the Blood Stealer, but about Elsa and her father and this child.

Myla looks down at her stomach, peeved by the sour bile forming in the back of her throat, a disturbance she is starting to experience regularly. "I suppose we shall have to let him have the adventures while you and I stay here . . . how very typical."

Myla's voice trails off as she looks around the monastery, seeing it in a new light. Not just as a passing stop on her journey, but a temporary home now. She contemplates defying his request and leaving, but it occurs to her, she has nowhere to go. "Gods damn you," she mutters angrily, shoving the note inside her bodice. There is nothing to do but find something meaningful to occupy her time with. In the back of her mind, she knows this respite is Bryar's way of letting her breathe amid upheaval; something she should be thankful for.

The day drifts on slowly, and Myla wonders how these men live such ordinary and simple lives day in and out. For Myla, it has been years since her days have resembled anything close to simple. Before she was Queen of Falkmere, her father ensured her days were filled with lessons by the finest tutors. Myla can see now how her days pouring over maps, studying regions, learning various languages, and understanding the history of the monarchy set her on the path of queen. Even the efforts of her father, ensuring her training in the art of the sword and making regular visits with her to the Institute of Mystic Arts, honing her skill, all contributed. There was no amount of coin he was unwilling to spare on her instructions and refinement.

For years, this resulted in very few days passing when she was not accounted for from sunup to sundown. Were it not for Bryar's apprenticeship with the blademaster, Myla very well would not have encountered him until she moved to the palace. By the time her magic betrayed her, exposing her to Caius, Myla had far exceeded her contemporaries, and there was no other choice but her. Once she summoned the Voice of the Gods, it was as good as written in stone. All those days of working on herself for the *sake* of herself, turned into her gifts being used against her. That was the worst day of her life. Even now, so many years later, the thought of it scratches at a wound that has not yet healed.

Myla sighs, looking up from pile of dishes she has been assigned to. There is something comical about standing here as a queen, unbeknownst to those around her, holding a pile of dishes to be scrubbed. So, she scrubs, and when the dinner dishes are clean, dried, and put away, she joins Martin at a pile of linens needing mending. *Thank the gods for endless hours of needlepoint.*

"You have been helpful today," Martin remarks, with a curious glance taking note of her precise line of stitches. "I am afraid if your mending all looks like that, this will soon be your task."

Myla smiles. "I shall be sure to throw in a few botched stitches, in that case."

Martin lowers his work to his lap and watches her. Myla pretends not to notice, unsure of what exactly he studies. "You are expecting," he says finally, answering her question.

Myla swallows hard and looks up slowly. "What would make you say such a thing?"

"As you know, magic is not allowed within the borders of this establishment. I have a gift, however, that can not be suppressed. The brethren consider it to be an exception, as it keeps us safe."

Myla's furrowed brow draws a confused line across her face. "What gift is that?"

"I see auras and the energy within them, good or evil," he responds matter-of-factly. "You, my dear, have two auras."

Myla slowly inhales and asks, "What does my child's aura tell you?"

Martin's eyes focus on her stomach. His answer is simple.

"The aura of the unborn are usually all the same. Pure."

"And . . . mine?"

"Your aura is troubled, my dear. I sense no evil, but I do sense conflict."

Well, that is for fucking sure. Myla chooses to say nothing rather than confide the whole truth of her circumstances. Lately for her, there has been no middle ground. She bares her soul, or she says nothing. Nothing is the safest option. Unfortunately, her company is a prying type.

"The captain is the father, I presume?"

Myla bites her lip. If she says no, Martin will press for more information. Myla refuses to expose the child's parentage, lest that knowledge somehow turn Martin against her or endanger the child. Instead, she nods. A small lie is better than an exceptionally large truth, in this case.

"I must assume, then, he has a particularly good reason for leaving you here while he completes whatever business it is he spoke of. I assure you, my dear," his words are soothing as he reaches to touch her arm, "you are safe here and welcome to stay as long as you need."

"You mean, as long as I mend the clothes?" Myla answers with a playful smile. They manage to overcome an enormous mound of mending, mostly in silence. An occasional pleasantry is exchanged, but for much of the evening, Myla's mind wanders from one anxious topic to another, heavily pertaining to her parents.

Myla continues to visualize her father's crushed corpse lying in the throne room, an image which assaults her without warning nor reason. A prick of the needle to her finger followed by a small drop of blood is enough to catapult her imagination to the darkest of places. The young man with his face severed, bodies hanging above her throne, Elsa nothing more than a pulp of bone and flesh beneath slabs of the Queen's Blue, her father's skull split in half like a carelessly cracked egg. In the distance, wolves howl and the image of snapping jaws clamping around Bryar's throat assaults her mind.

Myla squeezes her eyes together, sucking at the smarting point on her finger and wills the images to leave her be, to no avail. *He is tormenting me.* Myla realizes these uncontrolled thoughts, the urge to hyper fixate on death, can only come from Vesperian. Myla may not always be the most cheerful of people, but she certainly is not morbid. Even here, miles from the palace, deep within the thickest part of the forest, at the base of a near unscalable mountain, his invisible fingers stretch to claw at her, to pick at her wounds and entangle themselves deeper into her being. Hiding does not dislodge him from her being. It merely isolates the problem in a too-simple setting with very few distractions.

From the direction of the mountain, wolves howl again.

Martin leaves when the hour is late. Despite the weight in her eyes, Myla is disinclined to return to her room and so she stays, hands folded across her lap and eyes drifting out of focus upon the lapping of the orange and blue flames. Nearly six years ago, she sat in a terribly similar state in a high back green armchair, her parents on either side of her, discussing her future as though she was not there.

"*Maverick,*" her mother had pleaded. "*Give her a moment to catch her breath!*"

"We do not have moments, Lavinia!" Myla recalls the way her father stood over her, clawing in a panic at his disheveled beard. *"Everything—everything we have ever done for you has truly come to this?"*

"Father, I had no idea this is what you wanted of me!"

"You knew!" he nearly snarled.

"Would knowing have changed anything?" her mother asked gently, holding her hand while flashing a fierce look her father's way.

It was this question which brought Myla to tears, the realization that king or no king, it did not matter a bit to her. She did not want the king. "It would have changed nothing," she had confessed beneath her breath, aware both her parents were watching in horror as their dutiful daughter warped into a transgression before their eyes.

Maverick breathed deeply, drawing from every deep well of composure he possibly had before responding. "Your mother and I married for love, child. I am no stranger to its fickle and unyielding power. But this . . . lover of yours is likely not a suitor the king would stand down for, there is nothing to be done. You will marry him."

"Father! You say the King is a good man. You can make him see!"

"Myla! I can not look at the King and tell him my daughter is to snub her nose at his proposal in favor of a—a what? You will not even tell me who he is!"

Lavinia had encouraged her husband to take his leave, sensing the matter was a delicate one. Myla trembles, even now, recalling the fear she felt when the door closed behind her father, leaving her alone with someone not known for leaving stones unturned.

"Have you lain with this man?" Myla had turned her face to the fire, focusing intently so as not to betray herself. As it so happened, her lack of response was all the response Lavinia needed. It was an admission of guilt. "You must tell me who it is, Myla. I will protect him and you, but I can not help if I do not know who."

"How will you help?" For a moment, Myla dared to hope her mother was going to offer a plan, something involving a carriage in the dead of night. What a foolish wish it was.

"I will take you both to someone who will make you forget. Heartbreak is the cruelest pain there is to endure. It will crush the human body beneath its weight."

Myla had stood, knocking an end table over with the motion, hot tears of anger and betrayal leaving trails down her cheeks. "I will have none of your so-called help!"

"Fine." Lavinia and Myla were made of the same fire, both able to dig their heels in and move not an inch. Lavinia had known better than to press the matter, so she simply added, "It is customary to examine a woman before marriage to a king. They will want to ensure you are a virgin. I will

see to it that is not in the contract. Fortunately for you, Caius needs you."

Lavinia held Myla's gaze until Myla finally answered, her shoulders slumped in defeat. "Thank you, Mother."

There would be many conversations to follow preceding the wedding and Myla's coronation as queen, during which time Myla would hold her tongue. She had feared that speaking too much would somehow somersault into her revealing Bryar's identity.

During the day, as wedding arrangements were brought before her for approval and visits to the King arranged, Myla's expression was placid and her words neither enthusiastic nor combative. Every emotion was carefully woven in check, crafting a blanket of suppressed emotions which would unravel every night as she cried herself to sleep.

She merely existed, drifting where her parents' current lead, inevitably right into Caius's bed. She felt like nothing but a carcass by the time she arrived at her wedding, but nothing prepared her for the ways she would break when thirty Council members and courtiers stood around the king's bed, prying eyes watching as a man twice her age bedded her.

Nor would she forget the way they all cried out in pain when she called upon the Voice of the Gods that night. It was the one and only time she defied the King. In his bed, with courtiers watching. The room had trembled violently, and the stones of his floors cracked. The courtiers left then, and he struck her. She learned that night the difference between love and duty, and how those were very different touches.

Emotions swell and her nose stings with tears. Myla has come to terms with her parents' agenda. She could rationalize that. The pain she still feels lies deeper than the places his body touched. There is a word for it, one she struggles to name, but the closest she has come is *betrayed.* And that is something she can not rationalize.

Myla recalls feeling, in that moment, that her marriage began with a betrayal. This powerful man, capable of making whatever changes he wanted to any situation he saw fit, allowed her, a scared young woman, to be a visual feast to the men of his court.

An evening, months after her wedding, over too many glasses of wine, Myla had confided these feelings to Elsa, who had responded profoundly, "Abuse and manipulation hurt no matter how pretty a package they are wrapped in."

Myla shudders and stands, throwing a handful of linens back into their basket before trudging outside, feeling like her insides need to be purged. Kicking off her boots, Myla wiggles her toes in the garden soil until they make an indent in the ground, rooting herself with nature. She takes a deep breath and urges the vile feeling to pass, as she has done so many times before. *One bad moment does not define the entire experience.*

She has tried to convince herself so many times that their consummation ceremony was supposed to be uncomfortable, a gruesome fact she can sometimes explain away, until she lands on the realization time and again that it was not just the consummation that was uncomfortable, but nearly every night after. This internal struggle always ends with her simply diverting her thoughts before they spiral into anger at her parents for allowing it all to happen. Anger that her father, a nobleman himself, knew exactly what would occur and allowed it anyway.

The following morning, Myla would wake up and sit across from the King, drinking tea and forcing herself to be pleasant while a dark cloud of shame built inside her. Shame she could not name or explain. Shame she now realizes was self-loathing for not having the courage to say, "I do not like this." Shame for averting her eyes every time she saw a face in broad daylight that was lit by candles, watching her that night. But most of all, owning a shame that was not hers to own, but *theirs.*

"I wish for you to be comfortable here," Caius had said with a

kind smile. What Myla wanted to say was: "*You should have thought of that before burning the image of my naked body in your friends' minds.*" Instead, she had sidestepped the uncomfortable truth and smiled. It had taken a long time before she was comfortable after that.

Overhead, an owl hoots, its dismal call caught up in the deep *whoosh* of wings as the bird of prey swoops down to dig its talons in a mouse. "Yes," Myla agrees, imagining she speaks to the Goddesses. "I agree. It is time to stop being the mouse and start being the owl. Or better yet, the *talons.*"

Two days have passed, and never before has Myla known time to drag on in such a way. Though she has found a rhythm, Myla discovers quickly that purpose and rhythm are vastly different things, quite capable of existing one without the other.

In the last two days, Myla has found a fondness for tending the garden. Solitary creatures as the monks are, forming friendships has proven difficult, although she feels she has made progress with Ethstan who tends the garden with her. His expressive features seem to make up for what he lacks in conversation. Myla has managed to learn he has two living siblings, but his parents are long since passed. He has not shared his age, but Myla figures he can not be less than sixty. He enjoys the rain more than the sun, and he has a favorite bard.

As it so happens, the young man Myla thought sang beautifully seems to rub Ethstan the wrong way. When the older bard sings, however, he wears a pleasant smile. When Myla asked him about it, he answered in the usual way: with a shrug. No amount of questioning seems to get her any closer to understanding why he does not speak, and Martin insists it is not his story to share, though he alludes to Ethstan atoning for something. Over breakfast, she brought Ethstan a quill and sheet of parchment, hoping he would answer with written words. He politely declined.

On the sixth morning, Myla steps outside the monastery to find the breeze carries a chill. Glancing up the mountain as she does every morning, hoping to see Bryar returning, she takes note of the yellow creeping along the edges of the leaves and a sense of contentment settles in her. To pass an autumn in this place, does not seem so terrible. Her green dress ripples in the breeze and her toes tingle, cold against the earth where a thin frost has collected. Today, she and Ethstan will harvest the gourds and store them, but first, offerings.

Since the night her soul raged and the owl came to visit her, Myla has begun her days with offerings in the woods. Today, she brings a small decanter of mulled wine to the base of a tree.

Some late summer flowers wilt in a twisted wreath from a few days' past. Other offerings include sigils, a pinecone, and various stones. Myla had washed the tree's exposed roots in moon water as an offering yesterday, and today, she places the wine beside the buns. This one is for Elsa. Mulled wine at the autumn equinox was her favorite, so today, that is what she will have.

Myla sits down, crossing her legs and begins drawing sigils and runes in the dirt, letting her fingers move as they will intuitively until she has enclosed herself in markings she has never seen. When she was a child, her mother taught her all of the runes and their meanings. These seem to be an entirely different language, something conjured from an unknown place inside her.

Myla stands, moving outside of the circle, careful not to disturb the intact swirls. Observing it from a few paces back, Myla's skin prickles. The earth rumbles violently, and a heat forms beneath her feet. The runes take on a life of their own. The dirt caught in the trenches of the designs begin rolling smooth like a stream until the entire circle is warping into something completely different than drawings in the dirt: a portal has formed.

A deafening crack, followed by a violent plume of smoke rises from the sky behind the mountain, presumably where the Seer lives. Myla gasps, her breath catching in her lungs as a rippling black mirage separates around the figure of a rounded woman. Her skin a dark bronze, with bright, caramel eyes peering out from beneath long eyelashes. Auburn hair, smooth as silk, drapes long down her body, cascading over the rounding of her breasts and past her curved hips. She wears a simple white frock fastened by gold rings at the shoulders and a crown of bones and forest foliage sits atop her regal head. She shimmers in the light, seeming one with nature. *The Spirit Mother.*

"What—" Myla presses a hand to her chest, and she steps backward, her free hand instinctively cradling her belly. "Where did you come from?"

Her voice is not that of a human. It is a siren, carrying words on the wind, an echo of a memory more than audible sentences. "I go where I am needed. Here, it seems, is where I am needed."

Myla ventures closer, hesitating at first. "Did I summon you?" Of all the incredible feats she has carried out in her life, Myla is certain that summoning the Spirit Mother would surely be at the top of the list.

"Not exactly," she replies, taking a step toward Myla, her round face full of a gentle smile. "But here you have been, night after night, in search of someone to give you hope. So, I came."

"Is Bryar with you?" Myla glances past into the portal, half expecting to see a small herd of armored men clamoring through.

"He must return to you the way he came. I do not come bearing your captain; I come bearing a path to set your feet upon." As her words drip forth like a slow spring, the earth around them prepares for the Spirit Mother's guidance, a deep wind stirring up leaves around them and the wildlife scattering and silencing themselves.

"I do not understand," Myla protests. "I have worshiped you my entire life, and I have never summoned you. You could come to us the whole time . . ."

"I could not," she corrects, her voice reprimanding. "You called for me, and I sensed the need, so I came."

"But how did I know to do . . . this . . ." Myla gestures to the still moving etchings upon the earth.

"These are not the answers I have come to give you. You must listen because your portal will not remain open long." Myla urges herself to be silent despite the questions begging to be answered. Content with her silence, the Spirit Mother speaks again. "When the captain returns, tell him to follow the fire. This will lead you both to answers you will need if you are to succeed."

"Follow the fire? And he will know what this means?" Myla feels a panic rise in her chest as the round cheeks of the Spirit Mother stretch into a warm smile.

"He will not. At first." Then she is gone, like a mist swallowed up in a vortex, the Spirit Mother retreats through the portal, leaving behind a cloud of disturbed dust and twigs.

Myla experiences a rush of anger. Her visit has left her with more questions than she had before. What was the purpose of telling her as opposed to Bryar? What could "follow the fire" mean? How did she summon the Spirit Mother without knowing how to do it nor intending to? Where is Bryar and how much longer will he be gone?

Feeling flushed and fatigued, Myla sits down, dropping her head into her hands with an exasperated sigh. Her moment of grounding for the day has instead resulted in feeling like a million drifting loose ends, billowing in the breeze without direction nor another end to fasten to. Her offerings lay scattered from the chaos of the portal forming. Myla retrieves what she can, arranging them once more at the base of the tree, before standing.

"I suppose we will just have to talk tomorrow; I have to go help pious men do pious work," Myla says, hoping her words drift upwards to wherever Elsa is and find her well. Even in death, Myla is firmly convinced whatever Elsa is doing, it is far more interesting than incubating a child in a woodland monastery.

It is well past nightfall, and Myla's body aches from a day of labor. Several of the monks commented on the tremble of the earth and the prominent smoke plume which still presides over the back of mountain. Myla says nothing, not wanting to admit she somehow caused it.

The monks made a celebration of their harvest. The bards sang, mulled wine was served with a simple meal, and then a 'gratitude ceremony,' as she heard it referenced, was held. They prayed over their harvest, and the rest of the day was spent carrying basketful after basketful of gourds to the cellar. Myla had watched the sun move across the sky, enjoying the minimal glow of warmth, which did not disturb the early autumn chill.

Now, she sits peacefully on a cushioned armchair near the blazing fire. As it has these many nights prior, her mind drifts to an introspective state. Something about the stillness of life in this place allows for deep contemplation. *Perhaps that is why they come.* She looks sidelong at Ethstan, who also sits staring into the flames. *Perhaps that is why he is silent.*

So often, Myla has found that pieces of the last six years have gnawed at her. Easily dismissible thoughts as they are, they still lurk in the places of her conscious where justice seems to reign.

"It is disturbing." She breaks the silence, drawing Ethstan's attention. "I feel as though I was conditioned my entire life to fall willingly into complacency, to never say 'no' lest it interfere with plans larger than my preferences."

Ethstan's brow turns upward, and the line of his mouth draws thin, his expression seems to say, "Well, that is a damn shame, is it not?" There would be a heavy emphasis on the *damn,* she is sure of it. He smiles when she says things the others grimace at.

Myla is still convinced he does not belong here.

"I can think of a lot of people to blame, people who made me this way . . . afraid to tell a man when I do not like his touch. Or afraid to speak up in a room full of men, my father included, making decisions in my name. But the only person I can truly blame is myself. I am a woman now; I have been for a long time. There is no reason for me to fear my words and how they make others feel. Especially when their disrespect glares in my face like a beacon, no effort to even hide it."

Ethstan nods slowly, his old face weighted with approval and his hands quietly applauding.

"I know I keep saying it, but I wish you could speak; I think you would have lots of answers for me."

At this, Ethstan shakes his head 'no' making Myla wonder further at the atonement Martin speaks of. What could silence possibly atone for? Her former statement seems to have struck a nerve. Ethstan stands slowly and with a weak smile, he leaves.

Myla watches as the old man shuffles toward the kitchens, and a small voice inside her begs for sweet buns. Not usually being one for treats, Myla looks down at her stomach with a soft smile. "Stop, little one. No midnight snacks. It will keep us awake past our bedtime."

It is not ten minutes later when Ethstan reappears, walking even slower to avoid spilling the cup of tea he carries. Myla expects him to sit down and begin sipping it himself, but he hands it to her instead with a kind smile and a reassuring touch of the shoulder. Prompted by memories of Elsa and Fern bringing her nightly tea, a swell of emotions lays just behind her smile. "Thank you."

Ethstan does not sit. He leaves her to her tea and her thoughts for good this time. Myla's eyes drift to the large window to her left, which faces the mountain of the Seer, an eerie outline glows red with embers, which she studies until slipping unknowingly into a deep sleep, lulled by the crackling of the fireplace.

Chapter 14

The black gloved hand descends, one icy finger after another, curling around her throat. Myla's eyes snap open and horror implodes within, as she sets disoriented eyes on the sharp features of Vesperian. Panic crawls through her body, and her hands grapple at his, which are currently putting a stop to her screams. Myla arches her back, trying to break free, but the devil smiles menacingly down on her, forcing her back deeper into the chair.

"You can not escape me, my Ruthless Queen. Wherever you hide, I will find you." His hands relinquish their grip and snake down her throat, past her breasts and to the dagger at her waist. A nimble fingertip grazes the sharpest point of the blade. Myla opens her mouth to cry out for help, but she is unable to conjure a sound. Her hands, free to fight back, lay pinned at her side by invisible chains. Her head screams out *fight,* but her body refuses to comply.

Vesperian, wearing a cruel look of satisfaction, moves his hand from the blade, bringing it to her belly. "You did not tell me you have a little antidote of your own here." His words spew like venom, the threat within them searching for her vulnerabilities.

Myla's chest constricts, something fiercely maternal springing to life. All at once, she sees herself from overhead, like a storyteller looking down upon its subjects.

With a twitch of his wrist, Vesperian takes complete control of her body in a way he never has. She is lurched to her feet, control of her limbs completely sabotaged.

"You see," he whispers, leaning in so his hot breath mists her skin. "I can not allow such a powerful child to live. You know it; it is why your pathetic excuse of a lover has hidden you here, and you have so stupidly stayed."

Myla quivers, every ounce of energy she has bubbling inside, begging her body to move; yet, it betrays her, surrendering entirely to the whims of the Blood Stealer. Her fingers twitch as an impulse to grip the blade takes hold of her. Sweat pebbles on her brow, straining to resist his will. A sob, instantly silenced by a tightness of her throat slips, her protests quieted at his pleasure.

A smile darkens his face, and he crosses his arms over his chest, watching with satisfaction as she retrieves the blade and turns it to point inward, pricking her abdomen.

Myla's eyes dart around the room, she is overcome with a silent plea for help, for anyone to see her and *help.* Out of the corner of her eye, she spies Martin, made small by fear and the inability to wield a weapon.

"His aura," he whispers, pointing a pudgy finger at Vesperian. "It is black."

Myla rages with anger as this man, someone who swore she was safe here, watches unmoving. Vesperian laughs, a sinister sound vibrating from deep within the blackness of his soul. "Her aura must be black too, watch how she lets this happen," he taunts, eyes lingering on her whitened knuckles wrapped around the fox dagger. "You do not want this child, admit it. The spawn of a king who could be killed so easily. What a shameful legacy to carry within your sacred temple."

Myla tries to shake her head, barely managing to mutter a plea. "N-*no. Please!"* Then, her hands do the unimaginable. A wrenching scream escapes her lips and as she plunges the dagger inside her belly, agony ripples through her body. Blood sprays, soaking through her white shift. A tiny cry of betrayal slips out from within her womb. The frail voice begging to understand, *'Why, Mother?'*

The vile deed done, Vesperian releases his grip on her. Myla stumbles backward, her shriek of horror and pain filling every humble corner of the monastery. "Wake up, Myla," Vesperian says. "Stop pretending to be something you are not."

Myla feels a firm shake of her shoulders, and a voice in the distance calls for her. *"Myla! Wake up."*

She lunges to her feet, her hands at once moving to her stomach. Vesperian is nowhere in sight, and her stomach is not flayed; there is no blood.

Before her, Bryar stands, gripping her by the shoulders with a furrowed brow. "The . . . he . . . Vesperian was just here," she chokes, grasping her neck where she could still feel the ghost of his fingers, the burning pain, gone now. "I—he made me kill . . ." Her voice breaks as she grows red with embarrassment. The background coming into focus, a dozen tired monks stand near inspecting the scene, awoken by her night terror.

"It was not real." Bryar wipes sweaty locks of hair from her brow, his fingers press reassuringly into her shoulders before taking note of the small audience. "There is nothing amiss," he says a little louder, urging the tired men to return to their beds.

Her trembling slowly subsides, and Myla takes in the man before her, earnestly looking her over for any signs that she may be hurt. Which Myla finds ridiculous as she conducts a more thorough inspection of him. His hair a tousled mess, lightly coated with dust. Blood is dried across his brow, sprayed as though he cut a throat in close quarters.

Myla gasps, taking note of a bandage wrapped around his shoulder. "What happened to you?"

Rhyland and Callum stand nearby, moving in slow, stiff motions as they shrug out of their armor. Each of them is battered and covered in ash. Rhyland coughs intently.

"What happened out there?" Myla demands.

Bryar reaches over his shoulder with a cringe, trying to loosen his breastplate. Myla intercepts his hand, unlinking the fastenings and listening as he speaks.

"The Raven's Veil scouts, as you know. Ever since you . . . since he got ahold of you, I have them keeping a closer eye on any territories the Blood Stealer may have a heavier hold on." He winces as Myla peels the breastplate off him, sticky with blood. Myla's eyes widen, and she peeks beneath the bandage, her stomach quelling at the sight. "He has wolves under his control, and a month or so back, a few of my men reported a pack traveling toward the Seer's lair."

Myla swallows hard, realization dawning. "That is why you did not want me to go?"

He nods, unbuckling his belt so a heavy blade falls from his waist. He grunts in relief as weight sheds. Martin and Ethstan, both now wide awake, appear bearing plates of warmed breads and meats. "We were apprehended on the journey back last night."

Callum cracks a weak smile. "Bryar blasted the *shit* out of them. I thought he was going to burn the mountain down."

Rhyland cackles between swigs of wine, nodding in agreement. "I have never seen a crater form in the earth like that. Now we have survived it . . . I will admit it was impressive."

"You have never done much sight-seeing beyond the various *bedrooms* you visit," Callum adds, rolling his eyes.

"Just because I am an equal opportunist, does not mean I do not have life experiences beyond those," Rhyland retorts "I just do not tell you everything."

"You tell me enough."

With a shake of her head, Myla looks to Bryar for clarification, surprised to see he is not enjoying his friends' banter in the least. Their exchanges normally liven him up.

"Survived the *wolves*?" she clarifies.

"No," Bryar answers gruffly, choking on ash. "Survived the crater."

"The earth looked like it split in half," Callum adds. "There was this moment when the rubble on the precipice of it started sliding in—it was an avalanche—"

"Yeah," Rhyland interjects, doubled over and leaning against his thighs for support. "And we were sliding in!"

Myla's breath catches in her throat, her eyes bouncing from one man to the next as they tell the tale as though it is something to be proud of and not a near death experience.

"The rocks falling a hundred feet down were red-hot with flames, and I thought I was falling into hell," Bryar confesses, seeming to conclude the conversation with the riveting statement.

Rhyland and Callum exchange humored glances and Rhyland leans in. “You can not mean to tell me you are going to leave out the best part.”

Bryar wipes an exhausted hand across his face, and he shakes his head, dismissing their enthusiastic retelling. “I do not see any of it as a good story to share.”

“Gods . . .” Ryland rolls his eyes and turns back to Myla. “It was *spectacular.*”

“What was?” Myla probes, feeling annoyed by the banter leaving her piecing the entire story together with the small tidbits they offer.

“He was,” Callum added flatly, nodding toward his captain with reverence. “I have never seen anything like it in my life.” He continues, setting an empty tumbler on the table, “There were no less than fifty of these wolves, and they were not regular wolves.” At this, all three men nodded in agreement, Rhyland emphasizing they were more monster than wolf.

Callum nods in agreement. “They were possessed. They were *massive.* Swords were pointless. So, we started running, but—”

“That was also pointless,” Rhyland interjects with a shiver.

“So,” Callum resumes, “Bryar just turns around—that is when he got bit—and this . . . this explosion erupts from every inch of him, blasting the wolves into the sky.”

“Yeah,” Rhyland speaks again sarcastically, “and our feet out from underneath us.”

He begrudgingly rubs his hips, to which Bryar retorts, “But you are alive.”

In unison, Callum and Rhyland blurt: “Barely.”

Myla smiles slightly, despite the anxiety building in her chest as the details of the journey become more and more grim. Callum goes on to explain the force of the blast split their corner of the mountain completely off. At first, it seemed as though Bryar had only created a deep crevasse. But as the seconds passed, the mountain moaned beneath the weight of its shifting side, and the earth began swallowing the rubble, caving the side of the mountain in deeper, an 'avalanche into the abyss', as Rhyland dramatically described it.

Myla feels a shiver of awe as Callum leans closer to her, his eyes alight in amazement. "I swear to the gods, there is no human explanation for what happened, Myla. He was not just emitting fire—he *was* fire. And the blast he loosed, it was God-like."

Myla looks to Bryar who seems completely disassociated from the conversation, his eyes fixed on the untouched meal before him.

Callum speaks, his words whispered now as though what he says next is a dark secret that should not be revealed. "There was this unbearably hot wave rushing off of him as he . . . stopped the avalanche. He *stopped it.* With fire. It melted the rocks and evaporated the snow. The entire side of that mountain is a slab of granite now."

Myla's eyes widen, wondering how that much power could come from one man.

Bryar stands suddenly, walking away. Myla moves to follow, but Rhyland stops her.

"Something about this has him out of sorts." Both men look to each other, nodding in agreement. "He has not said a word all day. We have tried telling him that it was *legendary*. But he thinks it was a monstrosity."

Callum interjects. "The only monstrous part was hiking out of that fucking gash in the side of the mountain. It took six hours to get out of it. He broke the Gods-damned mountain, and we had to claw our way out."

Rhyland shakes his head, fiercely agreeing. "We were so deep inside the mountain at that point, I could not see the sun. And the heat—"

"Fuck the heat," Callum interrupts, nearly spitting the words. "I never want to be warm again. Take me somewhere eternally freezing and leave me there. I will die a cheerful icicle."

Myla sits dazed, looking over her shoulder to where Bryar stands. He looks out the window, absently chewing his thumb. His demeanor entirely rigid and numb. Myla presumes he must be in a state of shock. Deciding to give him a moment with his thoughts, she turns back to where her exhausted friends sit.

"What of the Seer? What did she say?"

Both men look defeated now, each exchanging wary gazes.

"We did not see her," Callum confesses, smiling gratefully at Ethstan, who refills his tumbler. "And quite frankly, I do not think he did either."

Myla is about to demand an explanation as hopeless sickening forms in her belly, but Rhyland speaks before she has any time for questions.

"We hiked four days up the side of that horrible mountain, only for Bryar to turn a dark corner and pop his head back around and tell us he saw her and it was time to go." He holds up his hand, five fingers splayed. "Five seconds, Myla. I lost sight of that fucker for five seconds, and he had the audacity to tell me he saw the Seer already. Thing is . . . I turned the corner after him, and it was a dead end. No Seer. No where else to go."

Myla's brows turn in, forming a confused frown. "So, neither of *you* saw the Seer?" They both shake their heads and Callum shrugs, speaking with a mouthful of food. "He swears he did though." They both turn to their meals, devouring the remainder of their plates in silence.

Thinking back to the day before, when she summoned the Spirit Mother, Myla recalls how the earth shook and the way smoke drifted from the back side of the mountain. Myla wonders if Bryar's destruction of the mountain was the rumble she felt when she accidentally summoned the Goddess, not the Goddess arriving herself.

Myla has no sense of time at this point. It feels like hours since she woke from her horrific dream to find Bryar had returned, but as she looks past Bryar's rigid shoulders, she sees it is still an inky black outside.

The bite marks gouging deep into Bryar's shoulder are red and gnarled. His body tenses with each dab of the cloth, but he is silent, and for some reason, Myla is not sure what to say. She had envisioned an uncomfortable hike to the Seer and an uneventful gait back down the mountain. *This* is nothing like anything she could have ever fathomed, and it clearly weighs heavily on him.

Gentle strokes of the warm cloth begin to rub away the layers of blood and ash coating him from the neck up. The steaming water in the basin turns dark quickly, and a tinge of guilt probes at her, wondering how she could have been angry at him when he knew what was in store for them, and he chose to leave her behind and risk her wrath instead.

Wordlessly, Myla coats the wounds in a balm of crushed comfrey and calendula with beeswax before re-bandaging his shoulder in fresh linens. Once he is mended and dressed in fresh clothes, he turns to Myla, his tone stoic, bearing no hints of distress, a pretense Myla sees through.

"I am afraid I do not have clear answers from the Seer," he confesses, sitting next to her, fidgeting with a belt he has yet to put on. "She said everything you need to overcome this is already within you, but that we will see '*a thousand burning ravens*' as you defeat him."

Myla tilts her head, wondering if she heard him right and she can not help but wonder what kind of nonsense '*a thousand burning ravens'* is.

"The Spirit Mother came to see me," Myla says, much to Bryar's shock. He looks directly at her now, his face set firmly.

"She *came* to you?"

"Yes, and she told me something odd. She said we had to '*follow the fire'* if we are to succeed."

Bryar nearly laughs and drops his head into his hands, his arms leaning entirely on his knees. The arch of his back is stiff with exhaustion and his muscles look strained as though his body has yet to relax. "I am not going toward any fires, Myla. What does that even *mean?*"

Myla shakes her head and cautiously places a hand on his leg, worried he is near a snapping point. "I do not know. She also said you would not know what she meant at first, but that you would figure it out."

Again, he chuckles, sitting straight now. "Why is my path always one of fire?"

"Because it is who you are, and colossal amounts of it or not, I am proud of you," she whispers, moving to hold his hand. "Tell me why you are so upset . . . is it fear?"

He begins with a resolute shake of his head, which hesitantly turns into a nod. "I suppose, yes. But also, no," he admits, sighing heavily as he turns to face her. "I told you last week that I felt out of control. *This* is not just *out of control,* though," he says, his words flooding out with an exasperated sigh. "Myla, I think . . . I think I ceased to be human for a moment. I did not feel like myself, and Callum and Rhyland almost died. We all almost died. Not because of the wolves, but because of *me*."

Myla stops him. "Bryar, you must be realistic right now. It sounds like the wolves would have killed you all if they were not stopped. You stopped them. How you accomplished that is a mere detail."

"Yes," Bryar agrees, his voice taking on a tone of frustration. "And

I almost sent half of the mountain sliding down to crush whoever and whatever was beneath it—*that* is no mere detail."

"But you stopped it," Myla insists, holding his hand tighter.

"I stopped it by becoming a monster. It was not fear that woke up whatever *it* was. It was anger."

"You have a lot to be angry about, Bryar. It is ok."

He nods and releases her hand to stand, braving the pain of moving his arm to put the wet linens to hang in front of the hearth.

"Tell me what you were dreaming of when I came back. You were convulsing on the chair."

She shivers, drawing blankets off the bed to cover her shoulders. "I was there, by the fire. I woke up, or thought I was awake. Vesperian was choking me, and then he took control of me again." Myla grazes over the details, not looking to replay the horrors over again. "He made me stab my own stomach to kill her."

Bryar is stunned, his eyes wide and a grimace forming across his face. "That is horrible—but he does not know you are with child, does he?"

"No," Myla responds firmly. "I never told him."

With a deep, shaky sigh, Bryar comes and sits beside her on the bed, leaning back against the headboard. "If I can do again what I did on that mountain yesterday . . . Myla, I might be able to stop Vesperian."

Myla gasps, looking sidelong at him. "What?"

"He may be powerful but his bones crush like anyone else's. I just need to figure out how I did it, so I can bring a mountain down on him."

A smile teases the corner of Myla's mouth, and though she knows now is not the moment, she can not help but think to herself: *That is hot.* Bryar senses the flirtatious smile on her face and shakes his head, pretending not to be entertained. Myla bites her lip to right her face and then looks back at him, her eyes searching his as though all her answers lie there.

"So, how do we get answers about your magic? We can not go back to Falkmere, so the Institute of Mystic Arts is out the question."

Bryar agrees. "Myla, I have no idea where to go for this. It is nothing like the sort of magic they teach at the Institute. It is more akin to—" His voice trails off, and he slowly sits upright, startled eyes fixed on her.

"What?" Myla demands, mirroring his pose to be eye level with him, her pulse jerking ominously as the expression on his face reflects something reminiscent of an internal awakening. "*Bryar,*" she insists. The words of the Goddess echo in her brain, reminding her that he would not know at first what '*follow the fire*' meant, but he would shortly. "Do you know what we are supposed to do?"

His jaw grinds back and forth, and he nods slowly, his eyes glazed over as he stares past her, deep in thought. Moments pass before he finally speaks. "It reminds me of the Ashborn."

They are silent, both digesting the realization, Bryar in horror and Myla in silent awe. *He can not be Ashborn, he looks nothing like them.* Callum had told her earlier that he was not emitting fire, he *was* fire. Myla cautiously poses her question, watching his features shift in dismay as she does. "Do you think they can help you because they are masters at wielding fire, or because you think you may be one of them?"

Bryar chuckles, but there is no humor inflected. "I do not think I am one of them. You know what people say about my mother."

"Just because people say it does not make it true. People make up all kinds of stories in the absence of facts," Myla retorts. "Regardless, if Valyndor is where we need to go, then we will leave at dawn."

"It is a long journey, Myla. I do not like the idea of leaving you here again, but I worry about the toll this might take."

Myla stands and cups his face between her hands, assuring he listens. “I am not fragile, Bryar, and neither is this child. This time, I am coming.”

Chapter 15

Morning welcomes them with a deep autumn glow. The sun casts a shimmer off the back of the mountain, illuminating yellows, and oranges through the trees. Callum and Rhyland are preparing horses, kindly donated by the monks, as Myla and Bryar leave their room.

"I am afraid there are many here who will miss you when you leave," Martin says, nodding specifically toward Ethstan who sits, slightly slumped, in his space at the breakfast table. Myla manages a half smile of acknowledgment before moving to sit beside her silent friend.

"When I pass back through, what are the chances you will be speaking again?" Of course, there is no response but a slight smile and an old hand atop hers. "I am going somewhere I have never been before. I am afraid," she confesses, her voice low enough so only he can hear. "But, I will go see it anyway, so I might return here and tell you all about it—perhaps I shall take you with me, if you ever decide you would like to see new parts of the realm."

Ethstan nods approvingly, his old eyes glistening with hope, and gestures toward the door as if to say, 'get on with it.' Standing, she presses a kiss to the monk's cheek and steps outside.

"How far will we ride today?" Rhyland inquires, firmly fastening the straps of his saddle and sliding his sword inside its sheath.

"*You* will ride all the way back to Falkmere." Bryar transitions into captain mode, giving instructions which send Rhyland to assess the situation in Falkmere, and Callum to move a company of the Raven's Veil into Titonfall. "Once you have moved them into Titonfall, I need you to take a smaller company and scout out the Seam, gather information on this antidote, and return back to us with any answers."

"Why Titonfall?" Callum asks, cinching the straps of his saddlebag with a grunt.

"If there is to be a fight, I want to attack him from both sides."

"And when I have gathered information regarding Falkmere?" Rhyland asks, clearly at unease. Myla does not blame him; she would much rather make for wild and unknown places than return back to the destruction and political upheaval that will no doubt greet him in Falkmere.

"If there is anything you can do to help, do so. I trust your judgment. But if the Blood Stealer lives, and is still presiding over the palace, join Callum and send word my way."

"Which is . . .?"

Bryar clears his throat before he answers, "Valyndor," quickly as though he hopes to avoid any further discussion. Unfortunately, his comrades are cunning, and a grin claims Rhyland's face.

"That is brilliant. They will know how to help you."

Both men move to shake hands with Bryar and they exchange brief goodbyes before mounting their horses.

Rhyland sets off east, while Callum rides ahead of them, his path moving southwest toward the black mountains and the darkness they hold there. Meanwhile, Myla, astride a chestnut brown mare, follows Bryar west.

Myla has never been west. She has heard stories of the wildness, which seems to multiply the closer to the Seam one gets, but seeing it for herself has never been in the forefront of her mind. Especially over the past two years, her logical brain, when disassociating from her impulses, is very keen on staying *away* from the Seam. Now, they will ride past it. Granted, Bryar plans to add an extra day to their journey in order to give it a wide berth. Nevertheless, on opposite ends of the realm, she feels the pull. Closer proximity to Vesperian's stronghold will no doubt feel different.

For hours, their progress is slow as they maneuver the horses through dense forest. Myla does not mind; it affords her time to truly take in the beauty of the woodland terrain. Small creeks jutting off the river to the sea meander through the woodlands. Ebonbark trees, with trunks so wide in circumference five men could not circle them, rise from the earth like the towers of Falkmere palace. Their bark is darker than the trees nearer to Falkmere. If one has deep cuts, the sap of an Ebonbark tree is known to heal at a quicker rate than other natural remedies. Lichen drapes from their branches, resembling wild curtains, gently billowing in the breeze. Ahead, Bryar cuts a thicket of hanging Thornveil ivy aside to pass between two larger trees. The barbs of the ivy are sharp and known to ensnare prey, and certainly cut through flesh with ease. Blanketing the forest floor are Nymrien plants, a type of fern known to be used by the old Gods as a divination tool. Lavinia used to tell Myla that runes would appear on the fronds of the ferns when used in certain spells.

Appearing in an opening which offers an impressive view, Myla catches her breath, astonished by the treacherous landscape before her. The forest thins and gives way to a wasteland of ruins. Though trees and plant life still flourish, the growth is new and sprouts sporadically wherever the rubble of the flattened city allows. What used to be a stone roof is now cracked down the middle and mostly sunken into the earth. A row of pillars lays toppled, one over the other, being slowly consumed by the leafy claws of nature. Walls, bridges, arches, and towers alike, all in crumbled ruins, scattered across the earth as far as she can see. As though the ground beneath stretched open hungry jaws in an attempt to swallow the city whole.

"Is this safe for the horses?" Myla asks, taking in the sharp claws of rocks cleaving from the earth. One wrong step and she would be sitting on two halves of one horse.

Bryar draws his horse in with a hushed 'whoa,' assessing the situation before dismounting. "We will walk them through here," he answers, looking at the road before them grimly.

Myla dismounts and begins leading her mare by the reins, maneuvering across the jagged maze of black and gray, a few paces behind Bryar. "How far does this stretch, do you know?" she asks, trying to see an end in sight, to no avail. Even looking down from an incline, the bleak wasteland carries on out of sight.

"I do not," he answers simply.

They cover ground at a miserably slow rate, and Myla begins to curse her skirts, treading over the hems often. The deeper they submerge themselves within the ruins, the grimmer the landscape becomes. Bones protrude from between stone structures, the story of countless people caught in the wrong place at the wrong time.

A crumbling wall here, an archway there, a skeleton at her feet. They pass an abandoned shelter, appearing to have been built more recently, most likely by a traveler like themselves.   Myla takes in a deep breath and sidesteps a crevasse in the stone beneath her feet. "This is horrible," she mutters, dragging her free hand absently across the rivets of a cockeyed pillar.

Bryar nods in agreement. "We are on the outskirts of Old Falkmere. If we turned northeast and traveled that way for a few days, we would find the old palace."

"I did not realize how expansive the territories of Old Falkmere were. The city alone is the size of New Falkmere's territory," Myla remarks, thinking maps do not do the size of Myrnith, in general, any justice.

"We act like New Falkmere will go down in history as the greatest territory to have been reigned over. Most people do not realize we have already lost that battle by a long shot." He smiles halfheartedly at her. "Sorry to be the bearer of bad news."

Myla shrugs. "I missed the part of queen-training where I was supposed to care about such things."

Bryar chuckles slightly, glancing over his shoulder to watch that she and her horse maneuver around a difficult pile of rubble without harm. "I am sure your heir will make up for whatever ambitions of conquering you lack."

"I suppose she will not have much of a choice, will she?" Myla thinks what a shame it is to be born a queen. Her life is laid out before her already, and she does not even know what a *queen* is.

"I suppose not," Bryar agrees.

Memories of a mage who could pierce the crust of the earth with molten rocks from beneath the surface drift through Myla's brain in illustrations she recalls from a history book. He flattened most of the Old Falkmere Palace in mere seconds when the ground beneath it split open, making way for massive boulders, shattering the foundations of the palace and city. Legends told in pubs, or by cruel nannies before bed, state that if one examines the ruins closely, you can still find sprays of blood from where people were impaled in the process. Upon closer examination, Myla finds this to be true and shivers.

"You sent Rhyland back to Falkmere . . . not Callum." Myla says, after about a mile of silence.

Bryar glances back at her with a grim nod. "Callum is better at damage control than Rhyland, but . . . I could not bring myself to send him there to clean up the mess she died in."

Myla bites her bottom lip, nodding. "You were right to do it that way, then. Let us just hope Rhyland does not start another war." He has a certain sort of impulsivity which has served him well over the years. But in positions of authority, Myla wonders how that trait will function.

Bryar chuckles. "What is one more battle thrown on our plate?"

Myla smiles at his attempt at a joke, not daring to admit she is already weary.

"You know," Myla announces, "I do not feel like a queen anymore."

"Why is that?" Bryar asks, urging his horse to scale a small ledge. Myla mimics his path and accepts a hand up before answering.

"I guess the crown just seems to be fading from who I am, the further I get from Falkmere." She smiles slightly, hoping he can not hear how out of breath she is as she speaks. "You also have a way of making me feel like I am just a woman."

"I guess it helps I knew you for far longer as just a girl than as a queen," he responds. They both stop, each panting from the exertion. "I would rather you not feel like *just* a woman with me, though."

"No, it is a good thing," Myla assures, glancing past him to the never-ending stretch of rock and ruin. "I suppose maybe it is more that the time I have been away from Falkmere has allowed me to remember little parts of myself I used to appreciate—you are helping me see them again." Breathlessly, she steps over what appears to be a fossilized horse, cringing at the reminders of war beneath her feet. "Now, how far will we go today?"

Bryar turns to examine the path ahead of them, concern moving across his face. "I would rather not stop here tonight. Any manner of creature might call this home." Myla shivers as he mumbles a defeated 'but' and proceeds to state the obvious: the slow-moving path stretches for miles. A century of rubble has settled in place, some clattering to the ground and blocking potential paths. Weaving through the mess, while navigating in the correct direction, is time consuming. Myla begins to imagine they will spend days here. Then, an idea pricks the back of her mind.

Clearing her throat, hesitant to even mention it, Myla gives him a warming smile. "That thing you did to the mountain. Suppose you could do it on a smaller—*much* smaller scale. Could you clear us a path?"

Unimpressed and wordless, Bryar stares at her. His brows drooping almost comically over his green eyes. He does not need to respond. His face says it all. *You are fucking kidding me, right?*

"Listen, it is just that the entire point of going to Valyndor is so you can hone these skills. There is no harm in practicing."

"I am not looking to *hone* them, Myla. I am looking to *control* them. In any case, the harm is the attention it would draw." He pauses. "And that is not the only reason we go to Valyndor. You must try and form an alliance with the Ashborn, if we have any hope of defeating the Blood Stealer. I doubt the raven ever made it to them. Surely, they would have responded to Falkmere's aid if it had." With an air of finality, he turns back toward the rocks. There is no room for argument. With a sigh, Myla lifts the hem of her skirt, tying it in a knot which bobs at her knees, and follows Bryar onward.

It is past midnight when they finally stop. It is here, Myla realizes, that a difference in strength will show itself. In the way of magic, up until this point, that is, Myla has surpassed Bryar in every way. However, in sheer stamina, Bryar is every bit a warrior. He seems untouched by the many miles of road they have left behind them.

He has selected what appears to be an old pergola as their stopping place for the night. It is the first shelter they have found to be mostly covered on all sides in miles. Myla imagines it was once a lovely hideaway, but now it is piled deep in rubble, only a small opening allowing entry.

Bryar climbs in first, ensuring it is clear, before extending a hand to help her in.

"No fire," he instructs, retrieving thick woolen cloaks from their saddle bags. "We will have to make do with these."

Myla shrouds herself in one of the cloaks, watching anxiously as he leaves their shelter to tie the horses. It is pitch-black within the pergola, and Myla must strain to see anything. *No fire for warmth, no fire for light.* She looks at her hands, imagining summoning a small glow before shoving them beneath her armpits for warmth. *No light for light.* Bryar returns, the scuff of his boots kicking up dust.

"Get some sleep," he instructs, sitting next to her. His tone is unusually aloof, a characteristic he seems to have brought back down the mountain with him, causing Myla to pause. Disgruntled, aching, and not in the mood to dissect whatever foul mood he is stuck in, Myla lowers herself to the ground, ignoring the small voice in the back of her head which says it would be much softer to lie against him as opposed to the rugged earth.

Myla wakes to regret her decision. Her body feels as stiff as a board when Bryar gently nudges her awake. Opening her eyes to find it is still dark, Myla swats at his hand, pleading for another hour of sleep. As the words reach her lips, she finds his hand clamped over her mouth.

"Quiet," he whispers, "and look." Her gaze follows where his gloved finger points to something eerie: orbs of light flickering in various points across the rubble city, and nothing accompanying them to indicate life nearby. Yet, something has to be causing this.

Myla leans forward, quietly scanning the darkness for any sign of life. Nothing satisfies her curiosity, and both she and Bryar sit in silence. They watch the orbs drift past, like a parade of souls departing, each projecting a different light; some small, some large, each unique in its own way. Myla strains, certain she can hear a sad song in the distance, reminding her of that which was sung beside Caius's pyre. Flame wielders, Bryar included, had set the pyre ablaze while a chorus of haunting melodies were sung, serenading him into the next life. This moment feels similar.

"What is this?" she whispers, wondering if Bryar has met with anything like this in any of his adventuring. He shakes his head, equally awestruck, and together, they watch the ethereal lights drift by, by the thousands, until they are hushed away by daybreak. Their proximity to The Seam makes the hue of the sun a blood red, washing the terrain in a crimson tint.

"I have read nearly every text on lore and the fantastical that my father's and Caius's libraries held, save one or two," Myla declares later, still fixated on the scene as they continue their journey. "And I have never read of such a thing." Burned in her mind's eye, the bobbing orbs of light against the magnificent night sky may be one of the most magical things she has ever beheld.

"Perhaps it was in the one or two that you *did not* read," Bryar teases. "I will add it to the list of things we will ask the Ashborn."

"Now would be a wonderful time for the Spirit Mother to spontaneously appear," Myla adds. "She seems like someone who would know about them."

"You speak of the lights as if they are living."

Myla purses her lips in thought and shifts the reins, so she stands on the side of the horse closest to Bryar. "I think they are."

He flashes her a perplexed look. "Really?"

"They had energy within them, could you not feel it?"

He seems to reflect, his brows furrowed in deep thought. "Well, I suppose they did not seem inanimate by any means."

"See," Myla insists, "there was something to them . . . something that felt lonely."

The hint of a smile teases the corner of his mouth. "Surrounded by a thousand others just like them?"

Myla ignores the twinge of annoyance stabbing at her chest. "You can be surrounded by endless streams of people and still feel lonely. Believe me," she adds bitterly. "I would know."

Thoughtful remorse blankets his demeanor. "I know. I do not know why I said that."

"You have not been the same since you got back from that mountain," Myla says softly. "I wish you had not gone."

His jaw clenches followed by a growled string of words. "I went for *you. Believe me,* I wish I had not gone either. It felt useless."

It is Myla's turn to feel remorseful. "I am sorry—" she fumbles over an apology, feeling torn between sorry and seething. "I just feel like you left something up there, and I can not put my finger on what it is."

"Myla." He stops dead in his tracks, turning to face her. His expression is unlike any he is ever worn when addressing her. It is alarming.

"Can we just...not talk about this?" He points toward the path before them, his heavy chainmail clanking in the process. "Can we just...walk and get this over with?"

Get this over with. She plays the words over in her head as they walk on in silence, wondering what exactly could prompt the shortness toward her. A thought she would mull over for the next two hours until he speaks again, this time using a less aggressive tone.

"I see the end!" He points toward the horizon, their line of sight impaired by the glare of sunlight overhead. Myla squints, shielding her eyes with a hand, gratitude washing over her as the terrain slowly evens, and the ruins become more scattered, making way for quicker travel.

"We can ride the horses again in a few miles," Bryar announces. "We will make good ground today."

Finally able to ride and pass the miles with galloping horses beneath them, the scenery changes rapidly. At first, they pass through more barren wasteland, nothing but dusty ruins and young foliage. The dreariness, in time, transforms into a hillside scape, earth's green carpeting slowly evolving into a forest growing from the marshes.

In all her years, Myla has never seen a world so diverse, so spectacularly watched over by the gnawing teeth of mountains to her left. There is a chill in the air and a freshness of breath. It is wild, untamed, and less touched by civilization. While the ground beneath her feet is green and the trees all blaze with autumn colors, as her eyes travel the great height of the mountains, all she can see is snow and ice and billowing clouds. A long, skinny fox jets across their path, stopping briefly to blink its beady eyes in their direction, before dipping into a thicket of willows. Myla smiles, wondering where it is off to. How simple the life of a fox must be.

She wants to ask Bryar if he has been somewhere so wild before, but his face is unreadable, and the only words coming from his lips are prompts for the horses to drink and rest. Instead, she checks that he has the horses under control, and she walks downstream, balancing from rock to rock and enjoying the babbling of water over boulders.

Across the way, a deer dips into the forest, turning briefly to watch them, taking stock of the possible threat they pose. Myla wishes she could tell the beast she is a friend, but the spotted doe disappears as quickly as she appeared.

A bed of willows ahead catches sunlight on their thin, ice coated reeds. Behind, in the distance, the black mountains pierce the brilliant blue of the sky, a sight Myla promptly ignores. Without taking note of distance nor time, Myla immerses herself in her senses, experiencing everything nature has to offer her, until she has walked far out of eyesight and earshot of the captain.

There is an alluring glisten in the water and the way the current begins to violently crash, this part of the river picking up in speed and intensity. A sudden insatiable need to lie in the water, to soak in it—to *drown* in it—washes over her. A sensation that drives fear to her core.

"No," Myla says between gritted teeth, though her feet move against her will. "*No!*" she insists again, trying to resist the uncontrollable propelling of her body. She stumbles forward, her feet splashing into the water, and gasps at the shocking cold sending an aching through her.

Bryar is nowhere to be seen; she has walked too far. With the thundering of the river, he would not hear her scream even if she could, which she can not, though her throat tenses with effort. Somewhere, Vesperian sits, bored and burning with the need to torment her.

Myla realizes these past years, the little twinges of need and desire to appease him have been child's play. Somewhere in the back of her mind, she wondered why so many fell victim to him when suppressing those impulses had only been a matter of focus and mental strength.

Foolish thoughts, she realizes in a flash as she stumbles face first into the shallow water. Ice envelops her, stiffening her limbs and halting her breath with a *smack.* Something hard jabs her ribcage. Her mind, a jumble of panic, begs her to sit up and move toward the banks, while her body crawls through the rigid water, slipping painfully over the smoothed boulders, seeking a deeper water to die in.

A sob manages to slip from her lips as the water grows deeper and deeper until she is submerged. All that is left to do is lie down and take a deep breath. Hot tears leave her eyes to float away in the icy cold water, never reaching her freezing cheeks; her body trembles as the cold of the water paralyzes her limbs. Myla's only thought is of the poor child inside her, wondering why its mother's body is suddenly cold and tensing around what should be a warm, comforting oasis.

Like a newly sharpened blade, the cut of the icy water against her neck, then her chin, and finally her face, pulls her down until the light above merely ripples like a kaleidoscope, waving goodbye to her.

Fuck you, Vesperian. What a lovely final thought. Myla pictures him drowning next to her, his lungs aching like hers do. An overwhelming need to breathe tempts her, whispering, 'Take a breath right now; it is ok.'

She is ready to comply when the light overhead takes on an irregular pattern, disturbed by something crashing into the water. Not something, someone.

"What the *fuck,* Myla!" Bryar screams, on the verge of chastising when he feels her body resisting his rescue.

"Please, do not let me go!" Adrenaline squeezes the words from her lungs like gravel, while her body thrashes against his, scrambling to return to its watery grave.

Bryar's hands lock like irons around her arms, and he drags her to the bank, his face twisted with panic, assessing the slightness of her frame within the layers of dripping fabric. "Stop fighting me!" he demands, now wrapping his arms tight around her to combat her vicious attempts to break free.

Shivering and confused, Myla wills her body to calm, but it does not. It thrashes, fighting to return to the river. "I can not!" she manages.

All at once, his face shifts to understanding, and he mutters an angry '*fuck this*' under his breath. Though she fights him, it is more of a nuisance than a real struggle against his war-trained body. He manages to twist one of her arms into a position which locks her in place, sending a burning tightness through her joints. Meanwhile, he unfastens his belt and loops it around her, lashing her arms at her side, making it easier to throw her over his shoulder and move her as far from the edge of the water as possible.

The sensations fade at an agonizingly slow rate, all the while Bryar sits, back braced against a tree and both arms holding her in place. Somewhere in the chaos of her writhing, she hears him whisper, "It will be alright, just breathe."

Her full body convulsions subside to slight flinches until she releases the tension, Vesperian letting go. For now.

"Is it over?" Bryar finally pants, not releasing until she mutters a fatigued 'yes'.

At once, he unbinds her, moving to stand before her. "We need to get you out of these wet clothes." He fumbles with the clasp of her cloak. "Can you undress? I need to start a fire."

Numb, both physically and emotionally, Myla nods and wills her aching body to move, but her ribs scream against the motion. "Shit," she confesses. "I think I broke my ribs."

Frustration washes his features, and Bryar stands, neglecting a pile of kindling. "Relax," he commands, and she listens, her arms dropping at her side.

Myla never imagined standing naked in the woods in autumn would be warming, but the shedding of her drenched layers removes an element of cold. Bryar is quick to wrap his cloak around her for warmth while he digs for a change of trousers and a white tunic from his saddle bag. "Wear these while we dry your dress."

Chapter 16

Myla stands, wearing men's clothing, beside a raging fire, its warmth sending needles of pain across her body. Bryar wraps a firm brace of bandages around her ribs, before helping her sit on a fallen log, and taking up a crouching position across from her. He has no need to change, nor warm himself. Myla watches as he summons his magic, ripples of heat rising off his body, send steam into the frigid air around him. Soon enough, his clothes are dry, and his armor looks hot to the touch. Meanwhile, she sits shivering by the fire, hair wet and clinging to her face.

"What . . . happened?" he asks, eyes searching hers earnestly.

Myla bites her lower lip, mind bouncing from fear to anger to full panic, as she wonders if her child survived the incident. "I do not know," Myla lies, not wanting to relive what Vesperian's invasions feel like.

Bryar flashes her a glacial expression, as cold as the river, before pressing the matter. "It was him, was it not?"

Fighting a new wave of tears, Myla swallows hard, her silence all the answer he needs. Bryar stands angrily, tossing his gloves to the ground. "This has to end," he blurts, looking to her with kindness this time. "Are you ok?"

The question tips her resolve, spilling her emotional cup. "No," she hisses, through tears of anger. "I just went for a walk that ended in me trying to *kill myself.* My body is starting to do things my brain does not want it to! And now, it is doing things that could harm my baby." Her words are a flood, muting every natural sound around them, until all she can hear are her fears spewed and on display. "I dreamed he made me drive a dagger into my womb. Until this point, those awful things only happened in my dreams, I took comfort in that. But *now*? Bryar, I do not know when or how he will strike again, only that he surely will. So, no, I am not, *okay*."

Bryar moves around the raging fire to sit beside her, pulling her into his arms, his embrace a silent reassurance. "Alright," he says confidently. "We will ride one horse from here out, and I will keep watch while you sleep, so you can not hurt yourself. I promised to keep you alive, and I mean to see that through. I have you; do you hear me?"

She nods into his chest, taking a deep, calming breath. "We need to do something soon . . . I am a threat to the baby."

"I know," he answers, voice full of concern. "Let us just get to the Ashborn. According to the Seer, our next steps should take us there."

Myla does not feel herself. The hours fade into a bitterly frosty night, thankfully warded off by the rage of the blazing fire which Bryar keeps fed. Though the stars overhead sparkle gloriously in the sky, and the tree line creates an interesting pattern against the hues of midnight blue, her earlier sense of awe has vanished.

With a frustrated huff, Myla peels off her boots and stands, wiggling her toes deep into the cold earth. Closing her eyes, she presses two flat palms to her chest, and feels her breath come in steady waves. Moments pass and the quivering in her veins seems to still. "I am still here," she whispers comfortingly to the Spirit Mother. "Help me keep it that way." Tears fall freely, freezing against her cheeks.

"You look like someone I used to know." His voice is thick with a need for sleep, and Myla realizes the hour is late. Myla opens her eyes, catching the outline of Bryar, illuminated from behind the glow of the fire.

"*Used* to know?" she asks, rubbing her hands together and savoring the feel of dirt between them.

"It appears, I still do," he amends. "I just did not know she still worshiped the old Goddesses." He moves to stand before her, his deep green eyes studying her.

Myla breaches the small space between them, to takes his hand, wanting nothing more than to fall against his solid frame and feel his warmth. "I never stopped. It was simply, more discreet."

Bryar releases one hand to slip around her waist, holding her close. "Your tears . . ."

Myla nods, managing a small smile. "I fear there will be many more. I am scared for myself, the awful things happening to me, and . . . well, Elsa is worth an ocean of them."

Bryar presses a thumb to her swollen cheek and kisses her forehead. "I told you; I would not let anything happen to you; you will survive this. Dry your tears; between you and Callum, I fear the world might flood."

"I suppose it is a good thing I taught you how to swim all those years ago, then," Myla teases. Bryar laughs and his gentle hand shifts, digging fingers into a sensitive spot above her hips, evoking a brief squealed protest.

"We agreed not to talk about *that*," he whispers. "Suppose bandits were to hear."

"I would be more concerned about the *presence* of bandits, than of them hearing that you did not know how to swim twelve years ago," she teases in return, her hand pressed against his neck. "It seems we taught each other a great deal of things. Do you remember the night we first . . ." Her words drift off, innuendo sufficiently ending her question for her.

He scrutinizes their surroundings briefly before meeting her gaze. "It was a lot like tonight. We were in the woods, and you had just finished one of your rituals. I thought it was enthralling."

Myla presses herself closer. "You were *mystified.*"

He laughs, though it is more akin to a hungry growl, as his face lowers to hers, their mouths brushing together. Bryar pauses, his lips now barely grazing hers, and his words an ignition of flame. "Should we recreate it?"

She sighs a breathy laugh against his mouth with a playful nip, mimicking a younger version of herself. "Out here? For all to see?"

His hand gropes her trousers at the back of her thighs, holding her close against him, and he mutters against her lips. "Just the Gods and the trees." His mouth closes firmly over hers.

There is an urgency to their movements, a screaming passion and a need for fulfillment. Myla is pressed against the massive tree as Bryar's hand slides up her thigh, pulling her leg around his waist to brace her body against his. Her senses are overwhelmed with the fragrance of Ebonbark trees, wet soil, and the earthiness of dried river water on Bryar, each scent working as an aphrodisiac. Her breath catches in her lungs as she frantically yanks on the ties of his trousers. He wraps one arm beneath her and his other hand braces against the tree trunk.

"These damned trousers," she hisses, her words interrupted by the mingling of his tongue with hers. With a final yank, Myla unfastens his front, making way for her searching fingers. She does not have to search far at all; his length is hard and ready in her hand as he works at the fastenings of her pants. At last, they loosen and fall past her hips with a satisfied sigh from Bryar.

It is euphoric, the way her body shudders in acceptance as he pushes inside her. Myla wraps her arms around his neck and brings her other leg to his waist, linking them at the ankles behind him.

Fully supported by his sturdy frame, she relies on his strength to move her upward and back down again, pulling himself in and out of her. Completely different than the sacrament made at the monastery, this is feverish and animalistic. A tension coils between her thighs, she squeezes tight around him, ready to snap. Myla holds her breath, amplifying the sensation and is nearly tipped over the edge as his teeth find the soft skin beneath her ear. Her fingers grip his thick curls, holding him close, savoring every thrust and the ecstasy they bring.

Bryar's lips explore lower, his arms lifting her high enough to press kisses to the exposed ridges of her breasts beneath the loose tunic which has slipped off her shoulder. His lips create a trail of fire across her chest, which continues down to her core. Crashing together in a panting, sweating tangle, like a colossal wave, they finish in unison. This time, there are no thin walls nor monks present to stifle their gasps and moans for. Only the Gods and the trees to hear how she cries out her ecstasy.

It is only once the pleasant pulsing between her thighs subsides that Myla realizes the bark against her bare ass is sharp and pointed. Meanwhile, a lurching in her stomach propels her into a frenzy.

"Put me down," she pants, nearly pushing him away. Startled, he backs away, holding her elbow as she finds her footing just in time to vomit against the tree they just christened. Startled, Bryar steps toward her, swiping her hair away from her face in one swift motion.

The sickness in her belly leaves her weak and leaning against the tree, unable to subdue the heaving deep inside. Moments of silence pass as Bryar stands behind her, holding her steady and comforting her with silent, gentle pats. After what feels like an eternity of illness churning within, she stands, anxiously facing him and grateful it is too dark for him to see the red-hot embarrassment building on her cheeks.

"Well," he quips matter-of-factly, "I can not say that is good for a man's ego."

Myla laughs, still holding her upset belly, and sits on the forest floor, giving her weak legs a chance to recover from both exhausting experiences which have occurred in the last ten minutes. "I would say we failed the reenactment."

"Miserably," Bryar agrees. "In any case, it was not a tree last time," he adds coyly, expertly navigating the conversation away from her untimely encore. "It was a steep incline, with far too many insects." Bryar points a teasing finger at her belly. "When she arrives, we ought to tell the princess to time her tantrums better."

Myla falls asleep leaning against Bryar. There is no use asking him to sleep as well; he watches over her until dawn. Not even praying to the Spirit Mother and spontaneous sex can rid Myla of the feeling of a voyeur lurking inside her, violating her autonomy from afar. As she readies for another day of travel, she pictures the Blood Stealer, perched atop her throne, surrounded by the ruins of her palace, a dirty boot propped on the bodies of her dead subjects. All while playing her like a puppeteer to pass his time.

His grip is deep and bearing now, rather than a fleeting impulse, it feels like he is occupying her, like he *is* her. Unrelenting tension seems to coil in her chest, constricting her breath, an unyielding reminder, he is not just toying with her anymore. He wills her to surrender. If she would only submit to him, the battle would be over.

There will be blood soon, and Myla fears it will be hers.

Bryar insists they travel quicker now, only stopping to rest their remaining horse, then continue. They ride both day and night. Myla siphons her energy deep within her womb, forming a protective barrier, something she realizes she should have done two weeks ago when they left Falkmere. Now, she hopes it cushions the baby from the brutal gait of their travel.

During the previous two years, she has not formed an emotional attachment to the life within for a myriad of reasons, including uncertainty, and the fact the child felt out of reach—more like an idea than an actual being. Now, she can feel the energy, a contrast from hers, an entirely separate life, which she is responsible for. Now, she must protect it against herself for another five or six months, before she can assign it a more reliable caretaker.

At this thought, her mind drifts to the man behind her, stable and loyal. If she can only hold strong long enough to birth the child, she knows he will protect it, like he has protected her, even if, ultimately, they can not save her from Vesperian.

Myla wonders what would become of her child should she succumb; another mindless chunk of flesh in the Blood Stealer's army. Bryar would take the baby, and raise her far from the conflicts, Myla is sure of it. She makes a mental note to discuss it with him, when they are not riding a thundering horse into a thick, orange and yellow grove of trees.

The vibrant forest reaches upward toward the sky, spectacularly framed on either side by severely pointed mountains which pierce the skyline before disappearing behind fluffy, white clouds. Cliffsides gradually descend and are eventually hidden behind the luscious trees. The cliffs have man-made structures etched into them; beautifully carved belvederes positioned at different intervals of height. Myla assumes they are vantage points, or posts to watch from. The leaves of the trees glow with autumn colors, filtering orange and red patches of sunlight against the gently swaying golden grass blanketing their path. Compared to the way their journey began, surrounded by ruin, this sight strikes Myla as peaceful, safe even.

"Whoa," Bryar instructs the horse, pulling back on the reins. The panting beast halts. "I think this is it," he says, dismounting before helping her down.

"I think you are right," Myla agrees, continuing to take in the scenery with awe. "Look."

She draws his attention to something perched on the cliffside looking down on them and gasps. It is beautiful—*she* is beautiful. Even at a distance, the red-hot glow of her wingspan, tucking into itself as she lands gracefully is magnificent.

"Do you see?" she asks breathlessly before glancing to Bryar, no answer needed. He is transfixed. Something in his countenance has changed from a determined traveler on a mission, to someone seeking answers they have never thought to ask before.

As the creature swoops down off the cliff, disappearing into the trees, Bryar turns and the sunlight glints off the sword at his side. Dread pools in Myla's stomach as a vile feeling builds within her, this time with no intention of harming herself, but a need to kill him. Swift as lightening, Myla reaches to her waist, pulling her dagger free. The motion, though fluid, is no match for a trained soldier. Alarmed, Bryar ducks as her blade slashes the air where his throat was with a menacing *whoosh.*

"Gods-dammit!" he hisses, stumbling backwards to lunge out of her reach.

"I am sorry!" Myla barely manages to speak, her throat tightening once again around her words, stifling her cries for help. All the while, her body betraying her with a ferocity she has never been trained in.

It is reckless. Nothing in her technique resembles the discipline which Sir Roderick took pains to instill in her. This is a violent frenzy. It is *mindless.* Mindless, like the feeble attacks of Vesperian's soldiers.

Across from her, Bryar expertly sidesteps her attempts, his focus unwavering. With every assault, he out-maneuvers her. A frustration, not her own, grows within, until her magic tingles, begging to be released. Vesperian knows she will not best a trained captain this way, but her magic, even at its most spastic, is deadly. It only takes one accurate strike of her light and Bryar could easily be dead.

"Bryar!" she shrieks, the blade falling from her hand, replaced by a subtle light. Stars of gold flecks speckle her skin, until they collect at her fingertips, ready to shoot with lethal precision at her target.

"You have to find a way to make it stop," he says, clearly trying to calm his voice. "Myla, please try."

"I am trying!" she growls, feeling her body begin that terrible quivering of resistance against an impossible force. "You need to run."

He shakes his head. "Not without—"

He is interrupted by a blast of light, which sends soil and foliage flying out from underneath his footing. With a grunt, Bryar is splayed across the ground, barely rolling out of the way before another blast drills a hole where he had been. His features flush with anger and flames begin to crawl across his skin. They are small at first, a flame on his shoulder, a few at his fingers, then they grow. They encompass him, scorching the grass surrounding him and summoning an eerie, honey-red glow in his eyes. As if a ring of fire dances around his pupil.

In this moment, a look of deep, unfiltered fear stretches across his face. "It is happening again," he panics, holding his arms away from his body as though they are traitors. The flames dance and lap off his body violently now, like a fire to a watch beacon, a response to the panic and anger simmering within him.

Myla's ribs scream in agony as she twists to face him, her arms loosing a string of light meant to entangle him. Inwardly, her pain rages fiercer, fear for Bryar's life pulsing through her. Another volley of blinding light launches toward his face, deflected by a violent stream of flames, channeled from his palms. The dueling energies meet in the space between them, billowing, one against the other. Myla calls upon her light, darkness forms overhead, the particles of sun drifting and collecting inside her until there is no longer daylight around them.

"Leave me! I command it!" Myla heaves the words with all her effort, their force unmatched by the next wave of light. A shocked Bryar is flung high into the air, as the deadly blow releases Myla from the invisible hold. She feels her limbs lighten, belonging to herself again, just in time to see his ascent, slowly reversing into a fall. His body rolls midair as he plummets at a fatal speed toward the ground beneath him.

"No!" she shrieks, frantically digging her fingernails into her neck as she grips at herself, at anything, willing someone or something to help him. Just as she considers loosing a strand of light to try and catch him, an explosion of flames engulfs his body, swirling around him in a blazing inferno, one that ought to kill anyone, even a fire wielder. The light of his flames grows, as does the heat. Even from below, Myla's skin crawls in a rush of sweat. It feels as if the sun itself is colliding with earth. It *looks* as if the sun is colliding with earth.

He is not ten feet from contact with the earth, when his body splits open from behind, fire spewing forth in the shape of wings lurching him upward, away from the ground.

Gasping, Myla loses her footing and stumbles backward, eyes wide and mouth ajar in total awe. He is no longer a King's Guard; he is an ancient creature, magnificent and long forgotten by all, she presumes, *but* the Ashborn.

In this moment, as though summoned, beings emerge—some on foot, others by wing—from inside the forest, surrounding her in an impenetrable formation. They bear no weapons, which Myla finds more intimidating than if they surrounded her with spears or bows.

Bryar crashes a few feet from her, disturbing a great deal of dust, with an *oomph.* A few of the Ashborn chuckle, watching as he pushes to his feet, clearly aching and, even more so, clearly stunned.

The Ashborn are tall, and have a commanding and regal presence. They have a honeyed-amber glaze to their eyes, with a translucent and bird-like sharpness. Where their eyebrows ought to be is the start of a magnificently colored plumage, which fades into an even mixture of feather and vibrant hair, dancing in the breeze. Some have warm orange hair, others auburn red, and a few have platinum gold, but all of them match the autumn landscape and the fire that is their birthright. They have no need of cloaks. Magnificent wings of orange, gold, and crimson do the job, mostly shielding fine clothing, also the colors of fire.

One Ashborn in particular catches Myla's eyes. He is taller than the rest, and amid the plumes of his brow is a sapphire-blue crown. He appears both youthful and elderly at once; his being exudes wisdom.

"The first landing is always the worst," he jokes, looking to a woman bearing a similar crown; his queen, presumably. She assesses Bryar, golden eyes glinting with humor.

Both she and Bryar stand, temporarily frozen in shock, before Myla finds the wherewithal to speak like a queen.

"Please, forgive the intrusion," she says, with a respectful tilt of her chin. "We have come seeking aid."

The woman chirps a mocking laugh before gesturing with a delicate hand to the carnage around them. "You obliterate my forest clearing, then ask for help?"

Bryar, having collected his wits, bows deeply. "I fear we are in dire need of help," he gestures toward Myla. "The Spirit Mother sent us here. She said you could help us."

The Ashborn man's brow creases, the red feathers bunching at his hairline. "The Spirit Mother sent you? On what account?" His voice holds suspicion now. "Who *are* you?"

Myla nearly blurts her title until she realizes they could not care less who *she* is—all eyes are on him. Myla finds it oddly refreshing, though suddenly, she too would like answers regarding him.

"I am Sir Bryar Monroe, Captain of the Queen's Guard, and this is my Queen, Myla Alerys of Falkmere." It is now the Ashborn leaders cast a more speculative gaze her way, assessing her from top to bottom before the woman speaks.

"And tell me, Sir Bryar, why is your queen trying to kill you?"

Bryar chuckles, a nervous response, she realizes, when he takes a deep and shaky breath. "*She* is not. The Blood Stealer is, so it seems."

As though summoned, with the realization of her situation dawning on the Ashborn, that still, small voice tugs inside her, another onslaught threatening to break her. *Kill them. Kill them all. Kill him. Kill yourself. Kill someone.* It is a relentless string of commands which starts as a subconscious idea and ends with her clutching her own throat, desperate to speak, desperate to breathe.

"Help me," she whimpers now, feeling as though she can not physically survive another wave. Confusion seizes the Ashborn as Bryar lunges for her. He throws himself on top of her, pinning her hands, which simmer already, at her side.

"What—" the Ashborn queen begins, before her husband brushes past her, looking down at Myla's convulsing body, unbothered, as though he has seen it before.

"She will die if we do not get her inside. The Blood Stealer is done playing with her."

"*Die*?" Bryar questions, in disbelief. Myla strains beneath him, choking on something invisible, every muscle inside her tensing, trying to rage against the man pinning her down. A searing heat burns through her wrists as his own struggle to subdue her awakens that deep beast within him. She feels the agonizing burn on her skin, and she sees the way he grimaces as her light fizzles and nips violently at his hands. They are hurting one another.

"Yes!" The Ashborn king responds, crouching beside Bryar, speaking loud enough to be heard over her guttural cries. "He is consuming her. I have seen it happen many times. When he decides he has finished playing with someone, he either controls them or kills them." He tips a chin toward Myla. "It seems, for this one, he has chosen the latter."

A pain at her spine grows, claiming every inch of her body, as though on the brink of shattering or crushing in on herself.

Wild with urgency, Bryar looks to the man beside him. "What do I do?"

"Bring her inside!" His wife speaks before he can, and together, Bryar and the Ashborn King restrain her body, while hauling her toward the tree line.

Darkness swells, clouding Myla's vision. There is no telling if it is the pain, or something else more nefarious, but the blackness lures Myla into something that feels final, veiling the rest of the world from her senses, until she loses consciousness.

Coming to feels euphoric. She is the embodiment of something intangible, someone who should not still walk the earth, yet she does. A warm amber glow peeks through the thin drapes which enclose the bed she now lies in, hiding her from view of those who may pass in and out of the room. Myla sits up, her body aching from the abuse of the past days. Someone shifts beside her and Myla jolts, looking to her left.

Bryar sleeps upright in a chair, pulled close to the edge of the bed. He looks exhausted. His dark hair swoops into a mess of curls against his face, and his beard, no longer just a shadow across his jawline, is longer than she has ever seen it. He wears a casual black tunic, the sleeves are rolled, baring his forearms, upon which are gold-tinted markings.

Myla gasps, reaching out to trace the flame-like designs up his arms. The sensation wakes him, one groggy eye at a time falling open.

"You are awake." Relief floods his voice, and he sits upright. "Thank the Gods." His voice breaks with emotion as he leans forward, grabbing her hands to hold tightly.

"Of course, I am awake . . . why would I not be?" Myla asks, perplexed. His expression is haunted, a look that conveys hopelessness. "Oh," she says with a slight shake of her head. "That bad, huh?"

"Yeah," he confirms. "That bad. How are you feeling now?"

Myla takes a mental assessment, particularly pertaining to her ribs.

"Not great, but . . . not dead, so I will take it. How are you?"

He laughs slightly, standing to pull the drapes back. "I almost burned their grove down, but I am not dead either. So, I will take it. Let us get you up and dressed. There is a lot you would like to see here."

Myla hesitates, curling her knees to her chest, cringing at the warm light exposing her worn features. "Bryar, I do not want to get up. I do not want to see anything."

His brow furrows, her hesitancy calling him back to the bed, sitting near her. "Why?"

"I am scared," she whispers, her lips pursed in an effort to quench her fear. "I can not forgive myself for what happened yesterday, and I can absolutely promise you, it will happen again. You can not be here with me right now."

Bryar leans close and smiles reassuringly. "Myla, the Blood Stealer can not reach you here."

She tenses, the words falling on disbelieving ears. "What?" The idea of being untouchable to him feels foreign after so long. "How is that possible?"

"They say they have this territory warded. No dark magic is viable within its walls, including the Blood Stealer's."

Myla feels herself slowly unfold, legs relaxing and the tension in her jaw dissolving. The flex of stress within her stomach eases its way out, replaced with warm hesitation. "And, you are sure?" she questions. "How do you know they are genuine?"

At this, his eyebrows arch as he folds his hands, forearms perched on his knees. His eyes linger on the ornate tattoos, drawing her attention back to them.

"Because, I think my mother was one of them."

Chapter 17

The world they have entered is the art of dreams. Terraces glisten in the rain, stretch into winding staircases, weaving through trees and upward into layers upon layers of majestic stone structures, built into the cliffsides. From house to house, an ornately carved viaduct bridges the gap between each door front, providing a scenic route through the neighborhood overhead. The buildings are almost all graced with the creeping of lumelith ivy, the leaves illuminated in the moonlight, and Myla remembers her mother telling her how lumelith glows with the tears of the Dryad Gods, guiding lost travelers deeper into the woods.

From simple storefronts to manors and a grandiose ancient palace, the woodland oasis is bustling with life, a life Myla had no idea existed. Ashborn citizens clothed in bright silks, gemstone corsets, embroidered gauntlets, and even sea-glass skirts, move leisurely to and fro. Everything about Valyndor is mesmerizing and beautiful. There is not a dull color to be found—flashes of orange, gold, red, yellow, and blue move from here to there, all illuminated by ornate crystal lanterns dangling overhead from trees. Their glow is magical, casting various hues of color across their path. Myla catches her breath, amazed at the beauty hidden within the forest.

"This is . . . unbelievable." Myla points to a dome-shaped building, its roof made entirely of stained-glass; the rest of the structure is comprised of brilliant red bricks and tempered ruby tiles. Two great lampposts stand out front, welcoming guests through the oaken double doors, while the cobblestone path circles around either side of the cylinder building. A few paces beyond the perimeter, encircling the entire structure, is a loggia with benches every few yards. From the arches of the loggia, more lumelith drapes, shrouding the open wall romantically.

"What is that?"

"Their library." Bryar's eyes twinkle with thrill. "I have never seen a collection of this magnitude; the editions out date Old Falkmere." He extends a hand, his touch warm as his fingers lace with hers. "Shall we?" Bryar pulls her toward the magnificent library, their boots splashing against the rain drenched path.

Inside, lantern light glints off the spines of gilded books and rippling edges of scrolls. From floor to domed ceiling, ancient texts surround her on all sides. A fragrance, warm, like sweets in a kitchen, wafts through the circular corridor, and golden railings drift downward into a staircase, which disappears in the very center of the room.

This is where Bryar takes her. They spiral downward, a warm golden lantern every dozen or so feet lights their path. The steps are a hickory brown and creak with the slightest distribution of weight.

"What is down here?" Myla asks, wondering what could require being sequestered this far below the main library.

"Answers I did not realize I needed," Bryar responds, his hand still holding hers firmly.

Myla wonders if it is for practicality—helping her keep her footing—or if he longs to touch her as much as she does him. Considering the fact that she tried to kill him yesterday, she must assume it is the former.

"What answers? You said your mother was Ashborn. Why would your father not tell you?"

"I have not the slightest idea, but there are answers down here regarding the Ashborn's abilities and how they could play a part in destroying the Blood Stealer."

Myla stops dead in her tracks, studying his earnest features against the glowing cast of fire. "We need to talk about what happened yesterday."

His lips purse into a faint grimace, the topic clearly being one he wishes to avoid. "Let us not, Myla."

"*Let us,*" she insists. "I did unspeakable things."

"It was not you."

"Maybe not," she agrees. "But . . . it was my hands, nonetheless."

At this, he relinquishes his hold on her, crossing his arms stubbornly. "You can not make me angry with you."

"I do not *want* you angry with me. But you should be."

Bryar shakes his head, forcing out an exasperated sigh. "I am not angry. I am, scared shitless, if you must know."

"Well, that is reassuring. At least I know you are taking this somewhat seriously."

He reaches out, reclaiming his hold on her. "Believe me, I knew it was serious when you launched me a hundred feet in the air." He smirks, rubbing his shoulder for emphasis. "As if you trying to drown yourself did not do the trick already." He glances at her abdomen. "How are your ribs?"

Myla winces, then squeezes his hand. "They hurt, and I am sorry about hurting you . . ."

"I forgive you." He nearly leans in to kiss her and then stops himself, a fleeting expression of hesitance passing. Myla is about to ask why, but he speaks. "But that thing that happened, when I was airborne."

"Yeah, about that," Myla agrees, trying to ignore her wounded pride. Her mind lingering on the topic of *why the fuck is he acting so unusual.* It is not far-fetched to assume he feels in over his head when it comes to her, so she focuses on more pressing topics. "I would ask what that was, but it seems obvious. Did you know?"

"I did not," he answers, as they begin the final turn of their descent. "I had no idea. It does explain how out of control I have felt lately."

"But, why now?" Myla asks.

"That is what I asked. Their scrollwarden says similar accounts have been reported in times of dire need." He nods back at her. "Like when you first channeled the Voice of the Gods."

Dire need, she thinks. Like the stress of keeping an unhinged queen alive, or comforting your best friend through the death of his girlfriend. Or the brutal and relentless job of protecting an entire realm from an invincible foe. Dire need. More like disastrously impossible responsibilities.

"So, your circumstances have pushed you into boiling over like a volcano?" Myla surmises. "Sounds like you need Alaric to make you something for that."

He smiles halfheartedly. "My father never talked about my mother; this is why. I have been called a *half-blood* no less than ten times in the last twenty-four hours. Apparently, it is a bad thing."

"So why were you not raised here, with people who could guide you?"

Bryar shrugs. "According to a man in the palace last night, I am considered a disgrace to their kind. They referred to my mother and father's dalliance as my mother 'scraping the bottom of the barrel'."

"That is ridiculous!" Myla says aghast. "Your father was a good man." She fiercely defends the man she watched raise Bryar with every tool he could find; every deep pool of wisdom known to man, Bryar's father had scoured. There was not a single thing that man would not have done for his son. To refer to him as 'bottom of the barrel' was nothing short of treachery in Myla's eyes. By the look on his face, Myla can see his thoughts race similarly to hers. Something she has learned as queen is when to fuel the fire and when to let it burn naturally. Right now, she chooses to let the fire die entirely. He has enough of it, without her adding to the beast.

"So, where are we left?"

"Well," he answers hopefully, walking directly to a nearby shelf to scan for a text. "They say I must prove myself in some test. If I pass, they will allow me to train with them and learn to control it, summon it at will."

Summon it at will. It sounds frightening. It sounds fierce. It sounds exactly like what she would need, were she to defeat the Blood Stealer. Chills rush down Myla's spine. "It would have been easier, had the Spirit Mother just told us what you are."

"Not really," Bryar disagrees absently as he flips from page to page in a hefty brown book. "We would have had to make the journey nonetheless. Here—" He jabs a finger at an illustration on the page. It depicts a slight and slivering looking man, and at his feet is a pool of blood, seeming to drip from his fingertips. Behind him, mindless minions gather, awaiting instructions. A Blood Stealer. His face is twisted in agony as a winged woman above him, flanked by a score more of her kind, obliterate him in a bath of lava-hot fire.

"This does not stand to reason," Myla whispers, tracing the exquisite depiction with a light finger. "If the Ashborn can defeat Vesperian, why have they not?"

Bryar's eyebrows arch cunningly. "There is a caveat." He directs her to a small line near the end of the page. "It says here that in the absence of a Restorer, an Ashborn, when aided by the *essence* of a Restorer, might be strong enough to conquer the Blood Stealer, *or* the essence of a Restorer channeled alongside an Ashborn bond. I have no clue what that means, but maybe we can continue to read and find out more."

A voice from behind startles Myla. A scrollwarden approaches, shaking her head discouragingly as she walks by. "Do not put too much stock in those scripts." Her old voice sounds like a quiver, barely released from her lungs. "Those are theoretical; nothing has been tested, nor set in stone." She leaves them, abandoning them to more questions and frustration.

Myla stares blankly at the page, the crackling of flame drowning out any cohesive thoughts. "I do not understand. Essence? As in, you need to carry some of Caius's ashes?"

Bryar looks at her, disgusted. "Gods, Myla. That is morbid."

"*Well!*"

"No," he enunciates the *no* while pointing to her belly, visibly shrugging off the discouragement of the old Ashborn woman. "You carry a Restorer. Is that not essence enough?"

Myla slumps into the chair behind her. "I am not letting you carry my infant into battle, Bryar. Though I trust you implicitly, that is an excellent way for both of you to die."

Bryar chuckles and sits next to her. "No. I mean you. You must be there, with the baby inside you."

"And, when I am standing on the battlefield, aiming to kill him, and he turns me against my own? Are you prepared to kill me to save our people?"

Bryar's face stiffens, darkness swallowing his being. "We have to try something."

"In other words, *no*?"

"What do you want me to say?" he asks, holding up both hands helplessly. A spark of rigid defiance flashes across his face. "You want me to look at you, and tell you I am going to kill you, like your Council members agreed to? They are fucking power-hungry cowards; your death would not cause them to lose a single night of sleep. Your death, to *me,* would *be my death.* And I will not agree to that. I will do whatever I can to help you, but that does not include killing you. That is a solution I would not live with."

Myla balls her fists, both thankful for his commitment to her and also angered that he does not see the greater need beyond her own life. "I want you to tell me you will do what is necessary, Bryar. We wait until the child is born. Essence can be anything—nails, hair, saliva. We will make a potion from it that you can drink, or douse your blade in. We will go in to battle together, and if we can not defeat him, you will kill me. That is final! I will not exist as my own child's greatest threat."

Bryar stands now, slamming the book shut. "I will do no such thing!" Heat seeps from his pores now, and a red glow edges the surface of his skin, anger fighting to be released.

"Fine," Myla retorts, eyes ablaze. "I guess I will just have to fall on my own gods-damned sword then." And she walks away, leaving him to glare angrily at the book before him.

Not halfway up the stairs, she hears a clamoring of steps behind her, Bryar taking them two at a time.

"Myla, wait."

She turns to face him, her arms drawn around her middle, trying to ward off the nausea. Be it the child or the conversation, something has soured her stomach.

"I do not see us agreeing on this, Bryar. I do not want to fight with you. We never have, and I do not understand why we are fighting now."

With a pant, he runs a tousled hand though his hair, righting a few stray locks. "We are not fighting," he corrects. "We are simply disagreeing, and I do not want us to let a disagreement escalate into a fight so . . . let us talk this through."

Myla grinds her teeth, annoyed. "Bryar, we very clearly have problems."

"What makes you say that?" he asks, perturbed.

"I do not know, Bryar! Maybe it is the fact that you have avoided talking in situations where you would normally be an open book to me. Or maybe, it is the way you have been short-tempered and aloof with me at the strangest of times before you are warm again? Or when you almost kissed me on the stairs, but for some infernal reason, you stopped yourself. Now, Bryar, you tell me why I might think that?"

A somber look falls over him, and his eyes grow greener with sincerity. "Myla, none of that should be taken as a reflection of how I feel toward you, nor toward *us*."

Bewildered, Myla's shoulders slump. "Then how am I supposed take it? After all the time we spent apart, I have never felt more unsure of us, when I should feel unified."

Nodding in concurrence, Bryar takes a step closer to her. "Myla, you and I—neither one of us, are in control. I think yesterday was proof of that." They exchange brief smirks of acknowledgment, before he continues. "What happened on the mountain shook me, if I am honest. I have never felt so powerless to my own abilities. I have never doubted myself, as I do now. Meanwhile, you . . ." His voice trails off, no need to elaborate on what they both already know. "Anyway, I do not see how the idea of you and I in close proximity is safe. Not that I do not want you near me every second of the day. But I am afraid of what could happen should we both implode at the same time. In fact, we nearly found out yesterday."

Though she is inclined to argue with him, anything to convince him his distance is pointless, she simply responds with a quick kiss on the cheek. "So, what you are saying is you still enjoy me, even after I tried to kill you?"

He does not match her humor. On the contrary, his face is genuine as he speaks. "I do not simply enjoy you, Myla. I *crave you.* I can not even say it is as simple as love. No—this is complicated and messy, but I choose *it,* because choosing it, is choosing *you*. You could try to kill me time and again, and I would simply take out my own heart and ask what you want of it, for it is already yours." He speaks despite the shake in his voice, his hands limp at his side as though giving her these words is giving her everything he has left.

"Truthfully, I would burn this lifetime, and every other lifetime, to the ground. For you. I do not hesitate with you for a lack of love, Myla. I hesitate *because* of love, and I would like us both to live long enough to know a day together that is not tumultuous. The truth is, you could kill me, and I would claw my way out of the grave to find you again."

Myla closes the gap between them, a hand grazing the new tattoos on his forearms, feeling the pulse in her neck thud with greater intensity the further up his arm she navigates, until her hands rest on his neck. "I would rather ask the Gods' forgiveness, should we annihilate the ground beneath us, than know another day without your touch."

His hands move to her wrists, lightly grazing the burns left by his own hand, then he draws her chin upwards to meet his gaze. "You will never be without *me* again. But, the next time I have you, *all* of you, I do not want to worry how I might burn you, or you might accidentally . . . lose control."

Myla bobs her head, understanding. "I imagine it would be terribly indecent to fight for your life naked—suppose I killed you before I came to my senses and had to dress your dead body before anyone saw you."

Chuckling, Bryar takes her hand, and they begin up the stairs once more. "You would do that for me?"

"If I killed you? It is the least I could do."

The Ashborn throne room is different from Myla's in Falkmere. It is not a room at all. Rather, it is a semicircular ring of stone chairs facing a magnificent, wider-than-usual throne, carved into the body of a massive, petrified tree. The canopy of the trees merges overhead, leaving little sky above to be seen. Hanging at different heights, like those seen just outside the palace, are vibrant and warm lanterns illuminating the dark space above as night progresses.

Bryar and Myla both approach the throne where the Ashborn King sits, stoic and dignified. His wings are tucked neatly behind him, vibrant and starkly contrasted by the sapphire-blue armor he dons. He has deep-red hair, highlighted with streaks of silver. His nose, sharp and angled, is set between severe, soul-searching eyes. He wears a large sapphire amulet that pulses against his chest, Myla notices a matching one over the breast of the woman beside him.

"I trust you are feeling better, Queen Myla Alerys," he addresses

Myla, as she and Bryar bow respectfully.

"I am, thanks to your hospitality," Myla responds, hoping to reestablish any dignity lost the day before. "I am in your debt, Your Grace."

"Please, as my guests, I insist you call me Ivan." The latter is spoken chivalrously, and Ivan the Ashborn king stands, his immense height not lost on Myla. As he approaches, the feathered crown growing from his brow bobs in the breeze, catching the glint of the lanterns. The way light seems to exude from his being, not tangibly, but the illusion of it, is magical.

He extends a hand, leading Myla to a comfortable chaise to the right of his throne. She is left to sit with a warm glass of wine as Ivan turns to Bryar. "Your display yesterday was both impressive and alarming. I must admit, many of my people are skeptical, and even more feel threatened."

"How do I threaten them?" Bryar challenges, his lips upturned in defiance. "I simply defended myself."

"Yes," Ivan says. "About that. We will be discussing your queen's ailment next. For now, you threaten them because you are not like them. But you are also not like your kind either. You are somewhere in between. For the Ashborn, that is a disgrace; a ripple in our current of power."

Myla bites her lip, struggling and failing to remain silent. "Perhaps, your people could be less narrow minded."

Ivan turns to her. "Your Grace, this has nothing to do with anything more than magic. Your . . . *captain* here, is a perfect example of what happens when our powers go unrefined. They implode."

He turns to Bryar, once again addressing him. "You are lucky to be alive. I am surprised you have not set fire to your own veins."

Bryar takes a deep breath, briefly glancing down at the raised and irritated tattoos on his arms, not yet healed from when they were seared into his skin. "I feel like I have."

"Believe me," Ivan assures, glancing at his own tattoos. "I have seen someone absorb the fire rather than expel it. They were nothing but a puddle of slop and flesh by the time the flames died down."

Myla feels bile rise in her throat and she resists the urge to turn away. "So, what exactly do you want with him then?"

"I could ask you the same," Ivan retorts with a hint of annoyance, clearly wishing to dismiss her demands for answers. "I want to ensure you truly are Ashborn."

Glowering, Myla straightens her spine, sitting upright despite the ache in her back. Ivan forgets he addresses one of her subjects. Captain, lover, subject; they are all relevant to her, and Ivan's interrogation seems to only emphasize the impurities he sees.

"How do you do that?" she demands before Bryar can speak, her sharp eyes narrowing on the king.

Ivan glances at his wife as she stands. She too has traded her billowy dress for a set of sapphire armor. Hers wears differently, however. There are finer etchings across the neck of the breastplate and down the bosom. Delicate chainmail *clinks* with every step she takes, and the sapphire circlet on her forehead gleams with a fresh polish.

"Imogene will test you. It will be uncomfortable, but if you are of Ashborn descent, it would not kill you." He speaks directly to Bryar, a brief glance at Myla to pass it off as a response for her as well.

Myla stands abruptly, holding up a hand in protest. "And if he is not?"

Bryar appears less concerned than she, but turns to Ivan for an answer as well. "I imagine it will look similar to that puddle of *slop* and flesh you mentioned," he surmises.

"Those not of Ashborn blood can not survive becoming one with someone who is," Imogene coos, raising a hand to play with a flame between her fingers.

At this, Bryar, bearing a perplexed expression, is the one to protest. "I am sorry—can you expand on what becoming *one* entails?"

Myla nods fervently, refraining from demanding immediate clarification, at the risk of appearing tactless.

Imogene drapes herself across her husband's lap in spite of the space beside him, wrapping a slender arm round his neck and tracing a delicate tattoo beneath his ear. She seems unconcerned, but obliges an answer. "It is not what you think." Myla feels herself take a little sigh of relief. "But one could venture to say it feels more invasive."

Bryar, who is losing patience with the cryptic nature of their conversation, rubs his hands together vigorously before fastening the straps of his gauntlets. "Whatever it is, let us just get it over with." His chin bobs downward, as though insisting the Ashborn Queen step forward and get on with it.

"What—" Myla objects with a violent shake of her head.

"Absolutely not. Death is at risk here."

"Seems to be a common theme," Bryar puffs with a comical sidelong glance in her way, completely dismissing her objection. "But we need answers."

Given no time to respond, Myla is joined by two Ashborn guards, also wearing the same sapphire armor and chainmail. Their bodies glint beneath the lanterns as they escort her out of proximity. As she passes, Ivan says something about the test being too hot for a mortal human to be within the vicinity of trial. There is little use in arguing; the falcon-like men at her sides propel her out, only stopping once they have reached a steep incline of stairs.

"If you wish to watch, these will take you to our observatory, which overlooks the throne."

Heated, and heart thudding with anticipation, Myla hurries up the stairs, taking note of how breathless she is once she reaches the top. From her vantage point, she is unable to hear the words, but Imogene stands over Bryar, who is on his knees and shirtless before her.

It would be hot, if it was not a potentially lethal ceremony, she thinks to herself, watching as Imogene sprinkles something in a circular motion around the both of them. Her mouth moves and from what Myla can make out, she is chanting the same words repeatedly, until the circle comes to life, smoke beginning to coil and seep from the earth. Imogene's face lifts skyward, and her wingspan stretches to capacity in both directions.

Bryar lets out a deep cough as the smoke envelopes them, but Imogene seems untouched. The spark begins at the tips of her wings—what were previously feathers burn out, replaced by lapping flames in the shape of wings. Myla expects the flames to stop at her back, but they continue, stretching across her body until she is no longer anything resembling human. What was it Callum had said?

'I swear to the Gods, there is no human explanation for what happened, Myla. He was not just . . . emitting fire. He was fire.'

Imogene is no longer just emitting fire; she is fire. Her features change from human to falcon-like, and she levitates above the ground, an ashy blaze rumbling the ground beneath her as the flames lick at Bryar's body.

Myla resists the impulse to run back down the stairs and demand he put a stop to this. The muscles along his arms gleam with sweat, his head dipped against the heat and his dark hair sticking to his forehead. Tensed at the abdomen, he appears to struggle with remaining upright, a visible force accompanying the blast of heat emanating from the queen. *He looks fucking miserable.*

What happens next is inexplicable and leaves Myla stunned, her mouth agape with disbelief: Imogene presses a hand to his chest and, as though he is merely a pool of water, she falls *into* him, those same flames now spilling from Bryar's pores. Along his arms, the tattoos look as though they may boil and melt from his skin. A crimson red surfaces across his entire body, and the illusion of flames forming feathers is evident, even from this distance.

He collapses on all fours, his body strained beneath the visible pressure, and he cries out—be it in rage or pain, Myla can not tell—but, the response at once ejects Imogene from his body, spitting her out, like vermin. His body continues to sizzle on edge, and like the day before in the field, she watches as what looks like a puncture wound forms, and his back nearly splits, making way for a magnificent outreach of wings ablaze. While they were purely red and orange yesterday, there is a flicker of blue in his flames now.

Gasps to her left and right alert her to other Ashborn who have gathered to watch the spectacle. Some nod in admiration and approval, while others appear perplexed. *They must be the sort calling him a half-blood.*

Myla turns her attention back to the scene below, her heart pounding in her throat. Imogene soars above him now, each flap of her wings sending a pulse of heat in every direction. Like a fireball, she plummets downward toward him.

She is attacking him! Myla lurches forward to see where Bryar now stands, an inferno, angry and ready for the assault. They collide, Imogene slamming his body into the cliffside behind him, and a violent burst of ash and blue sparks swirl in every direction. The usual sounds of a battle are warped with what can only be described as falcon-like screams—not just from Imogene, but Bryar as well.

As the flames continue to eat away at his human flesh, the agony on his face melts into an all-consuming anger, and he appears reborn as a falcon or—no . . .

"A phoenix," she whispers.

The muscle in her jaw relaxes, as Myla realizes he is no longer struggling, his pain now replaced with passion. He pushes himself to his feet, the pieces of him that still appear human, his legs and torso, ripple with heat and strength combined. When Imogene descends with another onslaught of fire and force, Bryar stands still, legs placed firmly apart for takeoff. When she is mere feet from him, he launches himself in flight, and when the space Imogene intended on colliding with is no longer there, she crashes into the cliff, face first.

Myla is certain this ought to be the end of the test, but Ivan's body burns aglow now, and the amulet at his chest throbs more energetically than before. The fire is not a wild inferno like that of Bryar and Imogene's. It is an energy source, one Imogene begins to draw from; her body's light amplifying off the river of revitalizing flame, which trickles through the natural grooves of the stone flooring to where she is. Myla watches, amazed as husband fuels wife, the most holy of unities, resulting in a force not to be contended.

An Ashborn bond, she thinks, recalling the book in the library.

Imogene reels briefly from the attack, but with goddess-like speed takes back to the air, plummeting in a flash of color down on Bryar who, unsuspecting, is knocked to the ground. He lays sprawled, chest heaving with exertion, and seconds from pulling himself to his feet, Imogene is on him again, drilling a hole of fire in his belly.

With a deep yelp of pain, he rolls out of the way, sending a fiery blast at her feet, knocking her down beside him. He throws himself atop her, his features disappearing behind the mirage of heat radiating from them both.

With thighs on either side of her and a blast of fire choking her in place, Imogene seems as though she may be defeated until Ivan doubles over, a wing wrapped around his middle. A sphere of energy thuds from his body, shaking the ground around them up onto the cliffside where Myla watches.

The wave is sucked into Imogene's body and with a riveting gasp for air, she launches Bryar from her. An explosion of flames sizzles from his body, as he collides with a thicket of trees behind him.

Myla presses a hand to her chest, watching the searing hole in the woods dance with embers, waiting for him to emerge. He does. His flames have rescinded, and his body is covered from head to toe in ash and blood.

Finally, Ivan stands, motioning to his wife to cease her test of strength. His eyes turn to Bryar, who is knelt on one knee panting, his wings, the last sign of Ashborn, dissolving within his body. Myla realizes they are something he summons, like she does with her magic. They clearly are different from Ivan and Imogene's; theirs are constants, a physical attribute.

Myla turns and hurries down the stairs, rushing to hear what is said, and more importantly, to inspect Bryar closeup. As she approaches, inaudible words begin to clarify and form sentences.

"It is evident, though deeply concealed within your being, that Ashborn blood runs through your veins," Ivan speaks, glancing at his panting wife, a slight smirk washing over him. "Though you fought well, it was still as tactless as a fledgling."

Myla slips into the opening, lingering in the background and watching how Bryar is slumped slightly forward, one hand braced on the ground to keep him from collapsing totally. His shoulders heave with effort, as he sucks in deep breaths of air. She aches to go to him, but something inside her knows this is his moment, one she does not belong in.

"How is it you were unaware of this?" Imogene asks, sitting upon her husband's lap once more.

Bryar shakes his head, sweat dripping from the curls partially concealing his eyes. Breathlessly, he speaks. "I have always been a fire wielder. But my father never spoke of my mother. I never knew to look for anything more."

Ivan nods slowly. "You may have heard it spoken of before; Ashborn are not supposed to mate with humans. Can you imagine why?"

Bryar laughs, his tone nearly mocking. "I can only assume it has something to do with whatever you and Her Grace were conjuring together."

Ivan grins. "It is erotic, really. Watching your woman destroy her foe. But even more so is fueling her fury with your own. You see, when Ashborn marry, their magic becomes one; it pools together. I can draw from her energy, and she can draw from mine. *We* are one. So, our power is precious to us. When your mother mated with your human father, she compromised the strength the Ashborn built as a whole. Ask yourself why our territories are impenetrable. It is because *we* are impenetrable."

Bryar stands now, his frame straightening with defiance. "I did not come here to hear you speak of my father as though he is a lesser man than you."

Myla's skin prickles at his audacity. *That is erotic, really,* she mocks Ivan silently, admiring Bryar's gumption to speak his truth.

"I do not presume to make assumptions about your father. He clearly did his job well enough, as you stand here with what . . . integrity? Passion for your convictions? These are the premises with which we raise our fledglings." The Ashborn king and queen exchange glances. There is something hidden within their gaze, something Myla can not put her finger on. But it is unnerving.

"I do, however, believe I can speak for my queen," Ivan continues, "in saying, we would be delighted to offer you a position among our other trainees. You bear *remarkable* powers, and with time, we can help you hone them, should you accept."

Myla stiffens at their offer. *They are not doing him a favor. They do not want him taking that power elsewhere.*

Bryar nods in appreciation. "I am honored," he says, glancing briefly back at her. "I must take my queen into consideration, Your Grace. How long will she be protected within your walls?"

Ivan's eyes flicker to where Myla stands before returning to Bryar. "The Blood Stealer's tactics have not penetrated our territories in centuries. Your queen will be safe here, if she wishes to stay."

Myla feels a weight tumble off her shoulders, realizing she can lie in bed this evening and not worry about him haunting her dreams or tugging at her impulses. Everything within her screams at Bryar to accept.

Admirably, he simply says: "I thank you. I will have to discuss both of your offers with her before I give you an answer."

"Understandably," Imogene responds, wiping smudges of ash from her brow. "Will you attend a feast this evening? It is in your honor, Ashborn celebrating Ashborn."

Bryar's chin bobs and he bows slightly. "Thank you, yes."

He turns to leave now, making toward her first. As he approaches, she can see the ash buildup on his face and a cut along his abdomen which slowly drips blood.

"Bryar!" she hisses, examining him closely. "Are you alright? That was terrible."

"I am fine," he replies with an unconvincing chuckle. "Just a little sore."

"Let us get you cleaned up," Myla insists, taking his hand and leading him back to her chambers.

Chapter 18

Steam rises from the tub of water where Bryar is reclined. Myla had asked that two baths be prepared for him, the first to wash the grime off, and the second to soak in and ease his muscles.

She sits and watches from across the room, silently observing as his jaw grinds back and forth, his mind clearly racing, though his closed eyes could be deceiving. She wonders what it must feel like to be him over the last several weeks. *Years, really.* In the last hour, a darkness has washed over him; something is gnawing at him.

"Bryar," she says gently, almost hesitant to disturb the tranquility of the room.

He responds by cocking one lazy eye open and looking her way. "Hmm?"

"Are you thinking about what Ivan said? His offer?"

He nods, his sharp jawline catching the glint from the hearth. "I can not help but wonder if this is what the Seer wanted us to find. If I refine my magic, could it help defeat the Blood Stealer?"

Myla slips gracefully off the edge of the bed and makes her way across the room, crouching beside him. Her hands grasp gently at his on the rim of the tub, his curling around hers in response.

"I think it would be a disservice to you not to try. You spent so many years honing human skills and ignoring these. I think it is time you make way for new abilities."

"So, you *want* to stay here? For a time that is?" he asks, turning his face to hers, his eyes searching for any signs of hesitancy.

Myla nods slowly. "It would give me time to pass the pregnancy in peace. We would not have to worry about me trying to kill anyone, the child or myself included."

He smiles halfheartedly before facing forward again, his eyes seeming to scan the air overhead for answers. "Ivan said something I have to agree with."

"What is that?"

A devious smile stretches across his handsome features. "He said there is something erotic about watching your woman flatten her foe." He looks to her, his eyes full of hunger. "You have had some rather impressive moments in the last several weeks. They were erotic for sure, even if one of them was trying to kill *me*."

Myla blushes, pushing his hand off hers. "Do not flirt with me. I respect your boundaries, but toying with me makes keeping off of you too difficult."

Bryar leans forward, the heat of the bath rising off his skin and moistening her face. There is an odd look there, a mixture of longing, yes, but something deeper. Something confused.

"Yes," he says, "but that was before Ivan said you could be here, safe, for as long as you like. That was before I had more answers about myself. And that was before you were sitting here, looking at me the way you are."

Myla's lips part, tempted to lean inward and lay claim to his mouth. She resists and instead, reaches to her bodice, unlacing the front. The dress slips off, followed shortly by her corset. Bryar watches her undress, scanning unabashedly up and down her body. At last, she stands in an ankle length white shift. She lifts a leg over the side of the tub, stepping in to join him, straddling her thighs on either side of his hips until she has settled down upon him. He is already hard between her thighs, throbbing and aching for entry.

"Perhaps you should help me bathe before the party tonight?" she whispers, arms draped over his shoulders and lips teasing against his.

Strong hands travel down her back, past her hips, and grope her backside, pulling her closer against him. "I will not miss an inch."

"*Promise*?" she coos, leaning in to kiss his neck.

He smiles, his teeth nipping at her bottom lip. "I promise."

Steam rises around them as his body heat rapidly increases, warming the water significantly. Their mouths move against each other in a hypnotic slow dance of kisses, tongues rolling against each other, evoking moans, and gasps. It is not quick or passionate, rather a slow stoke of the flames, each gesture intentional.

"You did not last very long," Myla giggles between his kisses as they travel across her throat. "I thought it would take a lot longer for you to change your mind."

He bites the soft skin of her shoulder gently, a little punishment for her statement. "Are you complaining?" His hands slide between her thighs, finding a space even wetter than the bath.

Myla exhales, relieved by his touch and slowly shakes her head, her face turning upward as she melts completely in pleasure. "No. Not at all," she breathes. "Ivan was wrong."

"Do not bring him into this," Bryar commands, pushing his fingers inside her.

This is ecstasy. She finishes her thought, her hands finding his length, hard and aching to be touched. He throbs within her grasp, a deep moan escaping his lips as she rubs up and down slowly, teasing him with gentle touches. Water sloshes around them, rippling off the sides of the tub with their intensifying motions. Myla aches for more, and every second he is not inside her is a devastating one.

Myla rolls her hips, writhing with anticipation against his solid body. Bryar's hands dig into her thighs, and he lifts her body, urging her closer, before thrusting. He is as hard as steel and her body tightens around him, quivering in satisfaction. Just as she is certain he is there to stay, a wicked smile moves across his handsome features, and he lifts her once more, partially removing himself.

Myla groans miserably and leans down to nip at him, penance for the famine he puts her through.

"Denying your queen? I could punish you for that."

His strong arms tighten and resist as she fights to lower herself around him again. "Punish me how? Do not leave out any details," he teases and with a chuckle, his hips move forward, slamming himself deeper into her until she is fully seated around his hard length.

Myla can not seem to think now. As he teases, bringing her just to the edge of satisfaction before pulling away again, she is driven mad with the need to be bent over the tub.

"I shall stand up now and finish the job myself if you do not give me what I want," she hisses breathlessly, nearly squealing as he plunges deeper, throbbing against a sensitive wall of nerves inside her.

"You know you could not do the job half as well as I can," Bryar taunts, repeating the motion again and again until she is on the brink of igniting.

Then, something at his fingertip's fizzles and Myla yelps in pain as he sears her. She is inclined to giggle and keep going, but Bryar pushes her off of him.

"Myla, stop I—"

Myla freezes, slightly horrified. "It is alright," she insists. "What happened?" She swallows hard, meeting his tense gaze. "Are you ok?" She looks at the wound on his ribcage and then steps out of the bath.

Bryar stands, drying himself quickly before stepping into his trousers. He then turns to face her. His features are unreadable, stone-cold stoicism with a hint of suppressed deflation as he looks down at his hands, which seem to still burn with passion. With an angry sigh, he dries his hair in a towel and pulls a tunic over his head before speaking. "Do you know what today is?"

His question stops her in her tracks, her brain frantically sifting through any important dates that pop into her head, trying to understand what could be causing his sudden rush of anxiety.

"No, Bryar," she responds uncomfortably, wrapping her arms around her chest. "I do not know what today is."

He nods slowly, biting his lower lip in frustration. "Myla. Today is the day, six years ago, that I watched you walk down the aisle to Caius."

Myla flinches, the memory hitting her like a wall. She briefly wonders how she could have forgotten, but that question is quickly replaced by another. "And that is causing this? This response?"

He shakes his head. "Not exactly. I have tried to ignore the gnawing for hours now, and the thought I can not shake is this: when I help you win your kingdom back, and everything goes back to normal, where does that leave me? Does it leave me just your captain again, and the man you welcome to your bed under the cover of night? Am I to return to the barracks and lie to my friends when they ask where I was, because I can not even tell them that I am in love with the queen? Will I inevitably be pushed to the side when you remarry a titled man? Will I stand guard by your chambers then still? While I want to ignore it all and just enjoy simplicity with you here, for now, I am afraid we are setting ourselves up to repeat history."

Stunned, Myla stands silent and dripping wet on the floor, her wet hair clinging to her face. Raw emotions bared naked in the space between them, Myla finds her words tangled together in the mess of questions she feels unequipped to handle. She opens her mouth to speak but no answer arrives, only confusion. Confusion and hurt.

"I can not do it again, Myla." His eyes narrow and lines form across his brow in hopelessness. "Do you know what the guard on duty who stood by your door the night of your wedding came downstairs and told us at breakfast?"

Myla swallows hard, dreading his answer. Her eyes glisten with tears, hoping he will not say it aloud, but knowing their silence and dancing around the topic for years has led to this moment. She has known at some point, he would say something. Men like Bryar *always* say something.

"He told us: 'I do not think the new queen had a good first night.' I could hardly hide the horror on my face, Myla. All these men, who had no idea we had a history before you arrived at the palace, looking at me, wondering why I threw a tumbler of ale across the room!" His shoulders shake suddenly and his voice breaks with the following words: "I stood guard by your door night after night, as was my duty, and I listened to you cry as he raped you, and no amount of asking Elsa to talk to you could drag the truth from you."

There it is.

The word she has avoided.

The one she has renamed as *betrayal* or *duty.* Myla lets out a sob, covering her mouth and shaking her head fiercely. "Do not say that word, Bryar. Do *not* say that word! That is not what happened."

He steps closer, his eyes gleaming with tears and his mouth set in a firm line, fighting a rush of emotions. "Why will you not talk about it? Why will you not admit what really happened? You spend so much time defending his memory, but I *knew* the whole time. And I would be lying if I said I did not sigh a breath of relief the day he died because I knew he was done hurting you.

"Elsa felt the same way, you know. I once had to stop her from slipping poison into the king's nightcap."

His hands close around her shoulders, pulling her shaking body against his. "I can not do that ever again, Myla. If you tell me, at the end of this, you will return to that palace, and I will simply be your lover again—I can not continue like this. It is not fair to you, and it is not fair to me. I would rather love you from a distance than lose myself in a half-truth."

Myla looks up at him, raising a hand to his face to wipe a tear with her thumb. "I will not remarry, Bryar. I may not be able to marry you; that would start an entirely different war. But I will not marry anyone. I will always be only yours."

Her hand lingers and brushes against the stubble of his cheek. Words she has ached to tell him for years finally fall from her lips. "I love you."

Words which have been absent in the space between them for so long, though quenching, fix nothing.

The room stills and for an agonizing stretch of time, Bryar holding her against him in what feels like a final embrace. "I love you." His following words are soft whispers, as though he is afraid of what damage they will do if spoken at full volume. "Myla . . . I am not content to live half a life anymore. I wish I still had that in me, but I feel there is more to my life than supporting yours in secret. I will always be your greatest advocate. I will always be the person watching you succeed and smiling when you do, because to me, that is happiness. But I will not do it in shadows, afraid of someone seeing me smile too much when you are near, afraid that my eyes will linger too long on a woman who is not mine and that will be noticed." He swallows, his throat bobbing as he puts his emotions away.

"I will help you win this war. I promised to keep you alive and see this through until the end, but when it is all done, when I have seen you restored to your throne, I will resign as your Captain of the Queen's Guard, and I will be coming to seek my full potential here."

Myla stiffens, pulling away from him slowly, not daring to meet his gaze for the blinding tears that drip freely down her cheeks, burning what feels like eternal trails of grief into her skin. Instead, she wipes the tears with her palms, breathing deeply to steady her pulse.

"I never talked about what Caius did, because I thought if I did not say the words aloud, then it would stay tucked neatly behind closed doors. It would not be real. Because those are the only times I ever felt unsafe with him, and in truth, I understood where his desperation came from. I could rationalize it away, until I convinced myself what he did was not truly wrong. I could even smile at him when we were not in his bedroom. The Caius who wanted an heir was a different person than the Caius who walked the gardens or shared a meal with me. He was good to me in daylight. He made me feel like I had a friend in him, until it was time for bed . . . time to make an heir.

“I did not want to be seen as the poor girl forced to marry a cruel king, Bryar. I had already lost so much; my own self-respect was too much to sacrifice because he was *desperate.*” She touches her belly, thankful something good and pure and innocent will come of his abuse.

“If this is your final choice, Bryar, I respect it, and I will love you from afar, as you will me. But I will not spend another day holding you back.” She meets his gaze now, a trembling across her body screaming at her to say anything but this. “You have stood in this space with me long enough now. It is time for you to live for *you.*”

Myla presses her lips closed in finality and turns her back, allowing him to exit the room without a further word before she erupts in a shudder of sobs. Sobs for the life she feels her father robbed her from with Bryar, and sobs for the life she experienced within the palace.

She cries for the hundreds of times Elsa would fix her hair the morning after, asking how she slept, and she would lie, noting the pinch of Elsa’s nose as she would turn away. For the times she would ask Fern to leave the tinted cream behind and she would dab a bit onto her wrists, covering the little bruises.

'Why will you not talk about it? Why will you not admit what really happened? You spend so much time defending his memory, but I knew the whole time.'

Myla shudders, wishing she had the heart to ask him why he never talked to her about it before. But she already knows the answer. Bryar has never been a man to probe or insert himself where he has not been invited, especially when that probing would have opened so many doors they both needed to keep shut. Or when that probing would have called her integrity into question. He sat in an impossible situation, carrying grief of his own in silence.

Myla strips out of her wet shift finally after drying her eyes, and lies down on her bed, watching the gleam of the firelight cast eerie shadows on the walls. As she falls asleep, Myla pictures the moments of her youth which lead to this place, and she wonders: *can the worst day of your life save your life?*

The large double doors of the throne room swing open, two guards heaving them out of her way. She trembles, fingers wrapped around an exquisite bouquet of white hydrangeas and peonies. Beside her, Maverick Alerys stands, beaming. His gray speckled beard bobbing as he says something, words she can not make out above the thudding of her heart.

This dreaded moment has loomed in the near future, taunting her, yet seeming like a reality she would somehow escape. Now that it has arrived, decorated with crowds of smiling people and a man at the end of the aisle she does not wish to marry, a sickness seizes her, freezing her limbs in place.

She has not escaped it, and no one will help her now.

"Father, I—"

Maverick interrupts her, his words of encouragement a far cry from the warning within his eyes. "I am so proud of you, Myla. Everything we have worked so hard for has led to this moment. You will change the face of the Kingdom. The Alerys name will be written in history." His lips twist in the phantom of a smile and something lurks beneath the surface. Unspoken words that say 'do not make this difficult; we have come too far for you to falter now.'

So, instead of speaking up in one last plea for help, Myla forces the building tears back, smiles understandingly, and steps through the doors with the crescendo of the string quartet. To Caius's right, slightly behind him, ever the dutiful King's Guard, stands Bryar, his eyes fixed on something in the distance and lips pressed into a firm, expressionless line.

He does not look at her, and for that, she is grateful.

But she keeps her eyes fixed on him. His face is the only stabilizing force in the room. He is the only reason she does not crumple to the floor right here for everyone to watch her shame.

Then, his lips twitch and his fist tightens around his axe. His green eyes flicker to where hers are, and for a moment, they find solace in their quiet understanding.

He nods and those soft, green eyes seem to say 'well, this is bullshit, is it not?'

Myla's heart shatters.

The resolve she has finely formulated with deep breaths and lies of 'this is ok', seems to fracture. Tears form once more, and the pounding of her heart begins to sound like an angry battering ram on wood, or an urgent knock at a door—

Myla gasps, sitting upright in her bed, thankful for the sudden realization she is not reliving that horrible day.

"Queen Alerys," a timid voice questions from the other side of the door. "Her Grace has sent me to help you prepare for the party. May I come in?"

"A moment," Myla responds, flustered as she crawls off the bed, pulling the now dry shift over her head. She opens the door and a young woman—a girl, really—enters. Her golden and feathered head barely reaches Myla's shoulders. "Thank you," Myla says, examining the girl, who begins laying an armload of clothing on the bed.

"I am Felicity," she says, her auburn lashes lowering with a bow. "I am to care for you while you are here. I have brought an assortment of clothes at the Queen's command. Shall we pick one for this evening?"

Myla wants to insist she is not attending; the idea of seeing Bryar is too painful. *Queens do not hide in their chambers.* She corrects her train of thought, passing a brief glance over the options of dress before her.

Not wishing to miss an opportunity to form alliances, she merely nods and begins sifting until she selects a breathtaking, blush dress. *I would not dare to show up looking as bad as I feel, what would that say of me as a queen?*

Felicity helps her into the gown, lacing it tightly until her silhouette is sleek, tucked neatly into the form-fitting gown. The neckline scoops just beneath her collarbone, a tulle front providing a tease of what is beneath, reaching a scandalous point between her full breasts. Long sleeves of tulle bunch at the wrists, draping around her elbows gracefully with a delicate design of rubies swirling up her forearms. This same pattern of rubies trickles down the skirt, sparse at first and then increasing in frequency until they pool at the hem of her dress like a glittering red rain.

Felicity runs a brush through her hair, smoothing the tangles formed from the bath, then pulls loose waves over each shoulder, simple and natural. After a hint of rouge is applied to her cheeks, Felicity nods with approval.

"Is it to your liking, Your Grace?"

Myla nods. "I will not embarrass myself, at least."

Felicity eyes the dress around her middle before speaking hesitantly. "Shall I take any of the form-fitting dresses and have them altered, Your Grace?"

Myla glances at her reflection, and for the first time, she notices change. From tender breasts to a swelling in her stomach, it is evident: the child within grows.

"It is obvious?" she asks.

Felicity shrugs slightly. "Only to the trained eye. But I could have the dresses taken out a few inches to give you time to hide it longer, should you need to."

Myla smiles weakly, caressing her belly absently before nodding in thanks. "I do not need to hide it, but I would rather not struggle to make a dress fit. Please, have them altered."

Felicity bobs a curtsy and leaves with many of the dresses; a few simple and flowing ones remaining.

An hour later, after mustering every ounce of composure she has, Myla meanders through the halls. Every wall is adorned in art and expensive trophies of war or travel. The halls all graced with open-air balconies, which offer expansive views of the forest, the mountains, and beyond. From one vantage point in particular, Myla spies a thunderous waterfall cascading down the sheer side of the mountain, and she imagines bathing at its base.

After some exploring, she finds her way to the feast hall. Jovial laughter, shouts, and upbeat music reverberate through the palace; Myla discovers that Ashborn celebrations are boisterous events.

The room is crescent shaped around two thrones centered, providing an easy view of the entire hall. Heavy tapestries hang at even intervals, stretching thirty feet upward from floor to ceiling. Pictured on each are depictions of the Gods and their efforts in war, love, and justice. They tell stories, ones Myla could lose herself in. Thin chains fixed above each tapestry travel the length of the ceiling, meeting just overhead the thrones, serving as a suspense for vibrant lanterns which bring a warm glow to the room.

On either side of the thrones grow large trees, hot with autumn colors and branching out through the ceiling to touch the night sky. It appears as though some sort of mechanical ceiling opens and closes around the trunks, allowing for closure in poor weather.

Bryar sits at a table near the king and queen. To Myla's surprise, the majority of those sitting at the table with him are young Ashborn women, each aglow in their own way, beautiful, smiling, and certainly not carrying the weight of war on their shoulders.

Myla sucks in a deep breath, brushing aside any feelings of jealousy. *This is good for him,* she tells herself. *No holding him back.* But those words are more pretty lies she tells herself, to numb the pain searing through her middle. Pretty lies like those she and her father built together to make her journey down the aisle more convincing.

Myla eyes an empty seat at a table across the room and considers giving Bryar a wide birth. She is suddenly self-conscious in her choice of dress; it screams 'look at me, the woman that was on you hours ago,' not 'I am a confident queen, who did not just spend the last several hours crying over a man.'

Annoyed and tingling with unruly emotions, Myla graciously accepts a hot mug of herbal tea from a small Ashborn child who carries a simmering pot through the room.

"Fuck this," she whispers to herself, taking stock of her reflection in the windows. *It screams 'look at me, a ruthless queen who is not stopped by matters of the heart.'* Before thoughts of embarrassment or pain stay her feet, she takes several confident steps to stand before the thrones, bobbing a deep curtsy. The room grows hushed as she stands before their king and queen, all in company watching. Someone behind whispers, "It *is* her. The Queen Who Bleeds Stars, look."

Only now, does Myla realize that her emotions take form, speckling her skin in an array of magnificent starlight. Her hands seem to sparkle as light spills from her pores.

"Your Grace," she acknowledges both Imogene and Ivan before standing tall once more, as the blademaster once told her to. Well aware that all eyes are on her, she squares her shoulders and tilts her chin. "What a beautiful assembly." Myla gestures to the surrounding room, ignoring the heat on her neck where Bryar stares. "I thank you for the honor of experiencing life as an Ashborn."

"It is you who honors us," Imogene responds, gesturing to an empty seat behind her. Myla turns to sit, steadying her breath as her gaze passes over Bryar sitting across from her.

Observing the busy to and fro of party goers, paired with the lively music, is a sufficient distraction from the man before her. Myla watches unruly children soar overhead, scolded by their parents; young men and women flirt, banter, and sing. The occasional intoxicated Ashborn launches fireballs out the open ceiling, giving Myla something to awe over as the sparks scatter into blackness.

Two Ashborn ladies sit beside Bryar, one on either side, and Myla wills herself to tune out their meandering conversation. What is impossible to tune out is the way he clearly tries to avoid her gaze, yet fails each and every time they cast a glance around the room. Now, his deep green eyes lock with hers.

A battle of ocean against forest.

Myla lifts her chin, her gaze seeming to unravel him. It is an exchange that does not quite seem to make sense. Given how they parted a few hours prior, there is no reason for either to stare as they do now, full of something akin to rage. Yet here they are, fanning the flame. Daring to defy the agreement already. Silently, they search one another's eyes for answers, as if unearthing something new will void the words spoken only hours ago.

On closer examination, Myla's mouth dries, taking in just how good he looks. His hair falls tousled into his face, the shadow of a freshly shaven beard casts sharp angles across his jaw, and a casual black tunic is unfastened three buttons down; the sleeves pushed over his elbows, exposing trained arms and the fresh tattoos. It is a feverish sight, one spoiled when Ivan stands to speak, breaking the trance.

The king exudes a regal confidence which commands the attention of the room, and the music fades to silence. "We welcome a newcomer." Ivan gestures to Bryar. "I trust he is to be given the warmest of Ashborn welcomes." The crowd applauds, and Myla rolls her eyes at the bashful smiles flashing him from all directions.

Apparently being a half-blood is not such a bad thing anymore. Myla glowers at the flock of young women around him. His discomfort is blatant, a detail they seem to miss entirely.

"We welcome also to our court, Queen Myla Alerys. We are honored by your presence," Imogene adds, almost as an afterthought. Myla's lips purse and her eyes squint, scrutinizing the queen before her. *That would never slide in Falkmere . . .*

"Sir Bryar," Imogene speaks again. "It is the Ashborn way to shield our kind, to keep our power strong and pure. We are, however, deeply impressed with the strength of body and character you show, for that is the *true* Ashborn way. Should you choose to accept our offer to train with us, we will welcome you permanently. You shall have a home, and in time, with effort and loyalty, a title." Ivan smiles with the charisma only a laid-back king dishing out women and titles could have.

He takes note of the female attention Bryar is receiving, whispers something to his wife, then speaks once more. "Phaenna." He gestures to one of the ladies, her beautiful red hair cascading down her back, which is bare save a delicate ribbon at her neck, holding the top of her dress in place. "I appoint you Bryar's personal companion for the party. I trust you will see to his every need this evening."

Myla does not like the tone with which the girl is given permission to sink her proverbial claws into Bryar. They are not just offering him a place to hone his newfound magic in peace; they are offering him a new life entirely.

She glances at him, not surprised to find his face unreadable beneath the courteous smile. The music resumes, and Bryar is summoned to speak with the king and queen, Phaenna trailing beside him, pleased as a newborn colt to be appointed to the handsome newcomer's side. Her fingers graze the inside of his arm as she latches onto him.

Gods, Myla hisses inwardly. *She needs a new profession. Court harlot looks bad on her.* Immediately regretting the all-too-human and not at all queenly thought, Myla bites her lip and wonders what they could possibly be saying. Judging by the intrigued look on Bryar's face, it is an offer unlike any he has received before.

Unwilling to watch the spectacle any further, Myla loses herself once more in a sweet of hot tea and observing. She moves across the room to recline on a cushioned bench, blissfully tucked away in the corner of the room. Her eyes watch the night sky above as stars drift slowly across her view, occasionally interrupted by a shooting star or a plume of ash from the playful mayhem below. Her tea and quiet nook seem like a brilliant antidote to the ache in her heart, until Imogene stands before her, extending a hand.

"Join me?" she asks. Her voluptuous body on display, the hot-red gown she wears hugging all the right places, a pleasing visual that Myla takes note of for half a second too long before responding.

"I—yes. Of course. Forgive me." She stands, immediately triggering a nauseous twisting in her stomach. The child plans to put up a fight this evening. Myla had heard her mother speak of morning sickness. It seems her child prefers to cause disturbances in the evening.

"You look unwell," Imogene remarks, linking her arm with Myla's. "Shall we take the air?" *How kind,* Myla thinks, accepting the offer and ignoring the voice inside her which asks *why is this woman so contrary? Frigid one moment and thoughtful the next.* It is not lost on her that another queen might have allowed Myla to sit in the corner while her husband laid claim to Bryar. This queen may house some empathy after all.

"Felicity reported back to me," Imogene says once they stand outside. "It seems you are expecting?" She glances at the roundness of Myla's belly, just barely passable as bloating. "How far along are you?"

"I believe about five months," Myla replies, knowing that after two years of suppressing the pregnancy and letting it slip from time to time, she has lost track slightly.

Imogene hovers a hand over Myla's belly, not making contact, but a warm vibration grows between her skin and Imogene's hand. "The child is strong."

"How do you know?" Myla asks, curiosity piqued.

"The vibrations—the flow of blood—there is nothing weak reverberating off this child. But I do not sense Ashborn blood."

Myla's brow furrows. "Of course not, why would there be?"

Imogene's face hints at a coy smile but is quickly corrected. "I made an assumption is all."

"No." Myla shakes her head. "This child is the rightful inheritor of New Falkmere. The late King Caius is her father."

"He passed a while back though," Imogene questions, her head tilting in curiosity.

"Yes," Myla answers. "The conflict with the Blood Stealer has been treacherous," she explains. "I did not want my child to be born into such an uncertain situation. So, I siphoned my magic into freezing her growth until the right time."

A look of admiration passes over Imogene's face. "A mother is willing to do many things for her child."

"Yes," Myla agrees. "My child will have Restorer's blood, you see. That makes her existence even more dangerous and equally crucial."

"You keep saying 'her'," the queen remarks. "I remember my own fledgling growing within me. I knew he was a boy well before his birth."

"And you were right?"

"I was." Imogene points to a trail leading into the forest, lit by torches every so often. "The captain will train in the arena at the end of the trail. His practice begins tomorrow."

"So, he agreed to your offer?"

"He did," Imogene states, clearly pleased. "He is strong, for a half-blood; it would behoove us to have him on our side . . . reintegrating his power back into the Ashborn bloodlines."

Myla takes a slow, deep breath. She could have guessed when Imogene invited her to talk, this is where the conversation might lead. "I am sure Captain Monroe will make the best decision for himself," she answers, hoping her expression and tone come off as an indifferent queen.

Imogene side-eyes her. Apparently, the statement did not have the desired effect, for she continues, a little more blatant this time. "When he begins his training tomorrow, it would be best if you were not there to distract him."

Myla turns to face Imogene. Host or not, Myla refuses to be instructed as though she, too, is not a queen. "Do not think that I fail to see the truth beneath your scheme," she whispers, stepping closer to the feathered woman before her. "I know very well that you do not offer Captain Monroe a place here because you admire him. You offer him a place here because you fear him."

Chapter 19

The sun has barely risen in the sky when Myla finds herself standing at the mouth of the trail, pacing back and forth. Imogene delivered her message with such audacity that Myla has spent all night seething in defiance. *Who is she to tell me I can or can not watch him train. She has known him all of a few days. I have known him for over ten years.*

"What are you doing?" Bryar startles her from behind, his eyebrows pushed together in confusion.

She opens her mouth to speak, some excuse lingering just out of reach. Instead, the truth spills out. "Imogene said I ought to leave you to train . . . without me as a distraction. I am mad that she told me I should not, so . . . here I am."

Bryar chuckles and brushes past her, no stranger to her stubborn inability to follow instructions. Thus, he motions for her to follow with a brief tug on her sleeve. "Come on, then, you can laugh as I get my ass handed to me."

"How did you know," Myla banters hesitantly, "I did not want to miss that." Together they walk in silence for a few moments, this sort of awkwardness only comparable to their brief interactions following her wedding to Caius.

Finally, Bryar speaks. "I think this will be a good place for me, Myla. If I do well in my training, I can hold an equivalent position here in a few years."

"Yes," Myla agrees gently, careful not to speak with too much confidence should he mistake her tone for acceptance. Nothing inside her likes what is happening. It is a breakdown that really should have happened years ago, but it did not. Now it is, it stings differently than it might have prior to becoming queen.

"Tell me about Phaenna. She seems like an interesting woman."

Bryar flashes her an annoyed look. He has never been one for conflict, and right now, that is all that seems to find them. "There is nothing to tell. They are putting a few potential mates on display, that is all."

Myla cringes. "That is all? Two weeks ago, we were lying in bed, determined we would figure this out *together,* and now you are casually examining Ashborn 'mates'?"

Bryar appears to flinch, the venom of her words striking deep. His response is even-toned, despite the heat building in her. "I am examining no one. You, of all people, should know I am not interested. But they have customs."

"Customs?"

"Yes," he clarifies. "Marriage is binding here."

"Is it not binding everywhere?"

"Gods, you are an argumentative little thing today," he says with an exaggerated eye roll before continuing. He seems excited now. "You saw yesterday when Imogene and Ivan seemed to battle together?"

"Yes?" Myla responds, trying to remain even-tempered, though she wonders how this relates at all to his *not* examining potential mates while adhering to local customs.

"They told me last night that when an Ashborn marries, they and their mate's magic binds together, forming one source of magic and energy to be drawn from by either party." His words falter slightly now, the tone shifting from a conversation to a confession. "Ivan gives the impression that my place here is conditional to my marrying an Ashborn and giving back to the bloodline."

Myla's steps slow and she digs her teeth into her lips, pinching her mouth shut until she can form a string of words that are not scathing. Any impulse to hurt right now, she knows, is only because she herself is hurting.

Finally, she responds, "Is that what you want? To stay here and start a family with an Ashborn woman?"

Bryar casts his eyes to the ground, focused now on his feet as they move him closer and closer to the clattering of the arena ahead. "I want to feel like I have a say in my future. If my future can not include you, then I have to start somewhere."

"Then you should choose this," Myla says, gathering her skirts at her knees to allow for a quicker gait. "I will be watching from over there." She points to one side of the circular arena where wooden benches are tiered, several layers of seating one after the other. "Good luck."

The arena is abuzz with more fledglings than Myla expected to see, and an instructor standing in the center, drawing runes in the strangest formation. It must be unique to the Ashborn as Myla's mother never taught these compositions to her. Settling into a seat, noticing that most in attendance as onlookers are barely older than she, Myla suddenly feels the urge to be invisible, her lack of wings and vibrancy drawing attention.

"Students! Assemble!" The 'students' are actually the fledglings Myla noticed a few minutes before. They align themselves in a straight row before the instructor, standing feet apart and hands crossed before them. They look fierce and serious until their new classmate reluctantly strides into the arena. Myla resists the urge to bellow in laughter as Bryar, hesitant at first, steps in line, eyeing the fledglings as they snicker at him. A faint look of amusement crosses his otherwise stoic features before his eyes dart to hers. She smiles and nods, hoping to pass along some encouragement in the wake of laughter, which builds not only among his classmates, but the audience as well. Or parents, she is realizing.

Myla fears the mockery will continue until the instructor, a severe woman who looks like she fell off the pages of a valiant battle retelling in Caius's library, stomps her foot upon one of the runes. A vortex of energy ripples through her body, transferring itself into the rune beneath her feet and sending a sobering tremor through the arena.

"Go on," she says with a dismissive wave of her hand. "Keep laughing. I am sure your flockmate will remember this moment when you are relying on him in battle." Little faces flatten into stoic expressionlessness. "You laugh, why?" She points to a young girl, maybe five or six years old. When the child does not respond, she steps closer, activating a rune beneath the child which knocks her onto her bottom. "Speak, fledgling!"

The girl clamors to her feet, steps back into position and tilts her chin upwards. "Because he is old, Elara." She answers obediently now.

Elara turns on her heels, pacing toward another fledgling, a fair-haired boy of similar age. "You laugh at someone older than yourself for trying to learn. Do you think learning stops as we age?" The fledglings shake their heads in unison as their instructor shines a spotlight on their shameful response.

"Learning can begin at any age, but I assure you, your new flockmate is at an advantage, and will far surpass each and every one of you within weeks, *then* who will be laughing?" She does not give time for response before she brings her foot down upon another rune, shouting instructions at the fledglings and Bryar to navigate the course she has arranged for them.

Myla expects the instructor to step to the side, observing the lesson. Instead, she stands in the center, casting new runes as a calamity of spells ensues around her.

Mere inches from Bryar, one of the runes takes on a devilish form, leaping from the earth in the shape of a Blood Stealer's wolf. Myla groans, wishing the lesson could have included anything other than the very beasts which had attacked Bryar on the mountain.

He recoils at first, raising an arm to block the snarling and snapping beast, entirely caught off guard. The illusion is hyper realistic and the wolf snaps and snarls, saliva flying from its hungry jaws across Bryar's arms. The fledglings respond in a mixture of glee and terror, setting the more experienced ones apart from those who might be newer to the experience.

Bryar seems to find his footing quickly. As another vicious and lumbering wolf appears before him, he ducks, rolling between its stocky legs to avoid its razor-sharp teeth. Myla watches as he begins to expect the unexpected, at which point he dodges effortlessly.

At first, Myla leans forward, elbows on knees, wondering how this is teaching him anything. He could dodge assault for hours without breaking a sweat. Even most of the fledglings consider this easy as well, for they begin laughing as though it is a game.

That is, until a wolf leaps from one of the runes like a demon loosed from the underworld, nipping at her forearm. A few feathers fall from her wings as she slips backwards, yelping in pain. At once, Elara lowers her foot on the activator rune, bringing the assaults to a halt.

"Dodging your assailant is useful at times," she says, pacing between fledglings, who sit or stand or continue to roll for the fun of it, until she stops before Bryar, who looks as though he is playing a child's game. She reaches for his wrist and raises it, putting his forearm on display. "Summon your gauntlet," she commands, evoking a perplexed look on every face in the arena, Bryar's especially. "One can only dodge for so long. All you will do is waste energy. You can not win if you are simply hopping back and forth like a rabbit. Face your enemy head-on when possible. Today, we will learn to summon our gauntlets."

Raising her arms, without so much as a grimace or a focused expression, Elara's arms burst in flame, the shape of gauntlets forming across her fists and to her elbows. "Strike me," she commands a fledgling before her, handing him her dagger. The little one hesitates at first, but with some prompting from his classmates, he raises the dagger over his head, lowering it with force upon her arm. The collision is met with a deafening *clang* and a burst of embers.

Elara drops her arm as though a mere fly has just landed on her and continues. "When I step on the runes this time, the beast emerging will be fiercer and angrier than the wolves; their bites *will* draw blood. Do not let them bite you. Most of you already know how to summon pools of flame in your palm. Now, control that flame. Visualize it forming a protective guard across your forearms. This will serve as your shield in battle, and in many cases, a shield is far more valuable than a sword."

She does not give her students a moment to gather their wits before she lowers her foot upon the activator rune again, this time releasing roaring and raging beasts that have not been seen in Myrnith in centuries. With wings reverberating gusts of wind down upon them—a force meant to flatten—and teeth the size of tree branches, three mid-sized dragons skyrocket before turning back, plummeting downward with barreling flames aimed at the fledglings.

First, they stun with heat, then they snap at anyone near enough to be caught between their gnashing jaws. Screeches erupt from the fledglings as the three beasts swoop down for their second assault. The rolling waves of flame engulf the entire class, evoking unanimous grunts of discomfort, before spiraling downward to take nips out of those beneath.

The class as a whole seems to look at their arms in a panic, wondering why their gauntlets are not appearing. Holding small arms in the air as though summoning the Gods, one fledgling curses the limbs to fall off and be eaten by wolves rather than continuing to betray him, and Myla smirks slightly as the child relies on humor to cope with his discomfort. Her attention is quickly drawn back to Bryar.

Come on, Myla urges, watching as Bryar crouches to brace himself. A dragon spirals his way at a terrifying speed. The nose of the great beast flares opens with a shuddering inhale before exhaling scorching blue flames. Myla thanks the Gods he is the very embodiment of fire, mostly unfazed by the melting heat.

He is not, however, unfazed by the razor-sharp teeth of the dragon as it snaps at him. A streak of red grazes across his forearm, chased off barely by the ripple of waves, intercepting the dragon's teeth with a chilling screech.

As though his victory is momentum to the others, two fledglings shriek victoriously as their forearms also blaze with gauntlets of flame.

Elara applauds, tilting her head slightly to avoid the swooping wings of a dragon as it descends upon a hunkering fledgling. Myla finds the nonchalance comical, watching as the instructor passes calmly through the fiery mayhem with little care. Her long hair, held back by a leather circlet, billows violently with every gust of flame and her freckled skin reddens, yet she appears as though she is walking through a market, deciding what she wants for dinner.

The lesson passes slowly with beasts of different shapes, sizes, and attack methods crawling, clamoring, and flying out of the rune portals at different intervals, sometimes many at a time. Each student is breathless and dazed by the time Elara seals the runes shut and sends them all away with instructions to return tomorrow.

Myla meets Bryar at the exit of the arena, taking stock of his battle wounds with a slight smile. "I did not see that coming," she says, greeting him as he falls in stride with her.

"The dragons?"

"No," she laughs. "The fledglings."

Bryar grins and drops his head in a humored shake, then presses his hands to his hips with an irked sigh. "That *was* unexpected."

"I was surprised you did not turn around and walk away."

His brow furrows, and he shoots her a knowing look. "No, you were not."

"No, I was not. You are right. But *I* almost got up and left when they started laughing," she teases.

"I see how it is." Bryar nudges her side, a cocky smile teasing the corners of his mouth. "Abandon me in my time of need."

"Never!" Myla gasps, at once regretting the coy exchange as a silence claims the space between them. Abandon him? No. Walk a path that follows his? Also, no.

I am a queen of crossroads, it would seem.

"Well," Bryar breaks the silence, his voice gruff with uncertainty.

"Thanks for being here today. It means a lot. I think I will come alone tomorrow though."

Understanding, though the proverbial dagger in her chest stings, Myla nods. The walk back to her room is slow, weighted with an all-too familiar ache brought back from its grave. Behind her, Bryar resumes his role as her bodyguard, wordlessly trailing her until she closes him out to stand guard beside her door. Her heart betrayed her before, when she and Bryar fell for the first time; that can be dismissed as adolescent bliss. This last time, Myla holds herself accountable for the weightlessness she allowed herself to find sanctuary in. It was a distraction, and it brought her back to a weakness she can never live in if she is to rule well.

I should never have reopened that door. She chastises herself, glaring at the hollow eyes staring back at her in the mirror. With a frustrated scowl, Myla turns away, determined to make something of her time in this place.

Chapter 20

Myla passes the days into weeks, scouring the Ashborn library. For the first several days, she finds nothing worthwhile, tales of their history and a few notes on the peaceable preferences of the Ashborn. Her goal has been to keep her whereabouts as simple as possible to avoid unnecessarily interacting with Bryar. It has become near impossible to pass through the dining hall without discussions of him babbling between young Ashborn women, let alone surviving dinner itself. His reputation as a valiant warrior grows, as does the enamor revolving around him. A strange, handsome man, now one of their own.

Myla thinks they need to spend more time in the library to occupy their minds with something else.

In the mornings, Myla leaves the palace hours before Bryar does, accompanied instead by a few Ashborn guards appointed to her by Ivan, and does not return until well after his lessons. Her schedule has proved successful as it has been four days since she came face-to-face with him beyond his trailing her to and from her room in the evenings to stand at his post while she sleeps.

Ultimately, she aims to make their severing as painless as possible. She has convinced herself her presence is a distraction to him and his new path; in reality she knows it is a matter of willpower. Should she speak to him again, she knows she would cave. She would chase every irrational need to be with him, abandoning her throne and responsibilities.

No. Studying and looking for any tools that may aid in defeating the Blood Stealer is the safest way to pass time.

About a month into her excavation of the library, Myla finds a thick text bound in pale leather, with fine lines burned in a breathtaking depiction of two phoenixes entangled. Something suggestive about the illustration causes Myla to swallow hard, her breathing growing heavy. "Well," she mutters flatly. "A phoenix sex book—fascinating."

With a thud, she flips it open.

The first page draws her in and for the next twelve hours, she stays curled in a pile of cushions, the pages lit by lantern light. The book speaks on the sacred unity of an Ashborn marriage, the burning of two souls into the Gods' Book of Sacred Warriors, resulting in the infinite draw of energy from one to the other. It is a union only documented between Ashborns.

Myla finds herself scouring the book, along with dozens of others, looking for some mention of an Ashborn and human match, as though finding that answer might justify her and Bryar's union.

After eight weeks of spending nearly every day in the library, avoiding Bryar as much as possible, and watching her belly expand, a young Ashborn woman enters, absently scanning the books. Myla watches her from her cocoon of cushions, packed heavily to support her aching back today.

The woman wears a purple silk dress, her belly also bulging with pregnancy, presumably more advanced than Myla. As she waddles, she leans backwards to offset the weight at her front. When she sees Myla slumped into her pile of soft pillows, she giggles.

"You have the right idea, stranger." She moves slowly toward Myla. "I have not seen much of you around since your arrival." She leans forward, her wings tucking at her back tightly as she extends a hand to help Myla up. "I am Lenore."

Hesitantly, Myla accepts her hand, ignoring the tragic image of them both toppling over into a pile of bellies and flailing limbs. "I am Myla," she greets the beautiful woman before her.

"Ah," Lenore sighs, "the Queen Who Bleeds Stars. Yes, Myla is less of a mouthful. I will go with that."

Myla grins at her new friend, then gestures toward her round belly. "When do you expect your little one?"

"I expected the fledgling last week. I suppose this one will come on its own sweet time." A resignation washes over Lenore. "I know better than to give birth a timeline of my own."

"Is it your first?"

Lenore howls in laughter, shaking her head. "I have enough fledglings to consider myself the commander of a small army. Eight young ones, not counting this one." She nods at Myla. "When will yours arrive?"

"If my timing is correct, in about two months."

Lenore nods toward the door. "I am famished, and nothing like a wholesome meal to bring on one's pains. Join me?"

Myla follows her out into the dreary day, rain thudding like hysterical tears of the Gods upon the ground. Her soldiers flank either side, clearly less than keen to follow two pregnant women slowly across town.

"Is this your first?" Lenore asks as soon as she has adjusted a drooping hood over her feathered head.

"Yes."

"You and your husband must be ecstatic," she remarks absently, her gait slow and lumbering.

"I am afraid the father has passed," Myla confesses. "But I am. Ecstatic, that is."

Lenore cringes, pressing a palm to her forehead. "Oh Gods, I forgot. I am sorry. I overheard some of the younger girls discussing who you are and where you are from exactly. What a terrible go of it you have had." Her words carry a weight of empathy—not as weak as sympathy, but a strength of character and camaraderie Myla has not experienced since Elsa. The face of her friend conjures in her mind, storming the barricades of her heart, a place she has reinforced as of late.

"We must all earn our place among the Gods," Myla responds, falling easily back into the rigid coolness of indifference which has been her solidarity for years.

"Must we?" Lenore challenges, beckoning her toward a bustling pub. The lax energy exuded from the place feels strange and nostalgic. She has not stepped foot in a tavern in years. She was with Bryar, Rhyland, Elsa, and Callum the last time. It was a night they would fondly dub the 'Night of Degenerates' for years to come. Mostly, because it was the night Callum lost his virginity to Elsa.

Who knows who Elsa lost hers to. It is the one secret she never shared with Myla, or anyone for that matter.

They enter and are greeted by a bustling crowd of drinking and meat-fat Ashborns who lounge, enjoying a midday break from their busy agendas. After instructing her guards to wait near the front, Myla follows

Lenore to a quiet table at the back of the pub, where they order warm tea and soup.

"What do you mean, you feel we must all earn our place among the Gods?" she asks finally once they sip their beverages, warding off the chill of the autumn day.

"Well, that every trial gets us closer to the Gods. Just as the Gods suffered, so must we."

Lenore smiles, rubbing her heaving stomach reverently. "The Ashborn believe there is a little bit of the Gods in each of us. To get closer to them, we must look inward. What do you see when you look inside yourself?"

Momentarily taken aback by the forward question, Myla stares at the rippling tea in her hands, watching the lights refract across its surface. Finally, she meets the steady gaze of her new friend and responds. "I see that I am angry."

"Ah," Lenore tilts her head in understanding, pacing her response with a long swallow of her drink. "Anger—an emotion the Gods work well with. Dare I ask why you are angry?"

Myla places her mug on the table with an unsteady hand, tracing the rim to distract her from the genuine aura emanating off Lenore. "I am angry because I underestimated myself, which allowed powerful men to, in turn, underestimate me."

Lenore shivers, drawing her wings around her broad shoulders for warmth. "Then, you must apologize to the version of yourself that you wronged, and you must do everything in your power to right those injustices. For her, and for you, and for every version of you which is to come."

Myla smiles to shield the sigh that aches to lurch from her lungs. "Yes, but how?"

Lenore leans forward, bracing her arched back with her elbows propped on the table, clearly uncomfortable. "You must ask what the worst thing you have done to yourself is and determine to reverse it."

Myla looks down at her rounding belly. "I do not think I can un-marry the king of Falkmere."

Lenore grins. "Considering he is dead; it seems you are not married to him any longer."

Myla resists the urge to smile, lest he see her in the life beyond and convince the Gods to smite her. "I suppose so. That does not undo the damage the marriage brought initially." Her mind drifts to the hurts Bryar hinted at, the way he grieved, alone with no one to confide in.

As if reading her mind, Lenore speaks, her voice all sincerity now. "You know, Myla, the Ashborn do not marry for convenience. Our kind has a history of lasting unities, with happiness for both parties, *because* those parties choose it. Not their kings, queens, or fathers."

Myla inhales deeply, her chest rising like a defensive wall against the probing. "It is not that simple for me, Lenore."

"On the basis of love, it should always be simple. Choose it, and everything else can fall into place as it does."

Their eyes lock, Lenore's brows arched with a knowing that should come only with age and wisdom, yet she wears it, etched in her sharp features.

Myla speaks, not averting her gaze. "What do you see when you look within yourself?"

Lenore's smile broadens, stretching infectiously from ear to ear. She appears as though she is about to respond with some answer of depth when she clutches her belly, a fierce gasp seizing her. "I see a fledgling that wants to get the *fuck out!*" Lenore stands, doubling over the table with a primal moan. Myla is temporarily frozen in shock, watching the woman before her grit her teeth together.

"Shit! Oh, Gods-dammit!" Myla mutters to herself, momentarily considering using the cloth linens to sop up the puddle pooling at Lenore's feet. She thinks better of it and offers Lenore an arm, the both of them making their way toward the door, where Myla's guards move to support Lenore. "Do you live near?" Myla asks.

Lenore shakes her head, letting out a humming noise Myla can only assume means she is focused. "No," the Ashborn woman answers finally, her body relaxing. "You must take me to the healer. She is only a few minutes away. Head back toward the palace."

A walk that should only take three or so minutes takes them ten with Lenore having to stop and pant her way through contractions. At last, they reach a small doorway tucked within the arch of a stone exterior. A sign hangs over the door, crudely written words read "apothecary" and Myla knows they have arrived when one good wail from Lenore sends a middle-aged woman barreling out the front. Her feathers droop slightly, perhaps with age. Wrinkles frame her eyes and a few at the corners of her mouth.

"Lenore!" she chides, motioning for Myla's guards to help her get Lenore inside. "How long has this been going on?"

Lenore attempts to answer but a grueling moan stops her, her stomach visibly tensing beneath another powerful contraction, so Myla answers. "About fifteen minutes." They guide Lenore inside, and Myla dismisses the guards to wait for her under the archway outside.

The healer rolls her shoulders backward and dips her hands in a steaming bucket, readying herself to deliver the child. "Lenore," she implores the woman to listen. "How are you most comfortable?"

Without responding, Lenore lowers herself to the carpet before the hearth, leaning on all fours, her back arched as waves of agony transform her from a woman to a wild animal coordinated with nature.

"That will do," the Healer states, gathering an armful of clean linens. "Please," she looks to Myla, "wash your hands and help me. The fledgling is not far off."

Myla shivers. It is such an intimate moment, and she feels as though she does not belong. Nevertheless, with the incessant moaning of Lenore and the way the healer moves the Ashborn's skirt above her waist, Myla knows there is not a second to waste on deliberating. Myla washes her hands and lays linens near the fire to warm for the babe before moving to Lenore's shoulders. Instinctually, she places a hand over the woman's and whispers encouragingly, "I guess little one has decided now is a good time."

Lenore grins in spite of the pain and nods, sending a droplet of sweat down her brow, which Myla is quick to wipe away with a damp rag. "The Gods smile on me this day, Myla. My fledgling is to be welcomed by the Queen Who Bleeds Stars, what good fortune—" her words are jarringly interrupted by a sharp wail.

"Lenore," the Healer's voice takes on a soothing tone, cooing her instructions while motioning for Myla to join her, "it is time to push."

Only thirty minutes before, Myla was having a conversation with this woman over a cup of tea. Now she is sitting on the receiving end of her fledgling's delivery, watching a midwife deeply massage the base of Lenore's spine to relieve pressure.

The next ten minutes are surreal, both emotional and enlightening. Myla watches the child enter the world, going directly from her mother's belly to her breast. Tears of pain and joy alike run down Lenore's cheeks as she lays back on a stack of pillows before the comforting fire. Watching the new mother effortlessly console her wailing newborn, Myla finds comfort in what is to come.

The sun has long since set when Myla leaves the apothecary. The Healer, Gertrude, spent the last several hours attending to Lenore and her new fledgling, until Lenore's husband was brought down off the cliffside from guard duty to take her and his new daughter home.

The evening air carries a sense of hope, drifting in with the chilly breeze which tumbles red and orange leaves along the glistening cobblestone path. The rain continues to fall from the sky in sheets of icy cold, and Myla cringes, considering the ten-minute walk she has back to the palace. She starts down the path, admiring the way the lights of the manors and shops overhead brings a majestic glow on the ancient trees, illuminating their leaves for all to admire in spite of the darkness.

She is strolling slowly, allowing the rain to drench her to the bone, when a familiar voice calls to her from behind.

"Myla! You are going to catch a chill." Bryar catches up to her, yanking a cloak off his shoulders to drape over hers while flashing the guards behind her a look that could kill. "What has you out at this hour?"

Her heart catches in her throat. Not expecting to see him and trying so hard these past weeks to avoid him, it feels as though they are back in her palace, painstakingly dodging one another to spare themselves this exact sort of moment.

Myla takes a trembling breath inward, before answering coolly. "I was at the healers."

"Are you well?" He quickly looks her over for signs of illness or injury before turning to face the guards. His words seethe like venom, and he stands toe to toe with them. "I am going to have *both* of your heads for not looking after her properly! It is freezing out here, and I see neither of you have done a damn thing to keep Her Grace warm or dry." He gestures to her rounded stomach. "Can you not see she is with child?"

"Sir—" A guard moves to speak but Bryar tips his head threateningly, as if their next words will determine if they are thrashed or note.

"Take pride in your job, *sir,*" Bryar warns. "I do not know what kind of oath you swore in Valyndor, but any guards assigned to the Queen of Falkmere are duty bound to ensure she is well at all times."

"Leave them be," Myla interjects with a sigh.

Bryar flashes them a final, icy glare, no doubt ready to have them punished for their failings. In any other situation, she would be enjoying the spectacle of the protective and angry man before her. Tonight, it feels like more of an insult. Pulling the cloak around her stomach, Myla offers them a weak smile. "They were only obeying my orders."

"You ordered them to let you freeze?"

"Enough, Bryar."

"But you *are* well?" he probes.

Ignoring the longing in his eyes, she turns her attention to the ground before her. "I am perfectly fine. A new friend of mine delivered her child today. I helped."

"You helped?" he repeats, astonished. "That is remarkable."

"It was," she agrees. "Perhaps, I would have enjoyed it more were that experience not looming in my near future."

"You will be alright," he assures, as he begins leading her back to the palace. His expression is unreadable, but the tensing of his jaw is a dead giveaway: he is enjoying this even less than she.

Myla squares her shoulders, biting down on the words that beg to spill forth, the confessions bottling up inside her. She yearns to expose her rawest feelings in hopes he will find a safe place inside himself to keep them. Instead, she nods, words failing entirely.

They walk in silence, their footsteps sending sprays of rainwater in every direction when her footing slips beneath her. Bryar's arms slip around her waist, intercepting the fall. His furnace-like heat a stark contrast to the icy cold of the rain absorbing into her skin. Bryar helps her straighten, finding her footing well before he moves to unravel from her. His hands linger, pressed to her back, their faces close. Myla watches as his throat tightens. It seems she is not the only one swallowing words.

"Let us get you back," he says finally, offering her a stabilizing arm. "We will have your maid draw you a bath." At the mention of bathing, Myla's mind sabotages all decency, flashing memories of the scandalously exhilarating touches exchanged. That is, before they ended their relationship entirely. She wants to agree to a bath on the condition he joins her and satisfies the beast of longing that has tortured her dreams for weeks. She also wants to say, 'you can not tell me what to do; you are not my husband'. But even then, she knows, husband or not, she makes a terrible listener and maybe that is why she is in this situation to begin with. Maybe the rebellious inclinations she has fed since her marriage to Caius have caused her to lose her ability to compromise. Whatever seems to be her problem, it will not be solved tonight, and saying something, anything, to him will only confuse their already foggy situation.

So, she stays silent, willing her fingers not to grip his arm too tightly and feed the sickness raging in her heart as the palace fades into view. They will be inside soon, and she will be alone in her room once more, hating herself for not saying what she wants to.

"Rhyland is expected to return tomorrow. He sent word to me last week with news of Falkmere. We should have breakfast together in the morning, so I may brief you."

Brief me. He wants to have breakfast, as queen and captain, so he can brief me. "Yes. I have been worried; it will be good to get some answers and make a plan. I will see you in the morning." She releases her grip on his arm and quickens her pace, trying to leave him behind before her resolve vanishes entirely.

"Myla—" he calls after her, a few quickened steps bringing him to her side once more. Myla internally curses the pressure forming between her legs, causing her to walk slower than she would like.

"When I said I needed to train alone, I did not realize it meant we would . . . drift so far from one another."

Myla stops, her back to him and her eyes closed, a sense of rage simmering and threatening to boil over. Careful to check her words and tone, she speaks. "I know. Surely you see how space is what we both need to move on from this. Soon, Gods willing, I will be returning to Falkmere, and you shall remain here. It is best that I do not greet my child, and a kingdom looking to me for leadership, with a broken heart."

He grabs her arm gently, moving her to face him. A gentle hand tips her chin upwards. Defiance or grief, whatever it is, she keeps her eyes closed, unwilling to meet his gaze lest she should find it as full of pain and yearning as hers.

"Look at me," he utters the command under his breath.

Reluctantly, Myla's eyes flutter open to find steam rising from his shoulders as the rain thunders down upon him. She is grateful for the rain which hides the tears pooling at her eyelids. "Please do not say anything confusing."

"I do not know what to say," he admits, his green eyes piercing deep within her. There is something boyish in his expression, no inhibitions, nothing of the fierce warrior lingers. Just a sad boy, who has carried his wounds into manhood and does not know where to lay them to rest. "But I know this should not be confusing."

"You are right," she agrees. "If the Gods willed this, it would not be confusing. Our love should not feel more impossible than the war raging around us."

His hand lingers, grazing the skin along her jawline. "It is not our love that is not simple." He releases her, taking what feels like a restraining step back, his warmth leaving with him. "If distance is what you need, then I will give you that. But do not fool yourself into thinking *we* are the problem."

"Who is the problem, then?" Myla feels her words lash off her tongue, landing sharply. "What would you have me do?"

"I would have you make a selfish decision for once. Pick yourself."

"So, you want me to walk away from my child's birthright now?" she questions, unfastening his cloak from around her and shoving it into his arms. "It is all I have to give this child, Bryar. My parents are both dead—am I to simply take her to my family's estate and hope nobody chases after the king's heir? You do realize that this is no longer *just* about me? The child inside me is counting on me to make the absolute best choice I can for her. Throwing her into hiding at birth and keeping her from her kingdom is not what is best for her."

Bryar shrugs, an unconvinced bob of his head nearly dismissing her words. "I do not want you to do anything that does not feel right for you and that baby." He nods toward her stomach. "But sometimes what feels right to you and what you think everyone else expects from you may be different answers entirely."

"So, what do *you* want?" Myla asks, hoping he has a less indirect answer.

"I want to marry you." His body squares and is steeped in a

confidence even the guards behind them seem unprepared to face. Myla hears them shift uncomfortably behind her.

Fuck. It does not get any less indirect than that. Myla stares mouth agape, listening as he speaks with confidence.

"I want to marry you, and I want to raise that child with you, and I want you to be *happy*. Do you think after all this time I actually give a fuck what any of your subjects want from you? They have had plenty of you, and now, I want you *back*."

Myla grinds her bottom lip between her teeth, the pounding in her chest drowning out the splattering rain drops upon the ground. "No buts?"

"There will never be any 'buts' about you or the baby, Myla. That is what I will always want, so long as I do not have to do it in secret." He steps closer now, moving wet locks of hair from her face. "You once asked me to hold on to her—to keep the girl you were tucked away safely in my memories. I did not just keep her in my memories." He presses a flat palm to his heart. "Who you were before all of this, she is still right here where you left her, and I *really* want her to come back to me."

Myla ignores the stinging in her nose and grinds her teeth together until the sensation passes. Not daring to look at him lest he crack her resolve, she lies. "That girl does not exist anymore, Bryar. You need to let her go."

Chapter 21

Breakfast is uncomfortable, to say the least. In his time here, Bryar seems to have formed many friendships, one of which being Phaenna. When Myla joins him in the morning, she finds the spot across from him is occupied by the beautiful Ashborn girl. They appear to be deep in lively banter that she wishes she could cut short with a swift clobber to the back of Phaenna's head. When Bryar sees her, standing back and waiting for a suitable time to cut in, he says something to Phaenna and she nods understanding, taking her leave.

You will not be a jealous bitch; do you understand me? She commands herself, pasting a pleasantly indifferent smile on her face as she advances, intending to claim the seat warmed by the intruder's perfectly round ass. Myla forces herself to exchange nothing less than a warm greeting with the girl as they pass one another.

"Good morning," her tone is impeccable, and Myla is pleased with her delivery until Phaenna responds.

"Mornings are always good after nights like last evening." Her brazen statement is followed by a flirtatious glance over her shoulder in Bryar's direction.

Myla stops dead in her tracks, watching Phaenna leave the now quiet breakfast hall. Her gaze drifts back to Bryar and a swell of betrayal ruins her appetite.

He did not. There is no way. Swallowing her wounded pride, Myla sits, avoiding Bryar's intent gaze as he analyzes her.

"What is wrong?"

"Straight to the point, huh? Seems to be a common theme this morning." Her voice trembles and her attempt at sounding comical fails entirely. Nothing but hurt is conveyed, causing a look of concern to wash over the disgustingly handsome man's face across from her. Of course, Phaenna is quick to lay claim. Any woman who does not is a fucking idiot.

Oh, me. That is me. I am the fucking idiot. The queen of idiots—get me a crown for that one, Father. I can wear it until I die beneath the crushing weight of idiocy.

"What do you mean?" Bryar probes, sliding a cup of tea toward her, steaming hot and prepared in advance for her.

Wooing two women at once. Get him a crown too, Father. We are all idiots here, it would seem.

Myla pushes the tea aside. "What did you do last night after we went inside?"

A crease forms in his brow. Confusion? Concern at being caught? Contemplating how best to answer? Whatever it may be, Myla does not want to hear it. "Never mind. What you do in your bedroom is no longer any of my concern. Can we just get on with this? When will Rhyland return?"

Bryar, stunned, leans back in his chair, crossing his arms over his chest. "No."

"What do you mean, 'no'?" she asks, annoyed. "Is that not why I am here right now? So, you can tell me whatever it is you need to . . . as my captain?"

"It is," he responds coolly, "but I am not going to answer your questions until you answer mine."

"You have to," she retorts. "I am your queen."

Bryar rolls his eyes and leans on his elbows, his words a taunting whisper. "No."

"Bryar!" she snaps, her voice an octave higher than she intends. "Please, for the love of the Gods, just tell me what I am going home to, so I can plan my return!"

He sighs, pushing her tea back in front of her. "Drink. You will not like a single thing I have to say."

The shift in his inflection carries a warning and Myla drops the petulant defenses. "What is it?" She takes a long sip of tea, refusing to admit she is grateful for it.

"Rhyland will be here by nightfall. He brings about forty percent of your armies with him—those who remain loyal to your cause." His words shatter around her, and questions spill from her lips before she can impart any patience on herself.

"What? Why? Loyal to me? Where will they—"

"In your absence, the Blood Stealer claimed about ten percent of your army before returning to the Seam. It is said he has captives with him, but Rhyland did not disclose who. Once the palace was uninhabited, various lords of the realm descended, and there was a battle for the throne."

Myla stands, the half-empty teacup before her sloshing to the floor and shattering at her feet. "*What?* This can not be."

He nods; his face grievous. "Myla . . . your father did not die. However, in your absence . . . he has claimed the Raven Throne for himself. There is no palace to return to now. Not without a fight."

Myla's chest seems to cave in on itself, the weight of his news heavy enough to bring her back to the seat beneath her. Her heart thuds in her chest. It is as loud as war drums and ready to explode in a shock wave from decades of anger and abuse at the hands of the man who just wanted to give her power, to then take it away. Astonished and sickened, Myla finally blurts, "He *survived*?"

Bryar reaches across the table, grasping for her hand, a gesture she recoils from, her entire body stiffening in disbelief. "And now half of my army belongs to my father? Lord Maverick Alerys, now sits on my throne?"

"*King* Maverick Alerys . . ." Bryar grumbles, distaste for the name causing his face to twist into a scowl.

"And Vesperian took what, a thousand of them?"

"And Rhyland is nine hours away, with another forty thousand, give or take," Bryar concludes.

A wave of hot stress washes over her, nausea threatening to put on display the less queenly side of her. Slow deep breaths still the turmoil in her stomach, and Myla rests her head in her hands, finally speaking. "I do not know what I expected. I left my throne unprotected. Of course, power-hungry lords would lay claim to it. That does not shock me. But my own *father?*" Myla briefly considers that he may be simply maintaining control, which she will reclaim when she returns. That, however, is not the Maverick Alerys way. No, he has stolen her throne. Perhaps this is the conclusion to his grand scheme. Perhaps she was merely his social ladder after all.

Bryar shakes his head. “I did not predict this. I was certain the Blood Stealer would occupy the palace for a long time, Myla. I certainly did not expect anyone to contest your rule.”

“What of Callum?” Myla asks, moving on from the topic of her stolen throne. “Have you had word from him?”

Bryar shakes his head. “I have not. I plan to send Rhyland after him if we do not hear in a fortnight.”

“And we have no idea whatsoever who Vesperian’s captives are?” Her first thought is of Fern and the other young women who served in the palace. They would be easy targets for his appetites.

“Rhyland did not say,” Bryar answers, studying her face. “Listen, we need to build you a new Council and make a plan. Fighting the Blood Stealer in his own kingdom complicates matters significantly.”

“Yes,” Myla agrees, lacing her fingers before her. “Please, find out who battled for my throne. I do not want to extend Council invitations to them. We can decide from there who would benefit our cause.” She presses fingers to her temple, willing her brain to still. “Where will the army make camp?”

“King Ivan has agreed to let them make camp in the clearing.”

“I must thank him,” Myla sighs. “Surely, he is wary of such a large army encamped outside his kingdom?”

Bryar tilts his head slightly, responding cautiously. “He trusts me . . .”

The next hour is spent discussing plans. Bryar reinforces that Myla’s best approach is to stay put within the safety of the ward until Callum returns with more information on the Blood Stealer. For all the battle savvy plans Bryar seems to effortlessly propose, a gnawing sense of dread lurks in the back of her mind. How is she to fight battles on two different fronts? For someone not under the influence of the Blood Stealer, nor pregnant, this would be a feat documented by bards. In her current condition, one battle feels impossible, two feels like a death sentence.

Bryar seems to read her mind, and reaches across the table once more, nearly touching her hand comfortingly before retracting. "We will deal with the Blood Stealer first. Falkmere can come second—a mortal king is easier to defeat than the Blood Stealer, and your father is an idiot. Let him rebuild the palace for you," he adds with a cocky half smile. "You can reclaim it in time for renovations to be complete."

Myla smirks, brushing stray curls behind her ears. "We focus on the Blood Stealer first," she repeats in agreement. "Everything else can wait."

Myla is tempted to spend the remainder of the day pacing the long halls of Valyndor Palace, but as her feet begin to ache and she passes lunch on an empty stomach, she decides her pacing may as well take her somewhere. A visit to Lenore seems fitting. So, she dons a blue cloak, and begins toward her friend's house, carrying a basket full of fresh sweet rolls from the kitchen to give to Lenore's fledglings. At Bryar's command, her poor, deeply insulted guards follow close behind.

She has yet to venture into the common part of Valyndor. Its unique layout is fascinating to her. Spiral staircases of wood are constructed around the base of enormous tree trunks, leading upward into exquisitely crafted homes tucked into the canopies of the trees, leaving natural openings beneath the homes for gardening and playing fledglings. Laughter fills this district, lighthearted family life taking priority over anything else. Fathers swing their fledglings overhead and mothers clap with glee as their little ones take flight for the first time. It is exactly what she would expect to see in a peaceful community, but the sight sends a tinge of longing through her, knowing she will not experience this sort of simplicity with her own child.

A barefoot fledgling crouches curiously, his wings drooping in a puddle of mud as he examines worms beneath a fallen log. His mother calls to him, encouraging him to keep clean. It seems they have somewhere to be. Myla smiles and turns her attention to a group of adult Ashborn a few feet ahead of her, hanging washing from a line.

"Excuse me," she addresses a young man who watches her with hesitant curiosity. "Can you point me in the direction of Lenore's home? Do you know?"

The Ashborn man gives her brief instructions and soon she finds herself knocking on the door of a noisy home. It takes a few raps before anyone hears her over the commotion of shouting and a crying infant. The door cracks open and nothing but a bright amber eye peeping out is visible. "Who are you?" A small voice demands. "Mama!" they yell, before she can answer. "There is a weird lady with no wings here!"

Lenore laughs, shouting at her fledgling to let Myla in. "Forgive them," she says with a vibrant smile. "My house is full of feral creatures." *Feral creatures,* is whispered as a playful taunt at an auburn boy who darts past her, rustling the hem of her skirt before clambering up a small staircase, and disappearing into a room overhead.

"You look well," Myla says, placing her basket on a simple wooden table, taking note of the hand-crafted furniture and simply woven linens. Everything in Lenore's home seems to be made by herself, or perhaps her husband. The tree trunk at the center of the large room partially obscures Myla's view to the other side, but she thinks she can see a few more children quietly playing on the floor. "How are you?"

Lenore pats the space beside her on a cushioned bench. The infant in her arms is fast asleep. "I am happy today, but all last night when she cried, I thought I might cry too. We arrived home late, and she was happy as could be, so quiet and content. And then into the evening, she decided she had something to complain about, and she wailed about it until an hour ago."

A genuine smile stretches across Myla's face, for the first in a while, and she reaches to run a delicate finger over the infant's upturned nose. "She is just confused," she encourages. "But I do not need to tell you that. You have done this many times before."

"Yes," Lenore agrees, her tired eyes gleaming. "I can not say it gets easier with practice. I suppose, you just learn to survive until the hard days pass."

Her words feel relevant. Surviving is all Myla has done for six years, and she wills the hard days to pass again.

"Can I get you anything?" she offers, retrieving Lenore's empty teacup. "I will freshen your drink for you. Do your fledglings need anything?"

Lenore laughs lightly. "I can not have a queen waiting on me in my home."

"Please," Myla insists. "Allow me to be here, as a friend."

Lenore nods, understanding quite well. "I see you have brought food; I am sure they would love you forever if you gave them some."

Myla spends the next hour ensuring Lenore's fledglings have eaten and are free of sticky fingers before they run off again to play. Her second to youngest, a red-haired boy, informs her his mother's tea is running low, so Myla leaves briefly to buy some more, returning with enough to last Lenore a few weeks. After tidying the main room, Myla sits again, sharing in some of the tea.

"You asked me yesterday what I see when I look within myself," Lenore speaks. "I see decisions. Some good, some bad. But all of them have led me here." She nods down at the child in her arms. "I do not regret anything that has brought me here. Someday you will like what you see when you look inside yourself, and I hope you do not regret any choices that lead you to that place."

"Lenore," Myla responds hopelessly, her voice wearies with too many unanswered questions, "I do not recognize myself anymore. If I had faced these trials six years ago, I know exactly how I would have responded."

"So, what changed?" Lenore asks inquisitively.

"I think . . . I changed."

"You are supposed to change, but what has made you uncertain?" she probes, shushing the baby in her arms with a gentle stroke across the forehead.

"Responsibilities," Myla admits. "I did not have the sort of responsibilities I have now to get in the way of my decision making."

Lenore shakes her head, sighing heavily. "I can think of very few responsibilities a woman of your station might have thrown upon her that should stand in the way of what you want. You are a queen, Myla. You have the power to say no. You can stand in a room full of men and say no—why do you not?"

"Because they would not accept it."

"They would not accept it, or they would not like it?"

Myla smirks, letting out a slow breath as the baby inside her shifts uncomfortably. "Both, I suppose."

"So, what choice is so controversial that you fear their anger of it?"

Myla blurts the response before she considers how it might make her look to admit that love is what afflicts her. "Marrying my captain, rather than some eligible nobleman for the advancement of the kingdom."

Lenore snorts, bits of tea dribbling from her mouth, back into her cup. "I swear to the Gods," she says with a girlish grin. "If you pick a room full of ugly, pudgy men's feelings over that . . . *fine* specimen of a warrior, you are doing women everywhere a gross disservice."

Myla allows a moment of laughter before responding practically. "I do not know how to defeat the Blood Stealer, I do not know how to reclaim my kingdom, from my *father,* at that. I do not know how to raise a child. Lenore, I am a walking disaster of a queen in the eyes of my people. Imagine, I resurface with intentions of marrying my bodyguard?"

Lenore's eyebrows raise. "I think I need some more context here."

Over the next few hours, Myla shares her story, explaining to Lenore all the complexities that have led to her being in Valyndor. Sparing no details, Myla is sure to include her and Bryar's history, finding it a relief to share the burden with someone who seems to care, genuinely care, for her as a person, not as a queen or a pawn.

For a while, Lenore is silent, visibly mulling over the meaty content Myla has shared before speaking. "If you could channel your child's magic, do you suppose that might help with your Blood Stealer issue?"

It takes Myla a few seconds to register Lenore's words. When she does, questions flood her mind too quickly to ask in a cohesive manner, so all she manages is, "*What?*"

Lenore nods, touching Myla's arm reassuringly. "The Ashborn can channel their children's magic from the womb. It is how we determine if they have an inclination for good or evil, so we might course correct at birth."

Myla shakes her head, still confused. "How does this help me, Lenore? I am not Ashborn."

Lenore hesitates. “I believe your struggles stem because you are refusing the gift of the Gods. You believe your loneliness, your suffering, is the only way to stay on the right path. The Gods have more in store for you, should you accept.”

Myla hides the aggravation bubbling within, wondering what Lenore could possibly be getting at. “Lenore,” she probes with a sigh, “I do not think I understand what you are saying. Speak plainly, please.”

A reluctance washes over Lenore before she flashes a brief smile. “I will speak to you as a friend, no reservations, but truly consider what I say before dismissing it.”

Myla nods in agreement, resting a tense hand on her belly. “Alright, I will consider it.”

“You are not Ashborn. On your own, you can not channel your child’s magic. But you love a man who *is* Ashborn. A man who has already told you he would marry you if he could.”

Myla’s skin crawls with goosebumps, the message Lenore sends clarifying.

“Ashborn marriages are powerful. I saw you reading in the library, so I do not believe I need to expand on it. You already know. But what would happen if you stopped refusing the gift the Gods offer you—the captain? From what you have just told me; it seems he has waited very patiently for you.

“I love my husband, but I can not say he would have done the same—few would. The unconditional loyalty you two share is unheard of. Perhaps, you take a leap of faith and see what the Gods do with it. Worst case scenario, you have lost the throne, but you have a husband you can count on for the rest of your life. Best case scenario . . . you have a husband you can count on, who helps you win back your throne, and you have lots of *really* hot castle sex after an invigorating day of ruling together.”

Myla bellows in laughter, pressing a palm to her flushed forehead. "Oh . . . Elsa would have loved you."

Lenore grins. "Based on how you speak of her, I believe I would have loved her too. I believe she also might have told you; it is time to decide which part of your story you will choose for yourself, and which part you will give to the will of the Gods to decide. You are a queen, Myla. Do not walk around here as anything less."

Myla's trek back to the palace is a slow one. Lenore's words echoing in her mind, pushing her to a place where she knows a decision must be made, and quickly. She smiles at she and Lenore's departing conversation.

"Lenore, what makes castle sex different than regular sex?"

Lenore had shrugged, a coy smile curling her lips. "I suppose the kind that does not require silence . . ." She glanced at the trail of fledglings plowing through her house, a look of desperation washing over her. "The kind where one is not afraid of their fledglings overhearing . . . or monks for that matter." Her face squished into a delightful laugh. "We are going to have to discuss *that* later. I do not know how I feel about it."

Myla departed with lighter steps than she arrived, but now, as she makes her way back toward Valyndor Palace, she is acutely aware of the choices looming before her. Rhyland will be arriving soon, if he has not already, and the choices regarding where men are sent and what attacks are made in the next few days will be greatly determined by what choice she makes in her personal life. Should she choose to stay the course, with eyes only for her child's throne, her plan of attack will likely be more assertive than should she choose to follow her heart.

Ashborn soldiers congregate before the palace steps, discussions of the approaching army passing, heated, between one soldier and the next. They make way for her to pass, eyeing her in a different light, perhaps wondering if she has played a weak queen and is truly here to infiltrate them from the inside.

"What say you, Queen Who Bleeds Stars?" A market-goer carrying a basket on his hip eyes her wearily now. "Do you truly believe your armies can infiltrate such a mighty stronghold?"

Myla eyes her contester, straightening beneath the scrutiny of those watching. "I would not dream of trying," she replies as she pushes past them. "You grossly misjudge me." With nothing more to say, she enters the palace.

Something in the air around her shifts. Regardless of what anyone thinks or says about her; forty thousand men march her way. Forty thousand men prepared to die for their oaths. Forty thousand men who looked upon her father and defied him.

That kind of loyalty can not be fabricated.

Felicity helps Myla dress in a fresh, formidable gown, her hair cascading down her shoulders and her sharp crown retrieved from its resting place in Bryar's saddle bag. When her soldiers arrive, Myla intends to stand before them looking undefeated. No longer does she intend to be perceived as weak or dismissible. Decisions have been made, and she intends to live by them, rule by them, and enforce them by whatever means necessary.

The silk black dress she wears hugs her body like a sheath, her belly on display and unmistakable: the queen carries *her* heir. Convincing them on the matter of the child's father might prove challenging, but looking in the mirror and seeing a growing strength glare back at her, Myla decides she does not care. They can accept her words, or they can question them.

How men perceive her is no longer her problem.

"You look . . . magnificent," Felicity awes, her round eyes wide in amazement. "Whatever you plan tonight, good luck." With that, Felicity leaves her to stare at herself.

As soon as the door latches shut, Myla lowers herself slowly onto her knees, pressing her palms flat onto the cold stone flooring beneath her. Her eyes fall closed, and she envisions the Spirit Mother before her in the woods outside the monastery. "Please," she pleads, her fingertips delving into the stones as if she can dig her way to where the Goddess lives. "Help me choose what is right, not only for myself, but my child. And if you can spare it, grant me the same unwavering strength you lead with." Across her mind's eye, the vision of a raven flying fast toward a trio of moons, before exploding into a flock of burning embers and feathers, flashes. Myla takes a deep breath, feeling in her bones that the Goddess smiles on her now.

As she leaves her chambers, Myla can not help take notice of the side-eyed, lingering looks from the guards and Ashborn courtiers. It confirms for her that she appears as strong and beautiful as she hoped she might.

Moving down the hall toward the entrance of the palace, the deep voices of men shift from a jumble of inaudible chatter to coherent sentences, and she sees the familiar face of Rhyland.

"Your Grace!" he says warmly, bowing informally before stepping toward her in an embrace. "You look well." He glances down at her belly, his eyes wide. "I will admit, after two years of you saying it was there but seeing no proof, I am glad to . . . well, see the proof."

Myla laughs, placing a grateful hand on her friend's shoulder. "I am *so* glad to see you." Her face sobers slightly. "Tell me, how are our troops?"

He nods slowly, inspecting her countenance. "They are ready to see their queen. The journey has been long and miserable. They need your encouragement. They are unsure of what they even march toward, but I assured them, their queen is worth the risk—" He is about to say more when his eyes dance and, with a courteous nod, he moves past her.

Myla turns in time to see Rhyland and Bryar in a firm embrace, not just fellow soldiers, but lifelong friends. There is relief between them, and Myla whispers a silent 'thank you' to the Gods for returning another friend to them in such uncertainty.

When Bryar catches sight of her, his somber demeanor shifts to a swell of pride. As he approaches, his eyes linger a bit too long on her belly and even longer on her crown.

"Your Grace," he whispers, kneeling before her in a reverent bow. "Your army awaits your commands."

Chapter 22

"We will not let anyone see this," Bryar whispers discreetly, drawing a rune on the back of her neck with charcoal. "It will likely feel overwhelming, stepping outside the ward. Should you find you are losing control, try and give me a warning. If I activate this rune, it will incapacitate you. We will explain it away as something to do with the pregnancy."

Myla nods gratefully, rubbing her hands together nervously before her. "Thank you," she answers. "I do not know what to expect out there."

"With the army?"

"Yes."

He turns her to face him, pressing firm hands into her shoulders. "They did not risk their heads abandoning their posts to march for two weeks in miserable conditions to throw pitchforks at you, Myla. They came here because they believe in you."

"Right," she laughs breathlessly, ignoring the pit in her stomach. "I feel like people keep misplacing their trust in me. I never seem to know what to do with it anymore."

"That is not true," Bryar says assuredly, strapping a breastplate to her chest, along with shoulder guards and gauntlets. "You are just afraid, and that is to be expected. But you are not alone. Are you ready?"

"Yes," Myla answers, catching a glimpse of herself in the arched windows before the entryway. She looks fierce. "I am ready."

The night is late now and, in the distance, in a clearing beyond the forest that conceals Valyndor, hundreds of small fires flicker, no doubt warming the soldiers' meals and drinks.

Flanked by Bryar and Rhyland, and behind them, Ivan and Imogene, Myla walks briskly toward the exit, not daring to show anyone in procession how afraid she is to step outside the ward. Each step closer to the perimeter brings her closer to what could be her undoing, right before an army of forty thousand soldiers who have marched on good faith to come defend her. *I will not let them down.*

Ahead, the clearing looms into clear view, its entrance a pale yellow beneath the moonlight, contrasting against the black of the forest shrouding it. A few steps more and she stands at the edge. One step more, and she will remove herself from the protection of the ward. Behind her, Bryar and Rhyland shift, no doubt exchanging wary glances, wondering if their queen will falter.

Myla sucks in as much air as her lungs can house, holding her breath a few seconds before slowly exhaling, centering herself with as much determination as possible, and banishing all memories of nearly dying out here two months ago.

"Okay," she whispers, taking a step forward.

With a force unlike any she has ever experienced, her body aches. Her spine feels heavier, a need to double over tempting her to turn around and return to the palace. The air, which had only moments go felt pleasant is now hot, sending nauseating flashes of warmth to her head.

"Come now, Myla," Rhyland says confidently. "Show that asshole how little he truly controls you." Bryar chuckles alongside him, a discreet hand brushing the back of her elbow in support.

"Yeah," Myla agrees, swallowing hard beneath the pain growing from her joints and expanding rapidly across the rest of her

body. "No control, right?"

Bryar leads her up the side of a slight slope, giving her a vantage point over the majority of the massive encampment, which stretches across the clearing and beyond, into the woods of the other side. Standing tall, arms folded over her belly, Myla allows her gaze to glide over the moonlight's glint on the heads of thousands of men here to support her. If this does not merit confidence, surely nothing can.

"Attention!" Bryar's deep voice shouts, commanding every soldier to rise from their places beside their fires to stand straight, facing her. The clatter of armor against armor is nearly deafening, followed at once by an eerie silence as they listen. "Queen Myla Alerys of Falkmere." He draws attention to her, then steps out of view, leaving her the sole focus.

For a brief moment, Myla fears her words will fail her, as she feels like nothing she says can convey the depth of her gratitude to their loyalty. Alas, a spark inside her seems to banish the pain and fear, replacing it with the need to reassure her men that she has every intention of doing right by them, honoring their sacrifices, and rewarding them greatly. They have not come in vain; a gift from the Gods, Lenore might call it.

With a quivering breath in, she speaks. "You have traveled on the wings of faith," she begins, her voice stronger than she expects. "Faith that you would find me here, awaiting you with answers. So, answers you will get."

With confidence, her voice grows to a shout, hoping to invigorate the ocean of warriors before her. "Tonight, we find ourselves on the precipice of a battle, which I believe the Gods will see to victory. For too long, the Blood Stealer has cursed our realm and brought our people to their knees. I do not know a single soul untouched by him, be it personally or through a loved one. It is time for his reign of terror to come to an end!"

A shout of approval erupts, silenced only when she lifts a hand in the air prompting it. "We have faced a grave defeat, and we have lost those we love. I stand here today, humbled by your presence, your resilience, and your loyalty. I thank you all for sacrificing all that you have to come to me in my time of need. Your efforts will not go unrewarded."

A tremble of pain trickles through her veins, a hot sweat collecting on her brow. Myla ignores it, clenching her fists for leverage against the increasing discomfort. "I carry within myself, the heir of your beloved King Caius. For too long, his blood has lived in my womb, frozen in time. I feared what might happen to the child—the *only* Restorer left—should I allow it to enter this world.

"I understand my absence has surely been alarming, I hope you see now that it has been for the life and safety of our future king or queen."

At first, grumbles of confusion ripple through the crowd, soon replaced with invigorated roars of excitement, and renewed hope when Rhyland raises a fist to the sky and screams, "Long live the heir!"

"Rest tonight," Myla commands once the roar subsides. "Rally your courage and prepare. Soon we fight." Myla feels there is so much more she could and should say to these road-weary men, but the tightness of her chest, and the insatiable urge to fall on the swords of the men before her, cuts her speech short. Quietly, she turns to Bryar. "I need to get back in the ward. Now."

Without a word, Bryar takes her arm, leading her quickly back toward the tree line. As a suffocating tightness seizes her chest, Myla realizes she does not remember walking such a great distance. Lifting her skirts, she takes longer strides, begging the Goddess to send her even a drop more strength. A mere minute passes, agonizing waves of pain coursing through her body, as the need to shut down and cease to exist overwhelms her nervous system.

When at last she stumbles into the safety of the ward, Myla releases her grip on Bryar, ignoring the watchful eyes of the Ashborn king and queen, and continues walking onward on her own.

Rhyland and Bryar catch up to her, Rhyland making some playful remark about the speed of pregnant women. Myla ignores it, her senses not yet ready to receive any level of humor. The trio walks back to the palace in silence, but instead of entering, Myla sits upon the steps, overlooking the tranquility of the various paths leading into the darkness of the woods. She now knows, one path leads to the heart of the city, the wealthy manors and shops above, another to the training arena, and the third to the residential district where Lenore lives.

She allows the stillness of the night to soothe her pounding heart, bringing it to a place of equal stillness. The black vignette, which previously threatened to close around her vision, fades away, leaving her with a clear view of her comrades watching her, waiting for her to speak. Looking at Imogene and Ivan, Myla offers the sincerest smile she can conjure, considering her aching body. "I am indebted to you. Thank you for offering my troops a safe place to rest."

Imogene nods graciously. "There was a time, many centuries ago, when your kind offered aid to the Ashborn. It is the least we can do."

When the king and queen have retired, Rhyland and Bryar sit next to her. "Tell me." She looks to Rhyland. "Who are the captives you spoke of in your letter?"

He shakes his head. "I could not tell you, Your Grace. Townsfolk reported seeing the Blood Stealer leave with a slew of hooded captives dragging behind. I sent Callum to scout out the situation."

"Good," Myla praises. "He will get answers, without starting another war." Her eyes sparkle slightly as she glances at the younger man, hinting at his impulsive disposition. "You have done well. Thank you."

Rhyland shrugs, his face flushed with exhaustion and the red beneath his eyes a combination of sleeplessness and dirt buildup. "It is what friends do, Myla." He stands to leave, patting Bryar on the shoulder in a silent goodnight.

Alone, the space between she and Bryar seems smaller now. What was two feet of distance before, feels like maybe two inches now. His proximity to her is a stark reminder that, unless something changes, there will be a great distance between them soon. Two to three weeks of travel, to be exact.

The notion sinks into the depressions of her stomach, bringing a different sort of urgency to her attention. The kind that Lenore might call a sign from the Gods. A call for her to make a decision.

In her peripheral, Bryar sits, forearms perched on his knees, supporting his arched frame as he watches the lantern light flicker across the trees before them. His jaw moves forward and backwards as though he is chewing his thoughts to a pulp. Myla waits, watching, studying the shadows cast across his features and where his toned body ebbs and flows. Things she should not be looking at, yet she does. She wonders what goes through his mind—is it thoughts of his future? His place here in Valyndor? Not daring to disrupt the contented still between them, she merely sits, waiting for him to speak.

It is a long while before he does.

"You were a queen tonight," he says finally. "You were not Caius's widow. You were not your father's daughter. You were just *you.* A queen who cares."

Myla reaches above her head, pulling her crown off and twirling it between her palms. "I could not face them as anything less."

"But you could have," he disagrees, "and you did not. For that, I am proud of you."

She allows herself to look his way, swearing not to slip into the abyss of his endlessly searching eyes. Soft green eyes, like the wildest parts of the forest. Eyes that invite her to melt into the softness and discover the version of herself he so fondly sees.

The version of herself that must be true, for he does not lie.

"I have not felt like a queen in a long time. I confess, I do not exactly know what it is to be a queen without Caius or my father. I was not prepared for how naked I would feel, wearing a crown alone."

Bryar kicks a small pebble with the toe of his black boot, the grinding of rock on rock a disruption to the peace of the crickets and wind. "When I told my father I planned to join the King's Guard, he said, 'Son, nothing will scare you more than what you do not know. So, pretend you know it until you are not scared anymore,' and I have lived by those words. I believe joining the King's Guard has been far less terrifying than being the queen." He smiles at her. "I think you have done well, with what you have been given."

"It is time to do more, though," Myla adds, daring to inch her fingers near where his rest on his thigh. Though not a surprise, Myla is relieved when his hand closes around hers instinctually. "I am going to ask something I know I do not have a right to."

He turns his attention completely to her, nodding in ready. "You can ask me anything."

Myla takes a deep breath, ready for the pain that might come from the answer. "At breakfast, Phaenna insinuated that something had occurred between you two."

Eyes squinting in confusion, he tilts his head. "Phaenna?"

"Yes," Myla elaborates. "She made it seem as though you shared a moment . . . perhaps an intimate one. I know I have no business asking about your private life anymore, but I feel as though I need to be prepared if you are moving on."

Bryar's eyebrows press together in disgust. "If by shared moment, you mean she was disappointed when I rejected her, and so she threw herself on one of the soldiers instead, then yes. A moment occurred. But that would be the extent of it."

Myla releases a sigh of relief she had not realized she was holding on to, her head lowering slightly, hiding the faint smile stealing across her face. *Thank the Gods.*

"For the record," Bryar adds, his hand still tightly around hers, "I did not remain alone and celibate for five years just to trip over the first woman a king sends my way. I have eyes only for you, Myla Alerys, and I always will."

Hesitant, slow at first, Myla leans close, testing the breath between them, longing to remove all restraints and kiss him. He does not move, his eyes fixed on the fullness of her lips as they loiter mere inches from his.

"I do not know how this works," she whispers, "but I know I once told you I would give everything up for a life with you. I meant it then, and I mean it now."

His voice aches as he leans closer, "I will tell you how this works. You may be queen, but you are still mine." Bryar closes the gap, his lips warm against hers. His hand finds the back of her neck, drawing her in for a long-awaited kiss, slow and savoring, the kind that apologizes and makes up in one breath.

If kisses could heal wounds, every single one of hers, past and present, would vanish.

"Yes," she agrees breathlessly. "I am yours."

Felicity has just left. The moon casts brilliant rays of light across Myla's bed as she lies, hands on her stomach, watching the shadow of the curtains dancing across the ceiling, warmed by the glow of the fire. Her mind races with thoughts of all the evening has held. From her army, a mere stone's throw away, to the kiss she and Bryar shared. Here she lies, a woman, well advanced in pregnancy, certain she has never been more aroused by anything than that kiss. Myla smiles at the notion, allowing her eyes to fall closed, heavy with a need for peaceful sleep, when a knock sounds at her door.

Sitting upright, she is lured from her bed by the disturbance of a second knock. On the other side of the door, Bryar's muffled voice whispers, asking for admittance. She moves across the room, and swings the door bar over to allow him in.

"Is everything alright?" she asks, surprised to see him in her room for the first time in months.

"Yes," he nods earnestly. "If now is not a good time, I will come back in the morning?" He takes note of her hair in a loose braid over her shoulder and her eyes heavy.

"No," Myla shakes her head reassuringly. "Come in." She bars the door behind her, then moves to the chest at the foot of her bed, drawing a loose shawl around her body, self-conscious of the ways she has changed since he last saw her so bare.

"My mind has been racing since we spoke earlier," he admits, standing cautiously on the opposite side of the room from her.

Myla sits on the edge of the bed, watching his countenance shift, teetering on the edge of baring his soul, and saying nothing at all.

With a breath of confidence, he takes a few steps closer. "You said you do not know how this works, between you and me. What I know is, they say men move on quicker than women. That love has an end. Maybe that is true for other men, but for me, I have not moved on at all. I have not taken a single step forward from that place I was left standing six years ago. Maybe it was foolish; sometimes it felt like sitting next to a grave, willing a corpse to open its eyes and speak again. Nonetheless, I have stayed here in this place, loyal to you alone. You say the girl I love does not exist anymore, but when I separate you from your fears, I see she is still there.

"I have wondered if I might regret saying something, because when I look at what I am asking you to choose, it is preposterous. But I know I will regret it for the rest of my life, and I *think* you will too . . . if I do not ask you to marry me. So . . ." Like a man, falling to his knees in a final plea, begging for his life, he kneels before her, grasping both of her hands in his, his eyes searching hers, ready to receive whatever he finds reflected in them. "Myla, please say you will be my wife, and we can figure everything else out together?"

Of all the questions Myla has ever been asked, this is the only one that has ever made her feel light, as though her heart has detached from her body entirely and is carried away on a dreamy wind. "It is not too late, after everything?" she asks, holding desperately to his hands, her eyes blurring with tears.

"My love," he confesses with a gust of nervous laughter, "call me a fool, but my deathbed would not be too late for us."

Myla nods fiercely, not caring that the shawl has fallen away, or that stray hairs now cling to her tear dampened cheeks. She does not care that she is defying the rules of men, nor that she is trampling the consecrated ground of her father's carefully laid foundation for her.

For once, she picks herself.

"Then, yes," she answers with certainty, falling forward into his arms. "I will be your wife. And regarding everything else . . . I can safely tell my daughter there are worse fates than not being queen. If there is no clear path back to the throne . . . then I shall consider her a lucky little girl, and we see what else the Gods have planned for her."

Bryar's arms coil tightly around her. "We will let her choose her own life, as is her right."

Daylight finds them in a tangle of bedsheets, groggy from a night of sleeplessness, but content.

"I must admit, I am surprised," Myla whispers, as though a louder voice may break the euphoric spell they linger in. Her fingers trace the gold of his tattoos, enamored at how they shine.

"What of?" Bryar asks, looking sidelong at her nestled in the crook of his arm.

She flashes a coy smile. "That you found the courage

to *conquer* me in my . . . mountainous state."

Bryar wears a lazy half smile as he rolls onto his stomach to face her, drawing a line down the curve of her nose. "I assure you, my love, I have conquered much larger mountains as of late, none so appealing as yours."

With a gasp, imitating insult, she jabs a finger into his finely conditioned abdomen, "When do you have to leave for training?"

He sits up with a groan, squinting with one eye open toward the curtained window. "Something tells me I am late already."

Bryar stands and retrieves his clothes from the foot of the bed, much to Myla's chagrin. She is, however, diligent to enjoy every inch of exposed skin until he is fully clothed, at which point, she falls back onto the pillows. Lazily, she looks up at the tapestries displayed on the ceiling, listening to Bryar give account of when and where he will be, assuring her of his return later in the day, and hinting at promises of more 'conquering'.

Britches on and tying the laces of his tunic, he turns to her. "What will you do today?" he asks, draping her discarded shift on the foot of the bed.

"I would like to check on Lenore," she says, beginning to dress. "I will meet with Rhyland as well. I want to go back over the details of what is happening in Falkmere. Then, I will meet with the queen, Imogene."

Bryar looks over his shoulder at her, blindly fastening the straps of his breastplate. "What for?"

"To arrange a proper Ashborn marriage," she answers matter-of-factly, looking at him with a confident smile. "I see no point in wasting time. We have wasted enough already."

Bryar clasps his cloak and walks to her side of the bed, pressing a gentle kiss onto her forehead. "You will find no argument here. Let me know what she says."

Before the day grows busy, flanked by two of her newly arrived guards, Myla arrives at Lenore's house bearing a basket of breakfast scones and hard-boiled eggs, a small feast which her fledglings turn to crumbs in no time. They are now outside, where Myla left her guards, taunting the armor-clad men and begging for shoulder rides, much to Myla's amusement. Watching from the window above, she sees her guards engaged in a fierce pinecone war with the fledglings. She can not help but wonder if the simplicity of this day is a relief, compared to the past few months.

Having saved Lenore a plate, Myla places it near where her friend sits along with a steaming cup of tea. From the bottom of the basket, she reveals a vial of ointment she obtained from Gertrude on her way here. "She says this will help with healing."

Lenore smiles thankfully. "I have birthed nine fledglings now, and this is the first time I have had someone look in on me. I will be sure to return the favor, when your time comes."

"It is not a favor," Myla says softly, smiling at her friend. "It is friendship. Though, I must admit I have been lonely for a long time. It might even be selfish, my being here."

"Selfish or not," Lenore emphasizes, "thank you for making these days easier." The Ashborn woman looks her up and down, a sly smile stealing across her face. "You look different. What has changed?"

"I listened to *you,*" Myla replies, hiding her flushed cheeks behind a long sip of tea.

"Which parts?" Lenore probes.

". . . all of them, it would seem."

"Myla!" Lenore says aghast. "You have been inside my home for thirty minutes and have failed to tell me that you are no longer as neglected as old Falkmere!"

Myla nearly spews a mouthful of tea, barely managing to swallow the hot liquid before joining Lenore in a brief fit of laughter. "Do not make me regret confiding in you."

"No," Lenore forces a pretend expression of solemnness. "It is just . . . first monks, then trees, and now, well . . ." She gestures to Myla's round stomach. "Pregnancy is a whole other stroke. You have peculiar inclinations, not to mention that man of yours."

"Desperate times," Myla defends, reaching for half a breakfast scone abandoned by the youngest fledgling. "I am famished this morning."

"I imagine you are," Lenore teases. "So, what will you do now?"

Myla sighs, chewing the rest of the scone before responding. "Try to find a way to convince forty thousand men to follow me once I marry a man only slightly higher in rank than them. Then, if I am successful there, I will beg the Gods to smile upon me, as I do the same assembling a new Council."

"The army will be easier to coax than a council," Lenore says, frankly. "Men fighting for something often cling to any semblance of hope, especially if it points to their kind making something of themselves. The Council, however, will be threatened. You must remain strong."

Myla nods, playing with a fray in the hem of her wrist cuff. "Like you told me yesterday, I have to decide which parts of my story I will choose for myself, and which parts I will give to the Gods."

"I think you have chosen well," Lenore encourages. "I was hoping this is what you would do."

Myla spends an hour and a half with Lenore. When she leaves, the clutter left behind by her fledglings is cleared, the dishes are put up, and the newest addition is bathed. Myla promises to come again in the morning, then returns to the palace to seek out Rhyland. Though it is later in the day than Myla usually takes breakfast, she joins Rhyland for a plate full of cured meat and biscuits, noting again the rapid increase in her appetite.

"How was the condition of the palace?" she asks, watching as Rhyland eats like a half-starved man.

"Well," he mumbles with a mouthful of biscuit. Swallowing hard, he washes down the food with a long sip of warm ale. "I would say the worst of it is in the throne room, but the Imposter King seems to be making quick work of it. Everything else, though a bit dirty and scuffed up from what looks to be magic play, is alright."

"And what sort of attitude does my father's army have toward him?" she asks, gnawing nervously at her bottom lip. "Could they be swayed to join our cause?"

He shakes his head, looking as perplexed as she. "I am afraid I do not know," Rhyland admits. "I have yet to send scouts in to get a read on the political climate."

Phaenna walks in, her eyes lingering a little too long on Myla with a look of disgust.

Myla fixes her gaze on the young woman, silently accepting the challenge. The Ashborn sits at a separate table, being the first to break the gaze.

Clearing her throat, Myla looks back to Rhyland, who watches the exchange curiously. "Send scouts," she insists, not bothering to answer his unasked question. "It will be good to know what we are dealing with. When do we expect Callum's return?"

"Within a week," Rhyland answers, eyes still flickering inquisitively to where Phaenna sits. "What was that?" he asks, unable to resist the question any longer.

"*That,*" Myla responds, "is the woman our lovely hosts practically force-fed Bryar when we arrived."

Unimpressed, Rhyland's eyebrows arch. "She does realize she is looking at a queen, right?" Myla looks back at Phaenna, finding her gaze hot and challenging.

"Let it be, Rhyland," Myla says in a low command. "She is not worth my time."

"Oh," Rhyland agrees, "absolutely not. But she is well worth mine." He stands, walking across the room until he is toe to toe with Phaenna, her sharp eyes piercing holes into his.

Myla stands, absently adjusting the black buttons on the cuffs of her sleeve, before approaching the two, arriving in time to hear the end of Rhyland's short and sweet threat.

". . . I have traveled through hell and shit alike to get here, and I am not in a mood to watch my queen snubbed. You would do well to control your face in her presence.

"Come," Myla says calmly, not bothered to meet Phaenna's impetuous gaze, "we have better things to do right now."

Phaenna stands, crossing her arms. "You realize it is an insult to the Ashborn kind for him to entertain a life with you." It is not a question, it is a statement, one she delivers with conviction.

Myla glances over her shoulder, looking down on the girl with indifference. "If you are so concerned about the purity of the Ashborn bloodline, then you have already contradicted yourself with your interest in *him*. Get your convictions straight, and *then* come talk to me. Otherwise, I will not waste my time listening to you make a fool of yourself." Myla walks away, leaving Phaenna to marinate in her self-inflicted humiliation.

Rhyland is close behind, a brief snort indicating he is incredibly satisfied with the outcome of the conversation.

"*Your Grace*," he says stunned, a grin on his face. "I think you just made a grown woman cry."

"Grown women do not behave like *that*," Myla remarks. "I made a child cry."

"Despicable," Rhyland teases, catching up with her fast pace. "Myla," he pleads breathlessly. "For a pregnant woman, you walk *really* fast. Where are we going?"

"*I* am going to visit, Queen Imogene," Myla corrects, stopping to face him. "I need you to report back to Bryar, and be sure the troops are to his standards. Tell him, I would like scouts sent to Falkmere and to figure out how he would like to accomplish that."

"I should report to him now? While he is training?"

"Yes," Myla answers. "We have no time to waste. He will be done shortly. You can wait there for him to be done."

Rhyland leaves and Myla motions to the guards behind her to follow her outside. It is unusually sunny, the leaves overhead looking like red, yellow, and orange stained-glass windows to the heavens. She follows the trail which initially leads to the city, jutting off to the left, then down a narrower trail, which brings her to Ivan and Imogene's throne.

Imogene sits, a young fledgling on her lap. The child gazes up at her, laughing with a bunched-up nose at something the queen says. When Imogene sees Myla, she gently slides the child from her lap, sending him off to play.

Myla bows before approaching. "Was that your son?"

Imogene nods, a soft smile stealing over her normally stoic features. "He has returned from a fledgling expedition and looks forward to showing his father and I all he learned."

Myla watches as the child disappears into the woods. "Do all fledglings go on this expedition?"

Imogene shakes her head. "Only those who will sit on the throne." Her attention passes briefly over Myla who stands, arms folded before her in waiting. "You have come with something specific on your mind. What is it?"

Myla takes a step closer, and postures confidently, knowing her request may not be kindly received. After a moment of deliberation, she chooses her words wisely. "I have read much on Ashborn customs in my time here. Marriages of an Ashborn must be approved and conducted by their queen."

Imogene's lips purse. "That is correct."

Myla tips her chin slightly in acknowledgment. "Bryar and I *will* marry," she states, leaving no room for negotiation. "I would like to honor his heritage by joining together in an Ashborn marriage, and I know that can only happen with your blessing."

Imogene's eyebrows arch and she appears unimpressed. "In the history of Ashborn marriages, never have we conducted one between a half-blood and a human. I was willing to marry him to a full-blooded Ashborn—a reintegration of sorts. I do not believe his marriage to *you* would be well received by those who have honored our unified power source for centuries."

Myla bites down on the reprimand that nips at her tongue, staying cool instead. "In all respect," she challenges, "Bryar is the most powerful Ashborn, half-blood or *not,* within this kingdom. It is why you and Ivan accepted him so willingly. I know it. *You* know it. We both know that something in his parentage makes him powerful, and I can only assume it is his mother. Her magic must have been similar to . . . say . . . *yours.*" She pauses; her fierce eyes boring into the stone-cold features of the queen before her. "What you do not know yet, is that I am someone you want as an ally."

"Why?" Imogene laughs, standing now to level with Myla. "How would the Ashborn benefit from an alliance with you?"

Myla watches the queen pace slow circles around her, looking for chips in her armor, any sign of weakness. Myla intends to give her none.

"Because," she responds, "I am the only being left in the realm who channels the Voice of the Gods."

Imogene's eyes widen slightly before she checks her expression, returning to a stiff blanket of neutrality. "Why have you not used it on the Blood Stealer then?" she challenges, trying to sniff out a lie. "Would the Voice of the Gods not stop a Blood Stealer?" Naturally, she would not know. The Voice of the Gods has not been heard in centuries.

Myla shakes her head. "It stuns him; it does not break his blood oaths."

"So, what you are saying," Imogene coos, her words heavily drenched in mockery, "is that you need us."

Myla tips her chin upward, eyeing the belligerent queen from the corner of her eye. "I do, and I am not ashamed to say it."

Imogene laughs, a light tinkling in the breeze. "It seems we bring far more to the table than you do."

A familiar rage sparks in her chest and her fingertips tingle, the sudden urge to entangle Imogene in a twist of blinding light, insatiable. "Let me ask you," Myla nearly spits between her teeth, "why do you think an army of forty thousand men just marched for weeks to camp on your doorstep in *hopes* that I would be here with answers?"

"Because they are fools, all of them." Imogene does not miss a beat, the words nearly dripping from her tongue. "And clearly lead by a man blind with love. Like his parents before him."

Myla spins to face Imogene, her hand swift in its grip on her chin, forcing them to stand, queen glaring at queen.

"What do you know of Bryar's parents?"

Imogene wears a disgusted scowl. "I know his mother brought shame upon this court, and I know his father died with many secrets that are not mine to tell."

Myla shivers and her eyes narrow in contempt. "Does he know that you know this?"

"Why would I distract his learning with unimportant details?" Imogene rationalizes.

"He has spent his whole life searching for his mother," Myla retorts angrily. "He deserves to know the truth!"

"Says a queen who knows nothing of duty," Imogene hisses.

"You underestimate me, and you insult my rule," Myla growls, her forehead nearly pressed against Imogene's, a demand for attention. "I arrived here weak, yes. But throughout my duration here, I have *not* been received with the respect owed to a queen. Had you showed up on my doorstep, wounded and in need of refuge, in no way would you have been left invisible and dishonored in my halls. Your court ought to be ashamed of their reception of the Queen of Falkmere."

Imogene's nostrils flare, her skin red where Myla holds fast to her face, releasing her only when Imogene's guards' approach, eager to aid their queen. Imogene waves them away, a ferocity in her eyes. "If you want to be respected, Myla of Falkmere, you must demand it."

"No," Myla retorts with a whip of her head. "I believe respect is earned *and* reciprocated."

Imogene watches as Myla paces back and forth, her intense glare never once wavering. After what feels like several minutes, the Ashborn queen speaks. "I have seen nothing from you that suggests you are anything more than a scared little girl, thrown into a role you should never have been given. You speak of power, yet I have not seen it; hardly any infamy follows you. You speak of earning respect, yet you allow yourself to be trampled over. I am unimpressed with you, and I am disinclined to perform an Ashborn marriage on someone so unworthy of their mate."

It is not the unrestrained insults that tip Myla over the edge, nor is it the suggestion she, as a queen and a well-rounded woman, is somehow undeserving of Bryar. It is the way she speaks, so similar to the way the men of her Council used to, as though she is an uneducated child in need of enlightenment.

It begins as a warmth in her throat, a buildup of magic materializing into waves of fury. Light drips from her fingertips, sizzling on the chilled stones beneath her, ready to unify in one flash of electric shock. The Ashborn queen takes note of the simmering power, a brief eye roll dismissing Myla entirely.

Imogene, back turned, is none the wiser, her words continuing to cast judgment until the final statement unleashes a beast she is unprepared for. "Go home to Falkmere, and ask the new king how you might best serve him. It seems that is where you belo—"

Without warning, two guards come barreling into the space between Myla and Imogene, flames balled at their fists. Before they can make it three strides closer, Myla loses her light, binding them in a tangled mess together, suspended by a rope of magic to the trees overhead. Particles of light by the millions hang suspended in the air around them, ringing and casting a blinding glow in every direction.

Imogene's eyes flair, a brief moment of shock passing through her before she steps backward, fixing in a crouched position, her hands pressed together, summoning her own flames of fury.

From Myla's lungs, unrestrained and fueled with hatred, the Voice of the Gods raises from her throat in a deafening bellow, which causes the earth beneath them to tremble, a deep crack forming beneath Imogene's throne. A light engulfs Myla, bright enough to stun the Ashborn queen to her knees, arms shielding her face from blindness as the light extends well beyond the circular opening. The flicker of magic Imogene managed before Myla's display dies between her palms, her energy distributing throughout her body to act as a shield.

"How *dare* you treat me as though I am less of a queen than you." Myla's words are distorted, carrying with them the voices of the Gods and Goddesses speaking in harmony.

Imogene screams, covering her ears and squeezing her eyes shut. A trickle of blood runs down her cheek as her eardrums rupture.

"Do not be so naive as to underestimate me, I *will* have either your allegiance, or your *submission.*"

The Ashborn queen, tall and regal only minutes ago, is curled on the ground, her knees to her chest and her arms cupping her head to ease the sensation of her brain splitting in half. Myla wills her magic back within herself, casting a glance at the crack, which is nearly wide enough to swallow the throne within. Ivan and two dozen guards' approach with frenzied shouts, but Imogene holds up a hand, ordering their halt. Her amulet strobes violently now, calling to Ivan for help. His amulet blinks in response and at once, Imogene appears less distressed. Her husband carries the burden with her.

"May I offer you a hand, Your Grace?" Myla hisses, extending a hand down to the queen, who struggles to rise. It is not a nicety. It is not an offer of friendship; it is a final warning. One which Imogene inspects with fearful eyes before accepting.

Once standing, she looks from Myla to Ivan, and then to Bryar, who comes running into the destroyed space, a look of horror on his face.

His first response is to reach for the sword at his waist. Rhyland is behind him, flanked by several of Myla's guards, who refrain from drawing their weapons at her command.

"Do you need assistance, Your Grace?" Bryar asks, standing a few strides behind her.

"No," Myla assures, her eyes never wavering from Imogene's. "It was a misunderstanding, was it not?"

Imogene lifts her chin, small bruises specking it from Myla's fingertips, and blood staining the yellow collar of her dress.

"Indeed," she agrees, a look of admiration slowly replacing the fear and anger. "I see now that I underestimated you . . . *The Queen Who Bleeds Stars*." She glances down at the crack separating them and steps over it. "Let us have no more rifts between us."

Chapter 23

"What *was* that?" Bryar whispers, voice heavy with concern as they walk away from Ivan inspecting Imogene for serious wounds.

"*That* was the beginning of an alliance," Myla hisses, pressing a flat palm against her stomach, breathing through a brief surge of pain. "It seems the little one does not appreciate my efforts on her behalf."

Bryar shuts the door of their chambers behind him, latching it closed, visibly stepping into problem solving mode. "Are you sure it was an alliance? Did you just start a war between us and the Ashborn?" His eyebrows are raised on his forehead and his posture is tense, ready to turn right around and go fight somebody.

"No," Myla's laughter sounds like long-withheld gusts of stress breaking free. "She challenged me, and I showed her I was not to be questioned."

Bryar purses his lips, deep in thought, pacing over to the balcony window which overlooks the front terrace, scoping for any signs of guards coming to collect them.

"She . . . also gave me the impression of knowing *exactly* who your mother was."

Bryar turns, stunned. "What did she say?"

"Only that your mother brought shame to Valyndor and your father died with many secrets."

Bryar shakes his head dismissively. "That sounds speculative. Anyone could say that."

"I am not so sure," Myla disagrees, but his body language screams an unwillingness to investigate further, so she drops the topic.

"So, what is your plan now?" Bryar asks after a moment.

Myla checks her reflection in the mirror, straightening her crown and the curls over her shoulders before advancing toward the door. "I am going to finish my conversation."

"Myla," he objects from behind, as she barges out into the corridor with purpose. "Stop. This is not necessary. We do not need an Ashborn marriage to—"

Myla turns to face him, her features sharp and fierce with determination. "We do not need it. But I will not leave here without their alliance. The only reason they will not join our cause is because they have gravely underestimated me, and I have no intention of allowing that any longer. Ashborn marriage or no, I will not walk away without their commitment to stand beside us in battle."

With a nervous sigh, Bryar follows her once more, the clank of his armor echoing through the halls and announcing their approach well before they come toe-to-toe with Ivan and Imogene, who presses a wet rag to her ears.

"Your Grace," Imogene says flatly, a begrudged acknowledgment of the queen before her. "It seems we have much to discuss."

Myla tips her chin, not daring to lower her eyes, lest she give the impression that she intends to concede in the least. "It seems we do."

Everyone is dismissed. Not a single guard, man, nor servant can be found, and Myla is received inside Imogene's personal sitting room, a warm reception area, full of plump chairs one could lose themselves inside. Arched windows face the forest with benches built into their frames. They are adorned in tasseled pillows and heavy red velvet curtains billowing at their edges. A fire crackles in the hearth, casting an orange hue on moody art which hangs on the walls, nearly every inch covered in beautiful paintings. Above her door hangs a majestic pair of metal wings, glinting in the light, scuffed with the scars of past battles.

Imogene sits, curling her feet beneath her. "Let us talk, Myla. Woman to woman."

Myla sits across from her, noticing the table cluttered in ink sketches. "Are they yours?" she asks, motioning to the art.

Imogene nods. "I enjoy drawing what I see."

Myla inspects the half-finished drawings, admiring the attention to detail. "I do not wish to be enemies," Myla says at last. "I feel we are very alike, you and I."

Imogene runs her tongue over her teeth with a hiss of wind seething between them. "A detail I seemed to overlook. How uncharacteristic of me," she admits, her eyes fixated on Myla. "Surely, you must see that breaking with tradition will cause an uproar."

"Will it?" Myla challenges. "Or will it show your people, you are a just queen who rules with reason, willing to change to meet the needs of *all* her people. What will it say to your people when you show a half-blood the same respect you offer them? I believe it will earn you a greater level of trust."

"Trust, perhaps," Imogene agrees. "But what of order? If I bless your union, what is to stop others from mating outside of the Ashborn race?"

Myla's eyes narrow. "As far as I am aware, yours is the only race in the realm that keeps to themselves. Perhaps it is time to change that. It does not say much about your trust in your own people's power if it can be so easily threatened by other *equally* powerful kinds."

Imogene inhales deeply, absently stroking a feather tucked behind her ear. "What do I gain from this proposal of yours?"

"My word that, should the Ashborn ever need the help of Falkmere, you shall have it," Myla assures.

"You do not sit on the throne, Myla."

"No," Myla counters, "but I carry a powerful heir nonetheless, and I come with a powerful army who will continue to follow me when they see the eyes of the Restorer in my child."

Imogene takes a deep breath, nodding slowly, her eyes fixed on Myla's stomach. "How can you be sure your child will be a Restorer?"

"Her father was a Restorer."

"Who died, nearly three years ago."

"My magic can do incredible things," Myla replies casually. "Question my child's legitimacy as much as you like. When she is born, her eyes will glow in rings of blue mist, just like her father's."

Silence fills the space between them, Imogene visibly mulling over Myla's proposal. At last, she stands, her plumage casting severe shadows across her face. "As one queen to another, I choose to believe your intentions are pure. However, our alliance will be made official with a betrothal. Your first child with *the captain,* will wed Ashborn royalty."

Myla tenses, her convictions challenged, as she imagines telling her future child who they will marry. Giving up her child's right to choose. Myla weighs the consequences. If she does not form an alliance here today, she and Bryar will not be granted an Ashborn marriage, and they will not face the Blood Stealer with as much force as they could if she *does* agree to Imogene's terms. Given the circumstances, it is likely Myla, Bryar, and the child inside her would not make it far anyway. Not to mention the forty thousand men encamped outside Valyndor as they speak, ready to sacrifice their lives to her cause. A sacrifice she can not take lightly. A good queen—at least the kind of queen she wants to be—would do everything in her power to ensure her people are given the best chance at life possible.

With a resolving breath, Myla nods, reaching out to shake Imogene's hand. "I accept your terms."

An alliance contract is drawn up by nightfall. Myla insists on a few dozen of her soldiers being welcomed into Valyndor to witness the beginning of the Falkmere and Ashborn union, so they might return to the encampment and tell the others what has happened: a tale of hope. A place for Bryar's signature is also included, per Myla's request, as it includes his future child.

As they make their way to the great hall where they will sign the contract, Myla wills her breath to steady.

"Are we making a mistake?" she asks, looking to Bryar for a word of confidence. "Signing our future child up for the same fate I endured?"

Bryar's jaw tenses as he glances sidelong at her. "Perhaps," he admits. "I do not see how we have an alternative. Defeating the Blood Stealer *with* the Ashborn will be challenging enough. Without them, I do not foresee it happening at all."

Myla stops before the entry to the great hall and looks down at her shimmering skirts, smoothing the wrinkles of the deep green material over her belly. "Very well."

Bryar clears his throat, peering past her into the hall. "I must admit, this is not exactly my area of expertise," he says in a low whisper. "I am used to standing behind you, watching your back."

"Now you will stand beside me," she replies curtly, linking her arm with his. "Where you have always belonged."

The room is fuller than Myla has seen it in the ten weeks they have been here. Ashborn courtiers and guards, Falkmere soldiers, fledglings and adults alike, stand lining the path leading to the table where Ivan and Imogene sit, blue sapphire crowns a breathtaking contrast to their fiery hair and plumage. With Bryar in step beside her, seen now as her equal, not her guard—much to the surprise of the men he has trained for battle—they approach.

The two couples exchange bows of formality, before Ivan addresses the crowd of onlookers, eager to understand the meaning of the meeting called to order.

"It is with great honor that House Ashborn joins in allegiance with House Alerys," Ivan announces, his voice booming with conviction. "To mark the beginning of our unity, my Queen, Imogene, shall bestow the blessing of an Ashborn marriage bond upon Queen Myla Alerys and Sir Bryar Monroe of Falkmere."

There is a ripple of murmurs which overtake the room, looks of both shock and delusion in equal measure pass over the faces of the onlookers. At this, Myla straightens and faces the room, locking her eyes with one Falkmere soldier after another, holding their attention firm.

"You wonder what has occurred that allows the marriage of a queen's guard to *the* queen herself." Some chuckles quiver awkwardly through the room, silenced by a severe look. "*I* have occurred," she insists, her words growing in strength with passion. "I will no longer perpetuate a system which says this is as good as it gets." She gestures to her soldiers.

"For many of you, achieving the rank of knight has been a struggle—an *honor* your fathers before would never have dreamed of. So, to see Sir Bryar stand beside me tonight as my equal, may very well feel an insult to your efforts. I ask that you take it as it is intended, a symbol of hope for your own future and that of your children.

"And I ask that when we march in to battle in the coming days, you will look at your fellow comrades, the Ashborn, and you will see no longer a separate army and a separate people, but you will see your own kind, and the kind belonging to your queen's husband. I ask you to defend them as you would your fellow brothers-in-arms.

"In those most desperate moments, unity is the only way we will defeat the Blood Stealer and live to see a morning in the Seam where the sun does not rise a blood red." Myla's words are met with a roar of approval, not only from her soldiers, but Ashborn as well. Turning back, she watches as both Ivan and Imogene sign the contract, before turning it to face she and Bryar.

"Before you sign," Imogene says, moving from around the table. "There is another matter we must see to." She motions to someone in the back of the room and with a screech of resistance, the roof overhead recedes, pulled by a lever until the night sky shines above, welcoming a cool breeze into the otherwise stifling room.

"I believe it is best that you sign this contract not as the queen's guard, but as her husband," Imogene says to Bryar, holding out a closed hand before unfurling her fingers to reveal two amulets of twisted gold in the shape of a fiery bird rising, each bird bearing only one wing. Within the intricate folds of the wings, carnelian and polished rubies glint.

"It is the Ashborn belief that a husband without his wife can not fly, and a wife without her husband can not either. Marriage customs include the exchange of a token infused with one's own magic." She places one amulet in Bryar's hand and the other in Myla's. "You must give of yourself today, and every day until death, starting with the sacrifice of some of your power into that amulet."

Myla pictures the years she has sacrificed her power to her child, how effortless it comes, to share your strength with someone you love. Closing her eyes, she wraps her fingers around the cold metal of the one-winged bird, envisioning the transfer of magic. A cold chill sweep through her veins and a tinge of nausea threatens her composure as a piece of herself separates, infusing with the amulet. The metal grows warm with life.

When she opens her eyes, she watches as Bryar does the same, his hands aglow with a flame she is certain will melt the amulet before he can give it to her. Alas, his hand opens, and the amulet is intact, glistening all the same.

"These amulets will glow only for your intended. Should they fall into the wrong hands, they will be nothing but decorative."

Imogene places a hand on each of their shoulders, her voice sweet like birdsong. "It is believed that the Ashborn never truly die. Some say, it is our ability to burn and revive; others, myself included, believe it is our loyalty to our people. When you step into an Ashborn marriage bond, it is not to be taken lightly, for the power you will wield as one is unique only to you, and it can not be replicated. You are each other's life source. The death of one Ashborn mate is the death of the other. You can not fly without each other. Are you prepared to weave your days, your life, your magic, and your fate together, entrusting your wellbeing to the other?"

Imogene looks first to Bryar. "If this is a bond you are willing to give your life for, give your mate the amulet and your magic with it."

Bryar looks at Myla, not as though he is observing, but *seeing.* Taking a step closer, the amulet dangles on a fine gold chain as he reaches around her neck, fastening it. "I have been willing to give my life for you since the day I met you," he whispers in her ear before he moves back, examining the amulet resting on her collarbone.

Imogene now looks to Myla, her eyes flicking to the amulet cupped between Myla's palms. "What of you, Queen of Falkmere? Shall you give your magic, and potentially your life for your Captain of the Guard?"

"*Oh,*" Myla says with a coy smile, "he is so much more, and I would die a hundred deaths for him." Myla secures the clasp of the amulet around Bryar's neck, metal clanking on metal as it meets with his breastplate. Her hand lingers, pressed flat against his chest, their eyes locked as Imogene speaks, completely oblivious to the hushed crowd watching, one face in particular beaming with pride as she hushes her newborn.

"In honor of your marriage, I bestow on you the gift of the Ashborn Flame—a marriage bond which welds your fates and magic together for eternity. May you meet the gates of death side-by-side, and may you feast together with the Gods in the afterlife."

Myla flinches as a blast of hot flame launches itself from Imogene's palms, bathing her and Bryar together in a glowing flash of orange and yellow, before slowly fading to blue. The flame, which should melt her skin from her bones, feels like nothing more than a warm summer breeze, and a light pulses from her amulet, Bryar's magic protecting her already. In turn, light spills from her body, millions of stars spiraling in the vortex of their magic, blinding all but Myla and her husband.

Within seconds, the swirling energy returns to its owners, and the room takes on its natural lighting again.

"May the Ashborn Flame protect you both, and may your marriage be a *legendary* one," Ivan says, standing beside his wife. "Now kiss your queen, and sign this contract so we can begin feasting." His voice is laced with a hint of humor as he retrieves the quill, dipping it in ink readied for their signatures.

Bryar pulls Myla by the waist, bringing her as close as her round stomach will allow, and smiles into a kiss. "I love you, wife," he says, as though the words themselves are a sacrament to the Gods. "Now, let us put a stop to that son of a bitch, so I can finally worship you in *peace*."

"Perhaps, winning this war will be our wedding gift to one another," she hums in response, allowing her lips to linger against his a little longer.

"I can think of more pleasant ways to celebrate," Bryar retorts before leaning in to offer something filthy and exhilarating, sending a rush of red to her cheeks.

"Promise?" Myla whispers in his ear.

Her probing is met with a sly grin and a tip of his sharp chin, "I promise."

Myla has barely finished her signature on the contract when the great double doors of the busy hall fling open, revealing Callum in a cloud of ash. He looks older, somehow. His hair is a mess, his eyes are heavy, and his armor is marked with new dents and scratches. He stands before them now, covered in a heavy layer of dust and soot from days of traveling through the Seam. His shoulders heave as he angrily throws two Ashborn guards off him. Both guards grunt in disgust, dutifully reaching to seize him, shouting commands of, “Stop in the name of the king.”

They are about to detain him once more when Myla twists to face them head-on. “Let him be!” she insists, her tone not to be defied. “He is with me.”

Concerned, Bryar maneuvers past her, followed closely by Rhyland.

Before either can ask any questions or make sense of his distress, a quivering plea for help brings Myla’s heart to a screeching halt. “Vesperian has Elsa.”

Chapter 24

Somewhere, tucked within the darkest parts of the Blood Stealer's vile castle, a two-day ride from Valyndor, Elsa has fallen victim to Vesperian. Across the room, Rhyland and Bryar strategize, Callum paces in an agonizing trance back and forth across the room.

"To make things worse," Callum spews, continuing a rant that has not stopped since his arrival, "the road between here and the Seam is *crawling* with devilish wolves. Massive things." He points to a bandage around his thigh. "*Fucking massive.*"

"We can handle some wolves," Bryar says, about to offer solutions when Callum interjects again.

"I had to come back over the Seer's Mountain to avoid a pack of them—we need to be prepared."

Rhyland groans and looks at Myla. "Do you want me to make him forget the last few weeks so he will *shut the fuck up.*" The latter statement is louder and enunciated, more of a command than a question.

"No," Bryar insists. "Callum, *focus*—where did you leave the Raven's Veil? Is Titonfall ready?"

"I can not focus!" Callum rages. "He has her, and he is hurting her!"

Rhyland now grabs Callum by the collar, pulling him upright, and bellows, "She is *alive,* man. That is more than you had a month ago! You can still save her! Now, pull it together."

With raised eyebrows, Bryar watches the exchange and nods at Rhyland in approval, before turning to Callum once more. "Titonfall. The Raven's Veil. *Talk.*"

Callum reveals that Titonfall waits for word to march on the Seam, but he has split the forces of the Raven's Veil between Titonfall and a camp at the base of the mountains in the Seam. Myla and her armies are to meet them on their journey and battle Vesperian, resulting in an attack on Vesperian from both the north and east.

Myla lowers herself to the edge of the hearth in the great hall. A fog of guilt sneaks through every corner of her soul, visions of Elsa manipulated and misused plays over in her mind. "I thought she died," Myla says finally, drawing the men's attention her way. "I can not believe, I have sat here thinking she was somewhere with the Gods, to find that all this time I have abandoned her to the brutalities of Vesperian."

Callum's pacing resumes, his hands a frenzy of motions, first tangling in his rusty-blond hair, then grabbing at his sword as though the Blood Stealer is already near enough to stab, and finally he launches a volley of angry fireballs through the open ceiling, chasing them with a string of curses.

"She did not recognize me," he admits, his voice breaking with emotion. "I went in with the Raven's Veil one night to try and get her, but it was a mess. I could not reach her, and even if I could have," his voice trails off into a sob, "she is his *plaything* now."

"His what?" Myla demands, though she already knows the answer. She feels a painful lump form in her throat, threatening to suffocate her. "We need to go now," she insists. "There is no reason to wait. We need to get her." Myla stands, making for the door with every intention of donning her armor and rallying the troops, midnight or not. Anger courses through her veins.

"Wait," Rhyland interjects. "Your Grace, you can hardly leave the ward without collapsing. We need a plan." Then under his breath, "Being the voice of reason is exhausting."

Myla nearly snarls, anger rising like a black monster in her chest, threatening to spill from her limbs in flashes of brutalizing light. "Do I look like I care? If I have to crawl, convulsing and suffocating to where Elsa is, I *will.*"

Rhyland sighs, closing his eyes in frustration, as tensions in the room mount. "Myla, you *must* think of the child. There is no telling what sort of strain the Blood Stealer will put on it at this point."

Myla slams a flat palm against the stone frame of the hearth, leaning toward the fire and letting its heat fuel hers. At least, she thinks it is heat from the hearth, until she catches the glint of her amulet, flashing red against her breast, and realizes it is Bryar's power, which she shares in now.

"Everyone out," she insists, pointing toward the double doors. Callum and Rhyland need no further command; they leave at once, but Bryar hesitates, walking toward her.

"You will not help Elsa by doing something rash."

"Please, Bryar," she says, sucking in a deep breath. "I just need a moment to think."

Wordlessly, and with an understanding nod, he leaves, closing the doors behind him. Something intuitive takes hold of her and she plunges her hand into the flames of the hearth, unbothered by the searing heat, and retrieves a smoldering length of charcoal. Similar to the runes in the woods outside the monastery, Myla's hand scrawls symbols onto the stone flooring. Only this time, she recognizes the symbols, for her mother taught them to her.

A curse.

A ruinous promise of death upon her enemies.

I am still here, Spirit Mother. Help me end this. Myla lifts her face to the sky, letting her fingertips grasp at the moon until she sees light travel down her arms, through her body, and into the stones beneath her, setting the runes aglow. They flash momentarily before disappearing from the floor

Her curse is given to the Gods, to do with as they see fit.

Myla watches the stars and temporarily considers visiting Lenore for more of her wonderful advice, when a thought strikes her. Something Lenore said resurfaces in her memories. *"If you could channel your child's magic, do you suppose that might help with your Blood Stealer issue?"* Recalling she and Lenore's conversation, Myla places a palm on her stomach, willing their spirits to unite as one

"Alright, little one," she whispers. "I need you to be strong. I . . . I need *you.* I know as your mother, I should not be asking for your help, and I promise I will not make a habit of it. But it turns out you are a powerful little thing, and your people need you." The request is met with silence.

Unlike other times, when her magic is summoned, there is no tingling, no rush of energy. It is still in her womb save the kicking of the child within, no doubt peeved by the prodding and demanding of favors.

Myla groans, willing her pulse to steady before trying again, this time with both hands caressing her stomach, bringing a warmth upward from her womb to her hands. Every molecule of her body seems to vibrate in response, and with the surge of a blue light flashing through her abdomen, Myla nearly believes it has worked. Until she lifts her hands, looking for the blue haze Caius used to show her. When he did it, it was a marvelous, purifying swirl of blue mist, stunting to the Blood Stealer and healing to those infected by them, banishing the blood oath from their veins. Now, her hands fall short, no sign of healing blue, no rescue for her.

Standing, Myla leaves the great hall in a slow trudge, discouragement making her limbs heavy. Two guards that watched her from a distance fall to her left and right, following as she makes her way up the corridor, through the spiral stairs, and to her chamber.

Inside, Bryar sits reclined on one of the cushioned ledges beside the balcony, watching the Ashborn guards patrol back and forth outside the palace. Hearing her latch the door behind, he looks sidelong at her, his own features weary with too many problems and no solutions in sight.

"Are you better?" he asks, willing his voice to sound less discouraged than he feels.

Myla sighs and sits next to him, her breathing labored beneath the weight of the child nestled near her lungs. "No," she admits. "Lenore told me of channeling a child's magic from within the womb. Needless to say, it did not work for me."

His brow furrows and his gaze returns to outside, to the patrolling soldiers. After a moment of silent consideration, he speaks, "What if we tried together? Did not she say it was an Ashborn custom?"

"Yes," Myla confesses. "But this child is not *of* you. I am not sure it will help in this case."

With a halfhearted shrug, Bryar leans forward, moving her hands to her stomach again and placing his atop them. "At least we can say we tried."

Reluctantly, Myla agrees. "Okay. Let us try."

Dawn breaks, its warm glow diffused through rising clouds of dust, disturbed by nine legions of soldiers—six of Myla's and three of the Ashborn's—marching toward the Seam. It is a surreal feeling to go from two years of surviving what feels like the impossible, to six months of waiting, biding your time and problem solving, to this moment. Myla wonders where along the way she became the kind of woman to lead an army of nearly sixty-thousand soldiers to fight on her behalf, especially when twenty of those lived in peace before her arrival. Looking to her left, where Bryar rides magnificently clad from head to toe in a full outfit of the Queen's Guard, she is certain much of it has to do with him. Visions of the night before tease her memory, and she is filled with hope. This is what an equal partnership feels like.

The Blood Stealer is a two-day ride for a small group of travelers. A traversing army of this size will take four, a detail which aggravates Myla and Callum equally. Between here and there, the terrain will wilt, slowly crumbling from the majestic and lush mountains, which the Ashborn call home, to an ominous trail of dead trees, slate cliffsides sliding underfoot, and, according to Callum, a pack of possessed wolves guarding a shallow mass grave; a resting place for the victims of Vesperian who have wilted and perished beneath his rule.

Myla pictures herself among them, wondering if they met their end in the same delirium she suffered when the Ashborn took her in. Images far worse than her own decay tell of Elsa's fate should they fail, and she too be thrown into an unmarked grave, left to decompose next to other such victims. Myla shivers, drawing her Queen's Blue cloak tight around her shoulders.

When he returned from scouting Falkmere, Rhyland brought back her raven armor. A smithy in Valyndor worked through the night to expand the armor, making room for her stomach. Even in her rounded state, when Myla saw her own reflection, a queen, a warrior, and a mother in one, she knew she would watch Vesperian's body implode beneath the force of her magic, or she would die trying; she would not return with anything less than victory, for her child's sake.

"Too long," Bryar had said with his hands on her stomach. *"This child has existed in the form of a question, a worry. Let her arrive in peace and safety. Let us fight to give her that."*

As they ride onward, watching the scenery change slowly, this is Myla's prayer to the Gods and Goddesses. Her hand fidgets with the raven brooch holding her cloak tight around her neck, wondering what Caius might say if he knew the armor he had commissioned for her would be worn in a battle *caused* by his death.

Ugly words loom in the back of her mind, pricking her conscious. *Blood Stealer or not, after three years of suffering . . . I am glad you are dead.* A lump catches in her throat, and she wonders if wishing death on a man who hurt you when no one was looking is a cowardice the Gods will punish on the battlefield.

Not fighting back is as good as being a willing participant. Her mother's words ring in her head, memories of the one and only time she confided in anyone. The morning after a particularly violent encounter in the name of making the next Restorer, Myla had crawled into her mother's bed before the sun had risen, her cheeks swollen with tears, hips bruised with vicious and hungry fingertips. She told her mother of the encounter, explaining that she was so scared and startled that her body simply conceded the fight.

Lavinia died shortly after, and Myla continued to concede the fight.

Not this time. Myla tells herself, watching a smoldering landscape come into view, a clear change in territories. She refuses to falter this time. She will soon face a man who wishes to ruin her; this time, she will fight back. This time, she will scream, even if she dies screaming. All will hear it and know she did not lie down and let it happen. For herself, for her child, and for her people, she will be sure no one can say she did not try. *Be the talons.*

"How do you feel?" Bryar interrupts her thoughts, his gaze trailing the length of her, as though checking for any signs of weakness or resistance. He looks tired, as though he has been on horseback for three days, not three hours.

Wrapping the reins around her gloved hand, Myla shrugs. "I have felt nothing yet," she assures him. "That is not to say I will not. There used to be entire weeks where I would feel nothing."

Unconvinced, Bryar leans toward her with an uncomfortable grunt, maneuvering his horse closer. "Let me see your amulet."

Curious now as to what he suspects, Myla reaches to the nape of her neck, loosening the amulet from its trapping beneath her breastplate until it has wiggled free, revealing itself. It glows a fierce amber. *Oh.* She looks to Bryar, his exhaustion making sense now. She is not fine—she is sucking his magic right out of him, and were they not bonded by the

Ashborn Flame, she would not be riding alongside her army.

"Bryar," she whispers pressing her hand to the amulet with a tinge of guilt washing over her. "Are you okay?"

He nods with certainty, then touches his own amulet. "I am alright. One obstacle at a time, my love, we are figuring this out."

They spend the evening camped at the foot of a cavernous mountain. Stalagmites reach up from its base, and a sharp overcropping suggests there was once more to it than currently remains. As late afternoon drifts restlessly into the inky darkness of nightfall, the stench of death seems to grow stronger.

Rising over the top of the mountain, fast traveling stars begin rolling down its sides, ominously drifting closer, until Myla can make out what they really are: the orbs she and Bryar saw when they traveled to Valyndor months ago.

"Look." She points from their place beside a fire. Bryar watches curiously, an arm closing around her protectively as they move closer. The orbs drift, lonely and wanting, through the encampment. "This must have something to do with Vesperian."

"Yes," Bryar agrees, hushing a group of his men who appear startled. "Gather your wits," he whispers a low command to them. "I believe these beings are just as afraid as we are." He leans toward Myla now, holding a wooden bowl in his large palm. The contents are inky black, charcoal crushed and mixed with a small amount of water. Bryar dips his index finger in the war paint and raises a hand to her face. Line after line, he draws protective runes and sigils across her cheeks and forehead. When her face is sufficiently covered in menacing black designs, she takes the bowl and draws the same symbols onto him.

Like the night in the pergola, the orbs drift by for the rest of the night, the number endless. There is something devastating and eerie about them, and the sad song they carry with them. For the next three nights, Myla will sleep extraordinarily little. Though her body is exhausted, her mind races, trapped with the knowledge that this may very well be the end. Not only for her and the child she now longs to meet, but for so many around her. In all of the times she watched Caius send troops off to settle some dispute over territories and borders, or fight on his behalf, she never heard him voice concern, nor guilt, for the lives lost. He would say that immense success rides on the back of great loss; he was proud to have men willing to die for him.

All Myla feels is fear. Fear that her fight is not worth the death of even one of these soldiers, who all seem so ready to meet their fate on her battlefield. The burden of responsibility Caius used to carry effortlessly; she struggles beneath. She thinks of the families waiting for their return. If the Blood Stealer is defeated, how will she face victory knowing some of those families will not watch their soldier march home?

The feeling perpetuates as night waxes into morning, and just before sunrise, the shallow grave appears. Scarce at first, a bleached bone here, a rusted sword there. Then all at once, a disturbing sight of body upon contorted body stacked, barely covered in dirt.

But no wolves in sight.

Rising from their bodies, some quickly, others struggling to wiggle free, are the orbs that have haunted their nights. The song is louder here, the words inaudible but nonetheless, conveying a grievous injustice and a need for vindication. As if they are asking her to kill the bastard who has them trapped in this Gods-forsaken place.

Myla stumbles from her horse, bringing the company to a halt. “We have to do something,” she demands, a wave of nausea rising in her. Somewhere behind her, someone vomits at the sight and smell of decay.

Bryar takes her elbow, pulling her back toward her horse. “There is nothing you can do, not until the Blood Stealer is dead,” he says quietly, consoling her with a gentle touch in the center of her back. “What we need to do is figure out how we will get an entire army through this. It stretches for miles, and we will only make it through if we keep our wits.”

A black mist, barely noticeable at first, begins to coil from the mouths and eyes of the dead, a silky voice speaking through the corpses, distorted and yet all so familiar. “*Oh, you will not*,” it coos. So confident, so certain of itself in the face of her army.

“Fuck!” Rhyland shrieks and leaps into the air as one of the dead seizes his ankle, trying to pull him to the ground with a strength that should belong to no one, the dead especially. He swings at the arm, slicing it off entirely. Blackened blood sprays and oozes, sizzling on the unholy ground.

“Callum—you *bastard*, you mentioned a mass grave; you did not mention its occupants would fight back!” Rhyland looks to Bryar for direction, and finds his captain equally perplexed, slamming the heel of his boot down upon a twitching corpse beneath him.

“Callum mentioned nothing of corpses fighting back,” he growls, angrily looking at Callum.

“They did not do that when I passed through!” Callum defends, horror washing over his face.

Ashborn by the hundreds take flight, launching themselves far from the grappling hands of the dead. Legions of soldiers, Titonfall and the Raven’s Veil included, who were previously marching in tight formations, now bleed together in frenzied panic as the ground beneath them rolls and lulls with the heaving of living corpses.

"It is a trap!" Lord Valen of Titonfall shouts from atop of horse, looking specifically upon his wife in warning. "We should never have brought our men here."

Horses lose their composure, panicked whinnies begin to echo far behind her, as a wave of concern washes over the legions. Though they try to await Myla's command, the black mist grows sizably, traveling through their legs, creating the illusion of an inky river, swallowing her army whole within minutes.

A member of the Raven's Veil, dressed in black battle leathers, face entirely shrouded in a cowled hood, rushes to Bryar's side. "Sir, this is madness. We must retreat."

Bryar flashes his subordinate a burning glare. "There is nowhere to retreat to, Tamsyn," he warns. "The Gods have brought us here for a reason, and here is where we will fight *for* them, or fight to meet them." Myla's husband turns to face her now, making no effort to hide his fear. "Remember the last night in Valyndor?"

She nods, her trembling hands reaching for the sword at her hip, gripping the raven hilt. "Yes." Before her, corpses struggle to their feet, animated by some vile force.

"We weaken him first, ok? Do not attempt *any* channeling until he is weakened. —*Circle up*! Shields!" The latter command is bellowed, the scattering troops begin to fall into formation, moving as one, until Myla finds herself surrounded by the massive, armored bodies of well-trained men. In every direction, as far as she can see, red from the bloody sunrise gleams off the black helmets of the thousands of soldiers prepared to die.

Overhead, shrieking like hungry birds of prey, the Ashborn circle, embers scattering from their wings with every swoop, falling to the ground like dying stars. Ivan and Imogene spiral into a graceful land, their vibrant blue armor contrasted by the blackened landscape. "There is no point trying to retreat to more solid ground," Ivan says grimly. "Vesperian's grave stretches across the entire valley, even into the sides of the mountain."

"We fight here," Myla concludes. "May the Gods watch over you both." The king and queen take flight once more, their instructions overhead barely audible, but Myla watches as their warriors ignite, ready for battle.

The venomous black mist rises, waist deep now, and with it, thousands of corpses in various stages of decay. Where the wasteland before was silent, screeches akin to protests, like metal grinding on metal, now fall from the lips of the dead. Myla wonders if it is the souls—something she thought died when a body did—begging to be released from their oaths.

The sensation is slow and slithering, like a snake creeping in to leak its poison into her veins. "He is here," Myla says forebodingly, her muscles tensing. Judging by the sweat pooling on Bryar's forehead, he can feel it too. A light from beneath the neck of his breastplate pulses, the amulet seeming to already be at full capacity, pulling energy from her to revitalize him. She feels weak and sick, and the battle has yet to begin. Pressing her hands to her rounded belly, she whispers a silent prayer to the Spirit Mother, visualizing her child grown and healthy and strong.

"How did you carry this for so long?" Bryar asks, through gritted teeth as they press their backs together, eyes vigilantly scanning and waiting for Vesperian to show himself and release his army upon them.

"It was not always like this." Her eyes frantically dart from soldier to soldier, ensuring those she can see appear focused and ready. They stand shoulder to shoulder, most remarkably still and alert, though some wear a childlike fear in their eyes. Fear for things they have never seen before, things they did not believe existed. The heaving of decomposing corpses from the earth, begging to crawl over one another, is a sight none should witness, not in a nightmare and certainly not in reality. "Bryar," she nearly whimpers over her shoulder, amazed by his composure. "I am scared."

A hand grasps hers and squeezes tight. "Me, too," he answers. "Remember, '*nothing will scare you more than what you do not know. So, pretend you know it, until you are not scared anymore',*" Quoting his father, Bryar swings violently as a premature corpse lunges from the ground toward him, cutting it down.

"What kind of black magic is this?" Rhyland hisses, dodging from the front line as another corpse plummets toward him. "And why *me*?" He shudders as Callum's blade buries itself in the back of its skull.

"Because you have the most meat on you," Callum jokes, yanking on the back of Rhyland's man-bun. "You would be a feast for like five of them."

"It is muscle, Gods-dammit." Rhyland defends, winding up with an anxious shrug of his shoulders, before finishing the corpse off with a swing to the neck. Soldiers on either side of Callum and Rhyland also swing their blades, a few laughing at how easily they fall. A deep voice behind her suggests that, should all the corpses succumb so easily, this battle will be over in a half hour.

Bryar chuckles in response, shaking his head, and Myla marvels at how these men are cracking jokes right before mass slaughtering occurs. *It must be a soldier thing.*

Now in full standing positions with eyes of hollow black, Vesperian's animated army forms rows before them, swaying slightly, their bodies humming that sad song. Glowing beneath the surface of their chests, orbs bob, trying to free themselves. *Their souls are begging to be freed . . . their bodies betray them, even in death.* It is disturbing, and Myla can feel not only herself, but those around her grow anxious, awaiting the storm.

"Is it not beautiful?" Vesperian's voice echoes. Heads turn as those surrounding her look for the Blood Stealer's location, to no avail. He does not materialize yet, Myla realizes, listening to his voice channel through the mouths of his army, a few at a time to disorient them from his true location. "My army is loyal, even in death." He continues, his voice, soft as honey, dripping like poison into the ears of any who will listen. He feeds off their fears—as the trembling of the army grows, so does the power of his voice.

"You leave me jilted . . . *unsatisfied* . . . then have the audacity to challenge me, on my doorstep? I will have retribution."

Wasting no time, Myla reaches within, drawing from every power reserve she can tap into to call on her magic. As it has done so many times before, but never in such a time of need, particles of light are sucked from the atmosphere, summoning midnight so her body can refract the stars. Her flash of light is the only battle cry necessary. In an instant, a violent clattering of weapon against bone, and the cracking and spraying of blood begins. Dead claw their way over those slower than themselves to bury their rusted weapons in the flesh of the living, screams of fear and pain erupting all around.

Myla is seized almost instantly, a creature behind her grabbing at her shoulders in an effort to pull her down. She spins on her heel, drawing from her waist a large broad sword. Her fingers tighten around the hilt as it swings, coming into contact with the skull of her attacker before the poor soul has time to lunge her way.

A swarm of bodies close in around her; some still look alive. Myla concludes these beings have been dead only a day or so. Ashen, but not yet shredded fibers of skin, tendons, and bone. A corpse with stringy red hair, matted in mud and covering most of the face, stumbles toward her at an alarmingly quick rate. Its blade swings overhead, lowering violently upon hers as she parries the blow.

A piercing, forlorn cry disrupts the already chaotic battlefield. Howls. Followed shortly by the agonizing scream of a soldier, who is quickly relieved of his jugular. Myla flinches, spinning around as a hungry snarl sounds somewhere behind her. A wolf prowls near, hunched and ready to leap. Its haunches are raised and it sways with the heat waves launching off the bodies of catapulting Ashborn. Just as it moves to hurdle into her, a blast of red flame pounds the earth where the creature stands, engulfing it in a personal hell. The wolf yelps and cries in pain, before silencing entirely.

Though Myla can not see Vesperian, she can feel him. As she fells corpse after corpse, her body feels shaky and weak. He sucks the energy from her, while she weakens herself further by fighting his army.

To her left, Bryar's arms expand, gauntlets of fire traveling up them, while wings unfurl from his back. He takes flight. The blast of heat from his body shrivels weaker corpses, they furl to the ground like dead plants. Their space on the battlefield is quickly replaced as living soldiers from Vesperian's army spill forth, following the impulses of their master to slaughter and destroy. Though their eyes seem lifeless, their bodies are very much alive, proving a more difficult foe to kill than the hunks of animated flesh rising from the earth.

It feels as though she has slain a hundred living dead when Myla finally sets her sight on Vesperian. His voice stabilizes into one cohesive stream, the body of its owner spat out of the mist, disillusioned at first, before taking on his true form within the circle of defense formed around Myla.

"This is adorable," Vesperian laughs, watching with delight as those around him, Myla included, scatter in any direction that is away from him, startled by his sudden appearance.

As he takes his place on the smoldering battlefield before her, she realizes he has warped from the handsome villain who infiltrated her palace all those months ago.

Before her stands the true form of the Blood Stealer: a grotesque figure who wears the shadows of his victims and an ancient, malicious need to fulfill prophecy. His form is twisted and hunched, his skin ashen and pallid, stretched taut over sinewy muscles that ripple with unnatural strength. His eyes empty and soulless, twin voids that devour the light from around them, leaving only a cold, chilling darkness in their wake.

The time has come. Every moment in the last three years, which Myla has feared and pondered and made herself small to avoid, has led up to this: an unavoidable moment, one in which she is certain she will die, trying to reclaim all the pieces of herself which he has stolen from her. Or perhaps, it is the pieces her father and Caius stole from her. Or the pieces the members of her Council stole every time they looked upon her with doubt. Whatever pieces she hopes to reclaim, she knows they will be found on this battlefield. She will take them back for herself, or she will die for them. But she will not leave this place without them.

Her magic tenses within her, ready to be loosed. A primal, otherworldly scream reverberates through the air, like a thunderclap, and Myla unleashes a wave of energy that deafens both soldiers and Blood Stealer alike. All around her, soldiers collapse, grasping their heads in pain. The ground shakes beneath their feet, sending them stumbling and disoriented, while the winds howl and whip around them with an almost sentient malevolence. Several shield wielders loose their magic, hazy purple buffers shielding their comrades from her inferno of rage. It is not just her own energy she conjures, but the Gods'

Chapter 28

As the Blood Stealer reels from the force of Myla's scream, Bryar spirals downward, a haze of ash and smoke trailing behind him, his body plummeting into Vesperian in a tangle of muscle and magic. The Fae God and the captain grapple at one another, each clawing for a stronger bearing on the other. Bryar no longer wields fire magic alone; there is something more to it. A rage, a force, a power which can only be seen as a gift directly from the Gods. It is her magic pulsing through him. Two more Ashborn warriors follow suit behind him, slamming their bodies into Vesperian as he lies sprawled on the ground.

"Archers!" the Blood Stealer screams angrily. His command sends sizzling black arrows into the sky, dozens of them landing with sickening *thunks* into the soaring bodies of the Ashborn above. The winged people nosedive to the ground, their lifeless bodies joining the thousands beneath them.

Bryar extends flexed arms, sending another volley of searing flames to lick at Vesperian's shadowy form, and Myla lunges in his direction, taking advantage of his turned back, a second too late.

From the Blood Stealer's palms, his razor-sharp wraith explodes, a screaming carried with it, replaying the agony of its recent victims and waging terror on the army around it. The black creature bobs and weaves through limbs of fighting soldiers, dodging some entirely, while cutting and killing others, before it lodges itself like a weighted punch, right into her middle, sending her sprawling, and the child within her kicking in defiance.

"Myla!" Callum screams, pulling Rhyland to his feet from an assault, before they both rush to her side.

"I do not want to kill you," Vesperian hisses, striding toward her with confidence. "You could bring me so much power. Submitting is still an option."

The wind knocked out of her, gasping for breath and unable to find it beneath the weight of her armor, Myla forces herself upright, willing herself not to be distracted by the bodies of her men slumping to the ground at an alarming rate. Her friends help her to her feet and Rhyland hands her the heavy broadsword that was thrown from her hand during the impact.

"*Never,*" Myla screams. From the earth beneath her boot, something grabs at her, and she realizes the ground is heaving, bodies buried beneath it clawing their way to the surface. In a panic, she wonders how deep into the earth he has victims buried. Slashing at the hand which pokes from the ground, Myla sidesteps the attack and twists, desperate to get eyes back on Vesperian, whose voice hums an eerie threat from Gods-know-where.

"*I will live another ten centuries. You are not the last remarkable woman who will cross my path. If I must kill you and wait for another, I will."* His voice normalizes once more. "Right here, my Ruthless Queen," he hums from behind her. Spinning on her heel, Myla extends her blade, ready to lodge it in his throat, but misses by a hair when he dissolves into a cloud of black mist, materializing a few steps to the right. Now, Matteo and Margot join him, appearing and disappearing as he does. Myla's mouth dries as she realizes they are all one: the wolves, the wraith, and Vesperian. He is in every place at once, snarling with teeth like razors, taunting her, again in the form of a charismatic man, and decapitating on a whim, as he travels in the form of a shadow.

It is a push-and-pull battle for what feels like hours. Drenched in sweat, her long hair clinging to her face, Myla tugs at her power, summoning that rope of light and launching it nimbly at Vesperian's throat. It holds, and the demon lets out a shriek of agony as the light burns away his flesh, melting a grotesque indent around his neck. Bursting from the wound, summoned to the spot, his wraith shatters her light into a million shards, splintering in all directions. It is a deadly recoil, and every sharp spear of light is aimed at her own men.

Watching the mayhem in slow motion, Myla closes her eyes, willing the shards to return to her, to feed her energy once more, rather than embedding themselves in those around them. The light stills midair as she commands it, her hands extended as though she calls to dutiful children, then with a sickening warp of power, the motion is reversed in a rush of energy, which brings her to a full standing position. The light reabsorbs into her pores. To her left, Callum bores his feet into the ground, bracing against a wolf who snaps hungrily at his face. From behind, Rhyland swings his blade, hacking the deadly beast in half, brutally.

Crashing into the heaving surface of the earth, Bryar and a dozen other Ashborn warriors, their king and queen included, loose an assault of vengeful flames, boring holes into the ground at Vesperian's feet, until it caves in around him completely. Splintered bones, of the dead beneath, slice at his skin, dislodged by the powerful blast. The Blood Stealer writhes and screeches in agony, his dark energy flickering and faltering in the face of Bryar's fiery assault. Myla sees the lapse in power and falls to her knees, pressing her hands into the ground, ignoring the dead fingers wrapping around her wrists.

"Now!" Already covered in sweat and blood, Bryar yells. The amulet flashes, blinding at his chest, every ounce of energy he has channeling to her as he presses his palms into the dirt next to her. A river of magic forms between them, trickling over the corpses and mounds of earth. Focusing, begging the Gods for mercy, Myla visualizes the methods they have practiced together every night since their marriage.

Slow and subtle at first, a tingling in her body tells her she is on the right track. From her fingertips, a shimmer of translucent blue rises, and the corpses beneath the surface of the earth cease to struggle; orbs fly from their bodies in reprieve, their curse broken.

"Good," Bryar whispers, as he clamors to her side, a hand on hers, surging energy through her.

Myla's focus wavers as Vesperian pulls himself from the wreckage caused by Bryar. Callum and Rhyland rush bravely in his direction, though they have little to contest him with.

"*Ignore him,*" Bryar urges, hoping any amount of Restorer magic summoned will help. His weary glance in his friends' direction is unmistakable and he shouts in a panic for backup, bidding a wave of soldiers to join them.

Myla forms a small ball of blue between her palms. Shaking and dripping sweat, she raises the stream of energy overhead, trying to strike the Blood Stealer with it. It is not enough. Though it lands on his chest, sending a foul, burning odor into the already overwhelming stench of battle, the assault merely brings their foe to his knees. The energy he pulls from his subjects is enough to revive him, but doing so cripples his nearby forces in the process. Several hundred of his army fall unmoving to the ground, replaced shortly by living armies and mad wolves spilling in, summoned, no doubt by the irresistible call of Vesperian. Battle cries and hungry howling deafens all.

All around Myla, trails of fire sizzle across pools of blood. Overhead, Ashborn wage war with fire, sending balls of furious flames down upon clusters of their enemies. All manner of injuries and fatal wounds flash before her eyes, a sight horrible and sickening. A few yards behind the Blood Stealer, Rhyland and Callum stand back-to-back, each struggling against their own foes. They fight as one, as friends who have had each other's backs since boyhood.

With a body heavy from exertion, Bryar takes to the sky again and unleashes another wave of blue flame, Myla's cue to summon the magic of the Restorer while he distracts Vesperian. As the black wraith hurdles in his direction, Bryar's assault does not last a fraction of the time it did before, and he lands with a crashing thud near her, slow to stand now. Both their amulets flash, each of them exchanging power and energy, neither of them tipping the scale for the other.

"This is not working," he yells over the calamity of battle. A flash of horror passes across his face as he yanks her to the ground to dodge the swing of a mace, his sword stopping it midair. Another thrust overhead and he has decapitated the wielder. Her husband expends another massive wave of energy from his exhausted body, a ripple of flames pouring from his palms as he incinerates a wall of corpses rushing toward them.

Taking note of the onslaughts which continue to bar them from focusing on Vesperian, Rhyland and Callum make their way closer, along with several other soldiers. Their bodies form a wall at Myla and Bryar's backs.

"I know," she responds breathlessly, bracing her body against his as a surge of light breaks free of her body, bleeding white across the entire battlefield. Holding the wave of magic, she watches as Bryar rips his amulet off, tucking it into his boot. *No . . .*

Her energy expands within her, though horror threatens to distract her as she sees Bryar struggling to summon his own magic, let alone stand upright. He heaves with labored breath and his body is frigid with straining. Those soft green eyes find hers, but they are not soft any longer. They are angry and they are scared. "Again!" he bellows to her, loosing a wave of weakened flames in Vesperian's direction. The inferno engulfs the Blood Stealer, and Myla places her palms to the earth, grounding herself and her child, once more conjuring the blue mist.

As the battle reaches its climax, the Blood Stealer siphoning another surge of energy; instead of feeling the drain like so many around her, Myla feels a birth of power unlike anything she has ever experienced before. It is vindicating. It is the fulfillment of old prophesies and promises. It is everything she has always known she could be, materializing in a desperate attempt to save the thousands of people here fighting for her.

Bryar holds off the Blood Stealer with inhuman ability in spite of his weakened state; a feat only described as a force of circumstance. Before her, he stands, his body the only shield between herself and Vesperian. His sword swings with deadly intent, aimed for the skull of his foe, stopped short by a flash of the Blood Stealer's own blade. Overhead, arrows sizzle and volleys of flame fall from the sky like rain. Wolves howl and snarl, while screams of death stab, small defeats, time and time again. Muscle against muscle, set jaws and gritting teeth, the captain and the Blood Stealer lean into one other, neither willing to surrender. One slip of a blade could result in Bryar's neck being severed. Unrelenting, Bryar lets out an angry growl and pushes harder against Vesperian, a slip of the villain's heel giving Bryar the edge needed to step back and swing his weapon again. Their deadly blades flash and clank against one another, Bryar holding the Blood Stealer off for now, a feat Myla knows he can not sustain in his declining condition.

"Are you prepared to die?" Vesperian bellows, his black wraith at work once more, launching Bryar to his back. "How many years have you sat back and been the pawn of a woman who would not choose you?" Vesperian plans to weaken Bryar's mind as well as his body. This is the moment—any longer and they will lose any edge they have.

Myla squeezes her eyes shut, a tremble of fear passing through her body. Her eyes burn as the warpaint seeps into her eyes, and Myla realizes it is not the result of sweat, but tears. Placing a hand on her swollen belly, she feels the will of the child seeping into her bloodstream. She chills with a power that is not her own. In a moment of clarity, Myla turns her eyes upwards toward the mountains, a red haze creating harmony with the blood on the ground beneath her. *I beg of you,* she whispers a prayer, *give me another chance to lead these people well. Give me another chance to love. Give this child a chance to live.*

At first, the sensation might be confused with the tightening of the throat felt before tears break free. Awaiting the answer of the Gods, a burning pain scorches her throat, and she realizes this is their answer. The Restorer's blue glow begins like a sliver of veins, starting at her belly and trailing up her body to her throat. Drawing from every drop of energy around and within her, her child's magic is condensed at her core, ready to be unleashed from her lungs, in tandem with the Voice of the Gods.

Her body straightens, Sir Roderick's instruction to always stand tall encouraging her to face this final battle with a dignity most have not believed her capable of. Both hands pressed against her belly, an urge to lift her face to the sky takes over, and Myla surrenders to the will of the Gods. Her body takes form as a powerful vessel for their righteous scourging of the Blood Stealer, and she channels the Restorer Magic in a magnificent marriage of blue light and white fire, all carried from her lungs on the vengeful voices of the Gods above. The same Gods who saw fit to put her on this earth. The Gods who saw fit to give her this gift because they knew she carried a strength others might not see. The Gods who saw fit to set her feet on this path. They are the same Gods she feels with her now as the ground beneath her melts, and the corpses even deeper below turn to ash, glowing embers of black drifting upwards.

With a sickening blow to the abdomen, Bryar is launched backward, Myla's magic faltering momentarily, but a familiar voice, the voice of the Spirit Mother, urges her to remain calm and focused. Vesperian strides toward her swiftly, black mist expelled from his body with every step, his essence slicing any soldiers near him with deadly precision. To his left and right, bodies slump over dead until he stands before her, looking down in mockery.

His voice is louder than the deafening bellows pouring from her like an undammed river. "If you continue to fight like *this*," he scoffs, kneeling to her level, "I might begin to wonder if you even *want* to win." Despite the earth trembling at her fingertips and Ashborn warriors landing because of the quake, Vesperian seems only mildly uncomfortable, flinching as she pulses a wave of light at his throat again. Through gritting teeth, he speaks. "Maybe you even want this—to look like you tried, so no one can blame you when you must join forces with me. A brilliant ruse really, my Ruthless Queen."

Myla screams, though the Voice of the Gods powers her, it is a cry of the most hateful rage. To her right, Bryar crouches, panting and unable to rise as his energy bleeds out, his life source pouring entirely into her. Hot tears of anger and fear run freely down her cheeks, and no amount of death around her seems to drown out the voice inside, the voice of the Spirit Mother begging her to dig deeper. Titonfall soldiers, the Raven's Veil, Ashborn warriors, and Falkmere soldiers alike clash violently against their enemy, fighting side-by-side, and dying in devastating waves.

Drawing upon the Goddess's strength and purity to fuel her final, desperate attack, Myla rises to her feet, the round of her belly illuminated and reflecting the hot, unruly fires dancing in every direction around her. "If I have to die screaming," Myla speaks with conviction, lifting her arms overhead to draw from the energy of those around her, as well as the strength of her child within, "I will; if only to meet my death with every single soul here knowing, I did *not go willingly."*

A lazy smile creases her tormentor's face and he unsheathes a menacing little dagger. "What a pity."

Energy courses through her veins like liquid fire, filling her with a divine power that transcends the mortal realm. Several feet away, Rhyland to his left and Callum to his right, Bryar is guarded by his comrades, each bringing a halt to assailants as they fly like rabid animals toward the group. But most shockingly . . .

Elsa. A vision of resilience, her best friend stands, very much alive, behind her husband, hands pressed on either side of his head, surging her healing essence *through* him, allowing his electric light of energy to travel at an inhuman speed directly into Myla's veins.

Unwilling to meet her end here, with a final cry, she unleashes a blinding burst of rich, unforgettable blue light and energy that engulfs the Blood Stealer in a searing blaze of purification. The scream from her lungs, though the tail end of the Gods, are her own. An angry, victorious bellow commanding all to hear her: *I may not have chosen this, and for a while, I may not have stopped it, but I allow it no longer.*

The Blood Stealer howls in agony. As his various forms begin to disintegrate, he pivots backward, arms flailing violently, and he is consumed by the pure, unyielding light of the Restorer Magic.

And as the last echoes of his screams fade into the air, a gasp like a wave washes over those of his victims who survive. Most fall into fatigued slumps, while others kneel, weeping with relief. Myla stands, not as a girl, nor a victim, but as a queen who has chosen her own fate. Hair clinging to her face from blood and sweat, her entire body trembling from the shock of magic released from her veins, her eyes trail across the ruin and tragedy caused on this bloody battlefield. Though the sweet relief of victory is potent, Myla feels a nausea churning, the child within heaving and protesting.

Unable to stand any longer, she lowers herself to the ground, pressing her palms flat into the crater caused by her and the child's efforts. "We did it," she whispers, silently thanking her baby, and the Gods for their mercy. "You are a resilient little thing," she says with a slight gasp, gently rubbing her stomach before glancing over her shoulder at the sound of footsteps.

Bryar stands behind her, his face blackened with smoke and blood. "Are you alright?" he pants, his hands brushing her hair out of her eyes as he helps her to her feet, supporting her fatigued body with his own trembling arms.

"Myla, you did it." Pride washes across his face, and his voice breaks as the realization of victory hits them both. His eyes rim with tears, be it exhaustion, relief, or the release of years of stress, she can see the strong man before her ready to crack.

"No," she answers, holding her belly. "This one did it . . . *we did it.*" Pressing a hand to his chest, she points to the sky. "Look, a *thousand burning ravens.*"

Overhead, the ashes of the battle continue to rise, carried off on a breeze into the golden sunrise. From their vantage point below, it does, indeed, look like a thousand burning ravens flying upward to greet the Gods.

Bryar lets out a shaky sigh, the gleam in his eyes filling more as he watches the remnants of Vesperian's victims return to the Gods. A silence has befallen the battlefield, death in itself. Turning to inspect the damage to his troops, Bryar holds fast to her hand, turning her to follow him.

A guttural wail breaks the silence, a beast-like scream, which could only be conjured by grief. Myla and Bryar whip around, only to freeze at the scene before them. Grief threatens to crack Elsa wide open as she leans over the convulsing body of Callum. Beside them, Rhyland holds his friend's hand, tears streaking his dirty face.

Bryar releases Myla, rushing to Callum's side, his gloved hand immediately pressing the oozing place at his neck where the Blood Stealer's loosed dagger is lodged—a final attack before Vesperian died.

Callum's eyes, red and glistening with tears, move slowly from one face to the next, finally landing on Elsa's. She leans over him with a face hidden partially by her tangled blond hair, her hands on either side of his face, diffusing a healing energy into him. She mutters incoherent words, something akin to an incantation. Carefully, Myla sits beside her, listening for some semblance of a chant she can join in on to amplify its power, when she realizes she is repeating something over and over: "*I have a heart, but you hold it, so sometimes I forget to use it.*"

Callum struggles, fading in and out of coherency and looking sidelong at Rhyland. His entire body trembles, and a gurgling sound fills his throat. His hand stiffens as he urges Rhyland closer. "*T-t-take* care . . ." Callum's voice fails. As he begins to drown in his own blood, he looks back to Elsa, a look of relief washing over him. Even in death, all he wants is her safety.

Understanding, Rhyland places his free hand on Callum's forehead and inhales deeply, his voice quaking as he speaks, "Do not worry about that, man. I got her, okay?"

"Do not talk like that!" Elsa hisses, denial etching lines of agony across her face. Desperately, she looks down at Callum as though she is missing some key factor in saving his life. "Should I try taking the dagger out?" Elsa's voice quivers, panic hiding just behind the futile attempt to remain calm. Her hands produce exhausted flickers of magic before the lights extinguish, a testament to her own fatigue.

"Darling," Myla whispers as she struggles against her own tears, seizing one of her friend's hands. "No . . ."

Bryar slowly retracts his hands from the wound at Callum's neck, allowing the blood to flow freely. A look of numb shock washes over him and is quickly replaced with something different. Anger. Grief. Disbelief. "This can not be . . ." he pants, looking to Rhyland, who reflects his same expression. A slow and wheezing release slips through Callum's parted lips; his hand, once tight, around Rhyland's now falls limp, and his eyelids drop closed.

"No!" Elsa shrieks, her thread of composure snapping. "*Come back.*" It is not a request but a command, and her hands fly to the place the dagger is protruding. With a swift pull, she dislodges it, sending a spray of freed blood across her face. She replaces the weapon with her cupped hands, attempting to staunch the flow with her magic.

"I lied to you," she wails. "I thought if I let you think he had me, you would let me stay to find the antidote! You can not die with a lie between us! Come back." Sobs fall from her uncontrolled as she curses, willing her energy to bring him back in spite of the sticky blood oozing between her fingers.

"You can not die," she repeats. "I love you." Her voice is a mere whimper, a weak period at the end of a sad story, add the '*I love you'* standing in the place of a dissatisfying 'the end'.

With one last burst of healing energy briefly illuminating the gouge at his neck, Rhyland moves behind Elsa, gently pulling her back.

"He is gone; do not give his soul a reason to linger in this sadness. Let him go with the Gods. They will feast in his honor."

Huddled over their friend's body, they break together, cries of grief creating the saddest choir to send him off. A glowing at his center rises to the surface, gently slipping from the skin at his chest, an orb drifting upward, carrying with it the same lonely song Myla had heard sung all the nights before. As the orb ascends, joining the others, the earth seems to sigh, and one by one, the souls flicker in and out of sight, until none are left to be seen. With Vesperian's death, they are released to seek out the afterlife in peace.

Heads bow in honor of the lives lost. Weary soldiers, Falkmere, Titonfall, the Raven's Veil, and Ashborn alike, some wounded, others broken, but none unscathed, stand silent, watching ashes continue to drift upward from the battlefield, wings like ravens fluttering as the Gods above nod in approval. Dazed and confused, crowds of people who do not remember arriving at the battle, nor much of their time in the Blood Stealer's service, examine their surroundings. Many, far from warriors, look at their bloodied bodies and the carnage beneath their feet, letting out shrieks of horror.

"They need you," Bryar whispers, resting a hand on her shaking shoulder. "They need you to tell them it will be ok."

Myla sucks in a deep breath, wipes the tears from her face, and stands. The weight of her armor feels heavy on her exhausted body and that of the child's, but she finds strength nonetheless to pull herself on top of her horse, eyes traveling across the wreckage and tragedy of the battlefield.

"I know you are afraid," she begins, her clear voice drawing the attention of those who have survived, most slumped in piles of exhaustion. "You have woken from a nightmare into something worse than what you were experiencing yesterday. For reality is oftentimes more terrible than the illusions we find ourselves stuck in. I have felt the weight and the ruin of the Blood Stealer for many years now, as have we all.

"I ask you now: dry your tears, and take the hand of the person beside you. It is our responsibility to heal this land, as well as our hearts, to wash away the blood and debris left behind by a monster that no longer terrorizes us, and never will again." A heaviness falls away from her words as soldiers and citizens alike link hands, forming one powerful body.

"Let us never again find ourselves in a situation where we are not in control of ourselves or our future. May we never fall victim to the idea that we are compliant with something happening *to* us simply because nobody can see us fighting back. I know your fight. I felt it within myself, and I honor it."

Her voice trembles as the words spill forth. "And for the lives we have lost, the souls we grieve, and the pieces of ourselves we may never get back, we see you, and we will continue living and breathing, so the wind of our breath may carry you to where you belong: with the Gods."

Meandering up the cobblestone street, carrying a basket of baked goods and a single Ashborn feather, as is tradition in Valyndor, is Lenore, arm linked with Elsa. Together, they walk to greet a new life.

News of the birth of the child with misty blue eyes has spread like wildfire, sparking excitement among those who have grown fond of Myla, as well as those who do not know a thing about her; she has birthed a new Restorer.

It is a miracle none thought possible.

Within the palace, a pure light bathes the room in liquid gold, a hue of orange diffused on the pillars of the balcony, which catch the brilliance of the winter sky. Beige linen curtains, draped from ceiling to floor, billow gently in the breeze, a privacy wall between Myla's place in bed, and the balcony where Bryar stands, back to her, cradling a small bundle. It is tranquil here, despite the excitement building outside.

Myla shivers, cold from the breeze, and blinks slowly, her eyes adjusting from what feels like a long sleep. Her body aches, and there is no telling if the soreness is from the difficult delivery she endured, or the still-healing bruises and wounds inflicted on the battlefield weeks ago.

From across the room, she hears Bryar humming an unfamiliar song; slow and sweet. He rocks back and forth slowly, eyes fixed on the infant in his arms. There is a reverence in the way he holds the tiny child so close, so tight to him. As though he may never let go. To him, there is but one place his gaze belongs, and it is on the child he has sworn to protect.

"Bryar," she whispers, causing him to turn. "Tell me she is ok. I want to meet my daughter." Hands extended from where she lies, Myla awaits the feeling of the warm, new infant in her arms. A yearning to be reunited with the soul she has strived tirelessly to meet face-to-face fills her chest, and every second he stands opposite her, holding the child, feels like torture.

Bryar looks to her, his face stretched in the purest smile she has ever seen him wear. One slow step at a time, careful not to disturb the baby, he makes his way to her bedside. "I am afraid you can not do that," he answers, revealing a tiny head full of brown curls.

"What?" she questions, alarmed by what he could possibly mean. "Why?"

"Because," Bryar answers, with a sly grin, "you do not have a daughter. You have a son."

A warmth of tears, joyful and overwhelming, rise to the brim of her eyelids, instantly spilling down her cheeks. "A *son*?"

"Yes," Bryar says, sitting on the edge of the bed beside her, leaning in to kiss her forehead. "A boy, as strong as his mother."

He places a palm on the boy's head and leans into whisper, "I know you have been waiting to meet her, so here she is." As though responding, like he and Bryar have an understanding already, a sweet coo peeps from the tiny pink lips, parted in a sleepy haze.

It is in this moment; Myla is certain the five senses are not enough. No amount of holding him, kissing him, smelling him, nor studying his tiny features and hearing his coos will ever be enough to match the unfiltered rawness of the love she feels. "He is so beautiful," she says, tracing the tip of his button nose with a delicate finger. "How long have I been asleep? I do not remember . . ."

Bryar smooths curls of brown from her forehead, smiling gently. "Not long. Only a day. The end was . . . treacherous, and you lost a lot of blood. You passed out as soon as he was born, but . . . do not worry," he assures. "I did not leave his side for a second." At this, Bryar looks to the baby. "I never will."

"If you say anything else of the sort," Myla says, attempting to steady the shake of her voice. "I shall keep crying, and he is going to think I am weak."

"Never." Bryar insists. "Nobody could ever think that."

"See," Myla whispers, smelling deeply the sweet fragrance of the boy's soft skin. "I have picked a wonderful father for you. He is going to be your very favorite person."

Bryar's jaw tenses and a light fills his eyes, tears flickering therein. "The greatest honor," he says, stretching himself into a lying position next to her. "I can not wait to see who he becomes."

Myla leans her head on her husband's shoulder, eyes heavy with a need for more sleep. "What shall we call him?"

"You have not chosen a name?"

"No," she confesses, an idea sparking within. "I have had three years with this child already. I have grown him, spoken to him, held him within me while we slept. I have had a lot of him already—he is fused from the very matter which makes me. I want you to give him a name. Let him have a part of you."

Bryar takes a deep breath and reaches to where the boy is cradled. Taking him gently from his mother and holding him close, Bryar speaks. "I knew a man . . . someone who would have made you laugh and made you feel safe. If you ever questioned who you were or where you belonged, he would have made sure you went to sleep reassured of your place in this world and your purpose in it. His name was Caspian, and I think he would have liked it if you had his name, too."

Myla smiles, nodding in agreement as images of Bryar's broad-shouldered, wide-smiling, infectious-laughing father fill her mind's eye. "Caspian . . . what an honor to have that name."

"A name fit for a King."

"A name fit for *our son*," Myla whispers, turning to kiss her captain. "Now let us get him a castle."

The End.

"These scars will *never* feel worth it. But they will serve as a reminder that we had something worth fighting for. That we *still have* something worth fighting for." – Myla Alerys

Book 2 in The *Queen Who Bleeds Stars* series coming December of 2025

www.ingramcontent.com/pod-product-compliance
Lightning Source LLC
Chambersburg PA
CBHW020652110726
47901CB00001B/158

9798992499902